BELINDA BENNA

EVERY *Step* I TAKE

vinci
BOOKS

Vinci Books

vinci-books.com

Published by Vinci Books Ltd in 2026

1

A CIP catalogue record for this book is available from the British Library.

Paperback ISBN: 9781036734107

The EU GPSR authorised representative is Logos Europe, 9 rue Nicolas Poussion, 17000 La Rochelle, France contact@logoseurope.eu

By Belinda Benna

By Belinda Benna

Every Step I Take

Love and Other Dreams

The Dreams We Share

The Sky We Seek

The Colors We Desire

The Dance We Remember

The Stars We Chase

Marie & Lukas

Promise Me

Show Me the Stars

Halifax Harbor Hospital

A Glimmer of Hope

A Twist of Fate

Miracle Glow

A Longing for Light

The secret to happiness is freedom, and the secret to freedom is courage

— Pericles

Trigger warning

Every Step I Take contains elements that may be triggering.

These are:
Miscarriage
Psychological Abuse.

If you associate these topics with personal, life-changing experiences, you may want to refrain from reading this book.

Chapter One

Hospitals make me nervous. They always have, and today is no different. My instincts tell me to run, but I still walk into the clinic and try to imagine it's a luxury hotel. At first glance, I really can't see much of a difference. The entrance area is clean and minimal, tasteful and classy. A synthetic orange scent hits me and settles on my palate. Still, it can't compete with the harsh smell of disinfectant, which robs me of my illusion far too quickly.

My knees want to give way, but I don't allow it.

I have no choice. So I force myself to stride in long steps toward the elegant reception desk. The brisk sound of my high heels on the marble floor draws the receptionist's attention. Her smile reminds me of toothpaste commercials, her updo of the opera ball.

I hastily bury my hands in the pockets of my charcoal pantsuit. No one must see how badly they're shaking.

"Sarah Wagner, I have an appointment at seven o'clock." My voice wavers, but I get it back under control quickly.

"Of course, Ms. Wagner." Her friendliness seems forced, her movements mechanical.

I can't look her in the eye; I don't want to show her my panic, and even less my doubts. Luckily, she lowers her head now and searches for my name on the tablet on her desk pad. My gaze follows the path of her perfectly manicured fingernails. Very stylish, just like this clinic.

"Here you are. Please take a seat; you'll be called in shortly."

She draws a check mark next to my appointment and looks up at me again. With a refined wave of her hand, she shows me the way to the waiting room and gives me an encouraging nod. She knows why I'm here, and still she treats me as if nothing more than a harmless massage awaited me.

I thank her; after all, it's important to be polite, no matter whether you feel like it or not. At least that's what my mother claims, and if anyone would know, it's her. I should really get going now, but once again my body refuses to obey me. Rigid as a board, I'm still standing at reception.

I absolutely cannot stay here.

Fight or flight, what should I do?

I bite my lip; I don't have that choice, and it's time I finally understood that. There's only one path for me, and it leads to the waiting room. When I get there, I'm overwhelmed by the feeling that I've landed in a glossy catalog that has lost its colors. Only the gray, the black, and the white are left.

The graphite-colored chairs are lined up so perfectly it's as if someone had used a spirit level on them. The glass table in the middle has no scratches, nor can I make out any fingerprints on its gleaming surface. On it stands nothing but a bowl from which an orchid grows. Its green leaves are dark, and the blossoms don't seem to have a single flaw. I walk close past them to see that they're not alive.

Silently, I slide onto one of the chairs and fix my gaze on the glass front, beyond which everything suddenly turns colorful. The last rays of the day's sun bathe the park on the other side in a soft light. If I were out there, I'd lean against the trunk of the weeping willow, listen to the birds singing, and forget my fear while looking at the sea of blossoms.

But I'm in here.

With cold sweat on my back and bones that feel as if they were as fragile as porcelain.

In search of stability, I cross my legs; my chair lets out a squeak. Although it isn't particularly loud, it drowns out every other sound for a moment. Right after that, it's quiet again; only the rustling of newspapers and the clacking of computer keyboards at reception can be heard. Embarrassed, I lower my gaze and let my shoes wander over the floor. It gleams in the almost horizontally falling sunlight. I look in vain for signs of wear even now, although I know where they should be. Here, between the seating area for patients and the frosted-glass sliding doors over there, behind which the treatment rooms are. They glide open and shut without a sound, swallowing one person after another and elegantly concealing whatever happens behind them.

Is there still black and gray in there too, or only white?

The truth is, I don't have to see the rooms to know that it's just as cold in there as it is here. This chilly atmosphere runs through the whole clinic like fog on a November morning. It greets its visitors with noble frost, makes their faces freeze and their bodies go rigid. The people here blend seamlessly into the picture, just like I do. All of us are colorless, made up only of black, gray, and white. As if we had lost the red and the green, as if we were without passion and without hope.

How does my heart still manage to pound with such force that I can feel it all the way up in my ears?

All I can do is hope that no one but me notices. And as long as I can resist the urge to wipe my hands on my pants, it'll stay that way. My facial expression doesn't give me away; I've trained it long enough for that. It has to obey my commands, and today I order it to be strong. My chin lifts just far enough not to seem arrogant, the corners of my mouth pull up. Just a little. It's not supposed to be a smile, just look as if everything is fine with me.

That should be enough; the makeup takes care of the rest. It hides how pale my fear makes me and covers the dark shadows the nightmares have left under my eyes. Just like the hundreds of freckles that are now, in early summer, especially conspicuous on my cheeks. They don't suit me, they make me look young and naive. I don't want to be either. No matter where I am, and least of all here, in the waiting room of this clinic.

No matter how hard I try, what usually comes easily to me costs more strength today than I have. Once again my feelings threaten to become visible on my face.

The forced smile slips, my eyes grow watery. I can't help it and smooth the hair on the top of my head to calm myself. My hairstyle has to be perfect. I wear it every day; I could put my hair in a bun in my sleep if I had to. Not a single one of my reddish-blond hairs is allowed to stray out of line, every one of my curls has to be neatly straightened and pinned up. I feel a loose strand, carefully pin it back, and check that my earrings are sitting right. They belonged to my grandmother and are as old-fashioned as she is. They're perfect for me. Not because they remind me of

Grandma, but because they give my appearance at least five extra years of life experience.

You might think I was in my early forties, even though I just turned thirty. That's fine by me. After all, I make my living by pretending to be something I'm not. And it helps me now too, right in this moment, as the fear crawls up inside me, unstoppable.

It has no place here.

I force it down with all my might. Once, and once again. Over and over it rises back to the surface, like a balloon you can only hold under water as long as you have the strength.

Slowly I uncross my legs and let my palms slide inconspicuously over the soft fabric of my pants to my knees. There I lace my fingers together; they tremble incessantly when they're left without support. Blue veins stand out on the backs of my hands. They should be swollen, with the blood rushing through my body like a torrent. But they look as they always do, smooth and far too skinny. My fingers remind me of a witch's, only the delicately pink manicured nails don't match. I can't keep them still, so I press the nails into my skin.

So hard that it hurts.

It's a pain I like to feel. At least for a moment, it manages to overpower the other one, and I feel safe enough to open my eyes again.

Even so, I don't look around; I ignore the other women in the waiting room. The risk of catching sight of a rounded belly is far too great. Nothing could throw me off balance as much as a single pregnant woman resting her hand protectively on her swollen body. With that kind of tenderness that doesn't exist a second time in this world. The sight would make my fear disappear and give way to a feeling I have even less use for. I've felt it deep inside me for days. It ambushes me in my sleep, precisely when I'm as defenseless and vulnerable as the tiny little person in my belly.

A sense of guilt that surpasses anything I've ever experienced.

My baby has to die today. I'm having it removed as if it were nothing more than an ugly mole in the middle of my forehead.

Chapter Two

"Career comes first," my parents say, and of course they're right. I've worked too hard to give up so close to the finish line. Not everyone manages to become a partner at one of Vienna's most prestigious law firms, and for me that moment is within reach. All I'm missing is the victory in this one case. I can win it, I mustn't let myself get distracted. By anyone. Least of all by the child.

The scenes of my breakthrough play through my mind like a movie. All my colleagues raise their champagne glasses to congratulate me. I hear the applause meant for me alone, I smile and celebrate more exuberantly than ever before. But nothing can compare to the warm feeling that spreads in my belly when I imagine my family's reaction. Above all my father's heartfelt hug, so tight I can barely breathe.

"I'm incredibly proud of you," he whispers in my ear, and my heart leaps. Being this close to him feels like coming home after a long journey.

My mother is standing beside him. At last I see that

sparkle in her eyes again, filled with recognition and love. "My daughter," she says in a choked voice, even though nothing ever really moves her to tears, "that's my daughter." She doesn't get any further because she can't find any other words. She blinks hard, the corners of her mouth trembling. She showers my cheeks with kisses and gently strokes my hair.

And of course Tom. He pulls me against him with a passion I've never felt from him before and is as happy as if he'd been promoted himself. The lines on his forehead have disappeared. He can look at me again, as tenderly as he used to.

I'm going to have everything I've longed for all my life.

The fact that I have to sacrifice more than just my own life for it today is something part of me still refuses to understand. It calls me a selfish murderer and shows me, night after night, in garish images how my baby dies in agony. During the day it grabs my heart and squeezes it violently so it will end the same way. I can hardly breathe when I imagine how this guilt will haunt me for the rest of my life. Will I ever stop asking myself whether my child's eyes are as moss green as mine? Whether it has my far too skinny legs or Tom's aristocratic nose? What its laughter sounds like, how its tears taste, and what scent its forehead gives off while it's dreaming?

If only I could ask the doctor behind the frosted-glass door for an ultrasound. He would be able to show me a picture of my baby and let me hear its heartbeat. At last I'd be allowed to put my hand on my belly without worrying that someone might be watching me. I would be like any other pregnant woman. Full of joy and love, with rosy cheeks and shining eyes.

But only until I realize that I've thrown my whole life

away for it. When my mother's lips are nothing but a thin line, frozen and cold. And Tom can no longer look me in the face without knitting his brows together the way he does when he has no idea what to do next.

My pregnancy shook him. I still remember the look on his face when I finally managed to tell him. He stared at me, his eyes wide open. His chin dropped so low it was as if his jaw had come out of its socket.

"Wow, that's what I call a surprise," he said, almost tonelessly. His cheeks instantly took on the color of the kitchen cabinets surrounding us. A cream shade, pale as a veil of fog.

"It was for me too." I nodded vigorously. For a brief moment I bit my lip. A single question dominated my thoughts; I had to ask it. Now. "What do you think about it?"

He shook his head, folded his arms across his chest, and leaned back in his chair. "I don't know. It's so sudden." He looked at me helplessly.

Although the waiting was almost unbearable, I gave him the time he needed. "Think it over in peace, I'll wait in the living room." I left him the kitchen so he could be undisturbed.

It didn't take long before he followed me into the living room. "Sarah, um…" Awkwardly, he ran his hand through his short brown hair.

He only sits down next to me on the leather sofa when I ask him to. He leaves so much space between us that I can't touch him. Why is he doing this?

Now he looks me straight in the eyes, his hands wandering over his thighs as if he can't keep them still. "It's really a terrible time for a child right now, don't you think? My business trips, your partnership. We're both in the middle of our careers and can't afford any distractions, you understand?" His tone is urgent, his gaze leaves no room for doubt.

I want to cling to this memory so that now, so shortly before my appointment, I can keep being strong. And still I can't manage it. Of course Tom was right, a baby would turn our lives upside down. But his views are just as devoid of feeling as the interior of this clinic. They're well calculated and undoubtedly correct. My mind agrees with him, everything else rebels. It doesn't matter how reasonable it is, because in the end it still can never be right.

Now the receptionist comes toward me. She fixes me with her gaze. It's time.

"Ms. Wagner?"

I almost wonder how polite her voice sounds, so harmless and light.

I take a deep breath, then I get up. My legs are trembling.

"Treatment room three, please." She points to the door on the other side of the waiting room and smiles at me, as artificial as before. But her eyes tell me that she doesn't approve of what I'm about to do.

Neither do I, and I'd love nothing more than to tell her exactly that.

But I stay silent, straighten my blazer, and smooth down my blouse. Mechanically, like a doll, I put one foot in front of the other. Behind the glass front, the last rays of sun wrestle with the darkness of the approaching night. They're going to lose the battle, yet with all their energy they still bathe the sky on the horizon in blood-red light. As if they refuse to give up, no matter how hopeless their situation seems.

I wished I had the same courage. Then I could still fight

too, right in this moment when the sliding doors slowly open in front of me.

Behind them everything really is nothing but white. The red on the horizon disappears and drags my last bit of strength with it into the darkness.

I can't do it. Involuntarily, I stop.

"Mrs. Wagner. Please, come inside." I hear the doctor dully, as if through cotton wool, his face a distorted grimace. Instinctively, I lay my hand on my belly and suddenly I don't care at all who can see me like this.

Under my fingertips I feel gentle warmth. I shake my head vehemently. I won't allow anything to happen to my baby. Because it's the only right thing. And I pray that everything will turn out okay.

Without another word I turn on the spot and start to run. I just want to get out of this waiting room, out of the clinic. The stylish décor blurs behind the tears at the corners of my eyes. I stagger outside, lean against the stone railing, and exhale in gasps.

The darkness of the night wraps itself around me. Still, it feels as if I had left all that black and gray behind me. My baby will live.

Chapter Three

"That'll be thirty euros, please." The taxi driver switches on the small light above us and turns to face me.

I lower my gaze and pretend I have to search my handbag for my wallet. He mustn't see the watery sheen that spreads through my eyes with such pressure that I can barely keep it from overflowing. I blink it away and feel a drop catch in my lashes.

Did I really do it? Without thinking about what that might mean?

A familiar old fear lurks behind my relief and threatens to overwhelm me.

I press a fifty into the man's hand, murmur a quiet thank you, and open the door. The mild May night hits me and dries the corners of my eyes. Vienna's air consists only of exhaust fumes and the stench of garbage, but that's exactly why I take a deep breath. The mixture flows through my body, and my attention follows it all the way into my lungs. I wish it would stay there. Forever.

“Have a nice evening.” With a satisfied smile, he turns back to the front and slips the money into his pocket.

“You too,” I say without lifting my eyelids and make sure to get away from him. As soon as I let go of the door handle, my fingers tremble more than on a frosty winter morning. I hide them in my pockets and let my gaze glide up along the wall of the apartment building on the opposite side of the street. The city’s diffuse light illuminates it just enough for me to make out the ornaments above the windows. They resemble the calm swell of the sea on a carefree day. Where they lose their momentum, they end in delicate blossoms shaped from dark stone. The entire façade is covered with the dainty decoration, right up to where the centuries-old wall meets the darkness of the night. The sky above me is black, the stars are hiding behind a veil of dark gray clouds. They refuse to shine for me, and I can understand why.

Yellowish light seeps through the curtains of the floor-to-ceiling windows on the top floor. Tom is at home. He’s waiting for me, probably wondering what’s keeping me so long. I didn’t tell him it would happen today, so we could both pretend nothing had ever happened. The guilt and the grief would have been mine alone. Tom’s thoughts would have remained unclouded, his heart light and his shoulders free of any burden. And that’s all I want for him.

I wonder how he’ll react when he finds out what just didn’t happen.

Sooner or later, I’m sure of it, he’ll be happy to watch our child grow up. Behind my worries, a shiver of joy runs down my back. I’m having a baby, and I’m finally allowed to love it.

There’s still a lot to do before then, and telling Tom the truth is my first task. I pull my shoulders back and straighten my spine. Then I set off without looking back. My steps echo through the narrow alley, rebound off the house fronts, and fade into the city's background noise. The closer I get to the wooden double gate of our building, the better I can control the movement of my legs. Only my fingers are still doing whatever they want, can barely hold the key, and even less get it into the lock. I try again, but I still don't manage to hit the small opening.

Everything will be fine, Sarah. There's absolutely no reason to be nervous.

With a deep breath, I grit my teeth and brace myself on both elbows. I hit the keyhole right away. For a moment I'm strangely euphoric, feel as if I've won a war, even though the next battle is looming right ahead of me.

The damp smell of the courtyard hits me. As the front gate closes behind me with a soft click, the elevator doors open. The same carefree waltz music as always drifts from the speaker. It doesn't match the grimace staring back at me from the mirror on the other side. My eyes look as if they would cry blood instead of tears, if I only let them.

There's no way I can let Tom see me like this.

I remove the smeared eyeliner and cover the gray with a thick layer of makeup. The eye drops complete the transformation. The red in my eyes disappears and makes way for an innocent white. I pull my shoulders back and see in the mirror the Sarah I can show Tom. The expression in my eyes is rigid, but my complexion is flawless and there's nothing wrong with my posture. I'm like a magician, trapped in her own illusion. My emotional world is more chaotic than ever, yet I look as if nothing in this world could shake me.

The elevator stops on the top floor and opens its doors without a sound. At last I can leave the forced cheerful waltz music behind and slip into the silence of our apartment. I slip off my shoes and feel my way to the coat closet. Without the heels I can feel the floor under my feet everywhere. The sensation steadies me, even more than I'd hoped. So I stay a little longer, gather energy, and breathe in the air that should be giving me a feeling of home.

The light from the open double doors of the kitchen paints bright stripes into the darkness of the hallway. Carefully I step onto the dark wooden parquet that runs through the whole apartment. It creaks with every step, terribly loud in some spots, only softly in others.

The closer I get, the more clearly I can make out what's happening in the kitchen. It smells like lasagna, a fork scrapes on porcelain. For a moment it's quiet, then a wineglass is set down on the marble surface of our kitchen counter. Before I even reach the kitchen door, the soft clicking of a keyboard starts up, if only for a few seconds.

One last step, then Tom appears before my eyes. He's sitting on one of the stools at the kitchen island and looks as if he's made himself comfortable in the middle of an exclusive furniture showroom. With a sigh he rakes his fingers through the hair on the top of his head. Now he lets his hands wander to his neck and holds it, as if he needed some support to think. He's wearing a midnight blue suit, only the jacket is off. The sleeves of his shirt are rolled up, the dark hairs on his forearms look groomed. They lie perfectly smooth in neat rows and grow finer toward his wrist. There, where he wears the gold Rolex, not a single one is visible. I love his slender fingers, which he now places back on the keyboard in one elegant movement. He's so absorbed in his work that he doesn't even notice how I lean against the doorframe behind him, looking for a bit of support.

I'm going to tell him. Now.

"Hey," I say, trying to sound cheerful. I come up behind him, touch his shoulder, and kiss his cheek. His skin is smooth and salty.

"Hi, darling." As so often, he talks to me without looking up from his screen. "Was there still a lot to do?" He puts his hand on mine and gently strokes the back of my hand with his fingertips.

In a moment I have to tell him the truth, and I don't know how he'll react. After all, it's his baby too, but I made the final decision on my own today. I turn away from him, stroll with exaggerated nonchalance to the fridge, and grab a bottle of mineral water.

"I had another appointment," I say in a steady voice and quickly raise the bottle to my lips to buy time for further explanations.

In fact, the whole act isn't even necessary; Tom is already typing something on his laptop again. He looks as if he were letting his slender fingers glide over the keys of a piano. But I always hear the same note, as if he were playing a song with no melody at all.

"Mmm, I see." He doesn't say anything more, and suddenly I no longer know whether I should feel relieved or disappointed.

I see how absorbed he is in his work. Something is worrying him; the crease on his forehead is especially deep today. His wonderfully warm brown eyes are almost completely hidden by his lids and the gracefully shaped lashes. They're like soft fans, beautiful and incredibly elegant when they move. They don't really fit with his otherwise so angular face, which right now looks far too tense. He presses his lips together, as if words were forming in his throat that must not leave his mouth. Instead, he just clears his throat and keeps typing away with renewed vigor.

"Were you successful?" he suddenly asks into the silence that surrounds me like a vacuum.

Instead of an answer, the memory surfaces in my mind. Once more I see the doctor in front of me, with the friendly laugh lines around his eyes and the gray-streaked beard. Again I feel that panic and flee once more from what, in my family's opinion, is unavoidable. How am I supposed to tell Tom that he's going to be a father after all?

"I'm not sure you could call it a success." My voice wavers a little. Despite the distance between us, Tom notices immediately. He tears his gaze away from the screen and looks straight at me.

I see the question in his eyes and shake my head so I don't have to say anything more. My hands clutch the water bottle, my knees threaten to give way. Still, I stay strong, don't let anything show, and square my shoulders. That's how we stand facing each other, surrendering for a moment, without a fight, the seemingly endless space between us to the silence.

"The appointment was today? Why didn't you say anything?" Tom sounds worried and loving, but his eyes look at me almost suspiciously. He gets up from his barstool, then hesitates.

I can feel his uncertainty from all the way over here. He's acting as if I were a wild animal whose mood you have to gauge first before you can safely approach it.

I don't want him to suffer; he doesn't deserve that.

"A slot opened up unexpectedly, so I wanted to just get it over with today." I'm surprised by how easily this lie passes my lips. Sometimes it's just simpler that way, and it doesn't change what happened anyway. "But then, when I..." I swallow and look at him, searching for help.

"Of course, I understand," Tom cuts me off. His

muscles relax. He smiles, and somehow he looks content as he's still standing there motionless. Almost happy.

Can it really be true? "You're not mad?" I ask cautiously, so I can be completely sure.

He shakes his head. "There's no reason for that."

Thank God!

Tom knows what's going on, my tension eases, everything is fine. I give him a grateful smile. Now I just need a bit of peace so the pieces of my world can find their way back into place.

"It's been a long day. I just want to take a hot shower and then fall straight into bed." With a long, drawn-out yawn, I knead my neck.

The last spark of Tom's uncertainty died away; he came over to me and took me in his arms. His warmth wrapped itself around me, I breathed in the scent of his skin. It was strongest right where my nose touched his neck, woody and sharp. I wondered if that was what home smelled like.

"Get some rest. I still have a bit of work to do, but I'll come after you as soon as I can," he said lovingly and kissed my forehead. "Sweet dreams."

I hadn't had sweet dreams in a long time, especially not at night. But it was better if he didn't know that. Besides, that would change again from now on. I looked up at him, rose onto my tiptoes, moved closer to him and nestled against his broad chest. A breath later we were kissing, as full of longing and passion as we used to. As if our hearts were beating in the same rhythm, as if we weren't two people but only one.

Plus one tiny one, made out of the two of us.

Maybe my smile was tired, but it was real. One last time I stroked his clean-shaven cheek, then I left the kitchen. My legs felt so heavy it was as if I had just finished a marathon.

Only when I entered the bathroom and closed the door behind me was I, for the first time since my escape from the clinic, completely on my own. Little by little I began to understand what had happened in the last few hours. The tension finally fell away from me, my shoulders went weak, my chin dropped. All the tiny muscles in my face had obeyed me long enough; I released them, even though I knew what was about to happen.

My eyes filled with tears of relief, very slowly, until I couldn't see anything anymore. I didn't want to hold them back any longer, closed my lids, and let the salty drops run warm down my cheeks. They caressed my neck almost tenderly and soaked into the collar of my blouse. They were completely silent, as if they had no words for what they wanted to say. They matched the stillness of the apartment, and I did the same. Not a sound came from me as I slid to the floor because my legs could no longer bear my weight. The underfloor heating beneath the cream-colored stone tiles warmed my body, but even that couldn't stop the trembling.

My baby was alive.

That was all I could think about. And nothing else mattered. Through my veil of tears I saw the bathroom from a perspective in which nothing seemed to fit together anymore. It looked distorted in an almost bizarre way, as if it were trapped in a hall of mirrors. I tried to understand why, but Tom's deep voice distracted me.

His words came dully through the vent in the solid wooden door, but I could still understand what he was saying. He was greeting someone.

"Sorry for disturbing you so late," he says, laughing artificially. Then his words take on a conspiratorial tone. He's almost whispering. "Listen, Monika…"

He's on the phone with my mother. Every time he says her name, he draws out the "o" especially long, and he does that conspicuously often. A sales manager must simply master this professionally friendly manner, along with the art of deceiving the person he's talking to. Tom can do both perfectly, but he doesn't need to manipulate my mother; the two of them always agree anyway.

Now I hear the words "today" and "taken care of," then a relieved laugh. I strain to hear what follows the laughter.

"The appointment was today. The matter has been taken care of." His voice sounds so unbelievably happy.

He didn't understand anything.

And apparently I understood just as little.

My breath catches. The baby in my belly, our baby, is nothing more than a matter to him? An annoying obligation you just have to tick off?

At least my mother never made a secret of her opinion. The memory of our conversation immediately forces its way into my thoughts, making my heart heavy and my stomach so hard it feels like it's made of stone.

Right in the middle of an upscale café in the center of Vienna, between pretty little flowers and waiters in tails, she hurled her standpoint at my head a few weeks ago. As if she were a machine, without feeling and without mercy.

"Don't make such a fuss, an abortion is nothing special," she says with absolute clarity, fixing me with her ice-blue eyes.

It's certainly not her fault, but because of the color of her eyes she naturally comes across as emotionally cold. And when she really wants something, she can freeze everything solid. Even as a child I couldn't stand that look and did everything I could to make it disappear quickly. Like an entire iceberg in the wintry polar sea, she sits across from me and sips her coffee as if she were the queen of Austria.

As so often in moments like this, a burning sensation makes itself felt in my esophagus. I have to swallow, don't know what to say. Awkwardly, I fumble with the crocheted lace on the cream-colored tablecloth.

"But…"

She instantly cuts me off. "There is no but, understood?" She presses her palms onto the table and leans dangerously close toward me. "Your father and I worked hard to get you this far. Don't you dare be ungrateful, Sarah!" She speaks very quietly, yet I can hear her over the background murmur of the other guests with absolute clarity. "You're only thirty. Your career has to come first, you can look after children later."

I know that if I don't agree, she'll use her coldness to freeze my whole world. She'll punish me with ignorance and silence because I lack perfection. Just like back then, when I cut my own hair at six years old even though she had forbidden it. It was as if I no longer existed for her, until the tips of my hair touched my shoulders again. What would she do if I chose the baby over my career?

"I…" I begin again, but I can't go on. Not when she looks the way she does now. She folds her arms across her chest and presses her lips together so tightly they lose their color. My heartburn gets worse, my heart cramps.

Still, it doesn't change the fact that I love this baby. That's what I actually want to tell her, because that's the truth.

Instead, I lower my gaze and nod timidly. That's what she expects from me. In the highly polished silver spoon next to my coffee cup I can see myself. I look just as exhausted as I feel. Even if I still had the strength, I don't want to fight her, because I know I can never win. As if that weren't enough, tears now also push out of the corners of my eyes with so much pressure that I can hardly hold them back.

"Come on, pull yourself together. What are people supposed to think?" She hisses like a snake, and I immediately feel like the defenseless rabbit that has wandered into her merciless sights. Of course, the others. That's all that matters to her.

Once again Tom laughs out loud on the other side of the door. He sounds cheerful, as if the two of them were cracking jokes now as well.

All at once I understand how everything is connected, see it in front of me like the solution to a riddle.

Tom sent my mother ahead to do the dirty work for him. That way he didn't even have to bother talking me out of having the baby. Our child, the one he didn't want. Not at any point. When I told him about the pregnancy, he slipped elegantly through the conversation like a mamba through rough terrain. Then he curled up on a sun-warmed rock and calmly watched while my mother cleared the way for him.

All at once the bathroom's hall of mirrors also stretches the perspective of my thoughts wide, showing me ugly images without edges or frames.

The stone in my stomach wants out. It lay there for so long, and now it forces its way up along my esophagus. It reaches my throat, makes me gag, pushes on into my mouth. I give in with every fiber of my body and let everything out until there's nothing left of me.

Chapter Four

The sky over Vienna is still dark, but on the horizon I can make out a pale gray. The cool night air doesn't move, the city below me is asleep.

I should be in bed too, surrounded by the beautiful dreams Tom wants for me. But when he crawled under the covers with me tonight, I was still awake. I pretended to be asleep and stretched my arm far enough away from me that he couldn't come close. Lying in the same bed with him felt strangely wrong. So I left him there alone as soon as his breathing became deep and even.

I've been sitting out here on the terrace ever since. In a softly cushioned teak chair, my arms wrapped around my legs and pulled tight against me. A thin blanket envelops me like a protective coat. It smells like the two of us, Tom and me. Back when we were still happy.

Sleep weighs heavily on my body. But whenever my eyes close, it all comes back. My baby, living and dying on an endless loop. The false relief, Tom's heartless laughter. As long as I'm awake, there's only a stale taste on my tongue and the empty feeling in my belly.

I have no idea what I should do next. About my baby, about my parents, and least of all about Tom.

Today the traffic noise is just a soft murmur, somewhere a lone bird is chirping. It's probably sitting in the crown of the tree that ends right in front of the terrace. I get up and step to the wrought-iron railing to watch the bird that's keeping me company. But it's still too dark and the courtyard lights only illuminate the ground. The paving stones encircle, in ever smaller rings, the spot where the tree grows out of the earth. It's amazing that it can live surrounded by so little soil.

I should take a leaf out of its book.

In just a few days I have to be big and strong like it, firmly rooted and ready to withstand any storm. Because the next hearing will decide the course of my life. It's the case that will make me a partner—or not. I have to win it, and I will. The last few weeks were difficult; I wasn't myself anymore. If I could turn back time, I'd do a lot of things differently. I certainly wouldn't let my thoughts drift off during a client meeting, and I definitely wouldn't mix up cases. I should have been much more of who I simply am. The perfect Sarah. Organized, determined, and eloquent.

No matter what happened, my darkness can still yield to the light, just like the long bands of cloud that are still stubbornly clinging to the sky. Behind them it's getting brighter with every minute. At last the first rays of the sun flash over the city's tiled roofs. They end this night and push the shadows back to where I can't see them. I feel their warmth on my face and close my eyes. Where everything was still black just a few hours ago, I now see the flicker of bright orange light.

If I want to be perfect the week after next, I still have to work on my litigation strategy today. I'm going to spend the day at the firm. The fact that it's Saturday doesn't bother me.

Right now, anything is better than being with Tom.

What comes next is just routine, and that's a good thing. I don't question what I put on, how I do my makeup, or how I pin up my hair. I just do it and enjoy the feeling of security that grows stronger with every movement. The helpless Sarah disappears. She makes room for the successful lawyer, the strong daughter, and the presentable girlfriend.

On my way out I pass the open bedroom door. Tom's deep, even breathing can be heard, interrupted by a soft snore every time he exhales. It sounds so innocent that my heart grows a little heavier.

Have I done him an injustice?

Am I no longer able to tell good from evil?

He only wanted to help me and told my mother about what happened so that I wouldn't have to do it myself and relive it all over again.

Is it his fault that I couldn't express myself clearly?

Whatever the truth is, I can't go to him now and press my lips to his as if nothing had happened. So I turn away, sneak off on tiptoe, and feel almost as if we'd just had an awkward one-night stand.

Chapter Five

A few minutes later I reach the place I'm inextricably bound up with. The law firm is on the top floors of a modern building in the middle of downtown Vienna. Many of my colleagues call it, with a mixture of awe and contempt, the Glass Palace. The ornate old-town houses are reflected in its façade. No one can see in from outside, but as soon as I enter the building, I can watch the whole world undisturbed, even from the elevator.

When I reach the top, I key in the access code for the firm's offices. With a soft click, the door releases its lock for me.

My footsteps are barely audible; they're swallowed by the carpet that usually greets clients with urbane elegance. Where sparkling life normally reigns, it's eerily quiet today. I feel as if I were alone in a museum. The expansive space offers no protection, the pieces of furniture give no support. In here, too, every single wall is made of glass; no one is ever truly by themselves.

The fact that I don't run into a single soul today does

me good. I stroll through the reception area and let my fingers trail over the scratchy fabric of the seating area. Three bonsai trees adorn the wall beside it, lined up like soldiers. Their branches are twisted by the burden placed on them to control their growth. Their leaves were trimmed for so long that they understood it was better to stay small. The result is fascinatingly beautiful. They're perfect miniature trees that bring an illusion of nature into the artificial climate.

Above them hang portrait photographs of the partners at my firm. Each of them has a winning smile and a trustworthy expression. Soon there'll be a picture of me in the row as well, there, in the empty spot all the way to the right. And my parents will be proud of me, no matter whether I'm pregnant or not.

A little farther down the corridor lies the next milestone in my career. The name is still missing from the sign next to the crystal-clear door, but the spacious desk is already waiting for me. Only last week one of the senior partners led me here. A telltale smirk played around his otherwise so serious face.

"This office will be yours," he says, gesturing for me to go ahead. I take in the light-flooded workspace, the generously sized area for meetings, and the cozy seating arrangement where I'll chat with our most important clients in a relaxed atmosphere. From the carpet to the desk lamp, everything is done in metallic tones. The furnishings, like the firm itself, are striking in their clean lines. "Come on, take a closer look."

I dare to step inside, my heart beating faster. A delicate scent of perfume hangs in the air, and it's noticeably warmer than it was out in the hallway.

My thoughts wander into the future. To the very

moment when I'll present this office to my parents. The anticipation overwhelms me.

"It's fantastic." With energetic strides I walk over to the window front that borders the room on two sides. Suddenly the most beautiful view in all of Vienna lies at my feet. Not far from me St. Stephen's Cathedral rises into the cloudless sky, and in sheer delight I let my gaze drift over the old buildings in the city center.

"We're not there yet, you know that." My boss raises his index finger in warning. "The partners expect top performance from you."

I nod quickly. "That's exactly what they'll get, don't worry."

His hand moves to his chin, he tilts his head to the side and studies me with his dark eyes. "Can I really?" he asks, and we both know exactly what he's alluding to.

"Of course, I'm ready." My back straightens all on its own, I lift my chin and give him a discreet smile.

I have to keep this promise. Right now the only thing that matters is the hearing date, and what I need is an unbeatable plan. And coffee, preferably a whole pot of it. Decaf, of course, I remind myself, catching myself as I unconsciously stroke my belly with a smile.

Even while the coffee runs through the machine and releases its wonderfully spicy aroma, my thoughts are on the case. It's about a horribly ugly divorce. As so often, I have to remind myself that it's not my job to judge my clients, so I shouldn't do it. I'm a professional, and I act like one.

Routinely I push the thought away and take a big sip of coffee. The hot liquid runs down my throat, bitter and sweet at the same time.

It can start. I have to forget absolutely everything now. I must not feel, hear, smell, or taste.

I can see the goal clearly in front of me. The target that has to be reached, and I'll find the way, just like I always do. Bent over my desk, I try to work as intensely as I used to.

My fingers should be flying over the computer keyboard as if in a trance. But no matter how hard I try, I can't force myself to do any of it today. All I see in front of me again is a mediocre concept.

Exhausted, I lean back in my desk chair. My gaze wanders downward, my hand comes to rest protectively on my belly. On the spot where the reason for my distraction is slumbering peacefully.

"Hello, little one," I whisper, letting my thumb wander tenderly up and down.

For the very first time, we're talking to each other. A warm feeling flows through my body and takes me over completely. Work, my parents, and Tom suddenly no longer matter. All that counts is the tiny little person in my belly.

"We belong together, you hear? No matter what happens, I promise!"

Chapter Six

The ringing of the phone tears me out of my thoughts.

There are only two people who could be calling me right now, and I have nothing to say to either of them. Still, I reach for my phone and see Tom's picture light up on the display. He beams at me, tiny lines crinkling around his eyes. The three-day stubble and sun-tanned skin make him insanely attractive. As so often when I see this picture, a wave of longing hits me. It grabs hold of me and shoots through my body like an electric shock.

I wish I could turn back time. I wish we were back there again.

Once more I hear the sea air rustling through the palm leaves, somewhere parrots are screeching in competition. My bare feet are buried in the lukewarm sand, beside me the sun is disappearing on the horizon of the Indian Ocean. We're dancing, without any music at all, far away from uncomfortable costumes, forced behavior, and ticking clocks. Just the two of us. Tom and I, the way we used to be.

The ringing of the phone grows louder, I shake the

thoughts out of my head and crash back into reality like a meteor falling unchecked from the sky. In truth, the world around me is glassy and cold. Because of the tight bun, my scalp hurts, my toes are squeezed into elegant high heels. I'm alone, I feel like a fish in an aquarium with no water.

Tom is persistent, and he'll keep trying until I pick up. So I answer the call and greet him in a neutral tone.

"Sarah, my love, where are you?" The tender sound of his voice sends a warm shiver down my back. It makes me soft and helpless, and Tom knows that perfectly well.

Right away I want to tell him everything, but I hold back. Because I want to look at him while I do it. I want to watch what's happening in his eyes and understand whether there's something hidden between his words that he can't bring himself to say.

I clear my throat to buy myself some time. "I'm preparing my case, the trial is already the week after next. Everything has to go smoothly, you know that."

"Of course." He sounds understanding, so much so that I no longer know what to think.

If I were with him, he'd be cupping my face in his hands right now and kissing my forehead. I don't want that closeness—and at the same time I long for it. I'm torn, my mind and my heart are drifting apart like the ice floes off Greenland's coast in spring.

"I'll come back as soon as I can," I finally say, and I'm not even lying to him.

"Take all the time you need, I'll be waiting for you at home."

For a moment I'm not sure what we're actually talking about here. Still, his words feel like a hug. They hold together what would otherwise just drift around loosely.

"I love you, Sarah," he says as a goodbye.

All at once there's a lump in my throat that robs me of my voice. My mind is at a loss for words. What am I supposed to say to that?

I end the call and let myself fall back into the desk chair. The sleepless night catches up with me, my body feels heavy. I feel my eyelids closing and I don't have the strength to stop them.

In slow motion the white turns to black, the darkness has me again. I jerk my eyes open. The hearing is in just a few days; until then I have to hold out. I can't disappoint anyone, I have to cross the finish line as the winner.

After that, everything will get better. I could just keep my secret to myself until then. What difference would it make anyway?

I can't deal with my mother's hatred right now. My father's indifference even less. And Tom? How will he react when he finds out?

I shouldn't waste my energy on hours of arguments with my family. What really matters is a clear head. And once I'm a partner, even my parents will understand that my baby simply has to live.

Exactly like that, and no other way, it will be.

With fresh courage I get back to work and finally lose my sense of time and of myself. My breathing is fast, my cheeks are glowing. I don't stop until everything is as perfect as it can possibly be.

Only hours later do I lean back in my chair again. Exhausted, I exhale, the text on the screen blurs before my eyes. Still, I check my concept one last time. There's nothing left for me to do. I have to go home, whether I want to or not.

Chapter Seven

At the apartment door I'm greeted by jazz music. Its leisurely rhythm and the smoky voice of the singer take away my tension. I wish I could lose myself in its beat and forget my worries while dancing. But I don't have it in me today. The smell of Asian food hangs in the air. My stomach growls, but my throat tightens.

I follow the music into the dining room. On the long table of dark wood more candles are burning than I can count. It's set for two, the long-stemmed glasses gleam in the light of the small flames. On the cloth napkin at my place lies a single gerbera. The floor creaks behind me, and a few seconds later Tom nestles against my back and wraps his arms around my waist. I feel hot and cold at the same time, I want to get away and yet also stay.

"I'm glad you're here," he says softly and pulls me tight against him. Then he covers my neck with little kisses. It feels as if a butterfly keeps taking off and landing on my skin. Pleasant and soft, warm and tender.

Part of me wants to push Tom away and pound my fists

against his chest. To scream at him so loudly that even the neighbors can still hear it.

Why? That's what I want to know from him. Nothing else.

But not a single harsh word leaves my mouth; that has to wait until after the hearing. It's better that way. For me, for him, and for our baby.

"Is all this for me?" I ask instead, slipping out of his embrace and stepping closer to the table. I let my fingers glide over the damask tablecloth and try to look pleasantly surprised.

"Of course, my darling. Sit down, the food will be served right away."

With his posture humbly bent, Tom disappears toward the kitchen and comes back with two perfectly arranged plates. He has ordered sushi and sashimi, even though he doesn't particularly like it himself. From the artfully carved carrot on the edge of the plate, I can tell it's from the best Asian restaurant in town. It's his way of showing me how important I am to him. And the fact that he does something like this for me after weeks of distance robs my doubt of its voice. He loves me, and if I give him a little more time, he'll love our baby too.

I sit down and force a smile onto my face. The leather chair's cushion is hard and so strongly curved that I always have to be on my guard not to slide off to one side. I wriggle around a little, but try in vain to find a position in which I can relax.

Tom sits down as well now. His forehead is evenly smooth, and I'm the reason for that. Even though I'm not hungry, I take a vegetable sushi roll and bite off a small piece.

The seaweed sheet tastes of the ocean, the rice sticks

clammily and soft to my palate. "Thank you, that's really sweet of you," I say in a conciliatory tone and take another bite.

Tom fills our glasses with wine and toasts me. "To us." A friendly smile plays around his lips.

I let his glass touch mine and listen to the bright chime it makes. After he has taken far too big a gulp, he wants to know everything about my day. Luckily, he doesn't notice that I haven't even raised my glass to my lips.

I tell him what my strategy for the negotiation looks like, and almost by itself the kind of normality returns between us that I've missed in recent weeks. Whether I want it or not, it gives me a sense of security and confidence.

"That sounds fantastic. You're going to show them all, I'm sure of it. The negotiation is on Wednesday, right? Then we'll celebrate your success on Friday evening. With champagne, caviar, and everything else that goes with it. It's going to be amazing!"

Tom seems as excited about my breakthrough as if it were his own. His euphoria settles on my shoulders like a heavy burden. It presses me down with all its weight, makes me small and unable to move.

"Tom, you know it's bad luck to plan a victory party before the race is won." I try to sound serious, to slow him down a little.

But he doesn't want to hear any of it and would rather chatter about possible venues, a suitable musical program, and guests who still need to be invited. It sounds as if he were planning an official reception for my inauguration as federal president, while inside I'm shrinking into my chair.

"What about your fellow students?" His cheeks are glowing. "It'd be great to invite them too. I bet none of them has gotten as far as you have!"

I don't like the sparkle in his eyes, even though I know exactly where it comes from. Deep inside him burns the ambition to lead a model life, one overflowing with everything he didn't have as a child. Status, money, and recognition instead of welfare, fear of survival, and hopelessness. He works harder for that than anyone else I know.

My hand wants to wander to his cheek all on its own, but I hold it back. Instead I smooth the tablecloth, even though it doesn't have a single crease.

"Do you really think so? I hardly have any contact with my classmates anymore anyway."

With a mischievous grin, he swings his glass. "Oh, absolutely. They should all come. Including that… what's her name again?"

"Simone?" I help him out, even though I don't really know who he means. The truth is, I didn't have any friends at university. While the others were rocking every party, I sat at home at my desk. With my brain overheating and printer's ink on my fingertips.

Tom furrows his brow and looks far too cute doing it. "Yeah, maybe. And then that one with the long dark hair. Plus that blond snob, we definitely need him there. He won't believe his eyes!"

"Philipp? You want to invite him too? I'm not so sure about that." My voice loses its strength, grows quieter, and fades away.

Tom doesn't seem to notice my hesitation at all. With a dreamy look in his eyes, he sorts possible guests and guests of honor. I can't stop him, so I nod now and then and try to smile. What I'd like most is to drink the wine in front of me in big gulps. Maybe it could ease the pressure Tom is so thoughtlessly putting on me. Because standing up to him feels impossible. As strong as I can be as a lawyer, when it comes to being loved, everything inside me turns soft.

"Good, then that's settled." He smiles at me, satisfied, and raises his glass again.

What else can I do but clink glasses with him? He doesn't take his eyes off me the whole time, so I take a small sip of wine. A warm feeling spreads in my stomach.

"You wouldn't believe what my day was like." Tom's cheeks start glowing again, and I know I don't have to say much now. I nod appreciatively from time to time; that's usually enough.

It doesn't take long before a heavy tiredness overwhelms me. The image of our dining room changes before my eyes, as if someone were putting a soft-focus filter over it and turning it up higher and higher. The candle flames merge with one another, the edges of the table grow rounder. Even the usually smooth white walls look as if I could sink into them like into a cloud.

Tom's voice grows a little muffled, but it sounds so wonderfully melodic in my ears, as if he were telling me a bedtime story. That makes me even sleepier, so that I finally have to interrupt him.

I thank him for the wonderful evening, explain that now I just want to go to bed, and kiss him goodbye. His lips taste of soy sauce and leave a tingling on my mouth. I'm too tired to figure out whether that's because of our love or just a tiny bit of leftover wasabi.

Without thinking about it any further, I drag myself into the bathroom and a few minutes later fall into bed like a stone into an oversized ball of cotton wool. My thoughts disappear on the horizon, where the gray of evening and the black of night merge with each other.

Chapter Eight

"What was going on with you this morning?" Tom's voice sounds so casual, as if he were asking about the weather report. He keeps his eyes on the road, even though there are no bends in sight and there's hardly any traffic today. Nobody wants to drive anywhere on Sundays; only Tom and I are polluting the air with our Mercedes.

I sink deeper into the seat and stifle a yawn. I've been awake for hours because the truth about my baby wouldn't let me sleep. When Tom then snuggled up to me at dawn and let his hand wander over my belly, it suddenly became too much for me.

I just wanted to get away.

We've barely spoken since. Tom answered his emails over a coffee and I caught up on the latest news from the legal world. Like on an ordinary Sunday, as if someone had turned back time by a month. All morning I've felt like an actress desperately clinging to her role. Since I slipped into my dark blue jeans, the white blouse, and the matching blazer, it's been working better. My hair is perfect, my makeup too. The shields are up.

"I guess the trial is getting to me more than I'd like," I reply in a steady voice and inspect my fingernails. They look flawless, just the way they're supposed to.

"Oh come on, you're going to knock them all dead. You really don't need to worry." There's pride in Tom's words. He reaches for my hand, squeezes it, and doesn't let go again.

I don't like it when he acts as if there were no human being under my skin but a machine programmed only to win. Still, I grunt in agreement. I'm not ready for arguments and I don't have the energy to fight.

Concrete buildings of Vienna pass by my window, lined with billboards, street signs, and parked cars. Nothing but metal and stone. That's all this city is made of.

Tom's clearing his throat jolts me out of my thoughts. "By the way, I let Monika know. You know, about Friday evening." The knuckles of the hand on the steering wheel stand out white. "At the clinic."

I hear only the long "o" in my mother's name, and the hairs on the back of my neck are already standing on end. "Oh yeah?" I ask as neutrally as I can.

"I thought I'd take care of that for you so we don't have to drag the whole subject out today. You prefer it that way too, don't you?" His lower jaw looks tense and he still doesn't look at me.

So many words push their way up inside me, and I swallow every single one of them. "Sure," I reply with a smile, because it's better that way.

Out of the corner of my eye I see Tom nod in satisfaction. He thinks he did everything right, and in his version of the story he did. My hand wants to wander to my belly, but I hold it back with all my strength. Instead I stare at the seat belt that touches my body exactly where my baby lives. We pass through the streets of Vienna in silence. A cheerful Spanish song is playing on the radio, the clouds in the sky above us draw together like the cotton-white curtain of a theater stage. I wonder which act we're playing right now and which one will come next. Can I even be sure that there'll be anything after this at all?

Little by little more green spaces appear between the concrete walls, a few trees, sometimes even flowers. The houses out here in the posh outer districts look as if they'd been polished to a high gloss. Their colors are muted but beautiful; even the gray houses don't look sad, but elegant.

Tom steers our car into the side street that leads to my parents' house. Coming here to visit every first Sunday of the month feels as if I were putting on a corset every five weeks. Then for a few hours I allow everyone to tug at the laces. My parents, the house crammed full of memories, and somehow Tom as well. I breathe without getting any air, and still I endure it. This is my life, the way it has always been.

Am I strong enough for it today as well?

I have no time to think about it; the driveway already appears before my eyes. We pass through the wrought-iron gate guarded by two stone lions. They sit on the posts on either side, holding their heads elegantly raised and their backs straight. Then we roll leisurely along the gravel path to the house. It isn't particularly long, yet my mother had an avenue laid out here. There are only three birches on each side; behind them stretches an English lawn adorned with perfectly trimmed box trees. In front of us the house rises up like a castle. A dream in antique rose paint from long-forgotten times, with white shutters and generous terrace areas.

Tom parks our car, I draw a deep breath once more and get out. The sun is blazing in the sky, but I have to wear the blazer if I don't want to have an argument with my mother. An intense smell of roast beef hangs in the air, as if the entire neighborhood were cooking the same thing today.

"Come on now, we're running late." Tom takes my hand and pulls me up the steps. It's exactly twelve o'clock. In truth we're already late; after all, it's only proper to arrive a few minutes before the agreed time. That's a gesture of politeness, my mother says, and she should know.

We sprint up the stone steps. While I cover the last few yards, Tom is already putting his hand on the old-fashioned brass door knocker. But he doesn't get the chance to rap it against the wooden door. It's already being opened by my mother, so quickly you'd think she'd been waiting for us at the window. Her light blue suit fits her like a glove over her barely existent hips, and her gold bracelets jangle in a hectic clatter.

"Hello, you two." Her voice is cool, and she pointedly squints at the watch on her slender wrist. For a moment she pulls down the corners of her mouth and shakes her head, as if she can't believe what she's seeing.

At once I feel the corset nestle against my body, completely harmless, as if it were nothing more than a good friend. I check that my hair is sitting right; at least that should be perfect, if I myself already am not.

Luckily, Tom takes the initiative. "Monika, I'm sorry. Our being late is entirely my fault. You know, work." With a friendly, open smile he hugs my mother, whose features soften again. That, of course, she understands. She pats Tom on the back, then it's my turn.

"Well, now you're here," she says, a little more conciliatory, and presses her cheek to mine without kissing it. Her perfume hits my nose. It's far too fresh, smells more like a woman in her mid-twenties than a lady who's heading toward her sixtieth year.

The touch lasts only a fraction of a second, then she looks me over with a scrutinizing gaze. I smile automatically, and the icy blue of her eyes grows a little warmer. "Come on, come on, everyone's waiting for you." With a sweeping movement she turns around. Her artificially blond bob withstands the motion as if it were set in concrete.

I dart after her. No one knows where she gets her energy from, when she's so thin she looks as if she might snap in two. She practically flies over the wine-red runner with the golden border that stretches the entire length of the entrance hall.

On the threshold to the dining room she stops and, with a hectic hand movement, signals that we need to hurry up. When she has that expression on her face, none of the rejuvenation treatments she's been having regularly for years do her any good. She looks hardened, but no one would dare tell her that.

I lengthen my stride even more and am even a little out of breath when I reach her. My mother smiles, satisfied, then puts on the radiant expression of a woman of the world that she so loves to present to the outside.

"Bernhard, just look, they're finally here." She practically sings the words, her voice suddenly so melodic. A whole orchestra on the radio accompanies her entrance with a powerful symphony. Together they sound as if they're standing on an opera stage, and the dining room looks a bit like that too. The furnishings are dark wood. Art

Nouveau furniture, of course, as my mother likes to emphasize, upholstered in fine fabrics in cream and red.

My father is standing at one of the windows that look out onto the garden, and he looks like a bear. Big and soft, with white hair on his head. He's wearing a brown checked shirt and brown dress pants, with his hands buried in the pockets.

"Bernhard," my mother says again when my father doesn't react right away. This time louder and faster. She pronounces his name as if it contained a double r. That's her trick to shut absolutely anyone up. She does the same with my name when necessary. A melodious Sarah turns into a ghastly Sarra. It sounds like someone scraping their fingernails over a slate board.

My father turns around and comes toward us. "Hello, Sarah, hello, Tom." His voice is just a low rumble, as if he were dissatisfied and weren't allowed to say why. He shakes Tom's hand very formally, touches my upper arm, and brushes a quick kiss against my cheek. He smells of pipe smoke, his full beard tickles my skin. Unlike my mother, he doesn't look searchingly into my eyes but turns away from me again.

"All right; then we can finally eat. Bernhard, Sarah, Tom, sit down."

As we sit down, my mother rings a bell. She loves treating the catering staff like servants. A young girl in a black apron appears in the doorway, presents us with the day's menu as if we were in a Michelin-starred restaurant, and serves the soup in gleaming porcelain with gilded rims. It's the promised onion soup, and I don't like onions.

"How's work, Sarah?" my mother asks in a sharp tone, and I already regret that I've just been staring idly at the soup. Now I don't have a suitable excuse, I have to answer.

"Everything's great." I pull the corners of my mouth up, and with the forced smile my corset tightens further. But I can still breathe.

She draws her eyebrows together. Thanks to Botox, not a single wrinkle forms on her forehead. The skin around her slightly too-full lips puckers only a little, although I can clearly see how hard she's tensing her mouth. "That's nice to hear. Tell me more. Have you prepared your case well? What are you going to wear to the hearing?"

It's always the same questions, and she always gets the same answers from me. After all, she doesn't want to hear anything else. "Of course, I finalized the concept yesterday. Everything's ready, including the outfit."

"You were at the firm on Saturday to work? Good, good." She seems a bit more satisfied again; I even think I see a brief smile flicker across her face. At the same time she nudges my father's arm with her elbow, and he gives an approving grunt, as if on command.

Then the interrogation continues with Tom. While I choke down the soup, he reports with great enthusiasm on his upcoming sales trip through Asia. He'll be on the road for a full three weeks, and just a few days ago the thought of it made me sad. Being without him had always been like standing defenseless in the middle of a whirlwind.

Did he really do anything wrong? Or am I the one who no longer knows what's good and right?

He makes an effort with me, gives me his love and more attention than in the weeks before. Even now he steps in for me, draws my parents' interest to himself and gives me time to relax. His expansive accounts of the travel route and the upcoming meetings make my mother's eyes shine, my father nods appreciatively.

"Well then, everything's just fine." My mother is overjoyed; this kind of perfect world is what she likes best. Everyone here assumes that the night before last a doctor scraped a living little human out of my uterus and then simply disposed of it. But no one says a single word about it. It doesn't fit the picture my parents have painted for me; in our fair-weather life there's no room for things like that. "At least we don't have any problems, do we?" she adds, patting my father's upper arm.

Right on cue, he chimes in. "Exactly right."

Tom reacts before I have to and asks the question the two of them want to hear. "So is someone in trouble?"

With a theatrical sigh, my mother shrugs her shoulders. "The Baumgartners across the way, you know, further up the street, were broken into last week."

"Do you think it was foreigners?" My father seems unsure.

"Or that criminal gang that's been making a racket at night with their motorcycles lately. I'm telling you, when I so much as see one of those things..."

"I'm completely with you, Monika," Tom cuts in again now. "Motorcycles are the devil's machines and, honestly, what kind of person willingly sits on something that filthy and dangerous?"

My mother lets out a cold laugh. "Degenerate idiots with self-tattooed forearms." She twists her mouth. "Drifters and ex-cons."

My father grunts in agreement. "Dead weight for our society."

How do they manage to end up on the same topic every single time? Together the three of them rant about welfare scroungers and the fact that all our incomes are taxed as well in order to support them. It's better for me to keep quiet. The memory of what happened a few years ago when I tried to do the opposite is still far too vivid.

I had just started studying, and for a moment I thought the wind of freedom was blowing around my nose. Ridiculous, but that's how it was. I believed I was grown-up enough to finally make my own decisions. It happened on a Sunday morning; with her back straight and her index finger sticking out, my mother drank her coffee and ranted about the progressive tax rates in Austria.

"Just because we earn more, we're supposed to give up more?" She snorts contemptuously. "As if we didn't have to work for our money too."

A strained groan escapes me, then I cut into her tirade. "Give it a rest."

Instantly she fixes me with her gaze. "Excuse me?"

"Not everyone has it as good as we do," I say with a shrug and take a bite of my jam sandwich. Some of my classmates have to work on the side to finance their lives. They live in tiny rooms and bring their lunch from home so they don't blow their budget. Every cent of tax they don't have to pay helps them.

Her jaw turns to stone; she braces her palms on the tabletop and leans over toward me. "That was hard work. And now we're supposed to be punished for it? You shouldn't judge things you don't understand," she hisses so coldly that everything around me freezes. "And now get to your room and study for the exam next week. I expect top marks, is that clear?"

For a few seconds I hold her gaze, stare back unyieldingly, and consider my next move. But before I can say anything, she comes out with exactly the words that bring every bit of resistance in me crashing down.

"Or do you actually want your father and me to be ashamed of you?"

Of course I didn't want that, I never did. Not today either. Right on cue, my heartburn makes itself known. While the rant about the scum of society goes into the next round between my parents and Tom, I quickly take a spoonful of soup so that no more than a nod can be expected from me.

Between the salad platter and the roast beef there's only one topic left. My mother reports, full of excitement, about the children of her friend Maria, who are apparently all geniuses. While she talks, she looks at me expectantly. As if Tom hadn't already put enough pressure on me on the way here. My breathing turns shallow; anything more is no longer possible.

When we finally get our dessert served, she suddenly falls silent. Her gaze rests on me and at once I feel as if I were an attraction at the zoo. I have to say something, give her something so she can be proud of her child too. But I can't think of a single thing I could shine with.

"That sounds great, please give Maria my congratulations." I try to sound enthusiastic and hope the diversion works. Because lately I haven't had any brilliant achievements to show for myself, quite the opposite. More than once there was trouble at the firm; I was far too unfocused and careless. My mother is still silent, so I start nodding vigorously. She stares at me as if she can't believe that she isn't hearing a new story from me today that she can brag about to her friends tomorrow.

My father is contentedly spooning up his chocolate cake. That seems like the best solution for me too; I lower my gaze and poke industriously at the little gold-rimmed porcelain bowl with my silver fork. I wish Tom would jump in again, but he's strangely quiet as well.

Doesn't he realize that he's only making everything even worse by doing that?

I put a small bite of cake into my mouth and chew on it until there's really nothing left of the sticky sweet mass. "The dessert tastes excellent." I speak only so the silence will finally end.

"I'm sure it does. Go on, have another piece." That's all she answers, and slowly I start to get scared.

I know what she's waiting for.

By now my corset has given me a wasp waist. The burning in my esophagus spreads across my whole chest. Her gaze pierces me like a lance; I have to come up with something. Now. But my brain is starved of oxygen; all I can think about is that my baby is still alive. And that's definitely not something anyone here wants to hear.

I have no choice, so I stick my fork back into the cake. This time I want to scoop up a big piece from the bowl so I can chew on it for a really long time. My nerves make me so clumsy that I can't even manage that anymore. I keep hitting something hard; this dessert seems to have a solid chocolate core. Just perfect.

My mother slides forward in her armchair, her dress scraping noisily against the delicate fabric. The tense silence is still drowned out by the orchestra on the radio, which is already racing toward its finale.

Now it's time.

The corset is cutting off my breath, the laces grow so long that they wrap around my neck as well. They tighten and make me gag, as if I were dangling from the gallows. With the last of my strength I scrape a piece of cake out of the bowl. Something glittering appears underneath. Out of the corner of my eye I see Tom sliding off his armchair. He lands on his knees beside me.

Oh my God, he's not going to…

My mother is shaking all over. My father sets his fork down. The orchestra ends its piece with a crash of drums.

Everything is silent.

Tom looks straight up into my eyes. "Sarah…"

No. That's all I feel. My head is better behaved than I am; it nods, or at least I think it does. Why is it doing that?

"…you're the love of my life," he says, unusually cautious.

My stomach rebelled; the roast beef wanted to come back up. It rose, but got stuck in my constricted throat.

"I can't and don't want to imagine a life without you anymore. I don't know how I'm supposed to survive the time in Asia if you're not with me."

Maybe he just wanted me to go on his trip with him? And in the shell there was nothing but a necklace with a pretty pendant. My gaze flicked back and forth between the sparkling thing and the hopeful look in Tom's eyes.

He cleared his throat several times, lifting his arms apologetically as he did so. "That's why I'd like to ask you…" I wished his voice would tremble less. He took a deep breath and took my hands in his. "Marry me, Sarah!"

Silence. Expectant looks. Excited gestures.

My mother nodded vigorously. Tom's body was tense; his expression reminded me of a puppy that wanted its toy.

In the middle of it all I sat, speechless, feeling ambushed and defenseless.

I felt sick, my heart was racing, but my vision didn't go black. On the contrary, I saw everything in razor-sharp focus and clear outlines.

"Of course she does," my mother cut in loudly; apparently it had already taken too long for her. "Isn't that right, Sarah?"

I didn't know. Maybe.

"Sarra!" My mother's shrill tone shoots through my body like an axe, severing my heart from my mind. I can hardly bear it when she says my name like that.

Yes, the wedding is probably the sensible thing to do. After all, Tom and I have been a good team so far. And on top of that, my mother would finally have the great story for her friends that she's been waiting for so long already.

I nod, very slowly. I can't say anything.

Tom exhales loudly, my mother blinks conspicuously hard. "I'm so happy for you!" she cries, getting up from her armchair. She comes over to us and hugs us both at the same time.

My father smiles in quiet satisfaction and congratulates us very formally. Seeing everyone so happy relaxes me too, in a strange way. The noose around my throat loosens.

Tom frees the ring from the last bits of cake and slips it onto my finger. There's still a little chocolate stuck to the setting, but it's stunningly beautiful. With a diamond as big as a pea.

My mother keeps on talking for me. "Tom, you chose it wonderfully, it's perfect." The rapturous note in her voice is impossible to miss. And in fact I have to admit she's right. It's perfect for the perfect daughter, who is now also marrying the perfect man.

Only nobody wants the baby that goes with it.

It's probably not perfect enough.

The glitter of the gemstone on my finger blurs before my eyes, my mother's words grow muffled. I swallow hard; there's a nasty taste on my tongue, flat and somehow furry.

Liar, a voice in my head screams.

What on earth have I done? All my life I only ever made decisions about things that clearly fit within the framework of my goals. And now? All on my own I've made a decision that affects everyone here. Especially Tom. I have to tell them, right now! My lips move, but not a single word leaves my mouth.

"Well, someone's overwhelmed," my father speaks up.

I blink the watery haze from my eyes and try to look happy. Either it works, or the others pretend not to notice how I really am.

"Still, my dear daughter, we also have a surprise for you." There's anticipation in his voice, maybe even emotion.

"Oh yes, we do!" I haven't seen my mother this pleased in a long time. "Bernhard, come on, go ahead! Give it to her!"

"Calm down," my father says without the slightest excitement, yet he can no more ignore my mother's commanding tone than anyone else can. He reaches for a white envelope that must have been lying on the armchair next to him the whole time. Now he rises ceremoniously, as if he were presenting me with a diploma.

"Sarah, very soon you won't just be Tom's wife, you'll also be a partner in the best law firm in town. Of course you'll then tackle the next goal, that goes without saying. Still, we want to celebrate this milestone. We—your mother and I—have a gift for you that I have the honor of presenting to you now."

With a slight bow he hands me the envelope. I catch myself thinking that his little speech would also suit one of his employees celebrating their thirtieth work anniversary.

But of course I show myself grateful, just as is expected of me. I take the white envelope, with my name written on it in gold lettering. Typical Mom— even a simple envelope has to meet her perfectionist standards and match the color scheme of the table decorations. I open it, and what I find inside makes me forget for a moment where I am.

"Wow," I stammer after pulling the certificate out of the envelope and reading the text on the first page twice in a row.

Out of the corner of my eye I see my mother watching every tiny reaction of mine. "We're giving you an apartment," she explains unnecessarily.

"Two hundred and fifty square meters, a luxurious penthouse in Vienna's first district. Prime location," my father says while I look at the pictures. There's a terrace with a hot tub and a rooftop garden, a library, and a walk-in closet that looks like a designer store. Altogether I count three bedrooms and just as many bathrooms.

My father is close to tears. "You've earned it," he says and pulls me into a tight hug.

The fact that I haven't won my case yet goes unmentioned; after all, for everyone it's nothing more than a formality now. And I don't want to think about it either. I'd much rather enjoy the warmth of his embrace and bury my nose deep in the fabric of his shirt. The smell of his pipe always makes me feel safe whenever I can smell it as intensely as I do now.

He's rewarding me for something that hasn't even happened yet. Still, his affection soothes a longing in me that has been with me for as long as I can remember. Moments like this are rare; I savor it for as long as I can.

I can see very clearly how everything can be made right

again. The right moment to reveal the truth about my baby really hasn't come yet. First I'll make partner and make sure my family can be proud of me.

I have to win my case; it's the key to my happiness.

Chapter Nine

I've been sitting on the roof terrace of the glass palace for hours. Far away from my office, which seemed strangely cramped to me today. I couldn't relax there, and even less could I think. It was as if the furniture were staring at me accusingly, as if the walls had ears and the clock a voice.

Out here I can look into the distance, the wind gently strokes my face. That takes the pressure off me, makes me feel light and free. Still, I can't manage to concentrate on my work. The words on the laptop screen blur, I can hardly read my handwriting in the files. My feelings have taken command, and the truth is that I don't want to push them away any longer.

Somewhere between hope and panic, between love and the desire to be loved, my thoughts are stuck like a record player's needle on the vinyl. Behind my mother's cold expression and the sober sound of Tom's voice, there where reason has nothing to say, that's exactly where my heart beats for my baby. Loud and hard, it shows me that I made the right decision. Even now I love this little being in my belly more than anything else in the world. In my mind I rock it in my arms, kiss the soft skin of its forehead and sing it a lullaby. A feeling of happiness floods my whole body. With my gaze fixed on the bright blue sky above me, I can only think of one thing. Everything will turn out for the best.

"Ms. Wagner!" My boss's voice makes me flinch as if I suddenly heard a shot right next to me. "So here you are. What on earth are you doing here?"

He fixes me with an angry expression, his hands clenched into fists. What did I do wrong?

"I'm working on my case." Smiling pointedly, I nod toward my laptop.

His eyebrows draw together. Countless wrinkles appear on his forehead, each of them as deep as a canyon. "Don't lie to me. Not again. I can see perfectly well what's going on here."

What does he mean? Instinctively I straighten up and lift my chin. "I just needed a bit of fresh air, I can work out here too," I say in my defense, in a voice as reasonable as it can possibly be.

His snort sounds contemptuous. "Oh really? You call that working? You're just staring at the sky and daydreaming!"

This can't be true, he's been watching me. For how long? "Unusual cases require unusual measures," I reply confidently and look at him kindly. "I learned that from you."

It might just be wishful thinking, but I imagine that his features relax. His eyes release me from their unrelenting stare, wander downward and suddenly get stuck on something. "Are you feeling all right?"

It takes less than a second for me to register what prompted his question.

My hand is resting on my stomach.

How long has it been there? And why? I quickly pull it away and smooth down my skirt. It feels as if he has caught me doing something forbidden. I have to be more careful.

"Everything's fine." I pull up the corners of my mouth; I don't have anything better to offer.

At once he turns serious again. "Then make sure you finally get to the firm," he snaps at me. "Your client has already been waiting for fifteen minutes. That's unacceptable. Absolutely unacceptable!"

Impossible, is the appointment really already now? My gaze darts back and forth between my boss's angry face and the time display on the laptop screen. Oh no, please no! "I..."

He raises his hand and silences me on the spot. "Spare me your excuses." The coldness in his voice could freeze even the clouds in the sky. "Go on, what are you waiting for?"

I shoot up from my seat, snap the laptop shut, and yank it toward me. "Of course, I'm sorry."

I dash toward the door, race down the hallway at a run, and hurtle down the stairs. The high heels are in my way; I need to be faster.

Faster, Sarra. Come on!

Once more I quicken my steps. By now my breathing is nothing but harsh gasps, and with a wet smack my laptop threatens to slip from my hands. I press it tight against my chest and keep running. Just one more floor. In a few seconds I'll arrive where I should have been a long time ago.

I practically fly around the corner, and the pea-sized

heel of my stiletto suddenly loses its grip out of nowhere. My foot twists. A sharp pain shoots through my ankle. I groan.

Then everything happens very fast.

There's no stopping it anymore. My legs stumble, I lose control of my body. The landing rushes toward me.

Marble floor, light with dark inclusions. Neon light. Stair railing. Grab on? Impossible. The stairwell tumbles past my eyes, over and over again. It doesn't stop, just like the piercing scream that leaves my mouth.

All at once, it's quiet.

Chapter Ten

For a moment I can't breathe, my lungs don't work. My whole body hurts as if I had broken every single bone. I gasp for air like someone who has been underwater far too long. My mind comes back, my sense of time doesn't. I have no idea how long I've been lying here, my cheek resting on the cold marble floor, my legs twisted at a strange angle. Slowly I open my eyes and look at my feet. My shoes are gone. Where the dark red of my painted toenails gleams, I spot a run in my stockings. It stretches over my ankle and up along my shin. Oh no, not that as well.

With effort I push myself up, check my arms, and cautiously try to shift my weight onto my legs. Everything seems to be intact, only my head is pounding like crazy.

I quickly tuck my hair back where it belongs and straighten my blazer. I must look awful. I can't face my client like this. Next I need to freshen up, and as fast as possible. But at the very first step my stomach cramps, as if a giant were squeezing it with his fist. The pain shoots into my belly, I double over instinctively, but it doesn't help at all.

In the next moment, I feel it.

A warm liquid runs down the insides of my thighs. Frantically, I let my hand wander under my skirt. Luckily, I feel only a little dampness, probably sweat from running.

Everything is fine. I can go on.

My stomach cramped nonstop, but I couldn't deal with that now. I pulled my hand back and tried to breathe calmly. When I wiped my fingers off on the fabric of my blazer, I went hot and cold at the same time.

Nothing is fine.

Blood. There's blood on my hand, blood on my thighs. Where in heaven's name…?

The red-flecked image in front of my eyes blurred, the stairwell began to spin. In the distance I heard a male voice. "Ms. Wagner, oh my goodness!" he shouted in a panic.

I wanted to calm him down and raised my hand. The pounding in my head grew even worse, the neon light above me seemed unbearably bright.

My knees gave way, my whole body grew weak. The last thing I perceived was my boss's distorted face, which seemed to be coming closer and closer.

Then everything went black.

Chapter Eleven

"She's coming to."

"Good. Give her another liter of saline solution and ask what's taking the CT so long this time."

"Will do. Should I take her with me right away?"

"Yes, it can't hurt."

The ground beneath me started to move, jolting and rattling deafeningly. Light and darkness flickered alternately over my eyelids like the wings of jet-black ravens against a cloudless sky. I tried to open my eyes, but I couldn't make anything out. My surroundings were nothing but vague outlines. Everything was white, an overly bright lamp dazzled me. Now a gray shadow came closer, a ghostly face appeared in front of me.

"Welcome back!" The voice was very warm, like a fireplace on a dark winter's day. Did it belong to the face that was still above me?

The rattling came to an end; instead, I now heard ringing tones.

What's that? My alarm clock?

A nightmare!

I understood. My eyelids grew heavy, far too heavy to keep them open any longer. The darkness had me again.

A monotonous beeping presses against my eardrum. I'm floating on a warm, soft cloud. Something has latched onto the back of my right hand, a beetle maybe. An intense orange scent surrounds me, but behind it lurks the sharp smell of disinfectant.

I know where I am.

But why? And whose voices are those, talking over each other so wildly? They're muffled, as if someone were pressing a pillow over my face. That's exactly how my head feels too, trapped and sore.

"Impossible!" I recognize my mother's tone. That's how she sounds when her plans are thwarted.

"Of course I understand that you're upset, Mrs. Wagner. But please, try to stay calm. It'll be hard for your daughter, she'll need you." Whoever is speaking, I don't know him.

My mother snorts contemptuously. "Nonsense," she says, completely sober.

"Monika, come on, this isn't helping." Tom. That's Tom speaking!

Now I'm wide awake, only I don't open my eyes.

"I'll come back as soon as Sarah wakes up. Then we can discuss everything else," says the unknown male voice. Then I hear footsteps, a hint of sporty men's cologne passes by me. A door is opened and a few seconds later closed again.

Who's still here now? Tom. And my mother. Is my father here too? I strain to figure out what's happening beside me.

"Did you know about this?" my mother snaps at Tom, a sharp undertone in her voice.

"For God's sake, no." He sounds as if someone has drained all his strength. "She lied to me too, made fools of us all."

My heart skips a beat.

They know.

It must have come up during the tests. Oh no, please don't. Not now, not like this.

High heels click loudly back and forth; with every step a stabbing pain pierces my head. "The child is no longer controllable. What on earth is wrong with her?" my mother wants to know. She's probably putting her index finger to her chin, her eyes narrowing to slits.

Tom exhales loudly. "I'd really like to know that myself." His voice sounds terribly sad. I'd love to comfort him, right now. "I honestly thought everything was fine."

The footsteps stop, thank God. "She betrayed us. And we were stupid enough to believe her."

For a brief moment there is silence.

"Whatever. It's all taken care of now anyway."

Done? What's that supposed to mean?

Tom doesn't say a word. My mother clears her throat. "So how are we going to go on?" she asks, with a conspiratorial undertone in her voice.

"There's no point in making a big fuss about it." He sounds helpless and tired. That's entirely my fault. "Why cause a scene?" he asks, and I can practically see him shrugging his shoulders.

What on earth does he mean by that? The scene has already been made, and soon everyone will notice. You can't just sweep a belly that round under the rug.

"Exactly," my mother confirms now, to top it all off. "The brat is gone. We'll pretend nothing happened."

My mother's words pound in my head. The brat is gone, gone, gone.

No!

My stomach clenches in painful cramps, my body grows heavy. Even if I wanted to hold back my tears, I couldn't. They force their way through the narrow slit of my eyelids, run hot down my cheeks, and seep into my hair. My senses stop reacting, I stop feeling, I can't think anymore. No smell reaches my nose, I no longer register a single one of Tom's words.

I'm falling, and no one can catch me now.

I hit the ground without braking. It's cold, hard, and blacker than any night. Curled up, I rock myself back and forth. Salty drops keep running down my face. They're everywhere. On my skin, on my lips, in my hair. As if they wanted to make it clear to me from all sides that it's true.

My baby is dead.

"Dead, dead, dead" echoes in my head and immediately the next cramp seizes my body.

No one is here. My room is as empty as I feel. They slipped away without speaking to me. Even now they still want to pretend that nothing at all has happened.

And they can have it that way.

I hardly feel strong enough to get up. Exhausted, I bury my head under the blanket. The pressure on my eyes increases, everything around me turns dark. Reality and illusion blur into one another. Like watercolors that come too close together.

Black and gray.

From far away I hear a baby crying, very softly, really it's just a whimper. I mustn't care about the child, I ignore it, I want to sleep. All at once it's next to my ear, screaming at the top of its lungs straight into my eardrum. The shrill sound hurts everywhere.

I turn my head, my cheek grows wet. Slimy and cold. Blood, there's blood everywhere. In my arms the baby, tiny as a dwarf, with black doll's eyes. It stares at me, speaks in a distorted voice. I don't understand a word, I wipe the blood from its cheeks, and underneath, freckles glow.

Its arm falls off, I catch it, it has to go back where it belongs. It doesn't want to stay there anymore. The second arm falls off, then both legs. I don't have that many hands, panic rises in me. The baby laughs at me, and now its head is opening up as well. It breaks apart. Right down the middle. Just like that!

"Murderer," it resounds from a thousand mouths all around me.

I have to save it, press the two halves together.

Murderer, the chorus grows louder. And faster.

It slips from my grasp, the baby is gone.

Murderer, murderer, murderer.

The blood is still there, all around me. My dress clings to my skin, soaked cherry red, my hair is damp.

"Sarah."

They know my name, they know not only what I am but who I am. I have to flee, get away from here.

"Sarah!"

I lash out, I won't let them catch me. They're stronger, force my arms down, hold me tight. Now I have to atone for my deed.

"Darling!"

They brush the damp hair from my forehead. Why? Who calls me murderer and darling at the same time?

Something's wrong here, where am I?

"Open your eyes," a deep voice says. It's soft, as soft as the hands that are shaking me.

Where did the baby go? I look around. I don't see it anywhere, but Tom is here. I blink in bewilderment. Is he really there? What's he doing here, when he doesn't want to know about the baby? There's little to make out behind him, everything is gray.

"You had a nightmare," he explains to me now, so slowly, as if I were an idiot.

Nightmare, what does that mean?

"But now everything's fine. Come on, Sarah, say something already."

"Tom." My voice is little more than a croak.

He looks relieved, lets go of my arms, and braces himself on the bed beside me. The bedding is white. So this is where we are, in the hospital. Makes sense, really.

I exhale, my heartbeat settles. I'm cold, the hospital gown is damp, my hair is sticking to my skin.

Tom pulls me toward him, wraps his arms protectively around my body, and hugs me.

"We'll get through this," he whispers in my ear. "I love you, Sarah, no matter what happens."

He's here and holds me tight, gives me peace and a sense of safety. As long as I can lose myself in the woody, tangy scent of his skin and kiss his lips, I'm not alone with my worries. With a sob, I let myself sink deeper into his embrace.

He catches me, and that's all I need to know.

"I love you too." The words suddenly slip from my lips again, as easily as before. Because they're the truth.

Chapter Twelve

Once again it works to my advantage that I've mastered the art of never letting anyone see what's going on behind my façade. For days now I've shown the whole world nothing but a controlled expression and an upright posture. My voice is steady, my diction flawless.

Inside me, though, just beneath the invulnerable outer shell, everything is soft. Not a single bone broke when I fell down the stairs, and yet I'm no longer whole. Because the most important part of me is missing. My heart hammers against my ribcage as if it wants to escape. Run away, somewhere it can forget. And I want to run with it, to the end of the world. Or even farther.

Then I wouldn't be sitting here. On the front edge of my desk chair, my back ramrod straight and my hair pulled tightly back. I wouldn't have to pretend I'm working when in truth I'm only staring at the time display on the screen. It counts down the minutes relentlessly in the same steady rhythm.

It'll be time any moment now. The case that will decide my future is about to be heard.

It won't be long now, then hopefully the adrenaline will be coursing through my body and make it forget how little sleep it's still getting. I have to be awake, focused, and ready to step into the ring.

"Sarah!" My colleague Jörg is leaning casually against the glass doorframe of the office. He has a broad grin on his lips, trying to look confident. Still, he can't even hold my gaze; instead, his eyes dart nervously over the desk. If I didn't know better, I might think he knows about my loss.

"What can I do for you?" I lace my words with a sugary tone. My lips curl up all by themselves, even though there's no reason to smile. I leave my fingers resting on the keyboard; maybe he'll take the hint and keep it brief.

At least he stays at the door and looks a bit as if he's frozen there. Now he runs a hand through his chin-length blond hair. Does he still think I don't know that he only does it to show off the signet ring flaunting on his middle finger?

"I came to wish you good luck." His voice is no less arrogant than the expression on his face.

"Thanks, that's so sweet of you," I reply with forced cheerfulness and give a brief nod. I play along with his game and pretend I don't know why he's here. All my colleagues are eagerly waiting for the day I fail, and Jörg most of all. He's also been promised a partnership. My defeat would be his victory.

Smirking, Jörg puts his hand to his chin. "Are you nervous yet? It's a huge case you've got there. And let's be honest, the odds aren't exactly in your favor. Your client cheated on his wife, everyone knows that. Accusing her of the same thing now is really weak and it won't keep him from having to dig deep into his pockets for the divorce."

"Let me worry about that." I look him straight in the eye and show him the confident, successful Sarah who can't be rattled by anything. This time he holds my gaze. I'd love to know where he suddenly got the courage to do that.

"Believe me, not a single one of my fraternity brothers ever managed to end his marriage without a scratch. And they had much better lawyers than you." Now he does enter the office and prowls around as if he were a lion circling its prey. His intense stench of cigarette smoke instantly pollutes the entire room.

"This is my case." I lay my hand on my chest. "Unfortunately, your opinion doesn't matter here in the slightest." I shake my head as if I pity him for it.

"Of course, you're the star here. But you know what, Sarah? Every star falls from the sky eventually."

He comes toward me and braces himself on my desk.

"And no matter how radiantly beautiful it once was, once it's lying on the ground, it's nothing but a plain little stone that nobody wants anymore." His expression is as unreadable as that of a serial killer on trial. He's dangerously close to me, but I refuse to let that intimidate me.

On the contrary, I can feel my fighting spirit awakening. At exactly the right moment.

Very slowly, and without taking my eyes off him, I rise from my office chair. Thanks to my high heels, I'm almost as tall as he is. "Let's discuss that in detail at my party celebrating my promotion to partner. Unfortunately, I have to go now." I point to my elegant wristwatch and grab the documents that have been sitting prepared on the table for hours.

It can begin; I feel ready. The fact that Jörg has even done me a favor by dropping by still doesn't put a satisfied smile on my face. How could it?

With impressively energetic strides, I march past him. "In the meantime, you can go ahead and put the champagne on ice," I say in farewell, leaving him alone in the office.

I'd love to see his dumbfounded face, but I don't allow myself to turn around again. There are more important things now.

I keep my victorious expression and walk down the hallway as if I'd already won the case. Just before I enter the conference room, I take a deep breath and loosen my neck. I can do this. All I need is concentration. I don't allow myself to think about anything but the case.

My client is already waiting for me; he sits oddly lost at the long designer table. Dressed the way he is, you'd think this was a funeral. The jacket of his black suit is a size too big for his gaunt body.

"Mr. Berger, good afternoon." I hold out my hand to him.

Groaning, he gets up from his chair. Beads of sweat stand out on his forehead, his fingers feel so clammy it's like I'm touching a frog. He reeks of an aftershave that would be too old-fashioned even for my grandpa. Now my hand smells like it too, no matter whether I wipe it on my skirt or not. I do it anyway, because otherwise I can't stand it, but of course I'm as inconspicuous as possible. You must never be rude. Especially not when you're facing a client whose fortune can catapult this firm into the top league.

He clears his throat, his voice trembling. "Ms. Wagner, how nice. So I guess the time has come."

I don't like him. At every one of our previous meetings he was arrogant and sleazy. And yet today he seems so small and weak that I feel sorry for him. Strange how people can change when the weather turns.

I have to encourage him, so I pat his hand gently and speak to him in a soothing tone. "We're ready to go. Don't worry, we're going to win."

Winning, in this case, means that he gets divorced without giving his wife a single cent. Considering his wealth, that's basically impossible, but I'm not the top choice for partner at this firm for nothing. There's always a loophole, and I've found it this time too. Whether I like it or not, this is my job. And I'm the best, just like my parents wanted me to be when I was still a baby.

Stop. No baby thoughts, just divorce and professionalism. Get a grip, Sarra!

Deliberately, I scold myself in my mother's merciless tone. And it works; my inner voice falls silent at once.

I take a deep breath.

Where were we just now? Right, I wanted to calm Mr. Berger down, and that's exactly where I pick up again. I give him a confident smile and nod encouragingly.

"You're certainly right, Ms. Wagner. Of course we're going to win; after all, I have you by my side." He looks at me gratefully.

Although I'm no less nervous than he is, he accepts my role as the self-assured lawyer without hesitation. Whether I like it or not, for a moment I'm as proud of my perfection as my parents would be if they could see me now. Now I just have to get my racing pulse under control.

While I prepare the documents, I hear my boss in the hallway. In a honey-sweet tone he directs someone to the conference room. It can only be Ms. Berger and her lawyer. So far I know Berger's not-yet-ex-wife only from wedding photos. They show the two of them as the perfect couple. Beautiful, successful, and happy. If my client's stories are to be believed, however, Ms. Berger is nothing but greedy and superficial. She seems to have married him only so she could live the luxurious life of a rich wife. Love was never part of it, at least that's what her husband claims.

Now she enters the room, elegant and gliding. She is stunningly beautiful, her chocolate-colored hair falling soft and shiny over her shoulders. I immediately envy her golden-brown skin and her full cheeks, which make her look as fresh as a rose blossom in the morning dew. She's wearing a trench coat in a light rose shade that doesn't reveal much about her figure. But that's beside the point, because everything about her radiates as if she were the happiest person in the world.

She walks up to me, but instead of just shaking my hand, she kisses my cheeks as if we were friends. A delicate scent of spring flowers envelops me and clouds my senses. If that's her tactic, I can only congratulate her. Her entrance is perfectly executed; I'm fascinated by her composure in the face of this unpleasant divorce hearing. Only my client seems immune to her. He remains seated, pulls the corners of his mouth down, and forces a curt greeting through his lips.

"Can we finally get started?" he asks right afterward, audibly irritated, glancing sideways at his wristwatch.

"Of course. Please, have a seat." I show Ms. Berger and her lawyer to their places. She smiles at me, completely open, as if she wanted to encourage me.

Her behavior unsettles me, but I don't let her see that. The opposing lawyer and I begin to present the case and lay out our arguments. This routine comes easily to me, even though I'm distracted today. I can't stop wondering why this beautiful woman seems so unshakable without showing even a hint of arrogance.

As if she were aware of her effect, she studies me with

her dark eyes. I run my hand over my hair; everything is in order. My earrings are firmly in place as well. My blouse is wrinkle-free, the blazer has no stains. I'm not giving her any opening for attack, yet her gaze rests on me without interruption. I feel naked, as if she could see through my protective shell.

With an extended clearing of my throat, I straighten my back. "Now let's put our cards on the table," I say insistently. "Your client deceived and shamelessly betrayed my client. She was repeatedly seen meeting a man in various hotels."

One by one, I lay the photos on the table, making my accusation more than clear. Mrs. Berger only smirks, gives an almost imperceptible shake of her head, and lowers her gaze. I follow it and watch as she loosens the knot of her trench coat.

Underneath, a small bulge appears.

She places her hand on it and strokes her fingers over the little belly. That is exactly where I'm staring now, and I'm instantly unable to keep focusing on my job. This cannot be true.

She is pregnant.

That's why she is so happy, has that blissful glimmer in her eyes, and shows her joy with every movement.

She has what I'm missing.

Murderer! the voice in my head screams.

The world around me collapses. Piece by piece, my façade crumbles, as if someone were taking away my perfect makeup, the severe hairstyle, and the trained facial expressions. All of it disappears. What remains is the wrecked little heap of misery that I truly am.

"Mrs. Wagner, are you not feeling well?" The worried

face of the opposing counsel looks distorted, like a grimace. His words echo in my head.

Not well, no, I am not well.

Now he's coming toward me. The room starts spinning along with him and there's nothing I can hold on to.

My baby is dead!

This certainty hits me now with ruthless force. It brings me down and breaks my will as if it were nothing more than a thin straw. I forget everything I'm supposed to still be fighting for here. I barely register the others' shocked faces or the cautious patting on my forearm. Without another word I flee the room.

Nothing matters anymore. Because I know full well that in truth I've already lost.

Chapter Thirteen

"Unacceptable!"

My boss is beside himself. So much so that he can't stay seated in his chair behind the impressively large desk. Gesticulating wildly, he paces up and down beside me while I sit silently on the narrow armchair. He smells like a whole ashtray; every time he storms past me, I have to hold my breath. His sparse hair bobs up and down excitedly in time with his steps. Whenever he puts a foot down on the dark gray carpet, the earth shakes beneath me. Magnitude eight on the Richter scale. At least.

Out of nowhere he suddenly stops next to me and scrutinizes me intently. One of his blue-green eyes has a brown speck in it. I focus on that so I can block out his twitching eyelid.

"What on earth was going on with you just now?" he asks with a sharp undertone.

"I suddenly felt nauseous and dizzy. I'm terribly sorry." I feel like I'm a dwarf. My voice is jittery, my body collapsed. The last bit of strength has left me; I'm as empty as a battery that finally gives up the ghost after multiple warnings. More clearly than ever before, the heartburn spreads through my esophagus.

"Absolutely unacceptable!" He lifts his gaze to the ceiling. Is he hoping for answers from up there? Then he loosens his tie knot and opens the top button of his shirt. A thick, swollen vein runs across his wrinkled neck, so pronounced it looks as if it's about to burst. "Do you have any idea what you've just done?"

I lower my gaze. "I'm sorry," I repeat, because I don't know what else to say.

Like all the rooms in this law firm, my boss's office is built entirely of glass. I can feel exactly how we're being watched from outside, even if everyone pretends to be busy with their work. They know what's happening in here and are reveling in the spectacle.

Flawless, successful Sarah is lying helpless on the ground.

First and foremost Jörg, whom I can see out of the corner of my eye casually leaning against the copier. He stacks blank sheets of paper and doesn't even try to suppress his obnoxious grin. To make matters worse, he can probably hear every single word. At the very least the ones my boss is bellowing. He's upset, I get that. But does he really have to humiliate me in front of all the employees?

"That wasn't just a top client, that was the top client of our firm!" He gasps for air, his face turning red.

I shrink even further and hope that at some point I'll be so small no one will be able to see me anymore.

"You don't actually think he'll ever hire us again, do you?!"

"Let me talk to him. If I explain it to him, we'll find a

solution." I sound like one of the Chipmunks. Very professional.

"Ms. Wagner, please. You've been unfocused for weeks and have been turning in substandard work. We both know this isn't our first conversation about this. I warned you, and you assured me I could rely on you."

He shakes his head, as if he himself can't believe he was so naive as to place his trust in me. Then he exhales slowly and drops into his leather chair. Arms folded across his chest, he looks at me in silence. The corners of his mouth hang lifelessly, his whole face is furrowed with lines.

I can hardly look into his eyes, which are now fixed on me with a mixture of accusation and contempt. That's even harder to bear than the thunderstorm from before. How could I disappoint him like this? He believed in me, supported me.

I ruined everything.

My eyes fill with tears, even though there really shouldn't be any left. For the gawkers behind the glass, a long-cherished dream is coming true. It can't possibly get any worse.

"Ms. Wagner, I don't know what's going on with you, but this can't go on," he says, looking just as worn out as I feel.

We both probably did our best, and yet here we are, sitting across from each other like a married couple that no longer has much to say. I'm bawling like a little girl and he hands me a tissue. As if that could help me. No one can, I'm too ashamed of everything. My weakness, my failure, and the disgrace I've brought on this firm.

Still, I mustn't give up, I have to set things right again. If only I knew how.

"I'll make it right again, don't you worry." My words

should sound more convincing, my expression more resolute. I need sleep to pull myself together, then I can carry on, even better than before. That's the only thing I'm willing to believe. What else could I possibly do?

The disappointment in his eyes is unmistakable. "I don't think so," he says, and now his voice is faltering too. "You were the best lawyer this firm has ever seen. Relentless, shrewd, and full of energy. I pinned all my hopes on your abilities alone. Even when all this started, I still wanted to believe in you. But now…"

"…you still can," I finish his sentence with an effort. I straighten up. He should see how right I am, and so should our observers. But only a few moments later my body collapses in on itself again, like a flower that has gone far too long without water.

What the hell is wrong with me?

"My trust is used up. What happened today shows even me that you're no longer acceptable for this firm." He takes a single sheet of paper from his drawer and places it on the table in front of me. Even though my tears blur my vision, I recognize it immediately.

It's a letter of termination.

A sharp pull shoots through my chest. I know it's only the heartburn, but it still feels as if I were having a heart attack.

"I'm very sorry, Ms. Wagner." He puts a pen on the sheet and pushes it closer to me. It says that we're ending our relationship with immediate effect by mutual agreement. I'll leave this firm today and never come back. That's unimaginable; my career plan doesn't allow for anything like that.

This job is my life; without it I'm nothing. I can't

possibly allow that. What if I tell him about my baby? Would that make him forget about the termination?

I search every inch of his face for answers and still don't find any. We're nothing more than distant acquaintances, we've never wanted to know anything personal about each other.

No. Feelings have no place here. There has to be another way.

"Don't you think I deserve another chance? You know me and you know exactly what a good lawyer I am. Just think of the Hinterleitner case, or the Edegger matter. Even you thought it would be impossible to win, but I did it! You remember that, don't you?" I beg him, because I no longer know what else to do. What have I turned into?

"Of course, that was fantastic." A smile spreads across his lips. "You impressed me deeply; I remember it as if it were yesterday."

"I'd like to impress you again—no, I want to blow you away. Let me try, you won't be disappointed a second time." I wish I myself could believe at least a little of what I'm saying right now. But the truth is that my strength has left me.

My boss folds his hands into a triangle, as if he had to collect himself for a closing argument. "There's nothing more I can say. The partners have decided you have to leave this firm. It would be best if you stopped making this any harder for yourself and for me. There are plenty of other firms, and with your résumé you won't have any trouble finding a place." He pushes the sheet a little closer to me, and his stern look tells me that I'm going to lose this fight.

Slowly he gets up and strolls over to the wall of windows, beyond which the houses of Vienna's old town gleam in the sunlight, each one trying to outshine the others. He can't stand the pathetic sight of me any longer; I understand that and don't want to disappoint him even more. The only thing I can still do right now is accept the termination agreement.

With trembling fingers I claw the ballpoint pen and put my signature on the paper in strokes that are far too angular. Right next to it, the heel of my hand leaves salty, damp marks. With faltering breath I push the document back to the other side of the table. So this is what it feels like to sign your own death sentence.

It's over. Everything my parents ever loved me for no longer exists.

Chapter Fourteen

The sliding doors of the glass palace close so quickly behind me it's as if they too are relieved to be rid of me. The sky is hazy blue and completely free of clouds. As if there were nothing it had to worry about.

Not once in the past four years did I stop here. I was always in a hurry, had to move on. Today my feet stick to the paving stones. They don't know where they're supposed to go, and I have just as little idea. My head is empty, without destination and without direction.

Only the hectic bustle of the city surrounds me. High heels clatter on hard ground, dogs as small as cats bark their heads off. It smells of fried sausage, sewage, and exhaust fumes. On the other side of the street someone is swearing into their phone, a few yards away from me a homeless man is sitting with an empty coffee cup in his hand. He looks at me pleadingly and whimpers unintelligibly to himself. He's probably hoping that there's something valuable in the little box under my arm. But it's only the remnants of my life so far. Everything I was still allowed to take with me from my office.

Of all people, Jörg was assigned to keep me company while I collected my personal things. I had already set aside a lipstick, an emergency manicure set, and a small bottle of perfume when he entered my office uninvited.

I don't buy his artificially contrived expression. And I can see perfectly well how hard it is for him to keep his mouth shut. "How can I help you?" I ask, still sounding surprisingly confident. I'm giving the performance of my life, and even now I can still pull it off.

"This is just awful, Sarah." Jörg hunches his shoulders and furrows his brow. "Honestly, I'm truly sorry."

All I have for that statement is a contemptuous snort. Shaking my head, I open the bottom desk drawer and look for the shoe polish.

For a while, nobody says anything. Whatever he's waiting for, he's not going to get it. "Anything else?" I ask, fixing my eyes firmly on his.

"No." He really ought to leave now, but he's still buzzing around my office like an annoying housefly.

As if it still mattered, I carefully sort my personal things into a box, one by one. "Well then…"

He clears his throat, as if he suddenly feels awkward about having to supervise my exit. "I wish you all the best for your future."

I don't even want to know what kind of future he means. He probably already sees me ending up in the gutter because nobody else will have me. With the last bit of my pride, I grab the box and march toward him. I stop far too close to him; his gaze flickers questioningly between my eyes. "I wish you the same." The corners of my mouth rise of their own accord; I sound surprisingly friendly. Not a single one of the feelings inside me makes it to the surface.

He's probably suppressing a satisfied smile right now. After all, he's going to make partner at the firm and won't even have to work for it anymore.

I'll never forget the way he looked at me in that moment. Even though probably no one is interested in me anymore already, I suddenly feel watched through the glass walls of the building behind me. I guess that's how it goes when you're speeding impressively along the fast lane and suddenly slam into the guardrail.

Supposedly no one wants to look at the bloody result, and yet everyone does.

At last my legs also understand what to do and jerk into motion. Any direction is fine with them, just not the one that leads home. At the next intersection I march into a narrow alley. It looks deserted, and that's exactly what draws me in. As soon as I turn the corner, it's quieter and even the air seems clearer. I try to breathe deeply, but it doesn't really work.

At the end of the alley I reach a gate, behind which a park stretches out. I leave the wrought-iron archway behind me and feel as if I'm diving into another world. In contrast to the houses in the city center, which line up tightly in every shade from medium gray to white, everything here is colorful. Shrubs with pale yellow and delicate pink blossoms stand out brightly against the lush green of the lawns. A warm breeze carries their intense scent toward me, the sparrows on the edge of the fountain are chattering excitedly with one another. Behind the stone youth who lets water flow from his jug into the fountain there is a children's playground.

I quickly turn my gaze away. I can't look at children. Never again.

I'd rather head for one of the weathered wooden benches. Once there, I check the bench for cleanliness and protruding splinters. Parks are dirty, at least that's what my mother says. That's why we never went there when I was a child, no matter how politely I asked. She didn't like it when my little dresses got stained and my patent leather sandals were full of sand. Besides, I could have hurt myself, skinned my knees or even ended up with a wound on my forehead. That leaves ugly scars, she impressed on me, looking at me meaningfully as she did so.

Although only a few centimeters of my body are touching the wooden bench, I feel uncomfortable. Only homeless people sit in the park in broad daylight, someone like me definitely does not. I quickly straighten my blazer and smooth down my hair. It's supposed to look as if I'm taking a late lunch break here, not as if I'm an unemployed failure.

And yet that's exactly what I am.

Dejected, I lower my gaze and look at the diamond ring on my finger. The sunlight refracts on its facets, and it sparkles in all the colors of the rainbow.

Will Tom even still want to marry me like this?

Once again tears push out of the corners of my eyes like water from a leaky faucet. This has to stop, but how? It's as if I've lost myself somewhere between the pregnancy test and today. If I now also lose my family's love, I don't know what will be left of me. How will they react to the resignation, I wonder?

The very thought of it makes me feel hot and cold at the same time.

Just like back then, when I brought the bad report card home. As on every last day of the school year, my mother looked at me full of anticipation and pride. Behind her a cake was waiting for me, with peaches and strawberries. Next to it was a small box with a golden ribbon.

"Well?" she says, impatiently stretching out her hand so I'll give her my report card.

It's one thing to be afraid of something that might never happen. But being certain that it will come is something else entirely. Any moment now she'll be endlessly disappointed in me. Ashamed, I look down at the floor, whose grain I already know by heart. Everything on me is trembling, even my braids.

My mother tears the paper out of my hand. Her smile disappears.

Her eyes turn cold.

"Berrnharrd!" Her voice is so shrill it's as if a train were slamming on the emergency brakes.

My father appears in the doorway. She holds my report card so close under his nose that he could read it even if he were short-sighted. Wordlessly he shakes his head. I don't dare take a breath. Especially not when he looks at me and, for a brief moment, runs his hand over my hair. Then he turns around, just like that, and leaves me as if I didn't exist.

The B in math was out of the question for all of us back then, but my parents were as ashamed as if I had had to repeat the school year. My mother decided that I needed a tutor during the summer holidays so I could study ahead for the next grade. She paid him royally. Not only for the home lessons, but also for his discretion. That had always been her way of solving problems. They get pushed under a pretty rug so that no one can see them anymore.

I wonder if somewhere in this world there's a rug big enough to cover the wreckage of the last few days.

My stomach cramps and, with trembling hands, I pull a tissue out of the packet. The wind makes it flutter before my eyes like a white flag over the edge of a trench.

Capitulation. Is that all I have left?

First I have to talk to Tom. That's the only way this can work. He'll help me tell my parents about what happened today and hold on to me when the storm breaks over us. But first I dry my tears. No one wants to see other people cry, and Tom certainly doesn't. My wristwatch tells me he'll be finishing work soon. After all, we have a dinner date. To celebrate the occasion, as Tom remarked with a wink this morning. The memory makes me feel sick, but there's no time for that now. I have to get ready. Hair, makeup, posture, smile. All of that has to be perfect, if I can't be.

Purposefully, I set off. I leave the damp tissue here in the park and wish I could dispose of my sorrow just as easily. But it follows me home like a dark cloud, chases me into the shower, and still clings to me while I paint life onto my face.

When I arrive at the restaurant later, the hardest part begins. The waiting. Every attempt to distract myself fails. I can't focus on anything except the conversation ahead of me.

The room could be packed, other guests could be laughing, wineglasses could be clinking together. Someone could be playing the piano, the waiters could be wearing black suits. I don't know. Because I don't notice any of it. I keep watching the digits on my watch display change in a remarkably precise rhythm. Sometimes they blur before my eyes, then I blink and my vision clears again. Over and over I repeat what I want to say to Tom and how I'll behave while I say it. What gestures my hands will make, how my head will move. So that everything seems smooth. As if there were no problem, just a small bump in the road.

After what feels like an eternity, I suddenly hear the waiter speaking very close by. “Here’s your table. You’re expected.”

“Thank you.” That’s Tom. He’s here.

A mute panic settles on my palms, damp and cold. My heartbeat stops for a moment. I summon all my courage and look up at Tom. He looks good, maybe a little tired around the eyes. Still, he beams at me.

“And?” he asks without sitting down, and he sounds so hopeful that it breaks my heart.

He comes toward me, I can see the excitement on his face and force myself to give him a smile. I feel sick, the room around me starts to spin.

“I told you you could do it,” he whispers in my ear as he pulls me into his arms so tightly it’s as if he’s ready to catch me if I fall. His hand strokes down my back.

That wasn’t how this was supposed to go; he was supposed to ask how the trial went. Then I would have answered that everything was different from what we’d expected. Now he’s ruined my opening, I have to improvise. “Not quite,” I say softly, clinging to him.

“What do you mean? You did win the case, didn’t you?” He stops his caresses and loosens his embrace.

“Not quite,” I repeat, like a wind-up doll.

I can’t stop him from pulling away from me. He takes a step back so he can study my eyes. His hands are still on my upper arms, and a deep furrow cuts across his forehead that reminds me of a crevasse in a glacier. His kind features suddenly look as if they’ve been flash-frozen.

“You didn’t win the case?” His tone is a whole octave

higher than usual, his eyes widen. In a flash he lets go of my arms.

As if I'd just confessed to him that I had leprosy.

The corners of Tom's mouth drop, suddenly looking as if he'd only managed to hold them up with effort until now. Confused, he walks over to his chair and sits down.

Any second now. He's going to get that one very particular look. I don't want to have to endure it, not today.

"No." I don't have the strength to keep looking at him. I bite my lip, the pain forcing my tears back to where he can't see them. A tiny drop of blood spreads across my tongue, metallic and bitter.

"Why?" His voice is as sober as a Monday morning. Still, I'm relieved. At last the conversation is getting to a point I had factored in.

I look him straight in the eyes and put as much certainty into my words as I can. "In the middle of the trial I suddenly felt really sick, from one minute to the next. It was a disaster, I had to get out right away." I lift my arms in apology.

"And what happened to the case?" His eyes won't let me go, registering every twitch and every hesitation.

Only now do I realize that I don't know. Did someone take over for me? Or was the hearing postponed? No one cared about that anymore when I crawled out of the restroom like a wet rag.

I have to tell Tom the truth.

But when I open my mouth, completely different words come out. "It's being continued next week," I answer with a matter-of-factness that surprises even me. I can't do it. Not when he's looking at me like that, as if the disappointment might pull the ground out from under his feet at any moment.

Tom exhales, laughing with relief. "Well then, everything's fine! We'll just postpone the celebration until I'm back from Asia. That's no problem." He stretches his hand across the table and lays it on mine. Gently he strokes my skin, his gaze softening. "And otherwise? How are you feeling, my darling? About… you know."

I lower my gaze and nod silently. Nothing more is possible; talking about it is unthinkable for both of us.

"I understand," is all he says, then he falls silent too.

Our speechlessness bonds us together. Invisible, but strong. We suffer together. That's enough to make me feel at least a little less alone. With gentle pressure, he closes his hand around mine, as if he wanted to protect me with it.

This moment is far too beautiful to destroy it. Maybe I'm a coward, maybe I'm weak. But Tom's warmth is exactly what I need right now. And if that means the truth has to wait a little longer, then so be it.

Tom's clearing his throat pulls me out of my thoughts. "Let's order something to eat, what are you in the mood for?" he asks, opening the menu. "I think I'll have the fillet steak. And you?"

I don't have an appetite, so I go for the first thing I find on the menu.

As soon as we've closed our menus, Tom looks around. "Where is that waiter? In a place like this you'd think you could expect decent service."

I watch him throw his arms up theatrically, snort in contempt, and roll his eyes. He's annoyed; I really shouldn't pile more problems on top of that. In a few days Tom will leave on his business trip. Until then I could just keep pretending I go to work every morning. By the time he comes back, I'll have a new job. That would make everything only half as bad. I wouldn't have to worry about my parents' reaction, and he wouldn't have to worry about my future.

If I keep quiet now, in the end we'd both win, albeit in a strangely twisted way. The longer I think about it, the more certain I am. This, and no other way, is best for everyone.

Chapter Fifteen

Tom is leaning against the kitchen counter reading the paper, looking like a model from a coffee commercial. His hair is slicked back, he's wearing an elegant suit and a winning smile. He's holding the handle of his espresso cup between thumb and forefinger as if he were a guest at the White House.

I'm already all dressed up too, wearing a summery suit and a light blouse with ruffles at the sleeves. My bun is rock solid. Still, Tom might notice a change in me if he really looked at me. I'm fidgety and exhausted at the same time, I feel as if I'd had a night of heavy drinking. But he's so focused on his paper that I could be standing in front of him in sweatpants and he wouldn't notice. So maybe I don't need the show at all.

Silently, I sip my coffee, wrapping my whole hand around the cup. Like a farmer, my mother would say. The steaming liquid burns my tongue, as if it wanted to punish me for my thoughts.

Tom doesn't react to my quiet cursing, but the stone lion

on the pedestal in the corner watches me. His eyes remind me of my mother's. They scrutinize me, criticize me, and challenge me.

Looking at him drives me crazy.

Almost as much as the question of where I'm supposed to go today when we leave the apartment. Endless hours lie ahead of me, all of them as empty as my head.

My phone rings, and a photo of my mother appears on the display. A call from her this early in the morning is unusual. Is my father all right? And my grandparents?

"Aren't you going to answer?" Tom's question is more of a prolonged growl than a proper sentence. The ringtone is bothering him while he's reading the paper. I nod, even though I know he can't see it, and take the call.

"Good morning." I try to sound fresh and think I manage it brilliantly. Not even I can hear that I paid my usual visit to hell again last night.

"Good? What on earth is supposed to be good about this morning?" my mother snaps at me instead of greeting me.

"Is everything okay?" Instantly I'm suspicious and move the phone to my other ear as a precaution, to shield the conversation from Tom.

"You tell me. Is everything okay?" She sounds incredibly stressed. I can practically see her in front of me, pacing agitatedly up and down the living room.

What on earth does she want from me?

An unsettling burn spreads in my stomach. "Of course." I straighten my back and instantly stand in the kitchen like a soldier on the parade ground. Tom looks up from the newspaper, his eyes asking me what's going on. With a shrug, I let him know I have no idea.

"How dare you…?" My mother sounds at least ten

shades nastier than usual. I'd better keep quiet now, this is getting too risky for me. "Sarra, I asked you something!"

"I don't know what you mean. What is this actually about?" Even though a storm is brewing in my stomach, I put as much calm into my words as I can.

"About you, of course, what do you think? Is there maybe something you'd like to tell me?" She spits the words out like sour milk. She's panting as if she were slogging away on the cross-trainer.

She knows.

No, she can't know, that's impossible. What if she does? Confess or run, what should I do? How high are my chances of getting away with this?

"Sarra, answer me already!"

I have to move the phone away from my ear just to bear the volume of her voice. My thoughts are racing. I'd estimate the probability at seventy percent; that has to be enough.

"No, everything's fine," I say, but only very quietly, while the stomach acid inside me forces its way upward.

The contemptuous snort at the other end of the line sends a cold shiver down my spine. "Oh really? You think getting fired isn't worth mentioning?"

She knows the truth. How? I haven't even told the usually so talkative traitor in my kitchen about it. This has to be a nightmare, and yet I don't wake up.

I immediately disappear toward the living room; Tom mustn't hear this. "It wasn't my fault," I say at last, glad that I've managed to find words after all. "I couldn't finish the hearing because I got sick. Maybe food poisoning."

"Oh please, you should have pulled yourself together. If you want to achieve something, you have to be strict with yourself. How many times have I told you that?" My mother's words sound icy.

I swallow and feel small and weak. "I'm sorry."

"You can spare me that. You failed, and thoroughly! Can you imagine what that means for me?" Her voice breaks several times; she has never been this upset. "What are people supposed to think of us? You're a disgrace to this family!"

Yes, I am. And I'd do anything if I could undo it. Powerless, I lean against the living room wall, my head heavy. "I'll make it right."

"That goes without saying."

Ice cold Monika.

"I already started looking for another job this morning." I feel miserable. Not just because my heartburn is burning me up from the inside out at breakneck speed. As if my failure weren't bad enough, now I'm lying to her on top of it. Can anyone imagine a worse daughter than me?

"No, Sarra, not another job. You're going to find a better job. Is that clear?"

I don't get a chance to answer. If you could still slam a receiver down on the hook these days, I'd probably have a ruptured eardrum now. She can't stand me anymore. How could I have made such a mistake?

Only now do I notice that I'm shaking all over, as if my blood sugar were low. The phone slips from my hand. I stagger to the nearest shelf to hold on to it. The living room is spinning.

"This can't be happening." Tom's deep voice is suddenly behind me, emotionless and distant.

How long has he been standing there? His words hit nothing but hollow walls inside me. They echo there without fading. I don't turn around; I don't want to look him in the eye.

"You're unemployed." He hurls the words from his throat like clots of phlegm he wants to get rid of for good.

Next I hear the floorboards creak, loud at first, then softer and softer. He just leaves me standing there as if I didn't matter to him. Yesterday he still wanted to marry me; he can't have forgotten that. I follow him into the kitchen, where he's just drinking the last sip of his coffee.

"Let me explain." Every part of me is trembling. I reach my hand out to him, but he doesn't let me touch him. Of course I understand why. Our success means everything to him, and anyone who knows his past can understand that. Only the scars on the knuckles of his right hand are left from his childhood. He has left behind his parents' poverty and struggle to survive.

"What is there left to explain? You don't have a job anymore, and any idiot can figure out that you're definitely not going to become a partner at the firm now. How could you lie to me like that last night?"

All at once I understand how wrong I am. He isn't angry because I failed and dragged our reputation through the mud. He's hurt because I didn't tell him the truth.

"I don't know," I answer with complete honesty and let my shoulders slump forward.

His features soften. "Don't you trust me?"

After the whole thing with the abortion? No. After the way he behaved at the hospital? Absolutely not. "Of course I trust you," I say gently. I try to close the distance between us very slowly and keep my eyes fixed on him.

"Then why won't you talk to me, Sarah?" There's a plea in his voice, his eyes fixed on me in utter confusion.

Again I take a step toward him, but the distance

between us doesn't shrink. "I had to get my own head around it first, you know?"

He won't let me get close to him anymore, flees to the sink, sets his coffee cup inside. "I'm your fiancé, not just some guy who happens to live in the same apartment as you," he says sharply without looking at me. He takes a deep breath and braces his hands on the counter.

"I'm so incredibly sorry." At least my eyes stay dry, even if I'm already failing across the board.

In my entire life I haven't apologized as often as I have in the last twenty-four hours. All that's left of me is a tattered shell. A worn-out remnant cowering in the corner like a wounded fawn in the roadside ditch.

Tom studies me in silence, the kitchen clock ticking off the seconds as if it were a countdown. The corners of his mouth twitch, the crease on his forehead tells me how at a loss he is.

I try one last time and move toward him. Just for a moment I want to lean against his chest, feel his strength wrapped in the scent of his skin and take a little of it for myself.

"No. Leave me alone. Please." Tom suddenly seems to be in a hurry. He turns around and leaves the kitchen as if he wants to run away from me. "I have to go now," he says hastily, not even looking me in the eye.

A moment later he is gone. I wish I could leave myself just as easily. But I'm rooted to the spot, unable to take another step, even though there's only one thing I want. To get rid of that pathetic loser inside me who took control without asking and turned my perfect life into a never-ending nightmare.

Chapter Sixteen

Ever since Tom found out about the termination, everything has been different. After our argument he came home late. When he lay down in bed next to me, keeping as much distance as he possibly could, the smell of cigars and whiskey crept into my nose. Before the sun even came up, he was gone again. Since then he has been sleeping in the guest room. He claims the only reason for that is my restless sleep. He has to be well rested for his job, which of course I understand. Especially so shortly before his trip, there seemed to be even more going on than usual.

In the last few days we've hardly seen each other. And even now Tom is racing back and forth between the bedroom and the bathroom as if he's on the run.

Probably from me.

And that even though I've already considerately withdrawn to the kitchen. I'm almost disappearing into the corner next to the counter so I won't disturb him, drinking coffee in my bathrobe. With every sip, the silk fabric slides coldly over my arm and leaves a loveless shiver on my skin.

My hair is already straightened and pinned up, a good layer of makeup hides my freckles. Getting rid of the shadows around my eyes doesn't take any effort anymore. I know I don't have the right to wish they weren't there in the first place. Still, I long for sleep. Just a single night without nightmares about my baby, my mother's ice-cold eyes, or Tom ripping the ring off my finger. That's all I want.

Tom seems stressed and dejected today. I'd like to do something nice for him, but every time I try to reach out to him, a wall rises up between us. He blocks me, and I don't know how to deal with it. So I try to make myself invisible so that the sight of me doesn't strain him even more.

"Where the hell are the tie clips?!"

Although I'm not sure whether Tom is angry with me or just with himself, I seize my chance. I jump down from the stool and hurry into the dressing room. He's standing there between three open suitcases, countless garment bags, shirts, and black socks. His hair is sticking up wildly in all directions, and beads of sweat are glittering on his forehead.

"They should be in the drawer." I try to sound calm and feel my way through the obstacle course to the dresser.

"Oh please, I already looked there ages ago."

Tom waves me off, but I open the drawer anyway and carefully search every corner. They're nowhere to be found.

"See?" he says snappishly, leaving me standing in the dressing room as if he couldn't bear to be in the same room with me.

I'm not that easy to shake off. I hurry after him and watch as he searches the bowl on his nightstand. He doesn't find what he's looking for there either. Tom lets his arms drop and groans again. Then he glances at his wristwatch and shakes his head in annoyance.

"Don't worry, I'll keep looking. You pack everything else in the meantime." Can't he hear that I'm trying to make peace with him?

He doesn't answer, so I get to work. I look everywhere, no matter how unlikely it is that the tie pins would be there. As if my life depended on being able to help him now. That's all I want for the time being. Then, at some point, maybe he'll be able to forgive me too.

I find the tie pins on the shelf above the bathroom sink, hidden under cuff links. Thank God. I pick them up as carefully as if they were a treasure and run back to Tom as fast as I can.

"Got them!" I hand him my find with a broad smile.

"Mhm," he says, cupping his hand so I can let them fall into it. He just stares at the tie pins, as if they were even more important to him than they are to me.

"Can I help you with anything else?" I ask hopefully. After all, I've just proven that I can.

"No, I've got this. You just drink your coffee." Even as he speaks, he turns his back on me.

There it is, our wall.

And again I have no idea what I can do about it.

I trudge back into the kitchen, make another coffee, and try to switch my brain on. There has to be a way to get through to him again. I can't keep disappointing him; I have to be honest and give him a reason to be proud of me again. Could the new job I promised my mother also help me with Tom?

It's worth a try.

I start up the laptop and go through my application documents. My résumé is still flawless, and it has to stay that way. If I don't manage to start at another law firm next month, an ugly gap will appear. I search the internet for all the law firms that might be an option for me. The fact that I have several areas of specialization undoubtedly helps. It would be best to join straightaway as a partner. That's what I should focus on first.

"I'm off, then." Tom is standing in the doorway, his laptop bag in one hand and the black suitcase in the other. His gaze falls on my laptop screen. Tiny lines form around his mouth, but he doesn't manage a real smile. It's enough for me to go over to him.

A few moments later I'm with him, trying not to let my insecurity show. I rest my arms on his shoulders; this time he doesn't pull away.

"Have a good flight."

He doesn't bend down to me, so I rise up on my tiptoes to kiss him. His lips are hard and don't respond to mine. At least he lets me touch him; I probably can't expect more than that.

He pulls away from me and takes a step back, as if he felt uncomfortable being near me. "Thanks. I'll get in touch when I've landed," he says flatly and turns around on the spot.

I don't let that faze me, so I follow him all the way to the elevator. "I'd wish you good luck, but I know perfectly well you don't need it," I say with a grin. It's nothing more than a feeble attempt to lighten the mood after all.

"Definitely not more than you." Tom's face is like stone, his voice sounds exhausted.

"Already working on it." I try to sound confident, but I have no idea if I actually manage it. Then I force a smile onto my face. The very one I usually use for my clients to signal courage and reassurance.

"Well then, I'm curious." Again he shows no reaction, as if he were a robot whose on-switch for affection I can't find.

I want to kiss him one more time, but he pushes me away from him.

"My taxi's waiting." Tom seems as if his thoughts were already on the plane.

I do him the favor and take a step back so the elevator can close its doors. We look each other in the eye until the gap is so narrow that not even light can pass through it anymore.

For almost four weeks our contact will be limited to brief phone calls. I don't know whether that's good or bad. For me and for the two of us. In fact, I don't know anything anymore, least of all what I'm supposed to do with myself all alone over the next few weeks.

I stroll back into the kitchen and step up to the window. The day beyond the pane of glass is hazy, dirty, and heavy. Just like the questions that have lodged themselves in my thoughts.

Who am I even, if I'm not working?

I've never lacked things to do. My parents constantly set new goals for me, and I was ambitious enough to reach them. But now, all of a sudden, it all seems pointless. I've already done everything for my success. And yet here I am, with nothing in my hands and even less in my heart.

My baby is dead, my parents are disappointed, and Tom is frustrated. I gave everything, only to lose even more in the end.

With an effort, I force myself back to the laptop and keep looking for a new job. But the longer I occupy myself with it, the more senseless the idea seems to me. Do I really want to go back there? Can I keep fighting for something that doesn't give me any peace?

My body feels terribly weak. Empty and completely

without drive. The engine that kept my life running has come to a standstill.

Then I suddenly see it, and in that moment it seems like the solution to my problems.

Images appear on the right edge of the screen. They show a world that's so wonderfully different from mine. There are lonely footprints in the sand, terraces that open up a view of a sea that seems endless, and women bathed in golden light, sitting on a rock and meditating. That's exactly the kind of peace I'm missing.

That's where I want to be.

Somewhere else. Anywhere but here. In this city, where guilt and memories lie in wait for me no matter how hard I try to hide from them. If I weren't here, they couldn't ambush me anymore. I'd sleep again, my shoulders would be light, and my stomach free.

Without thinking about it any longer, I grab the phone and dial the number of the travel agency. My heart is pounding so hard in my chest, as if it can't believe it might finally get what it wants for once.

"I'd like to go on a trip, to the south, preferably today," I say after a brief greeting, trying not to sound like a teenage girl buying tickets for her favorite boy band's concert. Still, the adrenaline in my body does whatever it wants. I jump up from the stool and rush back and forth in the kitchen like a caged predator just before the cage is opened.

"Of course. What exactly did you have in mind?" the gentleman on the other end of the line asks kindly. He sounds like the voice-over in a commercial, his voice velvety and clear.

I hesitate. I want to get away, that's all I know. But where to? Fortunately, it's his job to make suggestions.

"Peace and quiet," I say firmly. "I need peace and quiet.

Sunshine. No phone, no emails, no obligations." That's all I can think of. "What can you recommend?"

"I understand. Let's see what I can find." In the background I hear the clicking of a keyboard and a computer mouse presumably darting hectically across the pad. "Oh yes, you'll definitely like this. Provence, in glorious southern France. The scent of lavender, an azure sky, eighty-two degrees Fahrenheit. How does that sound?"

"Wonderful." The longing for all that floods my body, as soothing as a hot bath on a cold winter's day. I exhale, close to tears, because I feel that I can finally start to hope again.

"I have a cottage for you, far away on a hill. You'll definitely find the peace and quiet you're looking for there. I'd also recommend a rental car, that way you'll be absolutely free in your choice of activities."

My heartbeat speeds up even more, even though that's surely impossible from a physics point of view. A little house, just for me alone, that sounds fantastic. I'll leave my baggage behind here in Vienna; in France everything will be better.

"Fantastic, I'll stay for three weeks," I reply without hesitating for even a second. "When can I leave?"

The exceedingly friendly gentleman gives me the details of my trip. I can already fly out this evening.

I don't have to spend a single more night in this apartment. My body suddenly feels so light, as if I were a gas-filled balloon that has just torn free and is rising up into the sky.

Chapter Seventeen

The line in front of the check-in counter is almost as long as the one at the gates of Schönbrunn Palace on a cloudless spring day. It's loud and hectic. I keep getting jostled, and it reeks of a mixture of sweat, perfume, and plastic. I join the line and let my gaze wander through the departure hall.

Right in front of me there's a couple. Both of them have been swiping silently across their phone screens for minutes, as if they had nothing to say to each other. The group at the very front, by contrast, is having a great time. Next to them stands an old woman, staring blankly ahead, as if her spirit had left her body in search of a better place than this one. I probably look like her, as if only half of me were really here.

My adrenaline rush has ebbed away. I try to relax further, and in fact the underlying heartburn that has been with me for so many years eases a little. It's as if the vacation were already working before it has really begun.

Suddenly a single thought ambushes me, ruthless and with full force. A cold shiver runs down my back, feels its way into my toes, and races up the fronts of my legs straight into my lungs.

I'm going on vacation when I should be looking for a job.

I haven't done anything to deserve this. On the contrary, I shouldn't even be here. If my mother finds out about this, she'll gasp for air in vain until she drops dead. Pangs of conscience bore into my soul like a needle into the skin of a balloon. They want my longing to burst before it ever reaches the sky.

Restlessly, I shift from one foot to the other, my palms growing damp. With a hasty glance I scan my surroundings.

If someone here recognizes me… and tells my parents what I'm doing here…

Frantically, I rummage my sunglasses out of my handbag and perch them on my nose with trembling fingers. I forget my good manners, open the suitcase right there in the queue and pull out the straw hat I haven't worn since my last holiday in Sardinia. Only when it sits firmly on my head can I breathe again. In gasps, but at least I'm getting air. I rest my hand on my chin as if I'm thinking and try to cover as much of my mouth as possible.

The taciturn couple in front of me is just checking in; I'm up next. Even so, the seconds crawl by like thick, slow honey. I stare at the floor and shield my face from every possible angle as best I can.

"Next, please," I hear a squeaky voice call. It's my turn. Finally.

Without a word, I slide my passport across the counter and heave the suitcase onto the belt.

"Ms. Wagner, where would you like to sit?" asks the woman at check-in in a volume that makes me flinch. Why do I, of all people, have to end up with an airport employee who has all the discretion of a gossip columnist? I glance around hastily, but no one seems to be paying any attention to me.

"Anywhere is fine," I reply in a muffled voice and motion with my hand for her to hurry up. She looks at me longer than necessary, her face expressionless. Then her gaze drifts back to the screen, and I could swear she now takes even more time with her work.

It feels as if hours have passed before I finally have the ticket in my hands. I hurry off to the restrooms. No one is here; I breathe a sigh of relief, take off the straw hat, and pull the clips from my hair. It falls straight over my shoulders and I brush it forward so it shields my face from curious looks. None of my mother's friends would recognize me at first glance like this. At least I hope not.

On the way to security, I feel like a stranger. I've worn my bun for so many years that I don't even know who I am without it. I don't have time to think about that now. The only thing that matters is getting to my gate as quickly as possible.

When I get there, I find a seat where I can wait for boarding, sheltered from the crowds. The gate is still deserted; only a cleaner is emptying the trash cans and a lone man in a suit is reading an oversized newspaper. A glance at my watch tells me that my plane won't be taking off for almost two hours. Until then I have to kill not only time, but also my nasty thoughts.

So far I haven't had the chance to find out whether Provence has more to offer than the scent of lavender and an azure sky. I dig my phone out of my bag and look up my destination online. Little by little I discover pictures of historic buildings, peach blossoms, and flamingos in the Camargue nature reserve. There are stone cottages with colorful shutters, surrounded by lush vegetation and peacefully grazing horses. I forget more and more where I am and almost feel as if I'm already there. The anticipation returns and pushes my worries into the background. They don't disappear completely, though, and from time to time they make me look up from my phone. The gate is already filling up, but none of the faces looks familiar.

Just as I start to feel safe, the phone in my hand vibrates. A jolt shoots through my whole body. Only a moment later do I register what the vibrating means.

My mother is calling.

I look around. She can't possibly know that I'm here. Or can she? After all, she also knew about my resignation, however she managed that.

I cup my hand over my mouth and the phone to block out the airport noise and answer the call. "Hello." My greeting sounds almost like a question.

Without unnecessary pleasantries, she gets straight to the point. "How's the job hunt going?" she asks in a voice so icy it seems to come straight from absolute zero. Minus 273.15 degrees Celsius. I freeze.

"Sarra, I asked you something."

"Very well," I reply, even though I can barely move my lips, and press myself deeper into the hard plastic chair. It lets out a terribly loud creak that makes me stop mid-movement. Every muscle in my body is tense; they have to hold their position so my mother won't get suspicious.

"A bit more precise, if you please." She hurls the words at me, and with them her disappointment. I feel as if I'm six years old again and have to justify why my picture didn't win the drawing contest.

What else can I do but lie to her? I hold my breath and summon all my strength. "I've found some great positions, the applications are already sent. I'm sure a few law firms will get in touch over the next few days." I can only hope the words sound more convincing in her ears than they do in mine.

"That's not enough. I'm done being ashamed of you. Next week you'll have a new job, is that clear?" She sounds as forceful as a robber ordering their victim to hand over the money.

Immediately after that I only hear a beeping. She has ended the call.

My muscles release their tension, the plastic chair groans. I exhale all the air that had built up in my lungs. Then I feel it. A terrible sense of guilt eats its way through my body like a fat caterpillar through foliage that was already withered. Everything is devoured completely, no matter how tasteless it is.

I shouldn't get on the plane.

Stay here, find a job and focus on my career. That would be the right thing to do. But that very thought brings tears to my eyes faster than I can hold them back. I spring up from my seat, rush to the only refuge there is here, and lock myself in one of the toilet stalls.

So here I am now, without touching anything. My shoulders slumped and my head heavy. I have to keep drying my cheeks, my makeup smears, my nose swells up.

A colorless voice from the loudspeaker announces the boarding for my flight. My head is dull and empty. It doesn't know what to think, can't tell right from wrong.

What if I get on this plane now and in the end it only makes everything worse?

Chapter Eighteen

For as long as I can remember, someone else has decided what I have to do, where I have to go, and what I'm supposed to think. I follow every instruction without objection; I'm the good daughter, the strong lawyer, and the accommodating girlfriend. Whenever someone gives me a goal, I find the way there. In my memory there's only a single decision that I ever made entirely on my own and for myself. When I decided that my baby would live. And where, if not straight into this dead-end situation, has that brought me?

My flight is called a second time. Time slips through my fingers as if it were desert sand and I only had a child's hand. Small and powerless. In my head, reason is screaming; in my gut there is a longing, very quiet and yet so warm that I can't ignore it.

"Attention, this is the final call for flight LH3402 to Marseille. Passengers Ms. Sarah Wagner and Mr. David Rainer, please proceed immediately to gate G45. G45."

All of a sudden the restroom feels far too cramped, the

walls horribly close. I can no longer stand the stench of urine and cheap paper. Suddenly I see the right path before me in razor-sharp images. I have to get out of here so I can finally think straight again.

I burst out into the waiting area and hurry straight toward the gate to the plane.

As if in a trance, my hand places the ticket on the scanner at the turnstile. The green light seems command enough. I lose control, as if my body were refusing to take orders from my head. Fascinated, I watch it as it boards the plane, as if it had no doubts. My limbs move calmly while my mind is waving its arms wildly and protesting at the top of its lungs. But no one can hear me, not even I myself.

When I come to again, the airplane doors close behind me with a loud rattle. Sweating passengers hoist their carry-on luggage into the overhead bins and squeeze into their seats. Some seats creak under their heavy load, the bright click of fastening seat belts blends with the discreet background music in the cabin. It smells of unwashed people and air-conditioning.

My brain is working at full speed, understandably wanting to know what just happened. Even before I know the answer, it becomes clear to me that something else matters much more right now. If I want to remain unnoticed, I have to be especially careful now. I wait by the aircraft door until the aisle through business class is empty. Then I lower my head and march quickly down the rows of seats.

My senses are turned up to the max, faces flash past at the corners of my eyes, my ears catch every voice. None of them says my name, no one holds me back. Only when I reach the rear section of the plane do I feel safe again.

None of my parents' so-called friends would ever fly in economy; it would be far beneath their dignity.

When I reach my seat, the entire row is still empty and I wish it would stay that way. Planes are often full of strange people, and I have little desire for shallow small talk. Exhausted, I let myself drop into the seat.

I still can't believe I'm actually here.

While I'm trying to make sense of myself, a gray-green backpack is heaved up energetically right next to me. Its owner is wearing faded, baggy jeans and a light gray knitted sweater. From what I can see from here, he must be a tall man. I fervently hope he doesn't have the seat next to me. Tall people don't have it easy on planes, I know that. But with such a beanpole as a seatmate, there's only room left for a toddler.

I prudently slide closer to the airplane wall and prop my chin in my hand. The sweeping movement of the seat next to me shatters my hope. I don't even want to look, deliberately keep my gaze fixed outside, and let my hair fall even farther into my face. I don't want this guy getting the idea of talking to me.

"Hi," I hear a deep male voice say that instantly reaches the fine hairs on my forearms and makes them tingle in a shivery way.

A wave of panic swept through my body.

I knew that voice.

Chapter Nineteen

"Philipp!"

That's all I can come up with as I stare at him like some dumb country cow. At least my lips still manage a smile, but my thoughts are on a roller coaster. The wild ride is in full swing when he casually reaches out his hand to me.

"How great to run into you here." He grins at me, his eyes shining like sapphires. I can only nod and I'm glad when he quickly lets go of me again.

"How long has it been? Five years? You look incredible." Was that a compliment? He's probably referring to my hair being down; he's never seen me like this before.

"You're not hiding a black eye behind those massive sunglasses, are you?"

"Of course not." The words tumble out of my mouth far too fast. I can easily imagine how red my eyes still are. I'm definitely not doing him the favor of taking off my glasses. Instead, I pull up the corners of my mouth while I all but compulsively scan him from head to toe.

I have to admit, he looks pretty good. Even much better

than I remember him. His face is so tanned it's as if he spent the winter in Australia. The skin on his sinewy forearms is even darker. A bracelet stands out in bright contrast against the dark skin of his right wrist. It's braided from cords in different shades of blue, all of which remind me of the sea. A churning light gray, like after a stormy night, a deep azure, like on a cloudless day, and in the middle a bright white, like the spray when huge waves crash against a steep cliff. His delicate fingers are still far too beautiful for his otherwise strong, masculine hands, and a part of me immediately registers that he isn't wearing any rings. Naturally, I'm not interested in that, but I still can't suppress a smirk.

"Hey man, that's my seat." A teenager has planted himself in front of us and is pointing with his black-tattooed index finger at Philipp's seat. His head is hidden under a cap; I can barely make out his face.

"Sure." Philipp gets up from his seat and slings an arm around the boy's shoulders in a matey way. "Listen, would you mind switching with me? My seat is right back there, D35. I've got something to take care of here, you know?" There's an oddly conspiratorial undertone to his words.

The teenager nods, a knowing grin spreading across his face. Without another word, he shuffles to the back. It looks like Philipp and I are going to spend the flight together. I don't know what to make of that. Especially because the kid is probably also thinking we'll be disappearing into the airplane bathroom together any minute now.

Philipp settles back down next to me, turns to me with a smile and looks at me expectantly. It's clearly time to say something. "So, Philipp, what are you doing here?" is the only thing that comes to mind. Every other word seems wiped clean from my head.

He bursts out laughing, warm and far too loud. "I'm going to go out on a limb and say the same thing as you. This is the flight to Marseille, right?" His tone makes it clear that he not only noticed how much he's rattling me, but is also secretly delighted about it.

I nod in agreement while I search in vain for any words at all. Is there really nothing I can think of to counter that constant grin of his?

Luckily, the flight attendant chooses this exact moment to explain the safety instructions with a bored expression. Even though I've heard them a thousand times, I pretend I'm fully focused on what she's saying. It buys me the time I need to recover from the shock of running into Philipp here so unexpectedly. When the ashy-blond, somewhat aging stewardess wishes everyone a pleasant flight, I'm fully myself again. Neither his unreal blue eyes nor the little dimples that form on his cheeks when he smiles can do anything to me now.

The plane rattles down the runway like a carriage over cobblestones. Then we pick up speed, the acceleration presses us deep into our seats, and for a brief moment it's not so bad that no one is saying anything.

"So, tell me, what's happened with you since college?" Philipp asks once we're in the air, stretching his long legs casually into the aisle. His upper body automatically leans in my direction and I can't stop his scent from settling in my nose. He smells of fir needles and freshly cut wood, as if he'd just been working in the forest.

I shake the image out of my head, irritated. "Nothing special, I made my way as a lawyer. You know how it is," I answer, trying to sound as relaxed as if I'd just had the best massage in the world. "And you?" I ask quickly so he doesn't get the idea to keep digging.

"As long as you're wearing those glasses, I'm definitely not telling you." He grins, his dimples deepening. "Your choice…" he says with a shrug.

"Fine, then forget it." I lift my chin and cross my legs.

His gaze travels over my body. "Still the same old Sarah, huh?"

"What's that supposed to mean?" I tilt my head and study him, no matter that he can probably only see part of my furrowed brows.

"Just that you haven't changed since uni." Now he studies my features and I'm glad I'm still wearing the sunglasses. He makes me nervous.

"In your opinion, is that a good thing or a bad thing?" Why am I even asking? I shouldn't care what he thinks. Pretending his answer doesn't matter to me, I play with the tray table in front of me. Very slowly, I push the bolt into the horizontal position, only to lock it again before the table can fold all the way down.

"You tell me. Good or bad?" This conversation would be easier if he didn't keep grinning like we were on a quiz show where, unlike me, he already knows all the right answers.

"Good, I'd say." I quickly hide my uncertainty as if I were an experienced stage performer and today were opening night. I go to smooth my hair, but my bun isn't there. So I just check my earrings and the collar of my blouse. Neither of them is sitting right—why am I only noticing that now?

With his arms folded behind his head, Philipp leans back in his seat, looking relaxed. "You do seem very sure of yourself," he says with a smirk, looking as smug and world-weary as a university professor just before retirement.

"Am I wrong?" I sound very convincing, but I can see

on his face how little it affects him. Instead of answering me, he just lifts his shoulders mysteriously. It's clearly time to deflect from myself. "What about you?"

"What do you mean?" he asks, and suddenly he doesn't seem nearly as confident as before. His voice is quieter, his gaze drifts up to the airplane ceiling.

"Are you still the same?" I turn toward him as far as the narrow space to the seat in front of us allows.

He jerks his head around and looks at me expectantly. "You tell me."

This one goes to Philipp, again. How does he keep doing that?

I study him again from head to toe, focusing. It even surprises me, but I don't have to think long to answer. "No, you're not."

There's something I could feel from the very first moment we met again. Even though I can't pinpoint the change, it's still there. And it's far more than just his light blond hair, which he used to wear cut short. Now it's grown long enough that he's tied it back into a small knot at the back of his head. Combined with the five o'clock shadow, he looks like an artist. A poet, maybe, or a painter. But definitely not like the lawyer he is. If I look into his deep blue eyes long enough, I see melancholy. It might also be grief; it's hard to tell.

Philipp doesn't answer me, but keeps looking at me as if he were trying to make out something through the dark glass of my glasses. The silence between us starts to make me uncomfortable, so I turn my face to the window, but in the end I can't help myself. "What happened to you?" I ask carefully, without taking my eyes off the miniature landscape below us.

Philipp remains silent. Far too long. Then I hear him take a deep breath, and I manage to look at him again.

"A few things." Thoughtfully, he plays with the loose ends of his bracelet, as if his fingers needed something to do. "And a lot more." His smile has vanished, the cheerful lines around his eyes are gone. I sense that it's better not to ask any further questions. Unpleasant things are best left alone.

"I understand," I say, and squirm awkwardly in my airplane seat.

Just a few seconds later, his dimples are back. He suddenly seems so relaxed and content, as if he only had to press a button to switch on his good mood. I've practiced that all my life, but I'm nowhere near as good at it as he is. How does he do it? And why?

"Are you actually still with that loser?" He stares at me unabashedly, and although I can hear his dislike of Tom, I can't see it in his face.

"Tom is not a loser. And yes, we're still together. We're even getting married soon." To prove it, I hold my ring under his nose. I don't want to look at it myself; it reminds me too much of what broke between us back home. I really can't deal with that right now, and besides, my problems are none of Philipp's business.

He lets out a whistle, as if he were seeing a beautiful woman. "Wow, that's massive. Then Tom must be the right one for you, huh?"

What an absurd question. Still, the way Philipp now fixes me with a probing stare makes me feel insecure. I lace my fingers together and press my nails into my palms.

"Of course he is." My voice is so firm that even he can't doubt my conviction. "And you? In love, or already divorced?" Almost as provocatively as he did, I point at his bare fingers resting on the airplane's armrests.

"Free as a bird." A satisfied grin spreads across his face.

It doesn't seem to bother him at all to be alone. I don't understand that in the slightest, but it fits the enigmatic figure he's turned into. What on earth changed him so much? I don't dare ask again and instead look for another topic of conversation, as shallow as a women's magazine.

"Well then, why don't you tell me what this little bird is going to get up to all on her own in Marseille." I try to suppress the sharp undertone that forms in my throat all by itself. Something about him provokes me, whatever it might be.

With relish, he pushes his seatback down; the squeak of the hinges hurts my ears. "Not everyone is like you, Sarah."

I wish he would give a straight answer to even one of my questions. "You mean driven and successful?"

He lets out a laugh. "More like overthinking and inflexible."

Even though he's unbelievably rude, it sounds as if he were stroking my head affectionately. There's something wrong with him; by now there's no doubt about it.

"Oh yeah? We just studied together, that's all, and we haven't seen each other for five long years. Why do you even think you know me so well?" Defiantly, I point my index finger at him.

"Just look at you," he says in a conciliatory tone, "your whole body is stiff and tense. When you smile, you look like you're wearing a mask." His voice is very soft, but that doesn't change the impact of his words.

How dare he!

I cross my arms over my chest. Doesn't he know you just don't say things like that? He can't just look behind my façade, he's not allowed to shake my very foundations. Desperately, I try to patch up the crumbling wall inside me, but it doesn't work.

I have to get out of here; Philipp is too close. Much too close.

Impulsively, I rip the sunglasses from my nose and fix him with my gaze as if I were a crocodile and he my next meal. "Excuse me, please," I say coldly, unfasten my seat belt, and spring up. Then I claw my handbag with the same impatience and push past him.

As fast as my high heels will carry me, I flee to the back of the plane. The restroom is occupied, so I stop in the middle of the aisle, take the compact out of my bag with trembling hands, and check my eyes in the mirror. Luckily there's no redness to be seen anymore, only my eyeliner is a little smudged. Carefully, I touch it up and tie my hair back into a bun.

I wait until the flight attendant has finished handing out drinks and starts putting everything back in its place.

"Excuse me, please." Cautiously, I take a step toward her. "I'd like to change my seat, would that be possible?"

She shakes her head. "I'm sorry, we're fully booked. But we're landing in twenty minutes anyway," she says with an apologetic shrug and locks her cart to the cabin wall. "I have to ask you to sit back down. We'll be starting our descent shortly," she adds, giving me an expectant look.

Wonderful, just what I needed.

I don't move an inch, unsure what I'm supposed to do now. I feel uncomfortable in my seat; Philipp throws me off balance too much. With ease he turns everything upside down, digs his claws into my insecurity, and bores through my protective shell. And whatever's hiding there is absolutely none of his business.

With a dull chime, the seat belt signs light up all over the cabin. My ears pop.

"You really have to sit down now," the flight attendant says, even more insistently than before, and gestures toward my seat with her hand as if this weren't a plane but a labyrinth.

Do I even have a choice? I can't think of one.

Slowly I work my way forward. I only have to endure a few minutes next to Philipp; I can manage that. Far too quickly his blond back of the head appears before my eyes, as bright as a lighthouse signal.

The plane drops into an air pocket, the cabin jolts violently. I stumble, grab the nearest seat, and give the elderly lady I'm disturbing an apologetic smile.

"Ladies and gentlemen, the airspace over Marseille is very windy today, so there may be increased turbulence during landing," I hear a man's voice sound calmly from the loudspeaker. The flight attendants buckle themselves into their jump seats. That's not a good sign, so I quicken my steps. I'm by no means in distress at sea, yet my body sways in all directions. My legs feel like rubber cords, my thoughts whirl around loosely.

What am I supposed to do if Philipp simply carries on where he left off earlier? If he doesn't let up until he's exposed me?

And once I'm standing defenseless in front of him, what will he do?

Chapter Twenty

Before I can even come up with a plan, I reach my row of seats. I clear my throat thoroughly, Philipp turns to me and looks me straight in the eyes. In them I can see only myself; whatever lies behind seems as unexplored and deep as the Mariana Trench. Without a word he gets up and gallantly presents me with a clear path to my seat.

I have to thank him; it's simply the done thing. "Thanks," I say just loud enough for him to hear. Keeping a safe distance, I squeeze past him, drop into my seat, and buckle up. The plane lurches to the side, I clutch the armrests and look out the window to find a point I can fix my gaze on.

"You're not scared, are you?" In contrast to earlier, he sounds cautious. Maybe he already regrets how he just put the pressure on me.

But he can't fool me with that. I definitely notice how he once again seems to see more of me than I want to show him. Why can't he just stop? "Of course not," I reply firmly, my gaze fixed on the dense wall of clouds outside my window.

Another air pocket, my stomach shoots up into my throat. Luckily I haven't eaten anything.

"Do you actually know it's far less likely to experience a plane crash than to win the lottery?" He puts his hand on my forearm. Unbelievable that I'm letting him do that. But it gives me a feeling of safety, I need that right now and I don't care in the slightest where I get it from.

I don't answer, so he just keeps chattering away, telling me how pilots are trained, why landings basically aren't difficult at all, and why every car ride is more dangerous than what we're doing right now. He probably has no clue about any of this, but his rambling distracts me, makes me grin and occasionally snort in surprise. The whole time his hand rests on my arm. As if he wanted to hold on to me, even if only a little bit.

At last the treetops beneath us look so close I feel like I could touch them if I stretched my hands out to them. I relax a little and as silently as possible I breathe out all the air that has built up in my lungs.

As if he noticed my change, his expression shifts now. "I'm sorry, Sarah." Philipp suddenly sounds subdued. "I probably got a bit carried away earlier. I never meant to hurt you, please believe me." I see regret in his eyes, at least that's what I think.

"It's okay, you weren't completely wrong either." I give in for the sake of the good mood. Maybe there really is a grain of truth in what he accuses me of. Relaxation and spontaneity just aren't things you usually build a career on. "Let's leave it at that," I suggest, to end the topic.

He studies me and immediately I wonder what he can

see this time. "We could do that," he finally says, "or we could do something completely different."

The gleam in his eyes worries me. Whatever he has in mind, it just can't be anything good. No way.

He smirks. "You do realize you currently look like a deer frozen in the headlights of a car, right?" he asks me, looking as if he's having a great time.

Hurriedly I lower my gaze and pretend I urgently have to look for something in my handbag. "Nonsense," I mutter dismissively and shake my head vehemently.

"Fear can be a bloody bad advisor," he says intently and takes his hand off my forearm.

Where he was just touching me, it suddenly feels so cold, as if I couldn't warm myself. It's only a small patch of skin, but from exactly that spot a longing travels through my body and finally settles in my heart. That's where it lies now, like a fizzy tablet, bubbling through everything. It tingles in a wonderfully exciting way. Is that what he meant?

What if he's right? Maybe I really should try something different. Haven't I failed miserably with my strategy so far?

"All right, let's do something different," I hear myself say. He didn't expect that, and I'm no less surprised. Whatever Philipp is doing to me, a part of me wants more of it. Letting him have his way feels good, and I don't even know exactly where I feel it.

"Wonderful!" he exclaims, rubbing his hands together, his open laughter contagious. Even I start to giggle, though of course, unlike him, I do it very quietly. "I don't know what you had planned, but I don't have any plans for this trip. We'll just spend the next few days together, drift along, and see where it takes us."

Let myself drift, what is that supposed to mean? "That's not possible, a rental car and a holiday home are waiting for me. Everything's already booked and paid for." I don't like it when I sound this hectic, but I still can't do anything about it.

"That's perfect, we'll need both, and the house is surely big enough for two, right?" He could definitely speak a bit more quietly. I'm pretty sure someone is already feeling disturbed by us. Besides, he's just inviting himself to stay with me, you simply don't do that. His direct manner overwhelms me, yet I nod. Because I'm a polite person, that's all. Not because I'm relieved that he's setting the direction and taking decisions off my hands. Definitely not.

A rough jolt runs through the plane, loud screeching booms through my eardrums straight into my head. Until now Philipp has done a good job of distracting me from the bumpy landing, but now fear shoots through my body like an electric shock that throws my heartbeat out of rhythm. I forget to breathe, my muscles turn hard as marble. The seat beneath me shudders, gravity pushes me forward. I quickly glance out of the window.

We've landed.

My tension drains away and with a sigh I let myself sink back into my seat. Philipp looks at me; he seems proud, and he has every right to be. He managed to distract me from my fears, and that suddenly becomes clear to me as well.

Could it even be that his company is actually good for me?

Somewhere between my head and my stomach it tingles. Just very softly, as if I were carrying sparklers inside me that have just lit themselves. Faint sparks of hope spread through me. My plan to relax here might actually work out. And that alone is so much more than has been possible in the past few weeks.

The plane comes to a standstill and even before the

flight attendant opens the door, hectic commotion breaks out. Passengers push into the aisle as if they couldn't stand it in the cramped cabin for one more minute.

Next to me, Philipp calmly stretches his arms up toward the plane's ceiling. "As if it made any difference," he murmurs, relaxed, and I'm amazed to realize that he hasn't even opened his seat belt yet. I've never thought about that before. On the contrary, I'm usually one of those people who are in a particular hurry. "Do you see the man up there? The one whose complexion is hardly any different from the gray of his suit?"

I spot him immediately. The man is standing in the line that's moving as sluggishly as the cars on Vienna's Südost-tangente at rush hour. His gaze flicks nervously back and forth. The way his index finger races over his phone's display, he looks like an addict who has finally got back what he so desperately needs.

"Sad, isn't it?" Philipp actually sounds as if he feels sorry for the man.

To me he's just someone who doesn't have much time. He reminds me a bit of Tom. Maybe he has an important business meeting or urgently needs to deal with the emails that came in during the flight. There's nothing wrong with that.

"Maybe," I answer for the sake of peace and slide my hands under my thighs. I have to fight the urge to take my own phone out of my bag. It's still switched off; I'm cut off from the part of the world I can't see right now. What if my mother calls? Or Tom?

What will they think when they can't reach me?

The thought of the two of them settles heavily on my shoulders; I immediately feel powerless and small. The sparklers in my chest fizzle out, go cold at breakneck speed, and crumble. Just a moment later it already feels as if they had never existed.

"Come on, off to pastures new!" Philipp is standing in the aisle, his backpack in his hand. He holds out his other hand to me and looks at me encouragingly with his blue eyes. He talks as if he knew how much I longed for exactly that.

Only now do I register that the plane is completely empty. I smile tentatively, put my hand in his and let him pull me up. He nods and doesn't have to say anything else. I know what to do, and I just start walking.

Chapter Twenty-One

"Up there, on the right. It should be there." Philipp points with his hand at an inconspicuous driveway that lights up in the headlights of our car. Right after that he yawns loudly, and I'm also struggling to keep my attention up. This day feels so long it's as if there were at least two packed into it.

"Yes, that's right. Here's a sign, another five kilometers," I answer tiredly, without taking my eyes off the road.

The darkness doesn't make driving easy for me, but since the rental contract for the car is in my name, I have no choice. I narrow my eyes and steer the car onto the narrow track. The gravel crunches under our tires, the ground is rutted with washed-out grooves. I have to grip the steering wheel more tightly so I can keep to the lane. Everything around us is dark, only the full moon shines pale in the sky. Now and then trees appear at the side of the track; otherwise there seem to be only meadows and low bushes. Wherever we've ended up, one thing is certain. There isn't another living soul out here.

"The house doesn't have a basement, does it?" Philipp's voice holds mock despair.

"I don't know, why?" I have to concentrate; I don't have time to think about what he's getting at. To see better, I lean forward as if I were a short-sighted pensioner.

"Someone might think you're abducting me." His voice takes on a conspiratorial undertone. "You know, to somewhere no one can hear me," he adds, breathing in and out quickly.

"Scared?" I draw the word out especially long and press the central-locking button with a smirk. The click of the locks underscores my question like a special effect. All that's missing now is some ominously swelling music. I hum the theme from Jaws, but only very quietly. It's actually quite fun to tease him.

Suddenly Philipp unbuckles his seat belt and rattles his door as if he wants to escape. My fun takes off faster than a thief who's got what he came for. I slam on the brakes at once.

"Are you crazy?" He's not actually going to throw himself out of a moving car, is he? Negligent bodily harm does not also need to be on the long list of my misdeeds.

He takes his hands off the door handle and grins at me. Amusement flashes in his eyes. Of course. Once again he had more staying power, I get it. "Relax," he says, leaning back with his hands clasped behind his head, "I just wanted to see how far you'd go."

"Idiot." Without thinking first I hurl the word over at him, as if it had been lurking somewhere in my throat for ages, waiting for its chance. Fractions of a second later I realize how rude I'm being and clap a hand over my mouth. "Sorry," I mumble meekly, giving him an apologetic look.

Philipp laughs, so openly and warmly it's as if I've made

a really good joke. "Oh, Sarah…" is all he says, holding his stomach. What is that in his gaze? Surely not pity? "Come on, let's keep driving or we'll never get there."

This man is a riddle I have no way of solving. His reactions are strange, so out of line and outside all the rules. My mother would wrinkle her nose, call him an ill-mannered lout, and forbid me to see him. Good thing she doesn't know about any of this.

Wait a second. She doesn't know about any of this. Nothing at all. Neither that I'm in France nor that Philipp is with me. She wouldn't approve of either. Ever.

The thought settles heavily on my chest. It presses me into the seat as if it wants to bury me underneath it.

"Philipp to Sarah, come in," I hear a soft male voice say. "You okay over there? You look like you've just noticed a stain on your blouse." He laughs again. Does he actually find that funny? How does he even know I can't stand dirty clothes?

"Of course," I answer curtly. I'd better ignore his comment; anything else wouldn't help anyway.

Hurriedly, I fix my gaze back on the road and floor the gas pedal. A bit too hard; the car rattles so violently over the bumpy surface that I can feel the agony of the shock absorbers all the way up my spine.

But only a few minutes later our destination appears before our eyes. At the end of the dirty white gravel road, I spot the stone façade of a bungalow in the headlights. Turquoise wooden shutters adorn the small windows, with flower boxes hanging in front of them. They're tiny and almost completely overgrown with blossoms and leaves.

"Like a gingerbread house, just without all the wood," Philipp comments happily, rubbing his hands. "And hopefully without a cage."

"Very funny." I shoot him a reproachful look. Then I turn off the engine and get out.

All at once I feel as if I'm stepping into another world. The intense scent of rosemary and thyme tickles my nose, the night air is pleasantly warm. A whisper of a breeze brushes my cheeks, the stillness of the night envelops me. No artificial sound can be heard, only the wind rushing through the leaves of trees and shrubs. It sounds like the sea when it rolls in gentle waves onto a gently sloping sandy beach.

Beside me, Philipp closes the car door; the dull sound pulls me back to reality. Like a gentleman, he takes my suitcase and strolls with it toward the house. I lock the car and hurry after him. Even before we reach the front door, lights come on all around us. Only now can I truly see what kind of paradise we've ended up in. Our lodging is nestled in a lush world of plants; everywhere I see perennials and other greenery whose names I don't know.

Just as described in the travel documents, I find the key under the flower box next to the front door. I slide it into the old-fashioned lock of the blue-painted wooden door, which opens with a scraping sound. The smell of damp walls hits me, and with it the memory of home. Where the mailboxes hang in our apartment building, between the entrance gate and the elevator, it smells exactly the same.

I freeze.

All I wanted was to escape. But now it feels as if I'm ending up right back where I couldn't breathe anymore. What on earth was I thinking?

That a foreign country could turn me into a new person?

As if I wouldn't still be with myself, as long as I just run far enough away.

Deflated, I let Philipp go first. He boards the house, sets the luggage down, and switches on the light. Then he lets out an enthusiastic whistle.

"Nice. Really nice, actually," I hear him call, as if that would change anything. "Come in, you've got to see this."

I don't want to.

What I'd much rather do is turn around on the spot, get in the car, and drive off. No matter where. But my legs don't move an inch. As if they want to make me believe they're cemented into the step in front of the front door.

"Sarah?" Philipp turns to me and looks at me. Completely neutral, not at all as if he's wondering what's wrong with me. I try to smile, but even I notice how badly it works. With a sigh he comes over to me, takes my arm, and gently pulls me into the house with him. Helpless, I let it happen.

"So, what do you think?"

At first I only make out the stone wall of the façade, which is partly exposed on the interior walls as well. It's broken up by walls painted a creamy white and purple curtains that reach all the way to the floor. We're standing in a room that's entrance hall, living room, dining room, and kitchen all at once. The wooden furniture is crammed close together; on the little table in front of the blue sofa I spot a vase of wildflowers. The sight of them moves me. I don't know why.

"Very beautiful." Softly, I sink down onto one of the chairs at the dining table. The violet-striped cushion gives way and nestles against me, as if it wants to welcome me. Only now do I notice how tired my body is.

"Look, we even have an open fireplace. It's a shame it's already the beginning of June and we won't need it." Philipp is still walking through the room, exploring everything. He yanks open the cupboards of the simple kitchenette, marvels at the modern coffee machine, and tests the sofa for comfort. "Perfect. It's a bit short, but it'll do." He seems pleased, even though there's no way he'll sleep comfortably here. The sofa barely fits two people sitting side by side; not even a small person like me could lie on it and stretch out her legs.

"Up you get, we'll look at the rest together." He's as giddy as a little kid. How on earth did he manage to leave his tiredness behind in the car?

I stifle a yawn. "Let's do it tomorrow, in daylight we'll see much better anyway," I grumble and prop my head in my hands. I feel his weight, as heavy as my worries. If I were here alone, I'd curl up on the sofa with all my clothes on and never get up again.

Philipp seems to sense my exhaustion; very gently he takes my hand and pulls me up to him. Then he links his arm through mine. "At night you can see things the day will never show you," he whispers in my ear and steers me straight toward the massive blue door at the back of the house. He undoes the lock and nudges me over the threshold in front of him.

For a moment we're both speechless, and I'm glad to feel Philipp's broad shoulders right behind me. They can catch me if my legs still give way. As if he guessed that I need support, he places his hands on my shoulders.

So we stand there, both of us, captivated by the idyll unfolding before our eyes.

It's a garden, as wild and beautiful as any I've ever seen. Lanterns stand scattered everywhere, their yellowish light casting an enchanted atmosphere over the plants. They give off a strong scent of blossoms, herbs, and something sweet I've never smelled before. In front of us lies a gravel path with little stones that sparkle as if they were tiny diamonds.

I feel a bit like Alice in Wonderland. A lightness starts to spread, first in my feet, then in my legs. It feels its way into my stomach and farther on to my fingertips. Now it relaxes my neck and runs over the back of my head straight into my forehead. I want more of it. Intoxicated, I put one foot in front of the other and stroll along the path. Philipp follows me, his hands still on my shoulders. Between tall grasses and bushy shrubs a pale blue-tinted water surface appears.

"We have a pool?" There's a reverent tremor in his words; he lets go of me and sprints past.

What is he doing? He won't be able to stop in time! He's not actually going to…

With a jubilant shout he jumps up, curls into a ball, and drops into the pool like a bomb. Water splashes in all directions; instinctively I step back. That sort of thing leaves nasty stains, and there's really no need for that.

"Come on in, it's insane," he calls out excitedly when he reappears and reaches his hand out to me. His eyes sparkle as intensely as the churning surface of the water where the light of the lanterns shatters.

How much I'd love to feel just once as happy as he looks in this moment.

But every part of me resists the idea of jumping into the pool with him. The water could ruin my hair and wash off my makeup. My clothes would cling wetly to my body. He could see me as I really am. Without my protective layer. It would be anything but sensible and stupid on top of that. Downright primitive, my mother would call it, grab me by the hand, and drag me as far away from here as possible.

"No way, forget it." I fold my arms in front of me in a

show of defiance. Still, I stay and watch, fascinated, as the beads of water drip from the tips of Philipp's hair onto the skin of his tanned collarbone. It would be better to run back to the house. Then I wouldn't have to see it, my own longing, as it flickers in his gaze as if it wanted to hold a mirror up to me.

He swims toward me, rests his arms casually on the edge of the pool, and looks up at me. "Start living for once, Sarah." His voice wraps softly around my doubts but can't make them disappear. "What have you got to lose?"

Everything, flashes reflexively through my mind, but I can't say that to him. Instead, I stare at him and shake my head vehemently. I order my legs to run, but they don't obey me. I have no choice but to watch Philipp pull himself up at the edge of the pool. Now he comes toward me in slow motion and lays his wet hand on my cheek.

I recoil at once.

"Stop that," I hiss, punishing him with a poisonous look. Unimpressed, he makes another attempt; this time I slap his hand away. "I said stop that." I sound far less convincing than I'd like. In his eyes I can see a deep warmth, and in a flash I feel it on my skin as well. It makes me melt as if I were nothing but a lump of dirty ice. If I let him keep doing this to me, everything good in me will seep into the ground beneath my feet. I can't possibly allow that. This little bit of clear water is the only thing still holding the dirt together.

Again he comes toward me, as if he didn't care how much he's scaring me. He touches my cheek, wet and cold.

I flinch.

My breath stops.

Just like my heart.

For seconds we both stand motionless like statues in the middle of paradise. Philipp's fingers are the first to break free from the paralysis. With his thumb he washes away a piece of my protective layer, and I can feel something inside me giving way all on its own. As if in a trance, I step with him to the edge of the pool and can't believe I'm really doing this.

I let myself fall.

I dive under and sink deeper and deeper until my hands touch the bottom. Once I'm there, I push off hard and break through the surface of the water like an invisible boundary.

Water runs over my face, drips from my hair, and leaves the taste of chlorine on my lips. Relentlessly it sweeps everything along with it. What's left is nothing but me.

Chapter Twenty-Two

Murderer!

A jolt shoots through my body. My surroundings are far too soft and smell unfamiliar. I tear my eyes open.

Where am I?

It's dark, only the moonlight lays a gray veil over the room. But the outlines of the narrow wardrobe and the wooden chair beside it tell me everything I need to know.

I'm in France, and my nightmares are too.

Like the stench of onion, they cling to me and bring tears to my eyes. There's no point in holding them back, nothing makes sense anymore. Disappointment rises in me at once. How could I have been so stupid as to believe that being somewhere else would save me?

I curl up under the blanket, rock myself back and forth, and wait. At least I've figured that much out: that it's better to let the crying happen. As if you open the sluices of a dam, the pressure eases a little. Patiently I stay in position until everything inside me is empty. Then I crawl out of bed.

My unruly curls stick out wildly in every direction. Of course I straighten them and pin them up carefully. Then I make my freckles disappear and do my eye makeup. That way I can dare to go outside.

The bedroom door creaks as if I were lifting the lid of a treasure chest. I stop moving at once; Philipp is sleeping on the sofa in the living room. I absolutely mustn't wake him, after all I know exactly what I look like despite the makeup. My eyes are shot through with red veins, my lids swollen.

I wait a moment; I want to feel safe, at least a little. Only a loud snore can be heard, so I take my sandals in my hand and tiptoe to the back door.

In the garden I make myself comfortable on a lounger and watch as the sky above me slowly grows light. In the last few weeks I've seen more sunrises than ever before. To me they're nothing special; they only show how a night of torment clears the battlefield for a bitter day. The French sky also turns orange first, then pale yellow, then blue. Instead of the hazy gray-blue back home, here it's a brilliant deep blue; otherwise I can't make out any difference.

As if the light of the morning sun were turning a spotlight on my memory, my gaze wanders to the pool. The surface of the water lies flat and motionless beside me. So inconspicuous, as if it hadn't robbed me of my decency last night. A horribly sick feeling spreads in my stomach, because I can't believe myself what happened.

Philipp had been utterly thrilled when I showed up at his side, soaked from head to toe. He immediately jumped into the pool with me and held up his flat hand for a high five.

"Insane, I can hardly believe you actually did it." A joyful grin spreads across his face.

I can't help but laugh, openly and uncontrollably. Because I feel so relieved. As if the water had washed everything unnecessary off me. With a flourish I slap my hand into his, then I dive under again. And again. Every time I break through the surface, it's as if I'm crossing the boundary into something new.

"It's amazing." I'm out of breath, but I keep going anyway.

My blouse clings to my body, the wet pants drag me heavily downward. My clothes are like a burden holding me back, and in this moment it makes perfect sense to take them off. Wearing only my underwear, I glide through the water like a dolphin. When I reach the edge of the pool, I look around. Philipp hasn't moved an inch; apparently he's doing nothing but watching me, his features wonderfully slack with astonishment.

"What?" I ask, giddy, and plunge back into the water. I surface just in front of him and look at him expectantly. He shakes his head in disbelief, his amazed gaze fueling my courage.

"What?" I repeat, even cheekier than before.

"I… um… well…" His stammering is not only cute, it also gives me a real high. This round goes to me, and that feels fantastic. I splash water in his face, at first just a little, then more and more. I don't have to wait long for his reaction. Like little kids we romp around in the pool, and we laugh until we're out of breath.

Just the memory of it now makes my heart race. The daylight shows me, without mercy, what I've done.

I behaved like an out-of-control first-grader!

As if I had no manners and no upbringing. It's incomprehensible—how could I lose my composure like that?

"Shame on you, Sarra," I hear my mother screech, and I have to agree with her completely. I should be ashamed, and that's exactly how I feel. A heaviness spreads in my chest, slowly but inexorably. It makes my shoulders slump.

"Good morning, sunshine. Ready for the next round?" Philipp is suddenly standing beside me, as if he had appeared out of nowhere.

Embarrassed, I lower my gaze and shake my head. "Definitely not." The words leave my mouth with a sharpness I hadn't meant to show. I quickly get up from the lounger and head for the house. "Coffee?" I ask as I pass him, without looking at him.

I don't wait for his answer; I can't bear the closeness between us. I'm horribly embarrassed about last night, and because I can't think of anything else to do, I run away.

Once in the kitchen, I switch on the coffee machine with fumbling fingers. I hear Philipp following me far too quickly. Hastily, I turn my back on him and pretend to search the wall cabinets for cups.

"We don't have any milk or sugar," I say, to steer the conversation in the right direction.

"No problem." I imagine I can hear confusion in his voice, but the rushing my heartbeat causes in my ears is too loud.

"We have to go shopping today, that much is clear." Still facing the kitchen counter, I watch the coffee dripping through the machine. Its cozy, strong aroma reaches my nose, calms me down, and sparks anticipation for the hit of caffeine I so desperately need after this night.

Instead of answering, Philipp just grunts in agreement, then I hear him rolling up his sleeping bag and rummaging for something in his backpack. "I'll wait outside," he says flatly, and disappears toward the back door.

I don't know which of us is acting stranger. Fine, my behavior the night before last could be called a misstep, but there's definitely something wrong with Philipp. I'm constantly afraid he'll see right through me. He laughs, chuckles, and grins as if he were the sole entertainer at a hotel on the Ballermann. But sometimes he becomes so quiet, as if something were catching up with him too. Just like a moment ago. His voice was very soft, almost sad. Is it because of me? Did he leave because I was so dismissive toward him? What if my behavior hurt him?

Immediately I'm seized by the urge to make it right. Hurting someone else is awful; no one should feel bad because of me. I grab the full cups of coffee and follow him out into the garden. There I see him standing at the far end of the pool. With his back turned to me, he looks out over the hills and smokes a hand-rolled cigarette. Like this I have no chance of knowing whether my suspicion is correct. In fact, it doesn't really matter. Problems you don't talk about don't exist. Just pretending that everything is perfectly fine can't be wrong.

I step up beside him and hand him the coffee. "Here you go," I say, deliberately cheerful.

Still keeping his eyes on the landscape in front of us, he takes the cup from me. "Beautiful, isn't it?" He sounds dreamy, almost as if the lush nature were calming him.

I take a closer look at the densely overgrown hills. They're completely covered in plants in different shades of green, with red poppies glowing in between. On the opposite slope I spot a vineyard next to an estate whose stone façade looks as if it were from another time. The longer I let my gaze wander, the more awake my senses become. I notice the sweet scent of blossoms. A butterfly flutters past us, as white as the clouds scattered across the sky. Philipp is right, it's beautiful. Why didn't I notice that earlier?

"It is," I reply, probably sounding just as dreamy as he does.

He takes a drag on his cigarette. Only the constant chatter of the birds breaks the silence that's building between us. I can hardly bear the quiet, because it stands for the words that hang unspoken between us. They're far too heavy; they can't just flutter away like that pretty butterfly keeping us company. They can only disappear if we drown them out with other words.

"What are we going to do today?" I'm sure the question will take his mind off things, and in fact he turns his head toward me and grins. The cheeky version of him is back, that very special glimmer spreading in his eyes.

"We're going for a spin." He stubs out his cigarette in the ashtray and releases the last cloud of smoke into the sky with obvious relish.

I can live with that just fine. It's neither stupid nor inappropriate to look around the area. On the contrary, it's so wonderfully normal that it could even have come from Tom. I'm definitely not going to ask him what became of his announcement on the plane. What happened last night must not happen again.

"I'll just get changed, then we can head out."

His grin grows wider, and his expression reminds me of a thief charming his unsuspecting victim. "You're already wearing something, why do you want to get changed?" he asks, baffled, stuffs the tobacco into his trouser pocket and slips his feet into his flip-flops. Only now do I notice that he's been standing here barefoot the whole time. Very strange.

I look down at myself. My dark blue jeans, the golden

sandals, and the cream-colored top with the lace at the neckline might actually be perfectly fine. "You've convinced me, let's go. I'll just grab my handbag."

In the bedroom I grab my wallet and sunscreen. I also take disinfectant wipes; after all, you never know what you'll be forced to touch when you're out. My phone is still on the nightstand, the small white light at the top edge blinking like a warning signal.

Oh God, please don't let it have been my mother!

I sit down on the edge of the bed, take a deep breath, and press the button that will tell me who called me.

Tom. No call, just a message.

"Got here fine," it says. Nothing else. The more often I read the words, the colder I feel. It doesn't sound at all as if he's expecting an answer from me. I immediately feel bad. He still can't forgive me. Did I destroy our love?

No, I mustn't think like that. He was probably just in a hurry and it was still important to him to let me know that everything was fine. There's nothing more to it. Quickly I type a few kind words to him, write that I love him and already miss him. As I send the message, I suddenly wonder whether that's even the truth. Ever since he left me at the elevator door of our apartment, I haven't missed him for a single second. Can that still be love?

I shake my head; I shouldn't let my thoughts ride this roller coaster. Besides, it's time for me to get going. Philipp is surely already wondering what's keeping me.

I find my travel companion waiting by the car. He's leaning casually against the passenger door, wearing sporty sunglasses on his nose. A few blond strands fall into his face; he's dressed in a simple white T-shirt, shorts, and, to my surprise, not flip-flops but sneakers. Whether I like it or not,

I can't help noticing how attractive he is. With his look, he could be on the cover of any surfer catalog.

Why doesn't he have a girlfriend? It's hardly as if he were short on offers.

"I'll tell you the way," he explains as I start the car. Very nice, that way it's not my fault if something goes wrong. Relaxed, I put it into first gear and let the car roll forward.

A little later we reach a small village and Philipp asks me to pull over to the right. On the other side of the street I see a supermarket. "Do you seriously want to go shopping already? It'll go bad on the way," I say, shaking my head.

He grins, as roguishly as before. "Don't worry, that wasn't my plan."

As soon as I've climbed out of the car, he grabs my hand and pulls me along with him. As if he were afraid I'd run off if he didn't hold on to me. Something's not right here; a queasy feeling spreads in my stomach. Touching him makes me uncomfortable, my hand starts to sweat. I quickly try to free myself, but I don't stand a chance.

"Cut it out, I'm an adult and I can walk down the street on my own," I say firmly.

"Just relax, Sarah." At least his voice sounds loving. So I trudge along beside him and let him lead me into a side street. We've barely turned the corner when he tightens his grip on my hand, and a moment later I know why.

The shop he's heading for with such certainty is a motorcycle rental place.

"No. Definitely no." I stop dead. "If you think I'm getting on a motorcycle, you're very much mistaken."

"You don't have to be afraid, I'm a good driver." His gaze inspires confidence, I have to admit that, but it doesn't change anything. Doesn't he know how many accidents there are every year? No matter how carefully you drive, there's no such thing as safety. And that's far from the only problem. I'd have to hold on to him, our bodies would be touching everywhere. A nasty thought that also brings my mother's words back to mind. "Like a slut," she screeches disparagingly.

"We could just as well explore the area by car." Even though I hate sucking up like this, I put a pleading note in my voice. Only lunatics and drifters ride motorcycles. And I'm neither.

With a mixture of pity and hope, he looked at me. "Didn't you want to do something different for once?"

So he hadn't forgotten after all. Damn.

"You're wrong about that," I replied meekly. Even though I had little chance of deciding this in my favor, I braced my legs firmly against the ground. My look was supposed to show him how determined I was not to take a single step farther.

Unimpressed, Philipp tightened his grip on my hand. It was as if we were both tugging on an invisible rope in opposite directions. With my spaghetti legs, I didn't exactly have the best odds. He didn't let up until I was standing right next to him. Then he pushed me through the shop's front door.

In the old-fashioned tiled room it reeked of grease, and the coveralls of the man behind the counter were smeared with black streaks. He was talking to two scruffy guys in leather gear. Each of the three had a bottle of beer in his hand. At ten in the morning. My flight instinct kicked in loud and clear.

"There is no way you're getting me on one of those things," I hissed quietly so no one else would hear. With a violent jerk I tore myself free. Then I crossed my arms over my chest and lifted my chin.

My behavior didn't have the slightest effect. Instead, Philipp looked at me as if I had just cheerfully remarked how much I was looking forward to our trip. "We'll see." Grinning cheekily, he tapped me on the nose with his index finger.

He seemed sure of himself, but this time I wasn't going to give in. Definitely not.

Chapter Twenty-Three

A black monstrosity is standing in front of me. It's humming and looks a good deal more dangerous than I'd imagined it earlier.

Philipp is obviously not bothered by that. He's sitting relaxed on the motorcycle, bracing both feet on the ground and handing me a helmet. I've got my arms folded in front of my chest, the way I've been doing nonstop since I tore myself away from him in the shop. He can't seriously think I'm going to hop onto this death machine as if it were a kiddie carousel.

"Come on, take the helmet." His voice is muffled, almost swallowed by his visor and the humming of the motorcycle. Unfortunately, I can still understand him.

"I already told you, I'm not coming with you," I yell back at him so he can definitely hear me. "You can go on your own, I'll take the car and we'll meet there." A good suggestion, if you ask me, but Philipp shakes his head.

At last he switches off the engine, pulls his helmet off and brushes his hair back behind his ear. I like that he's giving in. He fixes me with his deep blue eyes and I immediately fear that he can see something that's none of his business. I lower my gaze; that's safer.

"No, we're going together." It doesn't sound like an order, more like an unshakable certainty. "And I'll tell you why. You're going to love it, I promise. Once you're sitting back here, you'll feel like you're a bird. Whatever's tormenting you so much, the rush of air will set you free from it."

His gentle words hit me where they have no business being. As if he'd thrown a stone into water, they send out a wave of longing that keeps spreading inside me. It makes me wobble. For a moment I even forget to keep my back straight and my chin up.

What if it really is true? If I could forget everything, at least for a brief moment, wouldn't it be worth overcoming my fear?

"It is." Philipp cuts through my brooding as if he could read my thoughts. "And much more. Trust me, just this once." Again he holds the helmet out to me, so far that it almost touches my arms.

Do I even have a choice? And if I do, what is it?

Philipp smirks and shrugs his shoulders. "You can't keep doing the same thing over and over and still expect different results."

"Maybe," I admit meekly.

What he says sounds convincing. I've experienced it firsthand over the past few weeks. I didn't do a single thing wrong, and yet here I am now. Unemployed, on a failed escape from a life that doesn't even seem to be one anymore. None of my ideas was helpful. On the contrary, every attempt to make things better only made me fall further. My feet grow restless, as if they, too, want to convince me to just do it.

"Well then, hop on." Philipp pats the seat behind him and winks at me. "You've got nothing to lose—quite the opposite, in fact."

It happens. I can feel it clearly. Something inside me softens and finally gives way.

Still hesitating, I pull the hairpins out of my bun and reach for the helmet. Just getting rid of the tight pull on my scalp feels liberating. There's no need to keep sending commands to my body; it knows what to do. Resolutely it takes a step toward Philipp and climbs onto the motorcycle as if it were the most natural thing in the world.

Philipp turns the ignition key, and the vibration of the engine runs through my body as if it wants to shake my worries out of me.

"Hold on, please," he calls to me. Luckily, I find handles I can cling to. Putting my arms around him would definitely be way too close. I don't want him getting the idea he might have a chance with me.

"Okay, I'm ready," I shout back, and in the very next moment Philipp lets the machine roar. A thunder rolls through me and, without thinking about it any further, I end up clutching his stomach after all. In the end, that's still better than falling off this thing.

Just as he promised, Philipp starts off carefully. We turn onto the main road and roll leisurely through the village. I try to relax, loosen my grip, and dare to look around. None of the houses is modern. Even the ones currently under construction have traditional stone facades and red tiled roofs. Flowers grow everywhere, ivy climbs over brick walls, and even along the roadside wild thyme is growing. People's faces shine almost as brightly as the sun above us. Everyone seems content, maybe even happy.

Only now do I notice how clear the air is and how vivid the colors are.

We leave the place and Philipp picks up speed. I feel the acceleration, the slipstream whirls through my hair and tangles in my clothes. It tugs at me, almost as if it wants to tear away everything that's only loosely grown to me.

Like a bird.

Philipp's words wander through my head, over and over again. I feel ready, loosen my tight grip and allow air to push its way between us. Adrenaline shot through my body, tingling all the way to my fingertips. The landscape flies past me. Green, red, and gold merge with the deep blue of the sky above us.

So this is freedom.

Not just having light shoulders and no longer feeling the burning in my esophagus. No, this freedom is everywhere. And strongest in my chest. Right there where my heart beats to a rhythm as if it had been hypnotized. Fierce yet calm, hard and soft at the same time.

All my tension gathers in my throat and with it my worries. I don't hold on to them any longer; I roar them out into the world until nothing is left of them. On this inconspicuous country road in the middle of Provence, I let go of my burdens. Then I race away with Philipp so fast that they can't catch up with me again.

Chapter Twenty-Four

Maybe we've been driving for hours, maybe only minutes. I've lost my sense of time and with it the compulsion to constantly know what time it is. That doesn't matter here; it had never been clearer to me than in this moment.

Philipp slows down and in the next instant we find ourselves in a line of luxury cars. The bright red Ferrari next to me lets out a growl that makes the sound of our motorcycle seem almost childish. Its driver looks as if he couldn't haul himself out of the low-slung car without help. Beside him in the car sits a youthful beauty, with lips as fiery as the paint on the hood.

Through my tinted visor I can watch her unnoticed. She's wearing sunglasses. I can't see her eyes, but her features are stiff, almost snobbish. I watch her tilt her chin up and twist her mouth. Again and again she reaches for the white-and-gold silk scarf on her head, as if she wants to make sure it's still there. Something about the sight of her makes me sad, but before I can figure out what it is, Philipp pulls the motorcycle out of the line and weaves through the column.

France's high society answers our behavior with loud honking and frayed-nerves comments. Instantly I hear my mother's strict voice in my head. The fact that we're annoying these people is definitely not okay with her. The drivers probably think we're ill-mannered scum or, even worse, disrespectful vagrants. I wish I could escape that image, but it keeps pushing more and more to the forefront. Embarrassed, I press myself against Philipp's back.

Far too soon Philipp brings the motorbike to a stop and takes off his helmet. His blond mane sticks to his forehead; with a single movement of his hand he brushes the strands back.

"We're here, you don't need the helmet anymore." His smile is cheerful and completely relaxed.

Something inside me balks at taking off the helmet. The annoyed drivers will see my face and know exactly who was so brazen as to just roar past them. But what can they really do? I turn my back on the cars and pull the helmet off my head. My hair falls into my face, and that's just how I want it.

"Well then, off we go. I present to you *Les Baux-de-Provence*. The beauty of Provence." Out of the corner of my eye I see his hand trace an arc over the place in front of us. "You have to actually look if you want to see something." Philipp places his index finger under my chin and gently tilts it upward.

My gaze travels over a stone wall that really doesn't have anything special about it. It's so high that above it I can see only the bright blue sky.

"Seriously?" With a long, exasperated snort he turns my

head to the right. What appears before my eyes makes me forget the drivers behind us in an instant.

So this is it, the beauty of Provence. And it more than deserves its name.

In front of us rises a village built of pale stone and light red tiled roofs. Paths, house façades, stairways, and drinking fountains, everything looks as if it were cast from a single mold. Handmade, lovingly designed, and adorned with colorful shutters. We take the cobbled path uphill, and as soon as we enter the village there is more to discover than my senses can take in. Soap workshops line up next to nougat shops and art exhibitions. At every corner the scent of lavender sachets rises to my nose. Matching the people's cheerful mood, sunbeams tickle my skin. There is a lively bustle all around us; this place is a tourist magnet, and I can see why.

"It's wonderful." I turn in a full circle to take it all in.

"Great that you like it." Philipp takes my hand. His firm grip feels good, gives me a sense of safety and security. "But it's going to get even better. Come on!"

With purpose, he heads for an ice cream parlor, towing me along, and the display case makes his eyes light up. It's fascinating how he can get so excited about something so small. I wish it were contagious, but for me it's just ice cream. Not exactly a healthy lunch, but I don't want to spoil his enthusiasm. So I order one scoop each of strawberry and vanilla; you can't go wrong with that. Philipp, on the other hand, goes for flavors whose names neither of us can make any sense of.

"Nothing ventured, nothing gained." With a radiant expression, he ignores the doubts that are probably written all over my face. He's so carefree and seems to follow only his impulses, without thinking about whether he's doing the right thing. Outwardly I shake my head, but inside I'm captivated by his behavior. Tom wouldn't even accept a simple ice cream as dessert.

We've barely got our ice cream cones in hand when he pulls me farther along the path. As we walk, I taste my ice cream. An incredibly natural strawberry flavor unfolds in my mouth, fruity and sweet.

Behind the next shop he turns into an alley. It's so narrow that I couldn't see it at all until the very last moment. Philipp slows his pace and I stroll along behind him. Just a moment ago we were in the middle of rush hour; now everything becomes very slow and quiet. I can't decide what fascinates me more: the calm or the view of the Provençal landscape that I glimpse at the end of the alley.

"How do you know this place?" I try to keep my ice cream from running away, but I keep my eyes firmly on Philipp. He makes me curious. As an ordinary tourist you definitely wouldn't get lost in this inconspicuous alley, so how was he able to discover this?

His dimples deepen promisingly. "It's very simple. You always find places like this when you take paths no one else walks."

That's too cryptic for me. It sounds ambiguous, but is it meant that way? "I see," I answer, so he doesn't think I'm stupid, and turn my attention back to the ice cream cone in my hand.

"Most tourists are only here because their guidebook suggested it. They trudge along the main street without ever really looking around. No one notices that there's more here than the shopping mile and the ancient excavations displayed farther up. Because no one wants to see it, you know?" I can tell he thinks that's a mistake. He sounds a bit as if he feels sorry for all the people here.

I nod, even though I feel as if he's speaking a foreign language. Of course, as a tourist you look at the town and everything worth seeing; that's how I do it too. What's supposed to be wrong with that?

Philipp doesn't seem to notice my confusion and keeps chatting away unhindered. "The good thing is, as long as people go through life with blinkers on, places like this will always be waiting for me."

With his arms spread wide, he takes a deep breath. What he's saying sounds interesting. Still, I have no idea what he's getting at. Should I ask?

While I'm still pondering, Philipp helps himself to a massive spoonful of his ice cream and closes his eyes with a sigh. "Fantastic," he finally murmurs, smiling in sheer enjoyment.

Suddenly I feel warm, somewhere between my stomach and my chest. For whatever reason.

I quickly avert my gaze and trace a semicircle on the ground with my golden sandals. It's made up of a row of irregularly laid paving stones and reminds me of the narrow paths in downtown Vienna. I quickly push the thought away. I can't use grief and worries right now. Besides, the feeling that I'm missing something important here just won't let go of me. I simply have to know.

"Why do people wear these blinkers?" I ask, cleverly masking my stupidity with a skeptical expression.

Philipp shrugs. "Because they're constantly focused on their next goal and think they have neither the time nor the energy to take their eyes off it." This time I can clearly hear the pity in his voice.

"I know that feeling," I hear myself say. The words just pour out of me, unfiltered and without sense. "I mean, having goals, that is." What a pathetic attempt to save face. I lower my head and bite my tongue.

Philipp's hand finds my arm and comes to rest on my skin in a soothing way. His touch is so gentle, it's as if he were making contact with a shy deer. "That much is clear."

"It's not wrong to have goals. On the contrary, it's even necessary. Anyone who wants to achieve something in life has to make sure they move forward and must never allow themselves to be distracted." My parents drilled this sentence into me so often that it's become as indelible a part of me as a brand on a thoroughbred stallion. The ice cream in my cone is melting, running over my hand and dripping onto the ground. But I refuse to let it distract me; stubbornly, I keep my eyes fixed on Philipp.

He exhales deeply before he goes on. "Of course it's not wrong to know where you want to go." I immediately feel more at ease. So it's true, I'm doing everything right. "But a lot of people tend to see only the goal and no longer the path. It's as if they strapped those blinkers onto their own heads."

I still don't understand what's supposed to be bad about that. The direction our conversation is taking right now seems dangerous to me. My instinct tells me to change the subject as fast as possible.

"Maybe," I say absentmindedly to placate him, and turn my attention back to my ice cream. I'd rather not think about it any further, but even the intense taste of vanilla can't make me forget the image in my head.

I see myself in a midnight-blue suit and a freshly ironed blouse, with discreet gold jewelry and my hair pinned up. In one hand I'm carrying an elegant smooth-leather laptop bag, in the other a coffee to go. Like a madwoman I'm hurrying noisily down the street, my heels clattering. My gaze is determined, my expression hard. Massive blinkers block my view of what's happening to my right and left. The path blurs before my inner eye. I see only colors, no contours. They blend together, first turning gray-brown, then white.

Philipp's clearing his throat pulls me back to the present. "Exactly," he then says weightily. Only now do I realize that he has been watching me the whole time. What did he see?

There's no way he can know what's going on inside me. Or can he?

I swallow, but I can't stop the fear from rolling over me like a freight train. It squeezes me mercilessly. None of this is any of his business; he has to stop poking around in my thoughts. Right now.

I turn to him abruptly. "What about you, anyway? What became of your goals back then? What became of you?" I demand, pointing my index finger at him, without actually touching him, of course. His body stays calm, but in his eyes I can see that my words are having their effect.

"You mean the lawyer career, as pretty as something out of a fairy-tale coloring book?" He furrows his brows, as if the idea were repulsive to him.

"That's exactly what I mean." I know I'm on the right track. It feels as if this were a trial and he were the opposing side's witness I'm backing into a corner.

"Wasn't the right thing for me," he answers with a shrug, looking as if it doesn't bother him at all. How is that possible? What happened to the determined, career-focused student he used to be?

I tilt my head to the side and look at him expectantly. "What are you doing instead?" Now he can't stay silent any longer. I'm finally going to find out what happened to him.

This time he doesn't dodge me, and I don't leave him any loophole to slip through.

Despite how sure I am, the fearful expression I expected doesn't appear on Philipp's face. Instead, a radiant smile spreads, as if it's taking over his whole body. "I'm discovering the world."

The grounded sound of his voice leaves no room for doubt. He's doing what he loves, even if that's unimaginable to me. How can you do nothing but travel and still be content? Where's the success, where's the recognition? Can he really feel valuable if he doesn't achieve anything?

"The answer is yes," Philipp says with a smirk, "even if someone like you doesn't get it."

I need to get my facial expressions under better control so he can't keep reading them all the time. Then maybe he'll stop acting like he's the enlightened one and I'm the pitiful bat that lives exclusively in the dark.

"Someone like me?" I quickly pull my body into a defensive stance and fix him with a serious look.

"Do you have any makeup with you?" he suddenly asks, as if that had anything to do with what we're talking about. He wants to confuse me, but I'm not going to let him get away with it that easily.

"Of course." I pull the compact out of my bag and place it in his hand. He opens it, then flips it over and holds the mirror up to my face.

"What do you see?" he asks me. I don't hear a sharp undertone. If I didn't know better, I'd think he's genuinely interested in my answer. What is he trying to achieve with this? Make me feel even more stupid than I already do? With every hour I spend with him, it seems more and more as if he really knows something I have no clue about.

Pointedly, I turn my gaze away and take a step back. "What's this supposed to be?"

Unfazed, he follows me. "What do you see?"

Something tells me he'll keep going until he gets an answer from me. "Myself, what else?" I say irritably, without looking in the mirror.

Of course he isn't satisfied with that; he's not that easy to shake off. "Describe your face to me as if I couldn't see it." He closes his eyes, which in a strange way takes a pressure off me that I hadn't even noticed before.

My gaze flicks back and forth between the image in the mirror and Philipp's face. He looks as if he had all the time in the world to wait for my answer. His lids rest motionless against each other. So I fix my reflection, but I can't see anything unusual. The makeup is fine, my hair too. "Reddish-blond hair, snub nose, small mouth, pronounced cheekbones," I finally answer. "Happy now?"

"Not quite, keep going." He still doesn't look at me. I have no idea what he means, and I don't dare ask. "What do you see in your eyes?" he finally asks. Is that supposed to help me?

"Green flecks?" By now I'm so annoyed you can clearly hear it in my voice. Still, he answers my words with another shake of his head. Whatever he wants from me, I can't give it to him, no matter how helpful he thinks his questions are. "All right, that's enough, we're done here." I snatch the compact out of his hand and tuck it into my bag.

Philipp opens his eyes. "You'll never find what you're looking for like that."

He speaks softly, but what he says is powerful enough.

For a moment my whole world freezes, and with it our bodies. Only his words dance between us, touching me with their clarity and leaving an imprint right in the middle of my chest. But in the very next instant they leave me, rise high up, and vanish into the sky of France.

Philipp takes a step toward me. "Don't worry, it'll be fine. But it would be good if you trusted me a bit more." In a friendly gesture, he puts his arm around my shoulders.

With everything I have, I wish he were right about that. But there's no way I can tell him. Not a single word passes my lips, but my head sinks, tired, against his shoulder. Because it has had to carry far too much for far too long and finds rest right there, against Philipp's warm skin.

Chapter Twenty-Five

This time Philipp doesn't have to wait for me. I jump onto the motorcycle of my own accord and wrap my arms around his waist. Being so close to him feels familiar; I like the smell of his skin and the sense of safety his nearness gives me. Hope seeps into my thoughts like moisture into the dry furrows of a desert floor.

What if he really does know the answers to my questions?

I'd probably just have to ask him, but that's exactly what's basically impossible. You don't talk about problems. On the contrary, you pretend they don't exist. Everyone only wants to see the perfect Sarah; no one is interested in my dark sides. That's the fabric I'm woven from; I can't shed it without losing myself in the process.

We leave the hectic bustle of Baux-de-Provence behind us. The landscape rushes past me, lush green with red dots and white-flecked corners. As much as I'd love to enjoy the view, I can't. Because the image from earlier keeps forcing its way into my thoughts.

With oversized blinkers at my temples, I stride purposefully down the street, as if I can hardly wait to arrive. I don't look particularly happy, not with my lips pressed together like that. More strained, as if I were running a permanent sprint. But who would even notice? I can't tell if there's anyone near me at all. Because I can't see the way. What would I notice if I slowed my pace? Maybe Philipp, grinning at me and holding out his hand?

Nonsense. I shake the image out of my head. Going crazy on top of everything else is the last thing I need. All that matters is forgetting. I have to bury the memory so I can look ahead again. Despite his strange behavior, Philipp is helping me with that. He steers my thoughts in a different direction. What might happen if I simply let it? If I opened myself up to his ideas and found out where that would lead? Just thinking about it sends a tingling through my stomach, so intense that I can hardly sit still.

As if Philipp notices my change, he slows down and finally turns into a gravel side road. We roll through apple orchards, past neatly planted rows of vines and juicy red cherries. Only a few yards farther on, he brings the motorcycle to a stop and switches off the engine. The vibration still thrums through my body as I climb stiffly down from our machine.

"Do I see a smile there?" Philipp flips up his helmet visor. From the dark inside, his eyes beam at me.

"Maybe," I answer, and my smile grows a little wider. He nods, satisfied. Is he really happy just because he can see how much fun I'm having?

He comes toward me, and suddenly he's so close that I can smell him even more intensely than before. "I knew you'd like it," he says, while my nose tries to place the scent. It could be hazelnut.

I wave it off. "It was okay." It feels strange to pretend I'm casual and relaxed. But it's a role I'm actually starting to enjoy. Not just because he looks at me in surprise, but because, without even trying, I really am loosening up.

He takes off his helmet. Leaning against the motorcycle like a supermodel, he sizes me up. "Okay, I get it." I don't like his cheeky grin. "Unfortunately, okay isn't enough. We need more than that." He puts his hand on his chin as if he's thinking, and yet I can tell he already knows exactly what's coming next.

"We don't need that." The words rush out of my mouth before he can go on. Who knows what he's come up with this time. I've only just started to feel comfortable; he's not allowed to ruin that for me.

Philipp laughs, but it just bounces right off me. All my senses are cranked up to the max and clearly set to escape. "Trust, dear Sarah. We talked about that, didn't we?"

Right. I nod hesitantly—what else can I do?

"Very good. Then hop onto this wild beast here, it's time you took the reins yourself." Unbelievable, but his fingers are actually pointing at the front part of the motorcycle seat.

I swallow. "I'm supposed to drive? You're insane, I don't even have a license!" I protest loudly.

"See that little path over there? It's private property, you don't need a driver's license there. We'll push the motorbike up to that point, then we can get started." He nods toward the spot where the orchard ends and turns into a flower meadow. In between there really is a track that looks as if only tractors usually drive on it.

"You really think you're very clever, don't you. If that's private property, we're not allowed to be there at all. It's not happening, forget it." How nice that my job saves me from this situation. Grinning at him in triumph, I look him straight in the eye.

Philipp doesn't seem to care; undeterred, he moves the motorbike into position. "Don't worry, I know the owner," he says casually and keeps getting farther away from me so he can't hear my answer anymore.

I can't do it. Or can I? Like a toddler who doesn't know what it wants, I stay standing exactly where I am. In the middle of fruit trees I breathe in the aromatic air of France, fold my arms across my chest, and stare after him, undecided. It would be nice if he could see it too, but he doesn't turn around to look at me.

"So, are you coming?" he calls over to me from a distance, just before he reaches the path. It sounds so harmless, as if he were inviting me to breakfast.

Damn. Restlessly, I shift my weight from one foot to the other. It takes all my willpower just to allow the idea of simply doing it into my head. What's the worst that could happen? Accident, injury, death? I should just leave it.

Oh God, Sarah, loosen up. Come on, it's not that hard.

Philipp and the motorbike are ready, and I could swear the two of them are looking at me expectantly. "Come on, I promise you it'll be fantastic. Of course I'll make sure nothing happens, that's a matter of honor."

Message received, once again he knows exactly what I'm thinking. Why do I even bother constantly trying to hide my innermost self from him?

He reaches his hand out to me; something about the sight of him draws me in like magic. "Promise?" All that's missing now is me fiddling with the hem of a pretty little dress while rocking my body back and forth like an insecure six-year-old. Then I'd look exactly the way I feel.

"What do you think." It isn't a question but a statement

that cuts through the warm June air and lands right in the middle of my chest. I can feel it clearly: he'll be there for me, no matter what happens. But I can't grasp it. Why is he doing this when there's nothing I've done to deserve it? I quickly blink away the tears that are rising. He doesn't need to see how moved I am as well.

"Sometimes you just have to start walking. Just put one foot in front of the other," I hear Philipp call. His voice stops the brooding in my head, and my legs start to move, hesitantly.

By the time I reach him, my palms are damp. My breathing is shallow and fast. Even so, his encouraging smile is enough to make me climb onto the motorcycle. I no longer ask whether, no longer brood over the why. It feels as if I'm moving in slow motion while the world around me is changing at triple speed. Suddenly Philipp is sitting behind me, pressing himself against my back and placing his hands over mine. A sweet hazelnut scent wraps itself around me. I feel hot and cold at the same time, even though the engine isn't even running yet. Is it Philipp's nearness that's giving me goosebumps all over my body?

"Ready?" All at once he's so close it's as if he were a part of me. I feel safe, as if he were covering me with his embrace and melting the panicked paralysis inside me.

I nod, and a few moments later I hear the engine roar to life. My world trembles. With Philipp's help I gently give it some gas, and we set off. I feel the power of the machine beneath me. Steering it—no, mastering it—makes me laugh with euphoria. We rattle along the dirt track toward a horizon that suddenly looks even brighter than it did a few minutes ago. With every meter my body is flooded with more adrenaline, as if it were crashing over my head like a wave. I savor the ride with all my senses, hear Philipp's shouts of excitement, and feel his warmth on my skin. With the wind in my face and the wild, romantic Provence before my eyes, I'm left with only one wish.

I want to keep riding forever and hold on to this feeling for all eternity.

But no matter how much I long for it, the end of the path appears far too quickly before my eyes. It opens into a field of olive trees. We can't go any farther here; our ride is over. With Philipp's help I slow down, and a little later we come to a stop. While he gets off with a jubilant shout, I stay seated. My elation ebbs away. I slump, growing a little smaller with every second. This must be how a flower feels that no one wants to water. Lost in thought, I take off my helmet and let my gaze wander over the green fruit on the little trees.

Why won't happiness stay with me?

"Why so sad?" Philipp takes the helmet from me and forces me to look at him.

I pull up the corners of my mouth. "Everything's fine," I say, trying to avoid his gaze.

He doesn't answer, the silence makes me insecure. Now he also carefully lays his hand on my cheek, as if I were a fragile chick. This tenderness wins me over, and suddenly I want to tell him everything. What I dream of at night with my eyes wide open, who I really am, and that I don't know where I'm supposed to go.

But a terrible fear locks my lips. I mustn't scare him away; he has to stay with me so that happiness can find me again. Silently I blink up at him.

"You can't hold on to moments, nobody can. But if you enjoy them to the fullest, a part of them stays inside you." His fingers stroke over my ear, I lift my head, our eyes meet.

I don't want to hide my doubts any longer; I'm suddenly sick of wearing the untouchable mask.

"How?" I hear the pleading in my voice all too clearly. It exposes me and proves how much I wish his words were true.

Philipp smiles. He has finally managed to make my façade crack and turn brittle. But instead of exploiting this weakness to make himself strong, he only comes closer and closer to me until our bodies are almost touching. Suddenly there's a tension. It pulls us together as if we were magnetic poles.

"I'll show you." It sounds like a promise. And without having any proof of it, I know he'll keep it.

At last I dare to ask that one question that has been dancing through my thoughts all day. "Why are you doing all this for me?"

For far too long a moment, Philipp bites his lip. "Because I can't help it," he whispers.

Now he leans over me and closes his eyes. Out of nowhere my heartbeat loses its rhythm. The air in my lungs stands still, and with it time. Everything around us blurs; there is only him and me. We're so close to each other that I don't know where my body ends and his begins. My eyelids grow heavy and I don't stop them from closing.

Seconds, minutes, or maybe hours later I feel his lips right in the middle of my forehead. Exactly where my worries usually sit, they rest softly on my skin. His sweet scent is everywhere, wrapping around my thoughts and silencing my mind. It doesn't matter whether or what any of this means. Because in this moment he gives me a long-awaited peace.

Everything goes quiet.

There's only the two of us and the warm French breeze that gently brushes my cheeks.

Chapter Twenty-Six

Philipp jumps out of the car. "Go on ahead, I'll sacrifice myself to haul the groceries."

Unlike him, I drag myself up; the long motorcycle ride aches in every bone. This must be exactly how a cowboy feels after a hard day's work. Exhausted, but content. Now that we're back in our little gingerbread house, one thing really hits me. Philipp has given me a wonderful day. Because even though my muscles are stiff, I feel better than I have in a long time.

I unlock the front door, Philipp drops the groceries in the kitchen, and I immediately start putting them away. The dark red cherries look fantastic, but they'll have to wait a bit longer. Philipp squeezes past me from behind, grabs a whole fistful of the red fruit, and bites a particularly tempting-looking cherry straight off the stem.

"Wow." His eyes are closed, a look of pure enjoyment on his face. I watch him chew on that one cherry for what feels like minutes. Then he spits the pit into his hand. "You have to try these." He holds one of the stems right under my nose, a single cherry dangling temptingly in front of my eyes.

I shake my head. "Later."

Philipp holds me back. "The right time is never later." His eyes look at me expectantly.

Whether I want it to or not, the image of me with the blinkers on suddenly flashes through my mind. Do they have something to do with this? Are the cherries a symbol of the beautiful things I can't perceive along the way?

"Sarah, you really have to stop overthinking all the time. It's very simple, you just have to ask yourself a single question. Do you want this cherry right now?" Again, he lets the fruit dangle back and forth in front of my face.

I want it, it looks so appetizing that I have to swallow. Instead of answering his question, I open my mouth and snap up the fruit.

As I lean back against the kitchenette counter, its aroma unfolds on my palate. Wonderfully sweet and refreshing. Like Philipp, I let it wander around in my mouth for as long as possible. At that very moment something strange happens. I can't believe it, I just know it feels as if I were sitting in a race car that has suddenly cut its speed in half. I'm no longer racing, I'm strolling. With this wonderfully light feeling, I take my time, alternating between enjoying more cherries and calmly putting the groceries away in the fridge.

Of course I notice how I'm being watched while I do it, but that doesn't bother me. I don't want to hide anymore and right now, in this moment, I make myself a promise. To trust myself more, to loosen the blinkers, and to pay less attention to my worries, fears, and doubts. The thought feels so good that I float toward the hallway as light as a feather.

"I'll be right back." With a broad smile, I squeeze past Philipp, who is still leaning against the dining table with a satisfied expression on his face.

I close my bedroom door behind me, toss my handbag onto the bed, and slip my sandals off my feet. My toes look like a miner's. Dirty and neglected.

I have to clean them, right now.

All of me has to be washed. My skin smells like a mix of sunscreen and sweat, and there can't be much left of my makeup. A glance in the mirror finally confirms how much I forgot to pay attention to my appearance while I was out. My hair is matted, and right in the middle of my top I discover a massive, earthy brown stain.

Did I really go shopping in this state?

I feel a familiar old panic rising inside me, paired with a sense of shame that sends the blood rushing to my cheeks. My exuberant thoughts from earlier suddenly seem like a fairy tale from another time. In their place, doubts and pangs of conscience push to the forefront. But all at once I feel it very clearly. Now, in this moment, I have to fight back against it.

I give myself an encouraging smile; my reflection nods at me with a conspiratorial expression. Then I saunter slowly into the bathroom, take off my clothes, and step into the shower. Satisfied, I watch the muddy brown water disappear down the drain. Gradually it turns clear; I feel fantastic and grab the shower gel. It wraps me in the scent of coconut and pineapple; I spread it carefully until I'm covered in foam everywhere. I only leave out my belly. I can't touch it. Still not.

Right after I step out of the shower, I dry my hair, put on fresh makeup, and slip into a clean dress. Exactly the way my mother would like it.

Only now do I realize that I haven't thought about her all day. What if she called and couldn't reach me? With long strides I hurry into my room and grab my handbag. Sure enough, the little white light at the top edge of my phone is blinking.

Damn.

What am I supposed to tell her? That I'm doing exactly the opposite of what she thinks is right? How much longer can I keep lying to her before she gets suspicious?

Instinctively I hold my breath, bite my lip, and unlock the screen. Only then do I see it. It wasn't my mother who called, but Tom. My tension eases, I let myself fall onto the bed and wait for my heartbeat to return to normal.

Why did he call, I wonder? Maybe he wants to make up with me, seriously and not just on the surface. It would be nice to know that everything is all right between us. Our love is the only thing in my life that's still holding steady. With my index finger I stroke his picture on my phone's display. He's a dream man, definitely. Good-looking, successful, and blessed with an incredibly charming aura. Still, something keeps me from calling him back. I'd have to lie to him; maybe that's it.

Indecisively, I turn the phone in my hand and let my gaze wander back and forth between Tom and the diamond ring on my finger. It would be rude not to get in touch. He'd worry instead of focusing on his work. I know how important this trip is to him and how much depends on his being successful in Asia.

The time display on the screen marches on relentlessly. As I watch the minutes disappear, it suddenly dawns on me that it's too late for a call anyway. The sun is about to set here, which means it's already the middle of the night in Asia. Tom is asleep.

"Couldn't pick up, I'm sorry," I type in a message. "You're surely asleep by now, let's talk on the phone tomorrow at noon. A thousand kisses. I love you."

It isn't a lie and still it's innocuous. Actually perfect, yet I feel uneasy. If he knew I was here in France, with Philipp of all people, he wouldn't like it. And if he had seen how close we were this afternoon on the dirt road…

I don't even want to think about it. We're engaged, but I let myself fall into another man's arms and even enjoy it. Wrong, that's wrong, Sarra, I scold myself in my mother's tone of voice.

As if my phone had suddenly turned red-hot, I fling it away from me on reflex as far as I can. Not seeing it anymore means not thinking about it anymore. The room is too small for that devilish thing and me; I have to get out of here. Blindly I rush into the living area and almost run straight into Philipp. At first he just stares at me, then he whistles appreciatively.

"Wow, I didn't know you were still taking me to a Michelin-starred restaurant tonight." Pushing his lower lip forward, he nods in approval and sticks his right thumb up.

"What? No, why?" It probably wasn't very smart of me to enter the room without thinking first. He caught me off guard, again. I look down at myself; the dress really isn't that fancy.

"What a shame. But on the other hand, it's good too, otherwise I might've had to change my plans in the end." There it is again, that grin that spreads all the way to his eyes and leaves a sparkle there. So dangerously indecent that I automatically step back and blink at him distrustfully. My three closest friends aren't so easy to shake off. Fear, worry, and doubt seem to be just as firmly attached to me as arms, legs, and this damn head. At least I manage not to fold my arms across my chest. Instead, I lace my fingers tightly together behind my back. As if my protective cloak were missing, I'm now standing in front of Philipp.

He smirks. "Well, my little doe, caught in the headlights again?" For a moment his hand twitches in my direction, but he immediately pulls it back. "Trust really isn't your strong suit, I get it. But tell me, honestly, has it really been that bad with me so far?" He sounds dejected, as if my mistrust offended him.

"No," I admit sheepishly and shift from one foot to the other to get the tension out of my body.

"Good." He beams as if he'd won the lottery. What is he so happy about? That I'm backing down?

Now he grabs his oversized backpack. "I'm gonna hop in the shower, then we can head out. In the meantime you should change again. Don't you have anything comfy with you? Sweatpants or loose jeans?"

Yeah, right, as if I'd ever wear sweatpants. "No, what for?" I ask, and instantly regret that I've once again asked him a compromising question. Before he can embarrass me, I wave it off. "Whatever, I'll find something."

Smoothly, I squeeze past him and hurry back to my room. Once there, I rummage through my suitcase, find a pair of light linen pants, a simple top, and a fine-knit dark blue cardigan. It's not going to get any better than that. I get changed and take one last look in the mirror. Satisfied, I note how perfectly my hair and makeup are done. Still, something's off; somehow I look different. Only after I've examined myself thoroughly from every angle do I understand what it is.

I'm smiling, without even trying. Just like that. Now my smile grows even wider, almost radiant. The ringing of my phone keeps me from finding out where this is going, because in a flash my expression turns hard as stone. Tom is still awake after all; I have to pick up. I grab the phone in a hurry and glance at the display.

It's not Tom who wants to talk to me, but my mother. There's no escaping her.

A lump forms in my stomach, so heavy it's as if all my guilt is gathering there and piling up. "Hi," I say, and immediately put my hand over the microphone so she can't hear my stressed breathing.

"Application status?" My mother's voice is pure poison; it seeps through the phone into my ear and spreads through my body. Every muscle cramps, I shrink.

Once again I lie to her. I claim I've already had interviews, that I've received more invitations, and I assure her that everything will soon be back to normal. It feels horrible, but anything else would be my downfall.

"Well," she finally says, contrite, nothing more, and hangs up at once.

I let everything drop. Phone, shoulders, head, and arms. What am I even doing here? I'm running toward my own ruin with open arms, as if I'd lost my mind. I'll never get out of this dead end. I'm going to be exposed, my parents will never want to see me again. They'd rather imagine I were dead than a crazy, unemployed good-for-nothing.

This room is too cramped, my worries are overpowering and occupy every corner of my body. I have to get out of here.

With all my strength I try to push the memory of the phone call far away, and with it the miserable feeling of being a bad person. I loosen my body as if I could shake off the burden that way, and I even imagine it helps a little. Then I head for the living room.

"Wow, you took your time." Fresh and clean, Philipp is

lying on the purple sofa, looking as if he had made himself comfortable in a lavender field. If his hair weren't damp and he didn't give off that lemony scent, I wouldn't believe he had actually managed to take a shower in such a short time.

"Not everyone has superpowers, Clark Kent," I say dryly. The only thing that can help me now is distraction, so I decide the best defense is a good offense. I want to go where Philipp is so happy. "So go on, tell me what you've come up with."

Can he hear the pleading in my words? I'm completely ready to let myself be drawn into his world. Whatever is waiting for me there, it can't be worse than what I'm leaving behind.

"Don't worry, it's something absolutely harmless." He peels himself off the sofa, walks into the kitchen with a promising smile on his lips, and puts wine, cheese, and bread into a bag. Then he adds two bottles of water and some chocolate.

Leaning against the doorframe, I watch him. "A picnic, how nice!" I'm delighted. Not only because my stomach is growling, but also because this time I already know the surprise and have nothing to be afraid of.

"Yeah, you could call it that. Grab the cushions and the blanket from the sofa too, it might get chilly."

I'm happy to, and we also take the remaining cherries, butter, and jam. Heavily laden, we amble to the car. As always, Philipp sets the course and navigates me to a parking lot at the top of a mountain. There's no one else in sight.

I undo my seat belt, open the door, and get out. Before I can open the trunk, Philipp holds me back. His hand rests on my arm, his gaze lost somewhere out there.

"Take off the blinkers," he whispers, "and open your eyes."

I just do it without thinking about it. Now.

As if there were magic involved, I can suddenly perceive things that had been invisible before. It's as if nature, with its different shades of green and its intensely aromatic scent, existed just for the two of us. In the light of the evening sun, the valley below us looks as if someone had dipped it in liquid gold. Together with the play of colors in the sky, the sight reminds me of a work of art painted by an angel. I allow myself to take it all in, because I sense that this could be one of the moments Philipp talked about today.

For minutes we just stand here and gaze out over the wide expanse. Neither of us says a word. It isn't necessary. Being silent together feels exactly right. All at once I notice how light my stomach feels. The burning is gone, probably already for days. This trip is good for me. Philipp is good for me.

Before I can think about it any further, Philipp shakes me out of my trance. "There's even more of that where we're going," he says, turning to leave. Everything about me feels strange, as if I were a different person. I narrow my eyes to pull myself together again, then follow him.

"Why do you know your way around here so well, anyway?" I ask as we take our bags out of the car. It's really time to find out more about him. There has to be more to him than that he prefers traveling the world to representing clients and that social rules apparently don't mean much to him anymore.

"I've been in the area once or twice," he answers, as if it were nothing special, and directs me to a narrow path that looks as if it leads straight into the middle of nowhere. "We have to go that way."

Philipp is doing it again. He doesn't answer my question, he deflects from himself. What is he hiding from me?

"What's that supposed to mean? How often? And with whom?" I call after him as he's already disappearing around the first bend. I run after him but only catch up when he's a bit farther on, spreading the blanket out on the ground. "Hey, why didn't you wait for me?" I ask, out of breath, my hands braced on my knees.

"So we don't miss this." He nods toward the setting sun, sits cross-legged on the blanket, and pats the spot beside him with his hand.

I do as he says and even feel a sense of anticipation rising inside me. "And now?" I ask impatiently. "Close our eyes and say 'om'?"

He laughs. "Do you know what your problem is?" he asks, sounding completely affectionate. "You think too much. You're constantly worrying about what's going to happen next, or your thoughts are stuck in a past that isn't good for you."

I look at him, but he stubbornly keeps his gaze fixed straight ahead. "Yeah, evolution gave us a brain for that. To think. So why shouldn't I use it?"

"You should use it, but differently."

I stay silent. Once again, I don't understand what Philipp is talking about. Still, he seems to be waiting for my reaction. His hands rest on his thighs, his face is covered in reddish light. He looks as if he were radiating more warmth than the setting sun.

What if I just asked?

I swallow, open my mouth, close it again. Then I take a deep breath. "Differently how?" I force out, tense and at the same time relieved because I managed to push myself to do it.

No twitch, no snort. Philipp doesn't move. "Let the past rest, you can't change it anyway. There's no point brooding over it."

Okay, that sounded reasonable, even if far too simple. I nod. "And what about the future?"

"Your future is made out of your thoughts today," he answers with stoic calm.

"So it does make sense to think about it!" Got him, he's contradicting himself. So I'm not doing everything wrong after all, like he claimed earlier.

"How you think about it, that's what matters. The way you're doing it now, you're only throwing yourself into misery."

At last he turns his head toward me. His gaze captures me, and I sense that the next thing he says will be very important.

"Imagine your future as if it were a white canvas. Your thoughts are the brushstrokes, your feelings the colors. Right now you're painting your picture, you alone. What do you think it will look like if you're constantly worrying and thinking about the worst that could happen?"

Immediately I have a painting in my mind, dominated by gray and black, with a massive red streak with dark shadows in the middle. I lower my head. "Terrible," I murmur.

"And what will it look like if you're full of hope and dreams? If you see yourself as the best version of who you are?" he asks in the same calm tone as before.

The picture before my mind's eye turns into a watercolor, all light blue, soft pink, and grass green. The brushstrokes are delicate, as if each one had been placed on the canvas with love and care. "Peaceful" is the first word that comes to mind.

"What do you want your future to be like? If you could choose between terrible and peaceful, which would you pick?" He takes my hands in his, squeezing them so tightly it's as if he wants to jump-start my heart.

"Of course I'd prefer the second one. But…"

"…there is no but," Philipp cuts me off. "This but exists only in your head, right there between your eyebrows." With his index finger he presses gently on the spot where Indian women wear their colorful mark. "You alone decide how much power you give it."

"But…," I repeat in disbelief. Fragments of thoughts rush through my brain. So fast I can't catch hold of them.

Philipp shakes his head vigorously; he doesn't want to hear the but. "Think about it, let my words seep past your rationally trained mind."

I look at him, not understanding. How on earth is that supposed to work?

The answer comes without my having to ask for it. "Just don't pay any attention to thoughts that contain but, and wait to see what happens," he says, as if he could read my question in my eyes.

Once more he taps my forehead, then gently turns my head forward.

In front of my eyes the sunset appears, glowing as powerfully as any I've ever seen. From dark red to violet, from medium blue to indigo, thin bands of cloud stretch across the horizon. Behind the chain of hills the moon rises, accompanied by brightly twinkling stars. A breath of air rushes through the bushes and strokes my forearms, soft and warm. The spot between my eyebrows feels as if Philipp had lit a fire there. With every breath my surroundings grow calmer, the chirping of the crickets becomes muffled. In my mind an unpainted canvas appears, quite a bit larger than I am. All the colors in this world are ready beside it. I alone have the choice. With every step I take, I paint my picture.

If I really could decide my own future, what would it look like?

Chapter Twenty-Seven

The tart taste of red wine and the sweet note of creamy chocolate lie on my tongue. Still, in my thoughts I'm standing in front of my unpainted canvas, looking indecisively at the colors and not knowing which brush is the right one. I lack imagination, ideas, and passion. I only know that my picture mustn't turn out terrible; I definitely won't be needing the black and the gray.

Beside me Philipp pokes at the campfire with a stick and watches the flames flare up in the darkness of the night. The crackling sound is all that can be heard. He stays silent, as if he doesn't want to disturb my brooding. Maybe he's just lost in his own thoughts; I don't know. His expression hardly lets me guess what's going on inside him. Still, I think I can make something out in his gaze. His usually radiant blue eyes are dark and closed off.

As if he, too, were stuck in a memory that robs him of his joy.

"You're supposed to be focusing on yourself," he says,

still staring into the fire. A smile plays around his lips. His dimples appear, sweeter than all the sugar in the world.

Only now do I realize that I've been staring at him. For how long? Embarrassed, I look away. "I'm sorry," I mumble hastily.

"Stop apologizing, Sarah. If you can't take your eyes off me, that's fine." He laughs and lets himself fall back onto the blanket. Propped up on his forearm, he turns to me and looks at me expectantly.

Quickly, I let my gaze wander back to the fire and shake my head. "That's not it. I was just wondering…" Like a teenager, I fidget with the threads of the soft blanket beneath us and feel incredibly stupid doing it.

"What?" There's nothing in his face to suggest he's judging me for my insecurity. On the contrary, he smiles at me openly. The play of the flames' light dances across his cheeks.

I swallow; you're not supposed to ask people about their feelings. They don't belong in real life. We don't need them, they make us weak and have to be hidden. That's how I learned to see things. Philipp surely has a completely different opinion about that. About everything I've learned about him so far. He seems to see life from a perspective I didn't even know existed. The canvas in my mind is still brilliantly white; looking at his picture might inspire me.

"Tell me about your life." Cautiously, I glance at him out of the corner of my eye. "Are you really traveling all the time?"

Philipp nods. "For three years now."

"You don't have an apartment or a job?" I try to sound neutral, even though his way of living is as far beyond my imagination as the end of the Milky Way.

"Nope. I live everywhere and work wherever something comes up." A contented smile spreads across his face. "It confuses you, doesn't it?"

For a moment I hesitate. "Oh, absolutely," I then admit openly. "Explain it to me. Please." I lie down right next to him and rest my cheek in the palm of my hand. The warmth of the campfire tingles pleasantly on the soles of my feet, but all my attention is on Philipp.

"After university I started working at a big law firm, just like you. I spent days and nights there, gave everything and in return got more and more. More work, more power, more money." Shaking his head, his gaze wanders into the darkness of the night, as if he himself can't believe he ever lived that kind of life. "At some point I realized what really matters in my life. Not a single one of those things. So I decided to leave Vienna behind." He shrugs, as if it were the most normal thing in the world to just turn your life upside down like that. "I've been on the road ever since."

Immediately a thousand questions pop into my head, but one pushes its way to the front. "What happened? What made you realize you had to change something?" I lean forward, not wanting to miss a single word.

Philipp rolls onto his back and looks up at the starry sky above us. He clears his throat, opens his mouth and closes it again without saying anything. What I can see of his face looks frozen despite the warm light of the fire. "That's not the decisive part," he finally answers. "What matters is how you deal with the knowledge."

He dodges the question and doesn't even manage to look me in the eye. What is so terrible that he can't tell me about it? What kind of experience can be so life-changing that you turn your whole life upside down afterward?

When you lose your child, for a life that then collapses in on itself like a house of cards.

That exact thought shoots through my head now. At the same time, I remember Philipp's words from earlier. Didn't he say I could decide for myself how the past would affect the rest of my life? No matter what happens, you decide yourself how you deal with it. "… how you paint the picture of your future, I understand," I say quietly and nod.

"Exactly. Once you realize that you're the one holding the paints and the brushes, everything is open to you." He turns back to me, shifting restlessly on the blanket. In the flickering light of the flames, his eyes light up. We're on to something important, together. I feel an exciting pull in my chest.

"How did you know that traveling was right for you?" I ask hastily.

"At first I just wanted to get away from my old life." I'd gotten that far too; after all, that's the only reason I'm here. "For months I backpacked through Asia, constantly searching for a life that felt right for me."

I nod. His silence is driving me insane; he has to finally solve the riddle for me. "And then? How did you find it?"

"I didn't."

My hope for answers disappears. It's a dead end; what Philipp is saying leads nowhere. I fall silent, disappointed like a child that has just found out that Santa Claus doesn't exist.

As if he didn't notice my reaction, Philipp goes on undeterred. "At some point I gave up. The search made me tired, and at the same time I hadn't moved an inch. In the middle of nowhere in Thailand I decided to stop. My strength was gone. I put up the tent and sat down in front of it, fully intending to protest against the whole world."

A silence grows between us, charged with Philipp's memories and the images in my head. I see him before me, with the short-cropped hair he used to have. He's squatting all alone, sitting cross-legged on the ground with his arms folded. Behind him rises a densely overgrown jungle, his T-shirt clinging damply to his chest. His lower lip is pushed forward, stubborn like a child's. In the middle of his cheeks, beads of sweat glitter that look as if they were tears.

"For days I didn't move, and no matter how fiercely the sun burned down from the sky, for me it was always dark. Until one morning something magical happened."

I prick up my ears; maybe I can still hope after all.

"When I opened my eyes, it was simply there. It was as if life had found me all on its own."

"What do you mean, simply there?" I ask, confused.

"I realized that right outside my tent the whole world was waiting for me. With all its wonderful facets, the treasures of nature, and the stories of people."

I still don't understand it, yet it won't leave me alone. "Why?"

"Because I'd stopped looking for it." A radiance spreads across his face, as bright as the glittering stars above us.

"How can you find something if you're not looking for it?" My head is overwhelmed, a sharp pain bores into my forehead. I feel almost sick, my cheeks are burning like I've got a fever.

"By opening yourself up, letting go of everything that weighs you down, and forgetting what others taught you. Stop chasing after some goal or other. Take off the blinkers. Stand still and recognize the beauty of the path."

I've already tried that in my head. The path can't be seen, my steps lead me through nothingness. "I don't understand," I admit quietly.

"When was the last time you were happy?" His intense gaze sends even more heat rising in me. "Think back from this moment, right now, into the past. Hour by hour. Keep going until you discover a happy moment. No matter how long it lasted."

I want to, but the memories tumble over one another in my head. I hurriedly go through today.

"Take your time," I still hear Philipp say, then I feel his hand resting reassuringly on my shoulder.

I close my eyes; maybe that way I can see better. Then I imagine I'm sitting in a movie theater, watching the film of my day run backwards. I make it back to eating cherries, and that's when I first start to smile. But that's not it yet, I can feel it, so I go further back.

All at once the corners of my mouth lift. "The motorcycle ride." I'm absolutely sure. I open my eyes in excitement.

Philipp's smirk is unmistakable. He's pleased, but there's more to it. "Very good," he says meaningfully. "Now you just have to figure out why you were happy in that moment."

That's easy. "I was only thinking about what I'm experiencing right now." I can still feel the lightness in my head and the intensity with which my heart has taken command.

Instead of answering me, Philipp just nods. Then he raises his eyebrows expectantly.

What is he trying to tell me?

"That's your answer." He sounds so convinced that I just have to believe him. So I go over my own words again. Very slowly, so I don't miss anything.

Right now I understand something.

In my mind, an image comes together from all the puzzle pieces Philipp has been slipping me bit by bit since our meeting on the plane. On their own I couldn't make sense of any of them, but seen together they reveal their secret.

"The most important moment in life is now."

My voice flares up like the fire beside us. I jump to my feet, a wave of energy surges through me, as if a dam had burst somewhere inside me.

That's the one answer to every one of my questions!

And I roar it out into the world with everything I've got. So loud they could still hear me in Paris. "The most important moment is now!"

My body wants to dance, my arms stretched high up into the air, to music only I can hear. Without thinking I let go and feel how the movement carries me away.

All at once Philipp is standing next to me. His eyes are shining with moisture. He nods, at first just a little, then more and more emphatically. "Yes," he says, moved, "that's exactly it."

In the middle of a turn I stop moving and fix him with my gaze. "You alone helped me see that. Thank you," I say, my voice choked.

Walking up to him and wrapping my arms around him feels like the most natural thing in the world. I snuggle up to him, hug him as tightly as I can. His hand wanders gently over my back, I let my head fall into the hollow of his collarbone and close my eyes. On my cheek I can feel his heart pounding. The only thing I can smell now is the sweet scent of his skin. Under the starry sky of Provence we sway together, back and forth. Tentatively at first, then more and more, until finally we're dancing as if we were lovers.

I savor the moment for as long as it lasts. But even after that I don't let go of Philipp, I only open my eyes and look up at him. "This night is simply wonderful."

"Then let's just stay here," he whispers in my ear. His three-day stubble tickles my skin.

A night under the open sky. Like savages, my mother would say, fixing me with her ice-cold blue eyes. She would shake her head and punish me with indifference. That woman has far too much control over my life. Never before had I been as aware of that as I am now. She makes demands and punishes me, pulls me around like a doll and wants to show me off like a trophy.

What kind of person ties conditions to their love?

"Gladly," I say with complete conviction. For my parents, nothing I do will ever be enough. For far too long I've blindly chased after their goals, twisted myself out of shape, put on masks and, in the end, betrayed myself because of it.

That ends now.

Philipp pushes me away from him and looks at me in surprise. "Who are you?"

I shrug and plaster a broad grin on my face. "Do we still have wine?"

Together we spend an evening I'll never forget. We dream and laugh, fall silent and argue. Together we figure out which star above us shines the brightest and how many craters there are on the moon.

I've never been this relaxed.

It's as if Philipp's presence clears the fog in my head. I sense what has been hiding all my life behind my externally controlled behavior. Being a star lawyer and model daughter definitely isn't it. The fact that I still can't clearly see everything else in front of me doesn't matter. Because that knowledge will come to me, just like Philipp said it would.

When my eyes finally close a little later, Philipp is lying

right behind me, his arm wrapped tightly around my stomach. His fingertips rest where no one else is allowed to touch me. Not even me. I feel his steady breath on the back of my neck, feel safe and protected. This night will be peaceful, without ugly images and distorted voices. Because he'll be watching over me as if he were my dreamcatcher.

Chapter Twenty-Eight

With Philipp, the last few days have felt as if they were only hours. We swam in the sea, watched flamingos, and spent whole nights philosophizing about the truly important things in life. By now, almost half of my vacation is over. I don't miss Vienna in the slightest, and I miss Tom even less. The truth is, I was glad he hadn't contacted me so far. But now it's time. The moment I've been dreading for days has come. I'm on the phone with Tom.

"It's fantastic—no, what am I saying, it's just brilliant! What do you think, how many new clients I've already acquired? Come on, you have to guess. How many, in the few days I've been here?" He sounds as if coffee were flowing through his veins instead of blood. "Come on, Sarah, what do you think?" he asks without having given me any time at all to answer.

"No idea, you tell me." I'm not in the mood for this game; just hearing Tom is pure stress. His tension crawls through the phone straight into my head and disturbs the peaceful, calm mood. As if I could get rid of the pressure that way, I pace up and down the bedroom. Thanks to the socks on my feet, he luckily can't hear it.

Tom snorts. "Guess you're not interested."

"Yes, of course I am." What a bad girlfriend I am, paying him so little attention. "Five maybe?" I say then, just to make him happy.

"Wrong!" His voice almost cracks. "It's twelve, just imagine that. That's an increase in sales of almost twenty percent. And that after only ten of twenty-five meetings."

I can picture in every detail what he looks like right now. His eyes are shining, his cheeks are glowing. All at once I notice something I've never seen in him before. It's obvious: he's wearing blinkers too. He doesn't look at any of the exciting cities he's traveling to right now. Instead, he adds up the commissions in his head, and the result makes him incredibly satisfied.

Why is money still so important to him now that he already has enough of it anyway? How long does he want to keep suffering from the fact that he didn't have much of it in his childhood? In that moment it suddenly becomes clear to me that both our lives are dictated by something that actually belongs to the distant past.

"Wow, I don't even know what to say. That's fantastic!" My words sound almost exaggeratedly cheerful. "I'm so happy for you, congratulations."

"Thanks. What's going on with you?" His voice changes abruptly, turning serious and demanding.

I bite my lip. My gut tells me I'd better not tell the truth. "Everything's going great," I say quickly, "I'm making good progress with the applications." Hoping I'll sound more positive that way, I smile.

It seems to work. "That's nice to hear," he says conciliatorily, sounding so tender and soft it's as if he's gently putting his arm around me. "I'm already looking forward to seeing you again. Less than two weeks and I'll be able to kiss you again."

My knees give way, I sit down on the bed and exhale softly. He has forgiven me, I know that for sure. Everything that happened at home doesn't matter anymore. The two of us will forget it and pretend that this massive boulder right in the middle of our shared path never existed. I should tell him that I love him. But my lips refuse to form the words.

Only after we've said goodbye to each other do I understand what has just happened.

Tom has already forgotten our baby. Checked off, like an item on a to-do list. Exactly one month ago today it had to die, and he doesn't even seem to remember.

All he cares about is my new job. And he assumes I'll have one soon. The prospect of continuing our old life has made him give in. He adores his strong, successful Sarah, and I can't even blame him for that. After all, that's exactly how he got to know me. Would he stay with me if I no longer wanted to be a lawyer? Does he love me as a person, or only what he thinks I am?

With Philipp it seems to be exactly the other way around; he constantly wants to look into my innermost self. And when I show it to him, he looks at me as if he'd like nothing better than to hold me and never let me go again. Professional success, social standing, and my perfect shell leave him cold. How would he react if I told him about my baby?

Stop. Have I gone crazy? I'm comparing Tom and Philipp as if they were two suitors I have to choose between. Philipp is a friend, that's all. And Tom? Ever since we said goodbye to each other in Vienna, I haven't missed him for a single second. On the contrary, for the most part our phone call made me feel uncomfortable.

Is that supposed to be love?

With a sigh, I put the phone down on the wooden nightstand next to my bed. Maybe it's wrong. But right now it just feels more right to go out to Philipp in the garden than to keep thinking about Tom and me. He's probably splashing around in the pool again, with all his clothes on. As if wearing swim trunks were the crazy thing, and not the other way around. I can't help shaking my head; so much of what he does I just can't understand.

I slip into my bikini and grab a towel. I actually find Philipp in the pool; he's floating on his back in the water with his eyes closed. In swim trunks, as I note with a smirk. His face looks so peaceful, as if he had no worries and no fears.

Suddenly I'm seized by an immense urge to surprise him. Just like he did on our first evening here, I take a running start and jump into the water next to him in a cannonball. I'm small and delicate, but I still manage to create an impressive wave.

When I surface again, a dangerous grin is on Philipp's face. "Looks like someone's asking for trouble!"

"Never." I immediately raise my hands as if I were about to surrender. "I was just afraid you'd fall asleep and drown. You could even say I saved you," I add with an amused smirk.

Philipp studies me as if he had to think about whether he should get back at me or not. Then he lets his arms drop and swims toward me with a strong stroke. "Well then, I guess I'm in your debt," he says, looking so deeply into my eyes that I start to feel queasy. "In return, can I offer you a trip to Marseille?" An open smile plays around his lips, which suddenly look as if they would feel soft and velvety.

I quickly fix my gaze on the water; it sparkles in the sunlight and chases away these strange thoughts. Honestly, I'd rather we took it easy today. But by now I know that behind each of his suggestions there's something hidden that helps me paint my picture of the future.

"Permission granted," I reply with a regal wave of my hand and head for the pool steps.

Philipp holds me back. "You're forgetting something," he says, and instantly I start speculating what that might be. It can't have anything to do with his lips, can it? "Come on, it's not that hard. Think back to your realization from yesterday."

"The most important moment is now?" My mind is racing, trying to find the connection that seems so obvious to him.

He nods. "Exactly. What were you just about to do?" he asks gently, without putting any pressure on me or making me feel guilty.

"Get changed so we can head out. We want to go sight-seeing in the city."

He says nothing, just looks at me. As if he could see in my face how close I am to the answer, he starts to smile.

"But that's later?" I ask uncertainly. He nods, those terribly cute dimples appearing in his cheeks. "And if the best moment is now and not later, then..." I'm confused; a city tour is nice, so why shouldn't we just get started right away?

"Marseille will still be there in an hour." Philipp lets himself fall back into the water with relish. "But this right here just feels too good right now to give it up straightaway. Don't you think so too?"

He's probably right. I copy his movement and end up floating on my back in the water beside him. Above me the sky is so blue it looks as if someone had put a filter on it. The sun tickles my nose and forces me to close my eyes. I hear nothing but the muffled rush of the water against my eardrums, feel weightless. My breathing is calm. My mind goes quiet. Then I suddenly feel a spark in my right hand, hot and electrifying. It runs up my arm and, without any detours, finds my heart with unerring precision. It contracts, just tightly enough that it doesn't hurt.

I tear my eyes open.

There, where everything begins in my fingertips, Philipp is floating in the water, completely at ease. So close that we're almost touching.

Is he the reason for the electric shock?

Impossible. If he were, he would feel it too, and that is clearly not the case. When I paddle away from him, my heart relaxes so noticeably that I can't ignore it.

Am I actually in the process of falling in love with Philipp?

That would be the end of me, flashes through my mind. But right after that I wonder whether it might not actually be the beginning of something new. I let my gaze roam openly over his face. Even from a safe distance, with his eyes closed and without his dimples, he still looks far too attractive. Just a moment ago I was glad that Tom and I had made up, and now here I am, pressed into the corner of the pool, and there's only one thing I want to know. What it would feel like to touch Philipp's lips.

Chapter Twenty-Nine

The drive to Marseille is silent. Philipp doesn't ask any questions and I don't want to say anything. The way I suddenly pulled away from him in the pool hangs between us, uncommented, like a wall of fog. Gossamer-thin, but murky. Again and again Philipp studies me from the corner of his eye, but I stubbornly keep my gaze fixed on the turbulent traffic. Luckily, the narrow streets of the city now demand my full attention.

"We can stop here." He points to an empty spot at the side of the road that's big enough for our car.

In silence, I pull into the space; without a word, we get out. We look at each other over the roof of our car. Really, someone ought to say something, and I decide it's going to be me. "Let's get started," I say in an overly cheerful tone and smile at him.

"Pick a direction." He smirks; I can see it clearly. "But don't forget, you can only discover something new if you take paths you wouldn't normally take." Whatever he has in mind, I'm sure there's a new insight waiting for me here.

Willingly, I take the lead. We stroll along the streets, turn into side alleys, and cut through parks. Tom would claim I'm choosing the wrong direction. Because by now the facades of the houses along our way are cracked and veiled in a dark film. Behind us, trains thunder past again and again. The farther we go, the dirtier our surroundings become—and the air as well.

Eventually we reach an underpass. It's so narrow that only cyclists and pedestrians can get through. The walls are covered in graffiti, and a musty smell wafts toward me from the dark interior. A cool breeze gives me goose bumps on my arms, but Philipp doesn't notice.

My fear radar blares to life. This is going too far; I stop and fold my arms across my chest. "We're in the wrong place."

He tilts his head. "Why?"

"You know exactly why." I take another step; we've lost our way. "Come on, let's go back, this is a really nasty area." My voice trembles.

"Don't be scared, little Sarah, I'll look after you." He sounds as if he's singing me a nursery rhyme. Then he reaches his hand out to me, but I don't move.

"No. God only knows what could be waiting for us in there. Just look around you. What do you think, what kind of people live here?" I shake my head violently. Even he has to realize that in this neighborhood I look like a brightly flashing neon sign screaming rob me. As if to prove my point, a gray-haired man shuffles around the corner at that very moment. His grimy brown clothes hang from his scrawny shoulders like from a coat hanger. His pants are full of holes, his T-shirt is missing a sleeve. He drags greedily on a hand-rolled cigarette and sizes me up with his menacingly dark eyes.

I clutch my handbag tightly, step back, and glance around in a panic for possible escape routes. It becomes clear to me at once that I can't feel safe even within several blocks. Philipp is my only chance, no matter how wrong that feels to me. I hurry over to him and demonstratively take his hand in mine so the old man knows I'm not available to him.

"Very good, I'm proud of you," Philipp murmurs in my ear and pulls me closer to him. The man finally comes to a halt, but he doesn't take his eyes off us. I don't dare look at him; it might provoke him, and in my pretty golden sandals I'm hardly dressed for a quick getaway.

"Forget him, he won't do anything to us." The calm in Philipp's words brings my heartbeat back to normal. I feel a wave of gratitude in my stomach; it warms me and torments me at the same time. He shouldn't put me in situations like this. I can't allow myself to be this close to him anymore, but this is definitely not how that works. With a firm grip he pulls me into the gloomy tunnel ahead of us. My breathing speeds up. Sweat gathers on my forehead.

"Please don't. Let's turn back, okay?" I stammer, putting a pleading look in my eyes. The fear of becoming a victim of violence here is so overpowering that I don't mind in the least coming across as small and weak.

He slips his arm protectively around my shoulders. "I told you, I'll look out for you. I'd never let anyone hurt you." He looks deep into my eyes. It's exactly that look that cuts through my mind and makes the voice of my common sense sound like a cartoon character. Small and squeaky, so that even I can't take it seriously anymore.

"Don't look at me like that," I croak awkwardly and lower my eyelids. The next moment I feel his hand on my cheek. Even though he barely touches me, my skin burns like a nuclear power plant. The heat runs through my body, all the way down to my toes and back again.

Right now I understand it.

His touch is far more dangerous to me than the rundown neighborhood we're in right now.

I shouldn't allow this closeness, so I tear myself away from him with all my strength. "Let's get this over with." I try to conjure up an innocuous smile on my face.

"With pleasure." His cheeky grin makes the charged atmosphere between us disappear. I'm strangely relieved, even though I know what's coming next.

Clinging tightly to him, I follow him into the tunnel, my heart pounding hard against my chest. Instinctively I hold my breath as I try to find my bearings in the darkness. It doesn't take long before I can make out the first shapes. The brightly painted wall over there looks as if the plaster is crumbling off. I narrow my eyes to see better. With a shudder I realize those can only be bullet holes. I quickly look away. But even the sight of the ground makes me flinch. Used needles and plastic bags are scattered everywhere, and I'm wearing nothing but my golden sandals with the thin soles. Just a fleeting breath of the tunnel air makes the nausea rise in me, as if the mixture in my stomach were fermenting. It reeks of urine, sweat, and charred wood. I clap my hand over my mouth and nose and urge Philipp on toward the light at the other end of the tunnel.

The whole way I keep my gaze fixed straight ahead.

Because it's easier to look away.

Reality can be so much uglier than the images my imagination shows me. My steps quicken and in the end it's me who drags Philipp back into the daylight. At last I can breathe again, but I can't get rid of the nausea so easily. I'd love nothing more than to sit down, but wherever I look, everything is horribly filthy.

"Are you okay?" Philipp puts his hand on my back. I nod, but I can't say anything. Why did he lure me here? What's the point of this test of courage?

Patiently he waits until I've pulled myself together, then he tries to take my hand again. He doesn't seem to notice the disgustingly sticky sweat that has gathered on my skin.

"I can walk by myself," I say brusquely, and regret it again the very same moment. "Sorry." I lower my head.

Philipp exhales audibly. "It's all right." He saunters off and gives me a sign to follow him.

Exhausted, I trudge after him and look around cautiously. Beyond the tunnel it doesn't look any different than it did before. The houses are shacks, with makeshift patched-up windows and garbage heaps in front of the doors. On a half-collapsed wall in front of us sits a girl, far too young for this harsh environment. What was probably once a bright red dress hangs in tatters from her cocoa-brown shoulders. Her black hair is matted and looks just as dull as she does. Behind her, small feet dangle a few centimeters above the ground, swinging back and forth. They're in worn-out sneakers, one sole has come loose and flaps in time.

Spellbound, I stare at this shoe. I don't want to imagine who it belongs to and what story it has to tell. Still, that exact question circles in my head while the rubber slaps rhythmically against the stone wall.

Now the older one in the foreground notices we're here; she lifts her head and looks straight at us. There's a sinister glint in her dark eyes. She immediately straightens her upper body as if she were posing for a photo in a men's magazine. Her smile reveals several gaps in her slightly protruding upper row of teeth. Deliberately, I press my handbag closer to my body and lay my arm over the zipper.

"We have to get out of here," I whisper to Philipp, but instead of speeding up his step, he stops. Of course he does.

Out of the corner of my eye I follow how the girl rises from her spot with serpentine grace and comes toward us. The child stays behind on the wall by itself, its dark mop of hair bowed as it plays absentmindedly with a broken plastic bottle.

"Philipp, I'm serious, come on." With my free hand I grab his upper arm and pull as hard as I can. Again I curse my weak arms and legs. How could a fly like me ever throw him off balance?

"You'll be surprised, trust me." Completely relaxed, he watches the girl come closer and closer. She fixes her eyes on him as if she were trying to conjure him. She doesn't seem interested in me or my handbag. Still, I hide behind my companion's broad shoulders as best I can. If he's going to get us into this damn dangerous situation, then he can help get us out of it again.

"Bonjour." Her voice trickles down my back like a shiver. It sounds so deep and smoky, as if she were a diva from the fifties.

Philipp smiles openly at the stranger and greets her as politely as if she were a good friend.

"I'm Suna," she says in slurred French and brushes her hair out of her face. Her forehead is covered with countless fine scars, and a tiny blue-green stone sparkles in her nose. She can hardly be older than sixteen, but she has the eyes of an adult.

"I'm Philipp, this is Sarah." He gestures toward me. "She's shy," he adds unnecessarily with a wink. I give her a brief nod; that has to be enough. She shouldn't feel safe—there's nothing to be gained from me.

The young woman immediately focused on my companion again and thrust her barely existent breasts toward him. "Are you still looking for company?"

Had this girl just offered him her body as if it were a brightly embroidered scarf and this horrible place here an oriental bazaar? For a moment I forgot my own fear, and suddenly I could see hers. She was afraid of his answer, no matter what it would be.

Philipp shook his head. "No, thanks. But maybe you can help us with something else?"

Suna instantly lost her suggestive air. With a mixture of hope and curiosity, she planted her hands on her hips. "With what?" she asked, suddenly sounding like a perfectly normal teenager. Now that she no longer needed the act, she looked even younger than before. I didn't want to think about it any longer, nor about how she earned her money. Even now, a feeling of pity bored so hard into my chest that I could hardly bear it. I knew I might break if I found out too much.

"We want to get to know your neighborhood. You could show us around," Philipp suggested with a smile.

Had he lost his mind? What was there to see here anyway? Sightseeing was supposed to be nice, not trigger depression. I pinched him hard in the side, but all that did was make him move a little away from me. Now I was standing alone in front of the girl, whose sparkling eyes were fixed on my golden sandals.

"All right," she answered without looking up. "Come with me." Suna spun around on the spot, her dress fluttering excitedly in a half circle around her scrawny legs.

"Are you crazy? She'll drag us off to her friends, then

they'll rob us, blackmail us, or who knows what else!" Despite my agitation, my voice was muted. I didn't want Suna to hear how much I distrusted her.

"You can stay here, I'll go with her." Philipp seemed fed up with my constant nagging. "If you only want to see the pretty façade, the center is over there, spruced up for the tourists. You'll definitely find a nice café there where you can pretend the sun is always shining everywhere in the world." There was no anger in his words and even less reproach.

Without waiting for my answer, he marched over to Suna, who had now reached the child that was still sitting on the wall with its head bowed.

He can't just leave me alone now, what is he thinking? Am I really that unimportant to him?

A sharp tug shot through my chest. His rejection bored deep into a bleeding wound somewhere in my heart. The pain numbed every other emotion. Whether joy, longing, or fear. It was like an old acquaintance who had been tormenting me since childhood. It was his fault that I didn't have any friends back then, because my ambition to please my parents forbade me to play. He chose my degree, pushed my career forward, and in the end let my baby die. Whenever I managed to please someone, he eased up for a brief moment. The feeling was wonderful, so warm and light that I wanted to feel it again and again. I was addicted, and my drug was recognition.

That has to stop.

I make my own decisions, and right now is when I start. Wherever the courage comes from, I turn to leave. At that very moment I see Philipp coming toward me.

"What do you actually think we're doing here, Sarah?"

he asks me, a soft undertone in his voice, and puts his hand on my shoulder.

Shaking my head, I look at him. "I don't have the slightest idea." That's the truth, and saying it out loud feels fantastic. Because right now I realize that being honest makes me stronger, not weaker.

For a brief moment a wistful sparkle flashes in his eyes, he clears his throat and takes a step away from me. "How far along are you with your vision of the future?"

"Still all blank," I admit, "I'm still missing a bit of inspiration."

"Then why not look for it here?" His arm traces a semicircle over our surroundings.

In truth I have nothing to counter that. I grab his hand. "Well then, let's get started."

As I take my first step, Philipp gives me a broad smile. I smile back. It's nice to see him so content. Much too nice.

Chapter Thirty

"This is Nahla, my sister." Suna puts her hand on the back of the little girl who is still perched on the wall. She seems so absorbed in playing with the plastic bottle that she doesn't notice us.

Philipp crouches down in front of her. "Hi Nahla, nice to meet you." He holds out his hand to her, but instead of taking it, the little one buries her face in Suna's dress. "I get it, so you're shy too," Philipp says, sounding as if he were trying to coax a wild animal not to be afraid.

I watch the three of them from a safe distance. Even though Philipp doesn't exactly pay attention to sensible clothing, next to the two of them he looks like a highly polished gemstone. Much too bright. There's no danger coming from the little one, at least that's what my gut tells me. But I can't trust the older one. Someone who's willing to sell her body for money is also willing to do all sorts of other things. Or isn't she?

"We'll start the sightseeing tour here." With her index finger, Suna points to a narrow alleyway. Philipp seems pleased, while in my head images of the two of us lying dead in a dumpster pop up in a matter of seconds. I shake off the thoughts, clutch Philipp's hand and press myself tightly against him as we follow the two of them.

"You and Nahla have a lot in common," Philipp whispers in my ear.

"Nonsense." I furrow my brow. What could I possibly have in common with a dirty street kid?

He smirks. "The way she's hiding behind Suna, scared and skittish, doesn't that seem familiar to you?" He points at the nonexistent space between us.

I don't like it when he shoots his arrows at me with such deadly accuracy. "You can't trust everyone, just look at those two. It's not only okay, it's absolutely necessary to be careful."

"You know, that exact attitude is the reason those two obviously don't even have a roof over their heads." Philipp quickens his pace to catch up with Suna and Nahla.

As so often, I don't understand him. If you welcome every beggar in, you'll soon have nothing left yourself.

Give them an inch and they'll take a mile, I hear my mother scold.

From a young age she taught me not to even look at them, so as not to raise false hopes. If you slip them some money, they just want more. Next they find out where you live and come and take it themselves. You only have to open the newspaper; you'll find more than enough proof in there.

That's my mother's opinion, but what's mine? Will I get the chance to find out today?

While I'm brooding to myself, Philipp wants to know more about Suna. "Do you live here in the alley?" he asks kindly.

Suna shakes her head. "We don't have an apartment,"

she answers, "but maybe soon." A smile flits across her lips, hopeful and sincere.

When Philipp nods encouragingly, Suna begins to talk. "We haven't been in France for long, just a few weeks. There's no help, we have to take care of ourselves."

"Did you come all by yourselves?" As far as I'm concerned, Philipp isn't too nosy at all. I wait eagerly to hear what I'll find out next.

Suna's eyes fill with tears. "Yes." Her answer carries more grief and despair than I've ever heard before. With her gaze turned toward the sky, she goes on. "Our parents had to stay, there wasn't enough money. Nahla and I came so we'd have a chance. They wanted to follow later." Her voice breaks; she swallows hard and exhales shakily. "Since we said goodbye, I haven't heard anything from them."

"I understand." Philipp's words cut through the tense silence. We stop; he puts his hand on her shoulder in a comforting gesture. With a harsh movement of her hand, Suna wipes the tears from the corners of her eyes. She wants to be strong, I can see it clearly. Maybe for Nahla, and so she herself doesn't give up.

"I'm sure everything's fine," she then says with a pained smile and pulls her silent little sister closer to her. I want to comfort them, give them hope and be there for them. But how? My helplessness paralyzes me; not a single word leaves my mouth. A feeling of being overwhelmed rises up in me; part of me just wants to get away, not hear any of this and even less feel it.

Still, we stroll on down the alley, past defaced house walls and rotten front doors. Behind a window frame that's been hastily sealed with plastic sheeting, pink flowers glow like a glimmer of hope in the otherwise gray surroundings. Right in front of us, a frail man is crouched on a folding chair with a black cat in his lap. She purrs contentedly while he scratches her head and whispers into her ear. I look more closely. It's the same man we met earlier at the tunnel. Suna heads straight for him now and raises her hand in greeting. He returns her greeting with a warm smile, and suddenly he looks anything but dangerous. On the contrary, his features even seem likable. While I'm still wondering where this change comes from, Suna steps through the open doorway beside him.

"Come on, I want to show you something," she says, motioning for us to follow her.

I get a queasy feeling.

The old man may seem harmless, but the building Philipp is walking into without a second thought is as run-down as the worst crack dens in Vienna. Who but addicts and beggars would hang out in a dump like this?

I step into the gloomy atmosphere of the large room and make out a bar in the half-light, along with a motley assortment of tables and chairs. The walls are draped with colorful fabrics, and in the corner stands an old, worn-out piano. We seem to be the only guests.

Suna gives me an open smile. "Do you like it?"

Out of politeness, I nod. It's less neglected than I feared, but the acrid smell of cigarette smoke brings tears to my eyes.

Like an experienced tour guide, Suna leads us to a table and orders Coke for all of us. The place seems to be something like her home, the grumpy man behind the bar her friend. They seem so familiar with each other that I catch myself worrying they might be plotting something against us. But when she comes back with the drinks, I get the impression instead that she's happy to be able to show us this place.

"It's nice with you," she says and, with little Nahla in tow, takes the empty chair next to me. "Otherwise no one's interested in us. Everyone looks at us with that particular look. Full of disgust and hate. They think we should go back to where we belong." A sad veil settles over her eyes, the smile on her lips withers. "They don't understand how wonderful that would be for us too. If we could live where our home is. Without fear and without pain." Lovingly she strokes Nahla's head, as if she wants to give her life at least a little bit of normality.

Her words move me. I can hardly imagine what it must feel like to be alone and unwanted in a foreign country. And if being here is still better for the two of them than being in their homeland, then unimaginably terrible things must be happening there. I don't dare ask about them. Embarrassed, I lower my gaze and take a sip of my Coke. The stone floor beneath my golden sandals is dirty, the table legs are covered in nicks.

Philipp speaks up for me. "There's no support?" he asks in a rough voice.

"Nothing. When we arrived here, we felt as if we'd won. We were safe, we could breathe and talk without constantly having to be careful. For the first time in years we were free. But soon we understood that no one here had been waiting for us."

Absentmindedly she wipes the condensation from the neck of her Coke bottle, an uncomfortable silence spreads. I'd so love to say something, but I can't find the words.

"People here have so much," Suna goes on, shaking her head, "and still they don't want to give anything. They throw food in the trash even though it's still edible, and at the same time they watch while others go hungry. I don't understand this world."

Inevitably, images of myself appear before my eyes. I see myself buying new things in the most expensive designer stores over a glass of champagne, even though the walk-in closet in my oversized apartment is already bursting at the seams. Plates with barely visible chipped edges end up in the trash, cushion covers are thrown out because they're not the right color. What I'm wearing on my body today probably cost more than the two of them would need not to go hungry for a month. I'm sure Suna can see that. She knows people like me. I'm like the ones who usually hurl their hatred and indifference right in her face. She'd have every reason to treat me the same way. But here we are, in the middle of her world, and she's opening every door for me. So obligingly, as if we were friends.

All of a sudden I'm ashamed, so much that I shrink into my chair until I feel as small as a raisin.

"Despite everything, Nahla and I make the best of it, and one day things will start looking up for us again." With a warm smile, Suna pulls her sister into her arms.

At last the little girl dares to lift her head. With her almost black, round eyes she looks straight at me. Still fearful, but also curious, with the expression of an innocent child.

I swallow, not wanting to let either the memory of my own baby or the thoughts about her life rise to the surface.

Philipp takes my hand and squeezes it tightly. Then he lets his thumb wander over my skin, as if he wants to give me courage.

"I'm convinced of that." My voice is brittle and quiet. Out of the corner of my eye I see Philipp watching me. He keeps stroking me, leaving warm, tingling traces on the back of my hand.

With an expectant smile on her lips, Suna lets go of

Nahla, crosses the room, and sits down at the piano. Reverently she runs her fingers over the yellowed keys, her eyes glowing.

Now she starts to play, at first very softly, then more intensely. Her fingers dance across the keyboard like those of a pianist. In the melody I can hear her story, sad and melancholic. My eyes fill with tears, and I let them run freely down my cheeks. No one can judge me for it, because I don't judge myself. And that feels unbelievably good.

Little by little, the mood of the music changes. The piece grows brighter and brighter, as if somewhere on the horizon the sun were rising. Suna's fragile body sways to the beat, I see the passion in her face and the joy in her eyes.

Right now she's happy, even though there's neither money nor a career nor social status in her life. The source of her happiness lies within herself, in her thoughts and in her heart.

My body starts to vibrate, builds up and finally swings in the rhythm of the music. I can feel how a once so mighty wall inside me begins to crumble. Stone by stone it turns to dust, and for the first time ever I can see the sky. Clear and radiantly beautiful.

At last I understand what my life is really missing.

Overwhelmed, I beam at Philipp, who immediately pulls me up from my chair to him and wraps his arms around me. The world around us disappears, as if it were nothing more than an illusion bowing to the truth. I feel his heartbeat and breathe in the honey-sweet scent of his skin. We look deep into each other's eyes.

Only the music and Philipp's whisper reached my ears now, velvety soft and silky delicate at the same time. "Beautiful, isn't it?"

I nodded, deeply moved. "A perfect moment."

Chapter Thirty-One

We sat together for a long time and had lunch. Suna told us how she managed to survive in a country that was so foreign to her. Even Nahla gradually lost her shyness and started to talk.

"Beautiful woman," she said, sounding like an angel. Then she let her fingers wander over my bare forearm. I let her, the fact that she was dirty didn't bother me. On the way, she stopped to inspect a mole. She tried in vain to scratch it off my skin like dirt, then looked up at me in confusion.

I had to smile. "That's part of me, you can't take it off."

The girl had eyes like a field mouse. Dark and shy. I wanted to give her a sense of safety and protect her from everything she and her sister were going through. But what could I do? Just giving the two of them money felt clumsy. Of course we would pay for the food, the drinks, and the sightseeing, but that wasn't enough.

While I kept thinking about it, Nahla curiously examined the hem of my dress as if she were looking for something. "Woahh," she said over and over, as if she were finding one treasure after another.

"Do you like my dress?" I asked, and my hand came to rest on her head all by itself. Her scruffy hair was surprisingly soft; I buried my fingers in it. A wave of affection surged through my body and crashed so violently against the memory of my baby, like the surf against the cliffs of Ireland. Exactly where they collided, a familiar pain shot through my body.

Nahla nodded and stretched her arms out to me. No matter how much it hurt, I pulled her up and let her sit on my lap. Her small body was very warm, but she smelled as if she had slept on a garbage dump. Still, I held her close, as tightly as if I could save her by that alone. I wished it were possible. The open wound in my chest tore wider, the pain spread, but I no longer fought against it.

Startled by the trembling of my body, Nahla looks up at me. "Don't be sad," she says, wiping the tears from my cheeks. "Everything will be okay, someday."

I swallow and can barely speak. "Yeah, it will," I force out and try to smile.

If Nahla, after everything she's been through, is still full of confidence, what reason do I have not to be?

The little one jumps off my lap and starts dancing right beside me. The surroundings blur before my eyes, but I can clearly make out the joy on Philipp's face. He looks as if he knows exactly what's happening to me right now, and I start to understand how much I owe him.

First I had to take off the blinkers, now my vision is gradually clearing. We look at each other, and my lips form a silent *thank you*.

He smiles, bites his lower lip, and nods. A watery film spreads over the blue of his eyes. I can't wait any longer and spring up from the armchair. As if he feels the same, he's suddenly standing right in front of me. I let myself fall into his arms and feel as if, after a long journey, I'm finally coming home. Pressed tightly together, we stand in the middle of the run-down bar and don't need words to know what's happening right now.

Only when we pull apart again do I notice Suna's enraptured expression. "How beautiful," she says, placing her hand on her chest and sighing. She thinks we're a couple, and a part of me likes that more than I'd care to admit.

Before I can lose myself in the thought, Suna points to the wall clock above the bar. "I'm very sorry, but we have to go now."

We leave the bar and stroll on through the neighborhood. Suna talks about her dream of working here in France as a musician.

"When I play, I'm in another world." Dreamily, she spins once in a circle in the middle of the sidewalk.

"You've got this, I'm sure of it," I say with complete conviction. Philipp also nods in agreement, while Nahla hops happily around us. Whenever I doubt myself in the future, I'll think of this life-loving girl with the broken shoes. No matter what happens, I'll remember what she said to me earlier. Everything will be okay, someday.

"Thank you, that means a lot to me." With a hint of a bow, Suna lowers her head. Then her face takes on a serious expression. "It's been nice with you, but now we have to say goodbye to each other."

We really have ended up right back at the spot where we ran into the two of them a few hours ago. I'm sure Suna has to go back to work. Thinking about that makes my heart beat heavier. As if a gray veil were settling over the city, the colors fade and the birdsong dies away.

"It was great meeting you. Thank you so, so much for everything." Philipp pays generously for the city tour and pulls Suna into a hug.

I clear my throat and shift uncertainly from one foot to the other. Should I hug her too? "I wish you all the very best," I finally say, taking a tiny little step toward her. Suna laughs, comes over to me, and nestles against me.

"I wish you the same," she whispers, running her hand over my back. "May all your wishes come true."

I feel awful. How can I just leave the two of them like this? They're on their own and need help. If I could at least give them something small, it would be better than doing nothing. As Suna lets go of me, I notice her eyes, as so often before, wandering to my sandals.

"Do you like them?" I ask without thinking.

She nods, a glow flashing across her face. "They shine so beautifully."

Her feet are in frayed flip-flops, dirty brown and at least two sizes too big.

All of a sudden I know exactly what I have to do.

I slip out of my sandals and hand them to her. "Please, take them," I say a little awkwardly, "as a thank-you for this day."

Suna hesitates, but her eyes give away that there's nothing she'd like more than these shoes. I place them right next to her feet and give her an encouraging nod.

"Really?" she asks in disbelief and slowly slips off her flip-flops.

"Of course, they're yours." My voice almost cracks with excitement. Making her this happy feels exactly right. A grateful radiance spreads across her face, then she puts on the sandals and looks down at herself in admiration. The golden tone of the straps stands out nicely against her dark skin. "They suit you much better than they do me," I say without a trace of envy.

Suna is clearly overwhelmed. "I don't know… what…" she stammers, lifting her shoulders helplessly. "Thank you."

"I'm happy if you like them." Once again tears gather in the corners of my eyes, but it has never felt this right. I hug her tightly one last time, then we have to say goodbye to each other.

On the way back we give the tunnel a wide berth just to be safe. As if it were the most natural thing in the world, I grab Philipp's hand. I skip and dance by his side as cheerfully as little Nahla did by mine earlier. The fact that my bare feet touch the dirty ground of Marseille doesn't bother me in the slightest.

"Looks like someone's happy." Philipp looks at me with a grin.

I spin in a circle under his arm with a flourish. "Maybe," I say, beaming at him. "Come on, dance with me!"

Now I can see it again, that smile on his face, so warm and loving that my whole body starts to tingle. Like a professional dancer, he puts his hand around my hips and spins me around. The house fronts of Marseille fly past me so fast that their colors blend together. I tilt my head back and look up at Philipp. The color of his eyes is no different from that of the sky above us. Just looking at them fogs my thoughts.

What would it feel like if our lips touched? What do they taste like, how does the tip of his nose smell? And if I kissed him right now, how would he react?

Chapter Thirty-Two

With every step we come closer to the end of our dance, and with every centimeter I lose a little more of my courage. I wish Philipp would make it easier for me. He could press his cheek to mine; then I'd know that he wants it too. But his head stays at a height I can't reach, and I don't dare pull him down to me with my hands. All that's left are the questions racing through my mind so fast that they make me dizzy.

Drunk on the moment, I close my eyes. Even now, when he gently brings our circling movement to a stop, I don't want to open them again.

"Wake up." He's so wonderfully close, his hand stroking down my back.

I shake my head and let it fall back onto his chest. "No, not yet," I mumble like a child being forced to end its afternoon nap, and bury my nose in his T-shirt.

In truth, it's nothing more than a pathetic attempt to stay close to him a little longer. He gently takes hold of my shoulders and pushes me away from him. Although he looks at me kindly, I know exactly what that means.

My gaze drops awkwardly to the ground. My feet look like they belong to a miner, but I don't care about the dirt. Philipp doesn't want to kiss me. That's all I can think about.

"Are you already hungry again?" he asks casually. At least he doesn't seem to notice my disappointment, and I slowly realize how stupid I was. What good would it do to kiss him anyway? Philipp isn't interested in me, at least not in that way. Besides, I'm engaged. I banish the last spark of longing for Philipp's lips from my mind. It's a figment of my imagination that doesn't deserve any attention.

"I could go for a little snack." My voice is sober and firm, exactly the way I want it. It's time to be strong again, at least when it comes to the blond pretty boy, who is now already leaning against the passenger side of the car, waiting for me.

Wordlessly I trudge over to the car; Philipp looks at me in surprise, but I ignore him.

"What are you in the mood for?" He can keep his good mood to himself. Otherwise he always seems to know what's going on inside me, and now he acts as if he doesn't notice a thing.

"I'm tired, let's just grab something to go somewhere." With a deep sigh I start the engine and maneuver the car out of the parking space. Driving barefoot feels strange, but it works. The whole time Philipp studies me and looks as if there are words stuck in his throat that are desperate to get out. Still, his mouth stays shut.

An hour later we're back in our stone house with the blue shutters and are sitting across from each other at the dining table. It's narrow; our knees under the tabletop almost touch.

Philipp bites into his pizza and studies me with furrowed brows. “Is everything okay with you?”

“It was a long day, I’m tired.” With a fake yawn I prop my head up on my hand.

Philipp nods. He, too, has been conspicuously quiet since we left Marseille. He sat completely still beside me in the car, his gaze lost in thought on the gentle hills and colorful meadows. He’s probably noticed the way I looked at him today. Now he’s afraid he’ll soon have to tell me that he’s not interested in me. And yet he already made it more than clear on the plane that he doesn’t want to commit to anyone.

It’s almost unbearable, the way we’re sitting here in silence, so I get up and put my plate in the sink. The pizza is sitting heavy in my stomach, even though I barely ate any of it. “Well then, good night.”

“Sweet dreams.” His words are quiet, and he looks a bit like a desert flower that’s about to lose its fight for survival. Whatever his problem is, it can’t have anything to do with me. At least that’s something I managed to find out today.

Without another word, I head for the bathroom. A strange feeling of relief takes hold of my thoughts when, a few minutes later, freshly showered, I close my room door behind me. I’m on my own, and for the first time since I got here, I’m glad about it. With a wistful sigh, I let myself fall onto the bed. The pillowcase smells of detergent and feels pleasantly soft beneath my head.

That’s when I realize how good I have it in my life.

I’ve never had to fear for my existence. So many people in our world today don’t know where they’ll get something to eat tomorrow or where they’ll spend the next freezing night. I, on the other hand, can close my eyes every evening without having to worry.

No matter what has happened in my life, against this backdrop it loses significance. I was born in a safe country and grew up in a family without financial worries. My starting conditions couldn't be better, and it's up to me and me alone to make something great out of them.

My eyelids grow heavy, the canvas appears in my mind, and all of a sudden I can see its colors. I can't make out what they depict, so I take a step toward it. Then at least I see one thing very clearly. Being grateful only for my own happiness isn't enough.

Chapter Thirty-Three

In the bright light of the morning sun, my bare face in the mirror looks different today. I try to figure out why, but I can't. I probably just spent more time in the sun over the past two weeks, which now makes my complexion look healthier. My green eyes shine like a cat's in the dark. The red-blond curls frame my face, making it soft and friendly. I pull one strand straight and let it go again. The curl immediately springs back into place, as if wanting to make it unmistakably clear that this is where it belongs.

The Sarah in the mirror doesn't have much to do with the woman I was before this trip. Who is this likeable person beaming at me right now, and who was the elegantly strict lawyer I turned her into every morning?

My reflection smiles at me. More and more intensely, until my lips part and reveal the gap in the middle of my lower row of teeth. I've hated it all my life and kept my mouth as closed as possible so no one could see it. Now I don't want to hide it any longer. Or anything else, for that matter. Because it suddenly dawns on me that, in truth, it doesn't really matter.

I want to be who I am, not who others want me to be.

A feeling of lightness swept through my body, as if I were a butterfly. I fluttered out of the bedroom and entered the living area. No makeup, no straightened hair. Just like that.

What I saw there changed my mood in an instant. I gasped. My palms grew damp.

Wearing nothing but boxer shorts, Philipp was busy in the kitchen. The sight of his athletic back caught me off guard, and his tanned, far too smooth skin drew me in like magic. My hands wanted to stroke the star-shaped birthmark on his lower back, my nose to nuzzle the hollow between his shoulder blades.

For heaven's sake, did he have to tempt me like this?

More than anything, I wanted to turn around on the spot and barricade myself in my bedroom until he had put something on.

"Good morning," he said in his melodically deep voice without turning to face me. My face went up in flames; surely he hadn't noticed my presence from my gasping for air? Or had he? I felt the butterfly inside me regress into a caterpillar, small and clumsy.

"Coffee?" he asked cheerfully.

I wanted to answer, but not a sound left my mouth. Only my lips opened and closed. Helplessly, I had to watch as Philipp filled two cups and lifted them carefully.

Any second now he would turn around.

I had to breathe out.

And urgently shake the tension out of my body.

In my distress I fixate on the coffee cups in his hands. I

probably look like an addict who hasn't had her daily dose yet. But who cares.

The moment he turns around, Philipp stops moving. I send up a quick prayer, desperately hoping he won't have one of his bright ideas right now of all times. But he stays silent, so I lift my head and look straight into his face. This moment doesn't last longer than the beat of a dragonfly's wings, and yet I see it. His features slackened, he looks at me full of warmth and affection, while his body seems frozen in shock. Before I can even understand it, he starts moving again. He comes toward me, I take one of the cups from him and wrap my hand around it, no matter how hot the porcelain burns into my skin.

"Thanks," I murmur, confused, my gaze fixed on the black, steaming liquid. "I'll drink it outside." I turn around on the spot.

"Good idea, I'll be right out," he calls after me, and my head reacts instantly. I rush into the bedroom and grab my sunglasses. It's one thing to show myself without makeup, but the idea that he could see in my eyes what he's doing to me is absolutely out of the question.

Under the protection of the tinted lenses I step out into the garden. This morning the scent of lavender hangs in the air, far more intense than on the days before. A glance over the wide landscape tells me why. Where everything was still lush and green when we arrived, stripes of bright violet now run across the gentle hills. With the coffee in my hand I sit down at the wrought-iron table at the edge of the terrace. The mosaic tiles of the tabletop sparkle in the morning sun. Only the cheerful chirping of the birds breaks the silence that lies over this place like a protective cloak. I want to savor this moment; with the bittersweet note of the coffee on my palate, I lean back, close my eyes, and breathe in the warm summer air.

I only open them again when Philipp sits down beside me a little later. Luckily for me he's wearing a T-shirt, and he can't see his blue eyes behind my sunglasses.

"What happened to your hair?" he wants to know, with his usual cheeky undertone. Grinning, he sips his coffee. The strange mood from last night has vanished, as if the night had carried it away. And what just happened was probably nothing more than an illusion my own longing painted into my head.

I don't ask why, I just exhale in relief. "Is that supposed to be a compliment?" I give my mane an exaggerated shake with my hand.

His features soften. "You look gorgeous." Out of nowhere he suddenly lifts his hand and brushes a stubborn curl from my face. "Without a trace of makeup," I hear him whisper.

His voice disappears into nowhere; all I feel is the warmth of his skin on mine, electrifyingly beautiful. He lets his fingers glide over my cheek, no longer than absolutely necessary. Even so, I have to force myself to suppress a sigh that rises in me far too quickly. I don't know how he's looking at me right now, but my heart still skips a beat. It shouldn't do that anymore, never again. And yet it just does whatever it wants.

"Thanks," I stammer and move a little away from him. Something like what happened to me in the streets of Marseille mustn't happen again.

With his gaze fixed on the horizon, Philipp also leans back in his chair. "What are we doing today?" he asks casually and pulls a pouch of tobacco out of his trouser pocket.

"Don't tell me you haven't come up with anything yet." I furrow my brow. Something's off here.

"Nope." Shaking his head, he rolls himself a cigarette. "This is your day, you pick something."

Ever since we met, he has been the one deciding the program. Even if I wasn't always thrilled with his ideas, in the end every single one of them turned out to be wonderful. Because he seems to know, in a strange way, what I need to move forward. Much better than I do myself. So why is he leaving the decision to me now, so shortly before the end of the vacation? Is this the next step I'm supposed to take?

"Phew," I say, just so I say anything at all. At the same time, I try hard to remember what I read back then at Vienna Airport about Provence. Images of cyclists, wine, and flamingos shoot through my mind.

"Take your time." Skillfully, he rolls the cigarette between his fingers and lets his tongue glide over the end of the paper. "And don't worry, I'm not as much of a spoilsport as you. Whatever you suggest, I'm in."

Strangely enough, I feel relieved. My gaze drifts over the lush green and the strong purple in front of us, a warm breeze runs through my hair. This brilliantly beautiful day is far too precious not to spend it right in the middle of nature. "Hiking," I suddenly hear myself say. When did that occur to me?

"Your wish is my command." A satisfied smile spreads across his face. Like a wonderfully contagious disease, it takes hold of me too. As long as he doesn't touch me, being with him is so wonderfully easy. The things that make my life exhausting at home don't matter here.

I want to get started right away. My feet twitch impatiently while Philipp calmly lights his cigarette. The flaring flame reminds me of his most important lesson, and all at once I know what to do. First I drink my coffee, then we can move on. Not rushing myself is new to me, but it feels fantastic. Proudly, I put my feet up and exhale audibly.

"Exactly right," Philipp comments, as if he could read my thoughts, even though he isn't looking at me at all.

I'd love to know how he does it. To him I'm as transparent as if I were made of glass. He knows what I'm thinking and he knows my feelings. Better than I do myself, at that.

He, on the other hand, still won't let me look behind his façade. Whenever I get too close, he shuts down. As deftly as a magician who distracts his audience while he slips the rabbit into the hat behind his back.

That has to change today, and I'm going to make sure it does.

Chapter Thirty-Four

In silence, Philipp and I walk side by side, reveling in the scent of the lavender fields and watching the fruit farmers at work. Before long the sun beats down from the sky with such force that we seek shelter in a forest. Wildly overgrown trees and grasses line the narrow path that leads us ever deeper into the thicket. I slow my pace and watch, fascinated, as patches of light dance across the forest floor. Its mossy, earthy smell reminds me of Nahla's dirty hands. Lost in thought, my fingertips glide to the birthmark on my arm that she touched as well. At once I remember her wise words. Everything will be all right, someday, I hear her bright child's voice say, and I can't help but smile.

At that exact moment I realize I still owe Philipp something. "I haven't even properly thanked you yet."

"For what?" Philipp looks at me in surprise, even though it's absolutely impossible that he doesn't understand what I'm talking about.

I roll my eyes. "You know perfectly well."

"Maybe I want to hear it from you though." The

dimples appear on his cheeks, and there's a sparkle in his eyes.

If I've learned anything in the past few weeks, it's that I don't have to hide anything from others anymore. "For all the experiences, your patience, and the food for thought."

The time with you changed my life, I want to add, but I hold myself back.

Philipp nods and looks as wise as a philosopher. "It was my pleasure," he then says, and I can't shake the feeling that he, too, is keeping part of his words to himself.

Something about him is different today. He's so passive, leaving not only the decisions to me but also the conversations. I haven't gotten any impulses, any thoughts, or any cheeky advice from him so far. Is he already looking forward to being free again soon? In a few days we'll say goodbye to each other, and just thinking about it makes my heart a little heavier.

I don't have much time left to finally see my future clearly in front of me. Bravely, I break the silence between us. "My picture isn't finished yet," I say and look over at him searchingly.

"What can you already see?" he asks without slowing his pace. For a brief moment he looks at me, then he turns his attention back to the soft ground that cushions our steps so gently that they can't be heard.

I don't have to think for long. "Myself, helping others. But I don't know how, the picture is blurry and just won't come into focus."

Philipp doesn't answer, he just nods knowingly and seems to be waiting for me to go on. And I will. Right now.

"There's a lot you don't know about me. Things that actually make that impossible…" the words suddenly burst out of me.

His questioning gaze meets mine. "Why?"

I can't keep it to myself any longer. "Because I'm a bad person." Dams as high as houses burst inside me under the pressure that had been building up behind them for far too long. I want to tell him, I just have to tell him everything.

The unvarnished truth about me and my life finally needs to come out. Never before have I opened up to anyone the way I'm about to do now. But I know that it's exactly the right thing to do.

For a moment I bite my lip and close my eyes. Then I say what I never wanted to put into words. "I let my baby die."

With a raspy voice I force the words out. Tears shoot into my eyes, my nose swells up. Still, I go on.

"Everyone was against the pregnancy, after all my career was in danger. Everything I'd painstakingly built up until then was about to collapse. No one wanted to support me, but I couldn't have it taken away and I hoped that somehow everything would still turn out fine." My stomach tightens. I take a deep breath before I can go on. "It didn't."

I sob, the memory hurts so much. Silently, Philipp hands me a tissue. In his face I don't see a trace of judgment or rejection. He feels what I'm feeling; I can see it clearly in the watery shine of his eyes.

"Soon after I lost my baby. And it was entirely my fault."

I prop my head in my hands, the memory crashes over me with such force that I can barely stand it. Murderer, it echoes in my head. Murderer!

Still, I go on speaking in a trembling voice. "My world lay in ruins. But where was I supposed to go, and with whom? My success came first, and that had to stay that way. For as long as I can remember, I'd been trapped in a vicious circle, always having to give more and more to reach ever higher goals. I could please my family with that, but this life had made me hard and cold. I couldn't be who I am. On the outside I showed only what others wanted to see from me. I even hid the little gap between my teeth."

Deliberately, I push my lower lip down with my index finger so he can see my flaw.

Philipp nods, his jaw going hard as marble, but he doesn't say a word. I dab my cheeks dry and take a deep breath.

"As hard as I fought for my old life, after the miscarriage everything was different. I lost the most important case of my career, I couldn't just forget about the partnership at the firm, I even got fired. In my mother's eyes I stopped existing, she's ashamed of me. Tom treats me like I have a contagious disease, and my father stays silent about all of it."

I blow my nose loudly and look at Philipp through my veil of tears. He comes to a stop and shoves his hands into his pockets, as if he didn't know what else to do with them.

"No one knows I'm here. They think I'm sitting at home, looking for a new job day and night. If I hadn't met you, I don't know what would've become of me. But you showed me what life can feel like and that it's worth it to face your fears." I bite my lip, but then I just let the words out. "You saved me," I whisper, lowering my gaze.

A few seconds later I feel Philipp's strong arms around my body. He pulls me against his chest so tightly it's as if, for once, he had to hold on to me.

Then he lays his cheek against mine, and my skin tingles as if thousands of tiny lightning bolts were discharging between us.

"If you're constantly afraid of making mistakes, you

forget to live," he murmurs. His lips keep brushing my ear, so soft and warm that I can hardly bear it.

"I know that now. Thanks to you." Gently, I run my hand over his back.

"Then you know everything you need to know. If your view of yourself is still blurry, you're just too far away. Take one step after another, and soon enough you'll be close enough to see everything clearly." Philipp doesn't move away from me; we're standing in the middle of the forest as if we were a single intertwined sculpture.

"What's your next step?" he asks, and I'm not sure whether his words sound tender or just profound.

His question buzzes through my head and multiplies into an entire swarm of bees. "My return flight is already the day after tomorrow," I reply, sobered, and can't help swallowing. "I'm scared of what's waiting for me at home. And of being without you." It feels good to talk openly about my feelings, because suddenly they seem to have less power over me.

Philipp pulls away from me and looks deep into my eyes. "You're thinking about things that might be coming your way while you sit there doing nothing and wait for them. But the point is to become active yourself. What is your next step?" he repeats his question, urgent and firm.

That's when I suddenly understand what he means. "I'm going to tell the truth. Tom and my parents need to understand who I really am." Right now, in this moment, I feel that I can do it. I'm going to break this terrible silence that has buried all our negative emotions for as long as I can remember.

Philipp nods, puts his hands on my cheeks, and brushes his fingertips across my forehead. "Exactly." He sounds proud of me, and I'm proud of myself too.

I look up at him, our gazes meet, and all at once I recognize my own feelings in his eyes as well. Far too clearly for me to be mistaken yet again. A thousand butterflies awaken in my stomach. My heart beats excitedly against my chest and there's nothing I can do about it. Philipp's lips curl, just a little, but the sight makes my mind melt away. In an instant there's nothing left of it; I lift my face to him, wanting to finally feel him very close to me.

No fear and no doubts are holding me back now. I'm going to kiss him. And it will feel like coming home after a long journey. To the place where I've always belonged.

We move closer to each other; I feel his breath right by my face. In slow motion, his hands travel over my cheeks, glide down my neck, and continue on to my shoulders. My eyes fall shut. This moment belongs only to us and to the longing that burns its way through my body.

I'm ready.

Chapter Thirty-Five

I feel his lips, soft and warm. Just not where I long for them to be.

He kisses my forehead as if I were his little sister.

He had definitely noticed my intentions, and I knew he had wanted it too. It was there in his eyes. Or was it only my own desire reflected in his pupils?

This has to stop. Right now!

In an instant my courage evaporates and makes way for a sense of shame that sets my cheeks on fire. Luckily he can't see it; his mouth is still resting motionless just above the spot between my eyebrows.

"Thanks," I say, because I can't find any other words. I take a step back to pull away from him and glance up at him from the corner of my eye.

As so often, his expression is a mystery to me. I'd love to just ask him outright; I want to scream at him so he'll finally show me everything about himself too. But how could I force him to do that?

He clears his throat and seems a little as if he too has

been struck speechless. "Don't mention it." The situation suddenly makes him uncomfortable; he takes his hands off my shoulders and marches off. "Come on, I want to show you something." Once again I don't even get the chance to find out anything about him. Instead I have to figure out how to keep up.

When I catch up with him, he points to a glimmer between the trees right in front of us. "Right there," he says and nods, satisfied.

"What's there?" I can't and don't want to hide the annoyed undertone in my voice. I'm disillusioned, I'm done with his games. Even so, I trudge along the narrow forest path, straight through the undergrowth behind him. Sharp-edged branches leave welts on my skin, spiderwebs wind silkily around my legs. "If I catch my death out here, it'll be your damn fault."

"What's gotten into you all of a sudden?" Philipp turns to me, but only for a brief moment. As if he wouldn't be interested in the answer anyway. I should've known, there's nothing between us.

"Everything's great," I mumble and push past him. Philipp looks me up and down, shaking his head, but I ignore that completely.

I walk on blindly. The forest floor swallows the force of my steps, making them soft and quiet. Our sparkling destination comes closer and closer, one last bend and then I'll be able to see it as a whole.

It lies before me like an emerald-green oasis. A lake, nestled between tree trunks overgrown with ivy and stones covered in moss. Leaves and small branches float on the surface of the water. So slowly that it feels as if seconds are turning into minutes. I'm defenseless against the magic of this place; I take a deep breath and sink down onto a stone.

The damp, musty air streams through my lungs, a cool breeze dries the sweat on my skin.

"Great, isn't it?" Philipp is right behind me, but he doesn't touch me.

"It is," I reply, deeply moved, my gaze fixed on the natural spectacle in front of us.

Without having to say it, we both know what comes next. We silently savor the moment, each on our own and yet together. My thoughts are on him nonstop; they refuse to understand how he can be so close and at the same time so unreachable for me. As if our souls were one, but our bodies weren't allowed to meet. Not knowing what's behind that is driving me crazy.

I just have to ask him. Now or never.

"Aren't you finally going to tell me what you're hiding from me?" Wow, that was pretty direct. Since when do I do things like that?

Philipp seems to be shifting from one foot to the other; I hear thin twigs snapping under his shoes with a crackling sound. Did my question throw him off balance?

"What do you mean?" His voice sounds as relaxed as a Sunday morning.

I'm wrong, again.

Still, I keep trying. Without hesitating, I say what I'm thinking. "Ever since we met, you've been avoiding me whenever I want to know something about you."

"That's not true. I told you everything about me." Philipp carefully sits down next to me on the rock, but I can clearly tell how hard he's trying not to get too close to me.

A thousand questions are buzzing through my head, and I just let them out. "Why are you afraid of getting close? What started your change? What happened that turned you into who you are today?" But more than anything, I want to know why he doesn't want to kiss me. I won't ask that question, though, because I already know the answer, no matter whether I like it or not.

Minutes pass. I fix my gaze on the movement of the clouds reflected in the water of the lake in front of us and wait patiently.

"There's nothing big behind it. Please just believe me, Sarah." The pleading in his voice tells me everything I need to know. His travels, the self-imposed solitude, all of it is nothing but an escape. But from what?

"How long do you want to keep carrying it around with you?" Bravely, I look him straight in the eyes. He can't hold my gaze, shoves his hands under his thighs and bites his lip. For the first time since we met, he looks the way I've felt far too often all my life. Weak and vulnerable.

"There's nothing to tell, there's nothing there. Believe it or not, but that's how it is." As if he suddenly had to get rid of energy, he springs to his feet and gathers pebbles from the ground. One after another, he throws them into the water. I watch the surface, calm just a moment ago, break into agitated ripples. The lake is in turmoil, just like he is.

"I understand. If you ever do want to talk about it, I'll be there for you. No matter when and no matter where." I rummage a pen out of my backpack. I don't have any paper, but I do have a chewing gum wrapper—that'll work. Quickly, I write my address and phone number on the colorful paper and slip it into his pocket. He doesn't fight it, which is at least some progress. At least I hope so. "I want to walk around the lake. Will you wait here for me in the meantime?"

Philipp nods in silence, and somehow he looks relieved as he does it. He's glad I don't keep digging, and probably naïve enough to believe he could have deceived me.

On the way I head deeper and deeper into the forest, the leaves of the trees and bushes casting a pleasant coolness. It feels strangely lonely without Philipp, but I'll have to get used to that anyway. The thought sticks bitterly to my palate and that's where it will stay, maybe forever. Meeting him was the best thing that could have happened to me. Now I have to go on without him, brave and unstoppable, just like he showed me. How can he be such a great teacher when he himself carries a story inside him for which he can't find an ending? His sad face from earlier won't let me go; I'd love to help him, even if he might think I couldn't.

The ringtone of my phone reaches my ear like a strange, unnatural sound. For a moment I flinch. Tom or my mother, who else would it be?

I pull the vibrating device out of my bag; from the picture on the display my mother's pale blue eyes look at me appraisingly.

It's not hard to guess what she wants from me.

My finger hovers over the answer button, but something holds me back. Not the fear of her cold anger and not the worry that she might see through my lies. No, this conversation won't lead anywhere and will do me even less good. Just hearing her voice will destroy the beauty of this moment, and I don't want that. As if I were surrounded by a protective shield, I firmly press the small red symbol on the display.

My heartbeat is calm; I can't feel even the slightest burning in my esophagus. Because there's one thing I know for sure now.

I alone decide about my life. I'm free.

Chapter Thirty-Six

The air-conditioned air of the airport hits us, so pleasantly cool that I can almost see something good in the end of my vacation. Everything else makes me feel melancholy, no matter what I think about. Here, far away from Vienna and everything waiting for me there, life was simple, free, and inspiring. I did so many things I never would have been ready to do before. Just to understand what I'd been denying myself all this time. Inevitably I shake my head and push the curls back from my unmade-up face.

"How can three weeks go by so fast?" I ask Philipp, who is trudging along silently beside me with his oversized backpack.

He smirks. "That's how it is for everyone who spends time with me. Don't worry, that's perfectly normal." He gives me a cheeky wink. A strand of his light blond hair comes loose and falls into his face. Despite the neon light, with his sun-tanned skin and three-day stubble he looks almost unrealistically attractive.

I stop and look up at him appraisingly. "Sure, mister. And it has absolutely nothing to do with the fact that vacations, on principle, can only ever be too short?"

"Nope." His dimples appear and I have to look away at once. I've almost made it; I can't let myself get weak now. I need a distraction, and fast.

"Which check-in counter do you need?" I spin around once, searching, as if checking in were the most important thing right now. At first, though, all I see are masses of people moving in every possible direction. The bustle reminds me of an anthill. From the outside it looks like pure chaos, but in reality every one of those busy little creatures is pursuing a very specific goal.

Philipp laughs and fishes his ticket out of his pocket. "You just can't wait to find out where I'm flying next."

Of course I'm curious. Besides, there's no reason not to tell me. Or is there? "Could be. So, out with it already," I demand in a serious voice, planting my fists on my hips.

"That's unfortunately not possible." He's acting coy, like a girl who doesn't want to admit which boy she's crushing on. If he's trying to seem mysterious, he can save himself the effort. He's already won first place in the category of secretiveness.

"And why, pray tell?" My words sound annoyed. Good.

He rolls his eyes in exaggerated fashion. "It's way too tempting for you. Trust me, you don't even want to know."

Of course he's afraid he won't be able to get rid of me.

"Idiot," slips out of me. Even I notice that it sounds like I'm using his pet name. "Don't worry, you'll be rid of me soon enough anyway," I add quickly, and a lot less jokingly than I'd like.

"What makes you so sure about that?" he asks, and slowly I start to understand what he's getting at.

Who decides that I actually have to fly back to Vienna? I'm free to do whatever I want, aren't I? My gaze wanders over the departure board. I could be in any of those places next.

"You mean…," I don't know how to put it. With a helpless gesture I try to make it clear to him how much I need him to find the right words.

"But of course." He grins at me openly. "Why not?"

I've never thought about it before, but the idea is as tempting as the smell of the first Christmas cookies of the year. Not going back, leaving everything behind and just letting myself drift the way I have these past few weeks. The thought feels amazing. Far too amazing.

What does Vienna really have to offer me? What future do I have there?

I steel myself; I want to know if it would actually be possible. "Would you take me with you, wherever you're going next?" I ask, studying him closely.

Not a single muscle in his face moves; I can't read anything in his eyes. Neither agreement nor refusal. Then he furrows his brow in a theatrically thoughtful way. "Hm." He taps his cheek with his index finger and turns his gaze to the brightly lit ceiling.

I already regret my question. "Forget it, it was just a joke anyway," I say quickly.

"No, it wasn't, and you know that perfectly well. Why won't you admit it?" Again he looks at me as if he were a philosopher and I his student.

"Right, I seem to have forgotten that for a moment. So, would you take me with you? Yes or no?" It feels amazing not to hide. I grin, as cheeky as I'm otherwise only used to seeing from him.

With a serious expression, he suddenly lays his hand on

my upper arm. “Is that what you really want?” he asks quietly, and strokes his thumb over my bare skin.

I lower my gaze. “I don’t know,” I answer honestly. “The time with you was so wonderful, how could I let it end now?”

Philipp slips his index finger under my chin and lifts it just enough that I have no choice but to look him in the eyes. The little bit of air between us grows thin; I can hardly get enough oxygen. “It was,” he says. “But be honest with yourself. Do you want to come with me to move toward your happiness, or to run away from your fear?”

His gaze won’t let me go, and I swallow hard. “Aren’t you running away from something too?” I ask hoarsely. If we’re going to stick to the truth, then it has to apply to both of us.

“Sarah, this is about you. My reasons for living this way shouldn’t have any bearing on your decision.” Again he evades me, and it drives me crazy. But even worse is that he’s right. I have to know what I want and why. No one else can make this decision for me, no matter what he says or does.

I nod. “I know that.”

In my head I weigh the two options against each other. Going with Philipp would be the beginning of a new life. The past couldn’t hurt me, the pressure from my family would be wonderfully far away. Even if they couldn’t understand it, they’d have no power over me. I wouldn’t even have to look them in the eye when they found out. But then there’s still Philipp, with his tempting lips, the magnetic sparkle in his eyes, and those dimples in his cheeks that are going to drive me insane one day. How could I keep secretly pining for him any longer and at the same time endure, day after day, the distance he tries so hard to keep between us?

At home I have Tom, he wants to be with me. He even wants to marry me, and I at least have to try to find out whether I want that too.

My thoughts drift into the future, to exactly the moment when I tell all of them the truth. A horrible feeling spreads in my stomach, as if I had swallowed acid that is now eating me up from the inside out. I see my father's frozen face and his bewildered shake of the head. He turns on his heel and leaves the room without looking at me again. Completely different from my mother, who beats me down with words as hard as stone. Desperately, she tries to force me back onto the path that seems right to her. Just picturing the situation makes me shudder. The idea of being to blame for their unhappiness settles heavily in my acid-filled stomach.

Simply not exposing myself to all of this is clearly the easier way. But is the easy way really the right one?

"What would you do in my place?" I look up at Philipp, seeking help; he has to at least give me a hint. Something that can help me make my decision.

"Where there's light, there's always shadow too. The only thing that matters is what your feelings tell you." He lays his hand on my chest and my heart immediately starts pounding faster.

What is it trying to tell me?

With a hasty movement I free myself from his proximity. "I don't know." Impatiently, I let my gaze sweep through the departure hall, as if that could help me. By now my head feels like it's about to explode. The booming voice from the loudspeakers does the rest; my stress level spills over. "It's a decision for the rest of my life, how could I just make it like that? Here, in the middle of the airport."

"What would you do out of fear, and what out of love?" he asks, continuing, but that doesn't help me. Each of the options makes me fear and hope at the same time. I feel torn, I want everything and nothing.

I bite my lip; rationally speaking, it's mostly my fear that tells me to go with him. "Damn."

Before I can change my mind, I grab my suitcase and start walking. To my check-in counter, where I belong. Philipp trudges along beside me without a word.

"Are you happy now?" I ask, making no attempt to hide my bitterness.

"If you are…" His gaze fixed on an Asian tour group in the distance, he shrugs indifferently.

How can he?

The decision is made; I handle the check-in with cold efficiency. "So, then finally tell me where you're going. Now you don't have to be afraid anymore," I urge him as I slip my ticket into my handbag.

"Ireland." His eyes sparkle.

I shake my head, curls falling into my face. "And you think that's tempting for me? Australia or South Africa, that would be great."

"That wasn't the point at all and you know it. But come on now, thanks to your dawdling I'm really running late." Philipp grips my hand tightly in his and hurriedly pulls me along behind him.

Only when we pass through security a short while later does he slow his pace. I gasp for air, but Philipp shows no mercy, and I know why. His flight is being called; he has to get to his gate.

Together we keep going, forcing our way through the crowds. Our steps thunder across the tiled floor, my heart galloping in time with them. Gasping, I lift my gaze to the signs above the gates until I spot the right number. The line of people in front of the exit is short. The moment has come.

Far too soon.

In a moment I'll have to say goodbye to Philipp for good. We only have a few minutes left and I have no idea how I'm supposed to survive them. Nervously, I pick at my fingernails. My pulse is racing out of control, even though I'm not moving anymore.

"Well then …" I begin, stammering, "… take care." Looking him in the eyes hurts me more than I want to admit. The fact that he then comes over to me and wraps his arms tightly around my shoulders doesn't make it any easier. On the contrary, the sweet scent of his skin and the feeling of safety do me far too much good. Everything inside me rebels.

It's wrong to let him go!

I'm going to say what I'm thinking, I'm putting all my cards on the table. "You brought the most beautiful colors into my life." My voice threatens to break, I clear my throat. "Without you …"

"… your world will be just as colorful as it was with me," he finishes my sentence. His hand strokes gently over my back. "You'll manage without me too, trust me."

"Sure," I say quickly and blink hard to keep the tears at the corners of my eyes at bay.

"I should get going." Gently, he pushes me away from him. Only now do I notice the shine in his eyes. Even for him this goodbye is hard, even if he doesn't want to admit it. "We had a great time," he murmurs with a dreamy smile.

I nod. "One I'll never forget."

With his typically cheeky grin, he swings the backpack onto his shoulder. "Bye, my dear Sarah. I wish you all the happiness in the world." He's trembling, even though he's trying to hide it from me.

All of a sudden I'm at a loss for words; there's nothing left I could say. So, reluctantly, I raise my right hand in farewell. As if he can't wait, Philipp spins around on the spot and hurries to the exit. Helplessly, I have to watch as, without the slightest hesitation, he puts his ticket on the scanner.

There's no going back.

And although I'm sure of that, I don't want to give up hope. In my imagination he suddenly stops. In slow motion he turns to me. His gaze is full of longing, his body tense. Now he comes back, jumps over the turnstile, runs toward me and takes my head in his hands. Loving warmth tingles on my cheeks. He's so close to me that everything else around me disappears. In slow motion he bends down to me. Then I can finally feel it. His lips touch mine. He doesn't have to say anything anymore, because even without a single word I know what he feels.

While I lose myself in my Hollywood-inspired fantasy, Philipp disappears in the real world without looking back even once. Disappointed, I watch him go; for minutes I refuse to believe that it's really happening. Only very slowly does the truth seep into my thoughts.

My dreams burst as if they were nothing more than soap bubbles in the wind.

Suddenly my body feels heavy, my temples pound like crazy. I wipe my sweaty hands on my pants and take a deep breath. Then I make my way to the gate.

When I get there, I take the phone out of my pocket and turn it uncertainly in my hand. Should I get it over with right away? No, not yet. I'd much rather think back to the precious moments of the last few weeks. That's where I want to stay for as long as I still can.

With a smile on my face and tears in my eyes, I finally board the plane. This time I'm alone as the aircraft lifts off the ground. Just me and my thoughts, which are straining to paint my future in brilliantly bright colors.

Chapter Thirty-Seven

Hours later I arrive at the place I fled from so hastily. The elevator's sliding doors open and the stale, dusty apartment air hits me. It's eerily quiet; all I can hear is my heart beating. I clutch the handle of my rolling suitcase. For a moment I stand still, unsure whether I really want to go in. In front of me lies the long hallway with its high-gloss polished parquet and discreet lighting. Elegant and simple, my mother would say, and until now that's what I thought too.

Hesitantly I step into the apartment, set down my suitcase and handbag, and slip out of my shoes. My feet leave damp prints on the otherwise immaculate floor. After only a few seconds they disappear again, as if I weren't really here at all. I stroll down the hallway and let my hand glide along the wall. It's made of narrow stones in a light beige, irregularly veined with fine brown lines. Whenever I touch one of the sharp edges, a stabbing pain shoots through me. Like an electric shock that keeps my heart beating.

It's our apartment. My home. And yet I feel like a stranger here.

It's as if I'm seeing the rooms with different eyes. Cold and uncomfortable are the first words that come to mind. Somehow fitting for the life I've led here so far. Philipp would surely have some interesting piece of wisdom ready for me now. But even without him I can feel that this ultra-chic palace has never been a real home for me. For all its spaciousness, it's like one of those high-waisted jeans that are far too tight to let you breathe freely.

Leaning against the living room doorframe, I look around. We spent more than thirty thousand euros on the leather couch. Why, actually? It's an amount that would keep an entire family from going hungry for a year. And that's just here in Austria—how many countries in this world would you be rich with that kind of money? To make matters worse, the thing is neither particularly beautiful nor comfortable. It looks classy and solid, and it's good for impressing guests, but that's about it.

Shaking my head, I turn around, and the next room appears before my eyes. The kitchen is equipped with everything a professional chef would need to conjure up ten-course menus every day. But neither Tom nor I have ever cooked here. What's the point of all this if we don't need it at all?

No matter where I look, it suddenly becomes very clear how thoughtlessly we've surrounded ourselves with unnecessary things. Superficial objects, nothing more than supposed rewards for a life that consisted only of work and career.

"No wonder you couldn't see what really mattered with all that glitter blinding you." That's exactly what Philipp would whisper in my ear now in his warm voice if he were with me.

A pleasant shiver runs down my back and I can't do anything about it. Instead of getting angry about my blindness, I smile. Recognizing it is what makes it possible to give my life a new direction.

And that's exactly what I'm going to do now.

Without waiting any longer, I get to work and pack up everything I no longer need.

Loaded down with heavy bags, I open the glass door of the drop-off center for people in need and step, in high spirits, into the spacious room.

The smell of cheap plastic and old shoes stings my nose. Clothes in every size and color, household goods, and dubious-looking electrical appliances are spilling out of the aging shelves. The floor is worn down and the harsh lighting is anything but inviting. Still, I feel welcome, because the woman with the gray hair back there at the wide wooden table is giving me a warm smile. She is just tall enough to rest her hands on the tabletop. Her face is furrowed with wrinkles, all of which prove how joyfully she lives her life.

"Can I help you?" Leaning on a walking stick, she hobbles toward me.

Dragging my bags behind me, I march to meet her. "A donation," I pant when we finally stand facing each other. I wipe the sweat from my forehead and push my lion's mane back.

"How lovely!" Her cheeks lift with excitement, her eyes turn into crescent-moon slits. Even so, I can still clearly see the sparkle behind them. She seems as delighted with my discarded clothes as a child with presents from the Easter Bunny. "You know, we hardly get any donations anymore," she goes on, shaking her head as she opens the first bag. She pulls out a dark gray suit, unfolds it, and holds it up. "Good heavens. Are you sure you want to donate this?"

"Absolutely." I nod vigorously as I keep going without

slowing down. One designer piece after another appears, most of which I've barely worn. After all, my mother had drummed into me how important it is not to be seen too often in the same outfit.

"You do realize you could get a fortune for these in a secondhand shop, don't you, sweetheart?" She looks up at me with the skeptical gaze of a grandmother. I could almost kiss her, her manner is so charming.

Unimpressed, I open the next bag. "Maybe," I say casually, stacking the skirts and blouses in piles on the table. "But I want to donate them. You can use clothes like these too, I hope?"

Out of nowhere, doubts suddenly shoot through my mind that I might be doing something wrong. Who needs business clothes when they don't have anything else? Uncertain, I bite my lip. What if I'm donating things here that aren't needed at all? In my mind I see women in Chanel suits warming their hands at a fire under a bridge. How inappropriate. What on earth was I thinking?

The old lady pats my upper arm and smiles. "But of course! We even need them desperately. Otherwise we only get faded T-shirts and torn jeans. That's okay to start with, but it's not enough."

I lay the next blouse on the pile and try to figure out what she might be talking about. But I have no clue. "What do you mean?" I ask bluntly, hang a blazer on a hanger, and smooth the finely woven fabric.

"We're here for people who can't take care of themselves. Thanks to us they have the bare essentials, but what they really need is help so they can manage on their own. What do you think happens when you go job hunting in an old tracksuit jacket?"

Of course, now I understand what she's trying to tell

me. A tingling rush of excitement shoots through my body. If even one woman can make a good impression at her interview thanks to my donation, I've already won. "I'm glad I can help."

She nods, satisfied. "There should be more people like you, sweetheart." She's still smiling, but her voice sounds distressed.

"Absolutely." I try to sound carefree to lift her spirits again. "I've got some blankets, cushions, and other household stuff in the car, could you use that too?"

A radiant smile flits across her face. "Gladly," she replies, swinging the last clothes out of the bags. "By the way, I'm Helga."

"My name's Sarah. Nice to meet you." I reach out my hand to her, but instead of taking it, she pulls me into her arms as if she were my grandma and pats me lovingly on the back.

An hour later my car is empty; Helga and I have sorted everything together and stacked it on the shelves. I'd love to stay longer, but my work here is done.

"I wish I could do more." Absentmindedly, I turn the car key in my hand.

"But you can. Wait, I've got something for you." Before I can react, Helga hobbles over to a dresser. Since she doesn't walk well anyway, I follow her. She pulls a simple sheet of paper from the bottom drawer and hands it to me. Her eyes watch me excitedly. "This would be perfect."

The first thing I see is the colorful drawing in the upper right corner, which is presumably meant to show a father, mother, and three children. The visibly clumsy lines, drawn by a child's hand, catch me off guard. My muscles tensed, I pressed my lips together and blinked quickly.

"That's a project a good friend of mine is running. Her

name's Renate. See, it says so here," I hear Helga's voice, muffled as if it were wrapped in cotton wool.

I skim the text. It's about the Snail Shell, a place that looks after children when their parents need time for other things but can't afford a nanny. Job hunting, German classes, training courses. All that becomes possible for them because volunteers watch their little ones for a few hours. I swallow. Am I really suited for this?

"Everything okay, sweetheart? You've gone a bit pale." Helga studies me closely.

I clear my throat. Once, then again, and again. Only then can I say anything. "I'm fine," I force out and pull my lips into a smile. "Why do you think I'd be the right person for this place?"

With a knowing expression, she points to the last sentence on the sheet. "It's right there. For everyone who cares about the future of our children. You're perfect for it, I saw that right away."

Mechanically, I shake my head. "How?"

"Oh, at my age you just know these things. You like children, don't you?" she asks bluntly, bracing both arms on the wooden table and looking at me steadily. There isn't the slightest trace of doubt in either her words or her face.

I nod automatically; of course I like little ones. "Kids are great," I admit.

My thoughts drift to Nahla, the dirty little girl with the matted hair and big dark eyes. Once again she's sitting on my lap, I feel her small arms around my neck and listen to her bright child's voice begging me not to be sad.

Philipp is very close to us and smiles contentedly.

No. I can't let that happen. Quickly, I bite my lip and turn back to Helga.

"Very nice. Here's the address, just drop by whenever

you have time. I'll let Renate know, she'll be over the moon." Helga is beaming like crazy and despite everything I can't help but beam with her.

I kept hearing Nahla whisper, "Everything will be fine, someday," and all at once I knew exactly what she had meant by that. I couldn't change my past anymore. But now I was getting a new chance to shape my future.

The anticipation flooded my whole body, making me carefree and content. In this wonderfully light state I said goodbye to Helga and floated home as if I were lying on clouds.

The mirror in the elevator showed me what I already knew anyway. I had a radiant grin on my face. Together with the freckles it made me look almost like a lovestruck teenager. My cheeks were glowing, just a little, but enough to tint the skin of my face rosy. They were competing with my head of curls and looked almost as if their light were contagious.

When I reached the top, the silence of the apartment couldn't get to me anymore. With sweeping turns I danced down the hallway.

Floor, walls, and furnishings flew past my eyes. Brown, cream, and white blended into one another and left a beautifully marbled image on my retina. In the middle of it I registered a navy-blue blotch of color that definitely didn't belong there.

Someone is here.

I stopped moving abruptly. The image before my eyes froze.

My breath caught. Beads of sweat gathered on my forehead in a matter of seconds.

It's still too early, flashes through my mind. Still, there's no stopping him now.

The moment of truth has arrived.

Chapter Thirty-Eight

"Sarah?" Tom looks at me as if he isn't sure it's really me standing in front of him.

"Hi, Tom." I force a smile and walk toward him. Am I supposed to hug him? Probably, after all, we haven't seen each other for so long.

He backs away and clears his throat. "Is everything okay?" he asks cautiously. His forehead creases, his eyelids narrowing to thin slits.

"Sure, why wouldn't it be?" I make another attempt, put my hands on the back of his neck, and pull him down toward me.

Tom still doesn't move to hug me. Instead, he looks at me with a mixture of suspicion and disapproval. "Well… um…"

I wait patiently until he has pulled himself together. "What happened to your hair?" he finally asks. His voice is charged with a reproachful tone, his jaw hard as stone.

I'm not impressed by that; I tilt my head to the side and grin. "You don't like it?"

Again Tom searches for words but doesn't seem to find any. He presses his lips together, looking unsure and distant.

"It's kind of cute, right?" I try again and shake my head so he can see my curls in action.

"Cute?" he asks, his eyes wide. "Since when are you cute?" He growls at me like a chained dog at harmless people walking by on the street. As if he knew he couldn't actually attack me. Still, his anger won't allow him to keep quiet.

Defiantly I look into his brown eyes, which are much less warm today than usual. "I like it," I answer stubbornly and pull away from him.

He takes my hand and holds it tight. "I'm sorry, but you look so different, and it's not just the hair. Something's wrong, I can see that."

This is the moment when I would have given an evasive answer in the past. The old Sarah would have run into the bathroom, done her hair and makeup, and then crept back to Tom with her tail between her legs to finally get her welcome kiss.

Even now I feel the urge to do exactly that. My legs twitch, I press my fingernails into my palms. I feel an energy rising up inside me, like magma in a volcano. I have to withstand this heat. There are no more excuses, no more lies, no more holding back.

"You're wrong, it's exactly the opposite. Now, finally, everything's right," I say, my voice shaking. This wasn't how I'd imagined it.

Every muscle in Tom's body tenses, as if he were a lion getting ready to attack. "What's this about, Sarah? What are you even talking about?"

I fold my arms across my chest to protect myself from what's coming next. We've never argued before, but now it's inevitable. It takes all my courage to stand up to him. Even though I'm sure of myself, I have no idea where to find that courage right now. "What I mean is that there's more right with me now than there used to be. I've changed, not just on the outside, but in here too." I tap my temple with my index finger.

Tom rolls his eyes. "Oh God, you've gone crazy," he says, exasperated.

"No, I see more clearly than ever in my life." My voice is unshakably firm, intoxicated by the adrenaline flooding my body like a tidal wave.

"Oh yeah? And what is it you suddenly see? That you'd rather style yourself like some out-of-control teenager than a grown woman?" With sweeping strides, Tom paces up and down the living room, his hands kneading his temples.

This isn't going the way I'd hoped. I have to try to get him on my side. But that's never going to work as long as he's angry.

"Tom, come on, let's talk about this calmly," I say, steering him toward the luxury sofa. At least he gives in and lets himself fall onto the cold leather with a deep sigh. Then he looks at me as if he were my father, trying to drum some sense into me.

"This isn't going to work, you understand? This isn't you." He gestures at me with his hand while his gaze wanders from my hair to my shoes and back again. It reaches my face; his eyes are cold and devoid of understanding.

I make an effort to stay calm; anything else would hardly make sense. "I know this is all a surprise for you right now, but at least try to understand it."

"Understand what, exactly? I've just come back from a long trip, I'm dead tired and simply glad to be home again.

And then you hit me with this weird crisis of yours. I just don't need that right now." He shakes his head and lets himself drop back into the hard cushions of the couch.

"Oh, I'm so sorry your little wife isn't conforming to your wishes." Did I really just say that? With an undertone as sharp as a warrior's spear? Instinctively, I want to clap my hand over my mouth, but I hold back. Tom finally has to take me seriously, and that's only possible if I don't back down now.

He exhales slowly and stares at me accusingly. "All right then, explain it to me. But make it quick, I need to get to bed."

I could see in his face how little he was interested in what I had to say. He was just looking for the quickest way to end this conversation. I skillfully ignored it; what was coming now was far too important.

"It was my fault to wait so long. I should've talked to you much earlier, but..." I needed a moment to pull myself together; Tom's annoyed snort stressed me out, and his hand gesture, telling me to finally get to the point, even more so. "It all started with the pregnancy. Our baby, Tom, it was our baby! When I lost it, my whole world collapsed. Do you have any idea what that felt like for me?"

He shrugged. "You were like always, everything was fine."

I went on, insistent. "No, it wasn't. It was the opposite, I couldn't sleep for nights on end. I wasn't capable of anything anymore, my whole life had slipped out of my hands. Of course that didn't stop at work either."

"Come on, that's enough now. You're just looking for an excuse for your resignation. I saw you, I was always with you. You were in a good mood, focused on your career. Just like I know you." He looked at me, as lost as a baby bird missing its mother. "Just like I love you."

"But that wasn't me, can't you finally understand? You could only see what I showed you. But inside me everything was broken, I just couldn't go on. Damn it, Tom, I let our baby die!" My voice was shrill and loud, and I couldn't care less if anyone else could hear our fight. I was sick of always posing with my fair-weather face in my glossy-catalog life. "And you didn't just keep silent about it, no, it even suited you."

He looked at me, bewildered.

"Exactly, I know everything. Absolutely everything."

"I… well…" he stammered, but I didn't want to hear his excuses.

"You're a coward, you hid behind my mother just so you wouldn't have to take me on. But what's even worse is that none of this touched you in the slightest. Why? Why couldn't you love our baby?" Tears of disappointment and anger welled up in my eyes.

I'm showing him all my feelings, and I know that to him it feels like I'm forcing him to watch a horror movie with his hands tied and his eyelids taped open.

"It was the wrong time," he says, his expression contrite.

I shake my head. "Because of my oh-so-important career, you mean?"

"Don't act like your success didn't matter to you." His voice grows firmer; he feels sure of himself. Because he knows how right he is.

I nod. "It did, but for the wrong reasons. It was never about me, what I wanted, or what makes me happy." My index finger keeps jabbing hard at my chest.

Tom runs a hand through his hair and groans. "And

that's what you want to hold against me now? Or what are we actually talking about here?"

"I'm not saying it's your fault. Just that it was wrong." Doesn't he want to understand, or can't he?

Suddenly Tom springs up from the couch. "This is all too much for me, Sarah. I'm going to bed now, we'll talk tomorrow." His frosty look hits me painfully, everywhere in my body.

He can't leave now, this is way too important. "Do I really mean that little to you?" I hear myself ask, full of disappointment.

"You're just impossible to talk to today. Let it go, please. We'll sleep on it, then we'll see." He sounds discouraged; with slumped shoulders and his hands shoved into his pockets, he turns around and disappears from the living room.

I'm left behind just as alone as I am. Maybe even as I've always been, I don't know. Tears are still running unchecked down my cheeks. The conversation with Tom went thoroughly wrong; I managed to get out only a fraction of everything I had to say. And apparently he can't even handle that.

Without warning, a heat rises up inside me like I've never felt before.

Who does Tom think he is, just leaving me standing there like that?

I was in the middle of telling him something important. About me, my thoughts, and my life. He can't just ignore that. I jump up at once and run after him. He's damn well going to listen to me, whether he wants to or not.

Of course he's taken refuge in the bedroom. Unsurprisingly, he's sitting in bed working on his laptop. Leaning against the doorframe, I watch him.

"So you're apparently not as tired as you just claimed you were." My voice is sharper than a freshly sharpened butcher's knife.

Without taking his eyes off the screen, Tom lets out a theatrical groan. "Work," he mutters, as if that explained everything. "You know, that thing you're not interested in at all anymore."

"That really gets to you, doesn't it?" My patience finally evaporates into thin air.

"Forget it, I have to finish something here." Tom is pounding on his keyboard like a madman. His eyebrows are drawn together so tightly you'd think he needed all his concentration for this work.

That's it now. For good!

At a run I cross the room and yank his damn computer out of his hands. "Away with that thing. You're going to listen to me now, understood?"

He stares at me in disbelief. "Have you completely lost it now? Give it back already, or else…"

"…or else what?" I ask, pressing the laptop tightly against my chest. "What are you going to do, huh? Run away again, this time into the kitchen maybe? Even if you lock yourself in the bathroom, I'll come after you. We have to talk. Now!"

Tom gasps for air, his hands flailing nervously upward. "Damn it, Sarah, get a grip."

"I most definitely won't!" I yell at him as loud as I can and pin him with my gaze. He's supposed to know how little chance he has. "Now I'm talking and you're listening, understood?"

He lets his arms drop and rolls his eyes toward the ceiling. "If it really has to be…" he says in a tone as cold as the nights in Antarctica. Leaning against the headboard, he looks at me with raised eyebrows.

Euphoric, I pace up and down in front of him. I've managed something I've never achieved before. I finally have his attention. How am I supposed to go on now? "So, where should I start…"

My hesitation makes Tom sigh dramatically. "Is this going to happen today or what?"

Now or never, this is my moment. The most important moment. I clench my fists so tightly it hurts. "I'm not going to keep working as a lawyer." The words explode out of my mouth.

Tom bursts out laughing and shakes his head in amusement. "What? You don't seriously think that's your decision."

"Of course it is!" I hurl the words at him, full of conviction.

His eyes narrow, looking like slits in his face. Deliberately slowly he rises from the bed and takes a step toward me. "I don't give a damn what kind of trip you're on right now, but it's about damn time you started being reasonable again. You're a lawyer, just do your job, like everyone else here."

I don't let myself be thrown off, not today and never again in the future. "But it doesn't make me happy," I say with utter conviction.

"Life isn't about being happy. Get that through your head." Tom's lips are only thin slits now, and he presses his index finger against my chest. "And now listen to me." His ice-cold gaze makes me shudder. "I'm willing to forget this conversation if you pull yourself together again right now, clear?"

Defiant and challenging, I hold his gaze. The spot where he touched me burns like fire. “And if I don’t?”

He snorts contemptuously. “That’s not an option for you.”

His finger digs further into my skin until it hurts. I stay where I am, stare back and clamp my teeth together. We stand facing each other like rivals in a fight to the death.

“We’ll see about that,” I force out and push my chest against his so he knows how far I’m willing to go.

His gaze flickers over my face, surprised and horrified at the same time. He searches for words but doesn’t find any. Unimpressed, I hold my ground. For the first time I’m fighting for myself alone and for no one else. It’s my dreams and my future that are at stake now.

For seconds we stand in our bedroom, silently waging a battle that has been overdue for far too long.

Suddenly the pressure on my chest disappears, and with words I can’t understand, Tom runs out of the room. He wants to get away from me again, but he can forget that. I march after him and see him getting into the elevator at the other end of the hallway. With a panicked expression on his face, he keeps pounding on the button to close the doors, as if this were a crime thriller and I were the murderer. While he stares at me with eyes wide open, I move toward him faster and faster. The elevator doors close slowly, I’m almost there, can almost touch them.

Now I feel the cold metal under my fingertips. The gap that still connects Tom and me grows narrower and narrower. I can no longer stop the movement of the doors. His face twists into a grimace. The last thing I see is a triumphant grin, as ugly as that of a criminal who was acquitted despite being guilty.

"Coward!" I yell and slap my flat hand against the metal wall in front of me.

Of course I know where he'll go next. I could follow him, but from one second to the next the adrenaline suddenly drains from my body. My head grows heavier with every passing second, my legs weaker. Suddenly I register a tremor in my hands; it spreads until it takes over my whole body. That's when it hits me what just happened.

Tom and I, that doesn't exist anymore. And it probably never really did.

Chapter Thirty-Nine

Utterly focused, I crouch at the kitchen counter. My ears register every sound, classifying it as dangerous or harmless. The whole time I don't move and I don't let myself get distracted. My eyes scan my surroundings, over and over again. They'll come; the only question is when.

The time display on the microwave's digital clock jumps to eight thirty, then to nine. The coffee in the fancy little porcelain cup in front of me has long since gone cold, but I won't give up my post. On the contrary. I'm ready, keeping the tension in my muscles and my senses focused.

What feels like an eternity later, it happens. Almost silently, the elevator doors glide apart; right after that I hear tentative footsteps and muffled voices. As if they were whispering to each other and, just to be safe, still holding a hand over their mouths.

Now everything goes completely quiet.

I can feel the tension all the way into the kitchen. The hairs on my upper arms stand on end, my heartbeat speeds up. An invisible band tightens around my throat.

I straighten up and take a breath, but I can still feel the fear boiling up inside me. Can I really withstand the avalanche of cold rage and merciless accusations that's now thundering down the hallway toward me?

My mother is the first to enter the kitchen. Her face is set in stone, her lips pressed together so tightly I can't see them anymore. Reflexively, I correct my posture so she won't scold me. Apparently I can't stop wanting to please her, no matter what it costs me.

She stops a few inches in front of me and plants her hands on her hips. "What is this I hear about you, Sarra?" is how she greets me.

I'm hot and cold at the same time, I can feel courage and fear wrestling in my head. "Good morning," I finally say, overly polite. "Can I offer you some coffee?"

"An explanation is the only thing you're allowed to offer me." The mood reminds me of a simmering volcano just before it erupts, but her eyes make me shiver.

"If looks could kill, I'd have been dead long ago, don't you think?" I'm surprised to realize how matter-of-fact I sound. As if her rage were just rolling off me like water off a lotus leaf. On top of that, I can't feel any pulling or burning in my stomach. Am I actually stronger than I thought?

My mother gasps; she clearly didn't expect that. "Bernhard!" she calls loudly, her eyes still chillingly cold on me.

Behind her my father trudges into the kitchen, his hands buried deep in his trouser pockets. He looks like a schoolboy being forced to go to church on Sunday. He'd rather be anywhere than here with his failure of a daughter.

"Oh, come on over here!" she snaps at him impatiently. He reluctantly quickens his step and is almost beside her when Tom appears in the doorway as well. He joins my parents. Cold and overpowering like a wall of ice, the three of them now stand in front of me, all of them with serious faces and closed-off body language.

My gaze wanders back and forth between their faces. While my father and Tom can't look me in the eye, my mother stares back so unyieldingly that it's enough for all three of them. The air between us is charged; even a kind word could ignite it.

This can't end well for me.

Or is there still a chance? I try not to let my doubts show, look at them with equally frozen features, and wait for their first move.

"You owe us an explanation!" The color in my mother's cheeks changes, the barely visible little lines around the corners of her mouth tremble.

I get up from my stool so I'm at least a little taller. Meeting her gaze feels as if I had to force myself to watch someone commit a brutal murder. "I tried that yesterday," I answer as calmly as I can, then turn to Tom with an accusing look. "You remember, don't you? That was when you didn't want to listen," I add firmly.

If he loved me, he would be on my side. He would have to fight for me instead of against me. But he prefers to hide behind my parents like a coward.

My mother quickly steps protectively in front of my fake fiancé as well. "But now we're listening. So go on." She clenches her fists again, this time so tightly that the skin on her hands turns white all over.

I feel the fear inside me swell, like a sail in the wind.

I can still turn back now; it's the last chance.

But if I do, wouldn't everything be just like it used to be? Everyone would be happy—except me.

Seeking help, I cling to the stool beside me, square my

shoulders, and suck huge amounts of oxygen deep into my lungs. My ribcage feels as if it's about to explode any second. Just like my heart, which is pounding irregularly. My strong shell doesn't give way; instead it lets all the air out until there's nothing left.

"I'm not going to work as a lawyer anymore." My voice wavers and with it my whole body. No one seems surprised. "But as I can see, you already know that," I add quickly and look accusingly at Tom, which makes him lower his eyelids at once.

"She really has gone crazy," my mother mutters in my father's direction. She shoots him a stern look; he grunts in agreement. He punishes me with his silence, the way he always has.

"I'm not," I protest. "On the contrary, what I've done up to now was crazy!" I know I should hold back; this mustn't escalate, that wouldn't help anyone. But I can't manage to keep my words under control. I've suppressed them for far too long; now they want to do exactly as they please.

Hurriedly, my mother fixes her glacier eyes back on me. "Oh, so you call having a good life crazy?"

I snort. "A good life? You think I had a good life?" My voice turns shrill and I let it.

Now the truth is coming to light; I'm lifting up the expensive Persian rug under which the unsightly dirt has been hidden for as long as I can remember.

"As a child I didn't have any friends. I wasn't allowed to play outside; my pretty little Gucci dresses might have gotten dirty. At school no one wanted anything to do with me. I was the nerd, far too perfect to be liked." The memory brings tears to my eyes, but I hold them back.

"Nonsense," my mother says at breakneck speed. "You

had a wonderful childhood." Stubbornly, she shakes her head.

Anger rises up in me. "No, I didn't!" I shout back at her with all my strength. "And it didn't get any better after that. You kept pushing me. It always had to be more, always more and even more. Nothing I ever did was enough. As soon as I'd reached one goal, you loaded the next one onto me." One after the other, I stare at the three of them, feeling as disappointed in them as they usually are with me when I've made a mistake. "Isn't that true?"

With her lips pressed together, my mother looks at my father. His expression doesn't change. He lifts his shoulders, just a little, but that's all I need to know. My mother snarls like a wounded lion that no longer knows what else to do. Then she turns back to me. "You wanted it that way and we supported you. That's the truth! And now stop lying, it's pathetic."

"Are you really that blind?" I fix my eyes on her, squinting. "I never even had the chance to decide anything for myself, you laid out the path for me and I just trotted along it like a mindless donkey." Now I'm the one shaking my head. It's unimaginable what I let them do to me all these years. I take my hands off the stool; I don't need its support anymore. Accusingly, I point my index finger at my mother. "Thanks to you I could never find out who I am. What I dream of and what I burn for."

"Pfff," my mother says dismissively, "dreams." Her contempt is unmistakable. "I don't recognize you. What's this about, Sarra?"

I ignore her interruption and pick up where my rage leads me. No matter how much it hurts, it has to happen now. "You didn't even want my baby." My voice breaks. Still, I want to get everything out before I'm interrupted again. "Yes, all three of you, together. Do you have any idea what that felt like for me?" My furious gaze darts back and forth between them. At the same time, a feeling of relief floods me. It's finally out, the pressure eases. As if on cue, my nose swells shut, I can hardly breathe. Still I don't give in, I don't burst into sobs and I hold back my tears.

"It was about your career!" My mother throws her hands in the air affectedly. "Please don't be so stupid, Sarra."

"Oh yes, my great career. Well, thank God it still managed to make sure my baby had to die. A tiny, defenseless creature. For what?"

I stare at her, my eyes wide open. No one answers me. They just look at one another in dismay, as if they can't comprehend that it's the otherwise so compliant Sarah who is suddenly screaming the unspeakable at them.

"For a goal that, once you'd reached it, would only have made you set the next one for me. So that other people would think well of us, right? No one's supposed to believe that something's wrong with us." My anger vanishes as if I'd used up all my strength. What remains is a sadness as deep as the ocean.

"Oh please, the way you behaved at the firm, it couldn't have worked out anyway." Annoyed, my mother rolls her eyes up to the so inappropriately pretty kitchen ceiling with its stucco decorations.

"You can't possibly know that." Something's wrong here; I sense it immediately. My muscles tense; now I have to be on my guard.

She answers my words with a contemptuous snort. "I know everything. You forgot appointments, you went into negotiations unprepared, and instead of working you spent hours staring out your office window."

I stare at her in disbelief, not a word leaves my mouth. Still, my question seems to be written all over my face. She nods and pulls the corners of her mouth down.

"Oh yes, I know everything." Triumphantly, she taps her outstretched chest with her index finger. "Even that you cried like a little child when you quit."

Everything in my head is spinning, I feel dizzy. Only the kitchen counter is still there for me now. I cling to its cold surface. Unable to form a clear thought, my lips shape the question I can't answer myself. "How?"

A self-satisfied grin spreads across her face. "I had my sources."

Someone watched me. Someone from the firm.

Frantically, I run through my former colleagues in my mind. Their faces rush past my inner eye like a film on fast-forward. Faster and faster and more chaotic I see them before me, the images merge with each other and suddenly I see the culprit.

Clearly outlined, in glaring colors.

"Jörg."

The ground under my feet shakes. She really did know everything, had her spies planted everywhere. At work Jörg, at home Tom. And back at university? What if it was Philipp?

Tom wants to take a step toward me, but my mother holds him back. "Don't you dare give in now," she whispers to him. She thinks she's finally wrestled me to the ground, and that's exactly how I feel.

For minutes we stand facing each other. We all stay silent, as if there were no words for what we're feeling. Seeing the disappointment in their faces hurts all over my body. Still, I have to be strong now; I mustn't give in, no matter how much I'd like to feel their affection again.

The way I am, without success, career, power, and money, that's how they're supposed to love me. I don't want anything else anymore.

My mother finally breaks the silence. "Your behavior is unacceptable. You'll find yourself a new job, immediately. In return, your father and I will forget this conversation ever took place."

I stare at her in disbelief. Does she really want to sweep even this under the rug, which is already far too full?

"I won't do that." My words make the air between us freeze for good.

"And what exactly are you planning to do instead?" she asks, a note of contempt in her voice, folding her arms across her chest. Then she moves even closer to my father. Is she afraid of the answer?

My heart is pounding in my throat, my hands are shaking. I gather all the courage I have left. Because I know that what comes next will deliver the death blow to my old life. Deliberately and with full force. "I want to be there for people who need help."

My mother's eyes widen. "You want what?" Her question sounds brittle.

"Do you have any idea how many people don't have enough to live on? They're so hungry they eat food out of garbage cans, they prostitute themselves just to survive." My thoughts drift to Suna; again I see her face before me. With those eyes, far too old for that young face.

"They have nothing because they don't want to work. That's the truth," my mother cuts me off. "Besides, there are already more than enough institutions that take care of people like that. Those are the ones you want to help?" My mother's voice breaks, her breathing turns rapid.

"You have no idea." I shake my head so hard it makes

me dizzy. "Do you have any idea how lucky we all were to be born here?" They have to understand that; who couldn't?

"Your father and I worked hard for this good fortune, nothing was handed to us either. I won't tolerate such lies, Sarra!" my mother snaps at me.

She wants to scare me, but it doesn't work. That turning point has long since passed.

"You don't believe me? Then come with me, I'll show you what I'm talking about." Maybe I can still convince her; if she can see it too, then she would understand. We would have a future together. Suddenly there is light where everything had been dark before. Hopefully, I look at her. "Please," I add imploringly, "do it for me."

Nothing stirs in her face, not even her eyelids move. Then she parts her lips and I send up a quick prayer to a heaven that hasn't existed for me until now.

"Never."

Everything freezes. The three of them, me, and the air between us.

"That's a real shame," I say sincerely, "but it doesn't change my decision." I stand in front of her as solid as a rock, washed around by the hope that there might still be a shared path for us. What mother would turn her back on her child?

"If that's your last word, you're dead to me." Coldly she hurls her judgment at me, then grabs my father so hard by the arm that he yelps in pain. "Bernhard, we're leaving," she orders him and drags him behind her. On the threshold she turns around one last time. "Tom, are you coming?"

My fake fiancé shifts from one foot to the other, his gaze wandering back and forth between my parents and me.

Again, and again. What did Philipp say about him? That he's a loser? How right he was.

"Go on already!" She sounds like an officer. And Tom looks like a humble soldier.

Suddenly his eyes go empty too, like a doll's. "I'm sorry, Sarah," he says, but neither his face nor his posture matches the apology.

Composed, I look at him. "Of course you are."

"You're not the Sarah I wanted to marry anymore." His shoulders lift in a helpless shrug.

"I'm finally myself, more than ever before." His words can't hurt me anymore; my voice is steady.

Silently, Tom holds out his hand and cups it. "Get on with it," he snaps at me.

"You wanted it this way, Sarra," I hear my mother screech from a distance. I know she's won. And she knows it too.

So far I've been strong, but now it's all too much. Because in this very moment one thing becomes painfully clear to me. Without my parents and without Tom, I don't have anyone at all.

Exhausted, I lower my gaze. Through the tears that finally well up in my eyes, I see the diamond on my engagement ring sparkle. I twist it off my finger and place it in Tom's hand without looking at him again.

It's over.

Chapter Forty

The shock sat in every part of my body, making it rigid and motionless. Helplessly I had to watch as the people who had once been my family leave the room. I was left behind on my own, feeling as small and unwanted as a cockroach amid the elegant wooden floors and glossy cabinets surrounding me. There was no one I could go to, no confidants and certainly no friends.

The adrenaline in my blood fizzled out and left nothing but emptiness. With my back leaning against the cool side of the kitchen island, I sank to the floor.

In my mind I fled back to France, back to the moment when Philipp, in the shade of huge fig trees, asked me the crucial questions of life.

"Who are you?" A gust of wind swept through his light blond hair, his tanned skin glowing in the morning sun.

With a piece of wood I drew circles in the sandy ground in front of me. "I don't know," I admitted with a sigh.

Despite my helplessness, he smiled at me. "The answer will come to you, it's only a matter of time."

Doubtfully I looked up at him. I wished I had his certainty and his strength. "Please tell her to hurry up. I don't want to wait any longer."

"Look at me." Philipp's hands rested gently on mine, he turned me toward him and fixed me with his gaze. "No matter what happens, promise me you'll never lose your trust. Only you know where your path will lead you. Listen to your heart and everything will be fine." He laid his flat hand on my chest and the spot immediately grew hot. The warmth spread in all directions, right down to the tips of my toes.

At first I hesitated, but one look into his eyes was enough to make me give in. "I promise." It was definitely not a good idea, but I still put my hand on his. All at once I felt the magic between us, so strange and beautiful, like something out of a fairy tale. What he said was right.

None of that certainty was left, that became clear to me now as I crouched on the floor. It was as if I were a different person here in Vienna. I searched in vain for the confidence I'd had back then. My heart was silent; I felt colorless and heavy.

I needed Philipp; without him only half of me was left.

It would have been so easy to call him. My phone was lying on the table above me. I pushed myself up, reached for it, and unlocked the screen. Then suddenly I hesitated. I absolutely didn't want to be a nuisance to him. Like a fly that couldn't be driven away, no matter what you tried. I chewed on my lips until I tasted blood, then I put the phone away again. Still, I couldn't help staring at it and asking myself the same question over and over.

What did I have to lose?

Nothing.

In a flash I dialed his number. With sweaty hands I

pressed the phone to my ear. I heard the ringing tone. My breathing was labored.

"Come on, Philipp, pick up," I begged into the phone, but there was nothing except the monotonous ringing. Then suddenly a click.

"Hello." Philipp's voice was so close that I could hardly breathe. My heart skipped a beat.

"It's me, Sarah," I said cautiously.

"Unfortunately, I'm not available at the moment..."

Voicemail Philipp is cheerfully chatting away at me, but I'm not listening anymore. Now comes the long beep, I should say something, but I'm at a loss for words. I hurriedly end the call and immediately feel even lonelier than before. No one, absolutely no one, is left to me.

My life lies in shards, and they're far too fine to ever be pieced back together. Exhausted, I bury my face in my hands. I curl up on the floor again, my gaze fixed on nothing. I stay like that until I finally fall asleep on the kitchen floor, completely drained.

When I open my eyes again, the sun is setting behind the floor-to-ceiling kitchen window. The hard parquet floor presses relentlessly into my side. I push myself up into a cross-legged position, my back aches, my eyelids are sticky. I feel like a crash victim, run over by a truck, or three at once. There's no going back anymore, and maybe that's even a good thing.

With a long, lingering sigh, I lift my gaze to the white ceiling, as if someone up there might be able to help me. The sight reminds me of the canvas of my future. Is it really colorless? I screw up my eyes, maybe that way I can see it. Then I force myself to think of Philipp's words.

"What's your next step?" I hear him ask, and I know

that even if I can't see the goal clearly yet, with every yard I leave behind, it will become more distinct.

I'll tell the truth. Tom and my parents have to understand who I really am.

That was exactly my answer, and a few hours ago I did just that. Now I'll keep going, and with every step I'll get closer to my happiness.

I push myself up off the floor. In the bathroom I wash my face with ice-cold water, then my gaze gets caught on my reflection in the mirror.

"What's your next step?" I ask myself and look at myself as kindly as Philipp would if he were here.

The reflection doesn't answer, so I repeat the question. Again the woman with the puffy face stays silent, but a sparkle begins to appear in her green eyes.

I take a step back and suddenly I see what had been hiding from me before. A tentative smile spreads across my lips, my chin lifts and drops in agreement. This elegantly streamlined bathroom with its superficial perfection doesn't fit the barefaced Sarah who's now beaming at me with her whole face. I don't belong in this apartment; it's too big and far too impersonal.

Moving out of here, that's the next step.

I immediately storm back into the kitchen. The decision is made, and now I can hardly wait to get away from here. Where's my phone? I spot it on the floor next to the kitchen counter. In one leap I'm there and grab it.

Then I see it, the small white light at the top edge of the phone. Did Philipp call back? My heart skips a beat; maybe he does miss me after all?

I quickly switch it on, the display lights up, but instead of a call it shows me a new message. From Tom.

"I'll come by tomorrow to pick up my stuff. Would be

good if you weren't there." Disappointment spreads through me. Not because of Tom's message, but because I realize what Philipp's silence means. I have to let go of him and this fake romantic idea of the two of us; he doesn't belong in my vision of the future. All I can do now is paint over him, and black is the only color that can do that. I never wanted to let it into my life again, but right now I can feel it threatening to take command one more time.

Stubbornly I fix my gaze straight ahead and promise myself that from now on I won't look back anymore. Out there, somewhere beyond the rising stars of the night, a new life is waiting for me, and it will be wonderful. Because that's what I want.

"OK," I type into my phone and send the message to Tom.

Then I start looking for an apartment. It should be small and cozy. Without unnecessary frills. I comb through the real estate ads and immediately find several interesting places. Taking my future into my own hands feels like I'm flying. My thoughts grow light and clear. Between calls and messages, searching and anticipation, my next step presents itself all on its own.

If I don't work, I'll soon run out of money. My savings are tied up in financial products my parents forced on me. I check my current account; thanks to the trip it has shrunk to barely three thousand euros. That won't last long. Especially not if I move. Just putting down the deposit for a new apartment will be difficult.

But that ridiculously luxurious apartment my parents gave me still belongs to me. Living there myself is out of the question anyway. I'll rent it out so I can use all my time and energy for what my heart is set on.

Excited, I hurry through the apartment, pack what I

want to take with me, and mark what I'm going to donate. The pain over losing my family is still there, but with every step the certainty grows in me that I did the right thing. Anyone who can only love me as a dolled-up puppet has no place in my life.

I'm free and so alive, as if I were a once-wounded butterfly that in the end can still fly.

At last I'm myself, for the very first time in my life.

Chapter Forty-One

Not even a week has passed since my return to Vienna. Still, the memory of the argument with my family already feels as if it had happened in another life. I've taken countless small steps since then, not only here at the childcare center Schneckenhaus.

"Sarah, could you give me a hand, please?" Renate makes her way through the room as if through an obstacle course. Building blocks, soccer balls, and books are scattered everywhere, with children playing between them. She blows a strand of her white hair out of her face in a flustered gesture. Her gray-blue eyes flick back and forth between the floor, the room, and the tray in her hands. Although her expression is strained, she looks as if she's smiling.

I gently lay my hand on Anna's shoulder; she's sitting next to me, concentrating hard as she tries to add apples and bananas. "Try to solve this problem all on your own. I'll be right back."

She nods, her emerald eyes sparkling. I'd love to run my hand over her pitch-black hair again, but Renate really does need my help now. I hurry over to her, move plastic tractors and wooden blocks out of the way, and clear a table so she can set down the water and cookies there.

"Thanks, that was close." She looks at me in relief and wipes the sweat from her forehead. "The cups are still in the kitchen, would you get them?"

I'm happy to do it; after only a few visits this place has already become my second home. The brightly painted walls with decorations of handprints in every size cheer me up the moment I arrive. Renate, the director of the Snail's House, is so warm-hearted that you just have to feel comfortable here. I admire her for what she has built up. With simple means she has created a refuge. Not just for the children, but for me as well. When I'm here, I feel good; what I do has a purpose. I used to be as lonely as a person can be, now I have more friends than ever before. It's not just the other volunteers, mostly retirees and students, but also parents of children who are here a lot.

I come back with the cups and immediately the children storm toward me like a swarm of bumblebees toward freshly blossomed lavender. Only instead of buzzing, they chatter excitedly in their bright voices.

I have to laugh; the children's cheerfulness is contagious. "We're about to start. First one to sit down is first served." Everyone hurriedly looks for a chair, I pour water into their cups one after another, then it suddenly grows quiet. Only the crunching of cookies and the mouse-like chewing sounds of the children's mouths can be heard.

Now that the little ones are taken care of, Renate and I lean back on the miniature chairs as well. My gaze wanders to the doorway, where Anna's mother now appears and waves at me with a friendly smile.

"Come join us." I motion for her to sit down next to me,

but she just taps her index finger on her wristwatch and beckons her daughter over. Of course, today the handyman is finally coming to take care of the damp spot in the hallway of her apartment. "All right then, see you Friday evening," I call to her. I'm already looking forward to our game night.

"Bye, Sarah." Anna's smile reveals a gap in her teeth. The fact that she can show it off so unselfconsciously makes me smile in satisfaction.

I keep watching her and see how lovingly her mother pulls her into her arms in greeting.

Renate clears her throat. "Thanks for your help. It's wonderful having you here. The children love you." She takes a blissful bite of her cookie and smiles at me. The sincerity in her eyes moves me.

I shake my head. "No, I'm the one who has to thank you. This place saved me," I reply, gesturing with one hand to the room, the children, and to her as well.

She tilts her head, studies me conspicuously long, and even seems to hesitate for a moment. "Do you want to tell me about it?" she then asks, as caring as a grandmother.

I can't help but smile. "It's not important anymore, I've long since let it go." I never would've thought I'd ever be able to say something like that. But it's true, my past can't hurt me anymore. Because now I have something much better. A future as colorful as a graffiti artist's work.

Renate nods, starts to answer, but is interrupted before she can say anything. Necmi, a four-year-old Syrian boy, runs up to me and climbs onto my lap. There are still a few cookie crumbs at the corner of his mouth, and a bright red streak adorns one cheek, looking as if it were the result of a drawing done with intense concentration. I hug him as tightly as I can and breathe in that incomparable child scent that surrounds him.

"Well now, my little star." Since he doesn't speak our language very well yet, I speak very slowly and clearly.

A bit awkwardly, he points his index finger at his own chest. "Star!" he says, his eyes shining. They're as dark as Nahla's and look at me just as furtively.

"Exactly, Necmi means star." I stroke his head. "Shall we play something?"

His delighted squeal is answer enough. I nod, the little bundle of energy jumps off my lap, takes my hand, and with me in tow heads straight for the building corner.

Once we get there, I sit down next to him and watch him stack the wooden blocks on top of each other. It's not the first time I've noticed his forearms, covered in scars, and again I wonder where they came from. I'm sure he has already experienced more in his young life than is good for him. The thought makes me sad, but instead of letting my pity overwhelm me, I just think about how wonderful it is to be able to help him now.

"Are you building a tower?" I ask, and immediately find myself looking into a pair of eyes that clearly doesn't understand what I mean. "Tower," I repeat, pointing at the crooked structure in front of him.

He giggles as if I've made a joke; maybe the word sounds strange to him. I'd love to find out more about him; his delicate face with the oversized dark eyes has really captured my heart. I don't have such a close bond with any other child here as I do with Necmi.

We keep playing for quite a while, stacking one building block on top of another and creating a huge city. When all the blocks are used up, the little one claps his hands proudly.

"Well done!" I call out enthusiastically and hold out my

open palm to him. He slaps it, just the way I taught him a few days ago. We grin and giggle because we're sharing something that only the two of us understand.

Just as we jump up to dance around the tower together, I hear a deep male voice calling for my little friend. Unimpressed, we keep turning, the room whirling past me; I make out Renate, then the narrow windows with the orange curtains. Next the door, and then suddenly a pair of eyes, bright like the sea on a damp winter's day, looking in my direction.

I stop, and in slow motion I let my gaze wander back.

Philipp?

I have to blink to see more clearly who's standing there.

Of course it isn't Philipp.

Disappointed, I let my shoulders drop. The man the eyes belong to is tall, with broad shoulders and narrow hips. His short, close-cropped chestnut hair blends seamlessly into three days' worth of stubble. Fine lines play around the corners of his eyes. His gray T-shirt is covered in green and brown stains, and on his feet he's wearing heavy work boots.

Now he walks toward us with slow steps, his eyes beaming with joy as he looks at Necmi.

The boy starts running, throws his arms around the stranger's neck, and lets himself be swung high up into the air. He squeals and giggles so much he can barely catch his breath. When the man sets him back down on the floor, he kisses the little one's forehead. With the way the two of them love each other, he can only be Necmi's father, even though they don't look alike at all. A sharp pain pierces my heart; that kind of love was denied to me. But that's the past, and I can't change it anymore.

"Hi, I'm Sarah." With a friendly smile, I hold out my hand to Necmi's father.

"So you're the new one Necmi keeps raving about at home." He chuckles, then turns his gaze to Necmi. While I'm still wondering why he speaks such good German, his son starts tugging at his hand like crazy. I don't understand what they're saying to each other now, but they seem to agree. They both give a thumbs-up and nod vigorously.

"Nice to meet you. I'm Mario." He wipes his hand on his pants before offering it to me. His handshake is pleasantly firm, and his smile is so likeable you just have to like him.

Before I can say anything, Necmi draws attention to himself. Just like before, he pulls Mario into a discussion. To me it sounds as if he's asking for something. He looks at his father pleadingly and repeats the same words over and over until he finally nods.

"Necmi would like to invite you to dinner," Mario finally says, turning to me. I watch the little one fidget nervously, his big round eyes imploring me so intensely that I simply have to say yes.

"I'd love to." I nod so Necmi can be absolutely sure he understands my answer too. Now he starts jumping up and down, grinning at me. I'm more than happy to let his enthusiasm rub off on me.

Mario and I sort out the details, then the two of them head off. Necmi seems to fully understand why he has to help get everything ready at home now. Busy like a grown-up, he leaves the room. I wave them goodbye, then they disappear through the door.

In that moment it hits me how genuine the people's friendliness here is. No one wants to be better, faster, or more perfect. There's no competition, no envy or resentment. A warm feeling of gratitude brings tears to my eyes. This is where I belong.

I'd love to tell Philipp about my new life. Would he wrap his arms around me, full of pride? Would he kiss my forehead and dance with me in delight?

In my imagination he does. Right now, in this very moment. And even though I shouldn't be thinking about him, it feels fantastic.

Chapter Forty-Two

"I'm sorry?"

In the middle of the sidewalk I come to an abrupt halt. I can't believe what the realtor just told me on the phone. It can only be a misunderstanding; the roar of the passing cars must have drowned out part of what he said. Or I just didn't listen carefully enough.

"Could you repeat that?" I force myself to ignore the panic spreading in my stomach. Then I press my index finger to my free ear and squeeze into a doorway.

That's better; I can even hear his breathing on the other end of the line now. "Ms. Wagner, you have to understand…" His tone is conciliatory, which is not a good sign. Not at all. "Of course we're doing what we can. But a property of this size isn't easy to place. Something like this takes time."

"How long?" Numbers are somersaulting in my head. The money in my checking account has shrunk thanks to the deposit for my new apartment. I can get by for maybe one, two weeks. And then there's also the money I wanted to send Suna and Nahla to support them.

"We should be able to find someone by the end of the year, don't worry," I hear the realtor say. His words hit my eardrum and immediately my head feels as if a balloon is bursting inside it.

I wipe the sweat from my palms. Even though it's not particularly hot this evening, they just won't dry. My body is doing whatever it wants anyway; my feet can hardly keep still and my throat seems to dry out every few seconds. "Half a year? That's too long!" I croak helplessly into the phone. "If I were to sell the apartment…"

"…that would be even more difficult. Unless you carry out some remodeling. Divide the space into several small apartments, then it might go faster." An interesting suggestion, but how am I supposed to pay for that? I could take out a loan. "We'll do everything we can, I promise," the realtor interrupts my carousel of thoughts.

"Of course, please get in touch immediately if you find someone."

We say goodbye, then I hurry off as if I could leave the problem in the doorway behind. My escape is unsuccessful; the money worries are with me, no matter where I go. Even when I'm standing in front of Mario's door half an hour later, I'm still agitated. Even my index finger trembles a little as I press it to the doorbell.

I hear a long, deep buzzing, followed by clumsy footsteps and a child's voice shouting excitedly.

"Sarah!" Beaming with joy, Necmi wraps himself around my hips; I run my hand through his dark hair and greet him at least as delightedly as he greets me. It seems ridiculous even to me; after all, we've only been apart for a few hours. But I don't let that stop me.

Suddenly Mario is standing in the doorway; he looks as if he's just jumped out of the shower. Droplets of water sparkle in his hair and he gives off a fresh scent of lemon and olives. Being near him feels like a vacation on a sailboat. "Hi Sarah, come on in."

Curious about Necmi's home, I stroll down the hallway toward the room from which the smell of freshly cooked tomato sauce is wafting toward me. It's so delicious that my mouth instantly fills with saliva. I swallow it down along with the memory. It mustn't surface, not now.

I keep looking around, focusing. The cramped apartment the two of them share has a charm all its own that overwhelms me at once. The Mediterranean flair is what strikes me most. It runs like a common thread through every room. Turquoise and dark blue cushions are scattered over the chairs, the sofa, and the wide windowsills. Together with the many photos of Mario on his travels, wearing his uniquely likeable smile, they make the living room feel warm and cozy. Green scarves flutter in the warm summer breeze from the frame of the glass door leading to the ground-floor terrace.

I feel at home right away, my money worries lose their importance, and I can focus entirely on Necmi, who wants to pull me over to his play corner.

Mario holds us back. "First we're having dinner." He balances two steaming pots in his hands and sets them down on the dining table. As I sit, I notice the bouquet of flowers in the middle of the table. It's made of daisies and blades of grass standing together in wild disorder.

"Necmi picked that for you," Mario explains to me with a smile.

When has anyone ever done something so sweet for me without expecting anything in return?

I have to clear my throat before I can speak. "Thank you, Necmi!" Moved, I lay my hand on my chest and give a little bow. The boy claps his hands in delight and his mouth stretches into a proud grin. "He's a great kid, I like him a lot. Would you translate that for me, please?" I ask, turning to Mario, who is happy to oblige.

Then the little one starts babbling, gesticulating wildly and laughing as if he were telling me a joke. Mario doesn't even try to translate everything, but sums it up for me with a wink. "He likes you a lot too."

With practiced movements he fills our plates with pasta, tomato sauce, and fresh basil. Even though I know what's about to happen, I take a bite. My eyes close all by themselves.

Behind my eyelids I see Philipp. Deeply focused, he winds spaghetti around his fork. His hair is loosely tied back, a few light-blond strands framing his angular face. Just as he brings the fork to his mouth, some of the noodles slip back onto the plate. The tomato sauce splatters in all directions, leaving an abstract work of art on his white T-shirt. His gaze drops, then shifts to me. With shining eyes and a mischievous smile, he winks at me.

Seeing him in front of me like that makes my longing flare up like a flash fire. I snap my eyes open and leave the memories where they belong. In the past.

Now I'm here and I should use my chance to find out more about Necmi. With Mario as interpreter, we can actually chat with each other.

By the time we put Necmi to bed after dinner, I know that he doesn't like chocolate, his dinosaur is called Minno, and the toothbrush with the crocodiles on it is his. Together we sing him a lullaby and then tiptoe out of the bedroom, which the two of them apparently share.

Without Necmi I don't really have any reason to stay; I should go, no matter how comfortable I feel here.

"Well then…" I say, just as awkwardly as I feel, and pick up my handbag.

"Do you have to go already?" His disappointed expression cheers me up. "I thought we'd have another glass of wine."

Happily, I let my bag drop again and nod. "With pleasure."

Mario opens a bottle of red wine and pours the ruby liquid into two round-bellied glasses. Outside, the sun disappears behind the roofs of Vienna, the rush of cars grows quieter. The city settles down.

I raise my glass and toast him. "Thanks again for the invitation, the food was delicious." Our glasses touch ever so lightly and produce a sound as bright and delicate as the distant laughter of a child's voice.

"How could I refuse Necmi this wish?" He takes a sip. I follow his example; the liquid settles on my palate, woody and tart. "He adores you, much more than anyone else we know."

I can't help it; I just have to beam at him. So this is what it feels like to be loved unconditionally, wonderfully light and warm in my chest. "I feel the same way." Carefully, I slide the glass back and forth on the tabletop. Is this the right moment to ask about Necmi's scars? Or about why Mario, unlike him, speaks German so perfectly?

"Normally he's very shy, he doesn't let anyone get close to him. But with you it's different."

Surprised, I lift my gaze and look straight into the darkening sea of his eyes. "Why is that?" I ask cautiously.

He shakes his head, his shoulders sagging. "I don't

know," he answers with a sigh. "That boy is far too often a mystery to me."

With my head tilted to the side, I study him curiously. How can he not know his own child? "But you're his father."

Mario takes a big sip of wine. Then he exhales loudly before he answers. "No, I'm not."

"What?" I slide to the front edge of my chair and lean over the table as far as I can. "Then why is he with you?"

Again he looks at me with that sad expression, as if the world behind his eyes lay in ruins. "It's a long story, much too long and much too tragic for such a beautiful evening as this."

My hand moves across the tabletop of its own accord, searching for his and resting protectively on it. "I'd like to hear it anyway."

For a moment he hesitates, his gaze drifting back and forth between me and the reddish bands of cloud outside the window. "Necmi came from Syria about two months ago. All I know is that he ended up all alone on the Italian coast. Wounded and with broken bones. Dirty and malnourished, as if he were a stray dog. That's how I found him, on one of my aid missions for stranded refugees."

A terrible image forms in my mind, my heart clenches. "Oh no…" I squeeze his hand even tighter.

"He had no one, you understand? No parents, no siblings, no friends. So there he was in front of me, a four-year-old boy, eyeing me suspiciously from the corner of his eye, his short legs braced against the ground, ready to run." He falters, pinches the bridge of his nose between thumb and forefinger, and takes a few deep breaths.

I want to make it easier for him, to say what he can't.

"You took him with you. He's here illegally. In Austria and with you."

His gaze pleads with me to understand him, though there's no need. I feel for him. "What else was I supposed to do? Report him? At best they would have shoved him into one of those run-down homes. I couldn't do that to him." The sound of his voice leaves no doubt: he's a man with a big heart, ready to fight for others, no matter if he puts himself in danger.

It doesn't even occur to me to pull my hand away, even if he has committed a crime in the eyes of the law. "Of course you couldn't, I probably would've done the same," I say soothingly, running my thumb over his trembling fingers.

A hopeful sparkle lies in his eyes, like gentle waves glittering in the sunlight. "Really?"

I nod firmly.

"But if they find us…"

His despair leaves deep marks in my chest, but at the same time a broad smile now spreads across my face. Because I know exactly what to do. "I can help you make it right."

"But… how?" he stammers, hunching his shoulders.

At last I can use my training for something good. I tell him about my profession and explain what options we have now. "It won't be easy, but if we hang in there, we can make sure Necmi can live with you officially. Without fear."

As if I'd just given him the six winning numbers for the next lottery draw, he looks at me. "Are you sure this will work?"

I chuckle. "You're looking at one of the best lawyers in the city, or at least that's what people say. Everything will be fine, someday," I quote, chuckling, the little wise Nahla from Marseille.

Mario raises his glass. "Thank you for your help, you're an angel. How can I ever make it up to you?"

I raise my hands defensively; he doesn't owe me anything, and that's exactly what I tell him. Of course he doesn't give up, he wants to do something for me too, at least a little something. "Is there really nothing at all I can help you with?" he asks intently.

I don't have to think long; of course there's something I could use his help with. "I'm moving this weekend," I reply, my gaze fixed on his strong upper arms.

"All right, I'm in." A relieved laugh flits across his face; after our serious conversation, he looks more content again. "When do we start?"

We clear up the details, and for a moment I wonder if I should prepare him for the palace I'll be moving out of. What will he think of me when he sees how I've been living up to now? Will he think I'm shallow and stuck-up? Maybe. Still, I'm not going to hide from him. I am who I am, and there's nothing wrong with that.

"Would you like some more wine?" Mario lifts the now almost empty bottle and looks at it in disbelief.

I shake my head and glance at the watch on my wrist. It's almost midnight, and I have no idea where the hours have gone. "No thanks, I've had enough. I should go anyway. It's late, and you probably have to get up early tomorrow, right?"

"Necmi's an early riser." He grins at me, but his eyelids are heavy. I can clearly see how hard he has to fight against their weight.

"Thank you for the lovely evening," I say, getting up

from my armchair. Then I help him clear the table and set everything down on the narrow counter next to the sink.

"I'll walk you out." Like an old-school gentleman, he even carries my bag for me, helps me into my summer jacket, and opens the door for me. "Thank you. For everything."

"I'm glad I can help." I am, and maybe it even makes me happier than it does him. I wave goodbye and set off.

"Get home safe," I still hear him call as I'm already reaching the front door. I turn around one last time; he smiles at me.

I smile back, and right now I feel it very clearly. This is the beginning of a wonderful friendship.

Chapter Forty-Three

With the back of my hand I wipe the sweat from my forehead and, with it, the tears from the corners of my eyes. It took all day, but now it's done. Tom already took what he wanted last week. The rest of my old life is in front of me, wrapped in cellophane and cardboard. Most of the boxes are going to Helga's collection point, many of the pieces of furniture will be picked up tomorrow. I'm donating them to an organization that looks after refugees like Suna and Nahla.

Content but tired, I let myself drop onto the floor in the middle of the spacious living room. As empty as it is now, it looks even bigger. Gently I run my index finger over the marbling of the parquet floor. Although you can hear with every step that the floor has survived many centuries and even more residents, you can't see it. When daylight, like now, falls through the floor-to-ceiling windows, its beauty really comes into its own. At night, in the artificial light of the crystal chandelier, it's dull and lackluster. As if it had two faces, one for the bright times and another for the dark.

Inevitably, my memory paints pictures from long-gone times in my mind. I see Tom and me when we moved in. Of course we had hired professionals; neither of us packed a single box ourselves or assembled any of the furniture with our own hands.

No matter how long I think about it, I can't find a single moment when I was truly happy here. This place was like my own façade. Pretty to look at from the outside, but cold and meaningless on the inside.

The doorbell rings; Mario is here. I jump up, buzz him in, and wait for him right by the elevator. The display above the steel doors counts the floors up; in a moment he'll know. My pulse speeds up. I wipe the film of sweat from my palms on my pants and fan air into my face.

A bright chime announces Mario's arrival. The doors slide apart like a curtain finally revealing the stage set to the audience of a theater. I spot Mario leaning against the mirrored wall at the back, an incredulous look on his face.

"Wow," he says tonelessly.

"I'm glad you're here. Come in!" I take a step toward him, put my arms around his shoulders in greeting, and hug him gratefully. "Back there are the things that need to go to the new apartment, everything else can stay here," I say as I let go of him and point first to the study, then to the living room.

With raised eyebrows, Mario's gaze wanders through the apartment and finally comes to rest on me. "Um…"

"I know," I interrupt him, "all of this here is…"

What is it, really? Over-the-top luxurious, horribly superficial?

"Why on earth are you moving out of here?" Shaking his head, he wanders on into the kitchen.

"The apartment doesn't suit me," I answer with a

dismissive wave of my hand. "It didn't before, and it suits me even less now."

His fingers glide over the stainless-steel surface of the fridge. "Too expensive, even for a lawyer?"

I clear my throat to buy myself time I don't actually need. There's no reason to hide anything. "I don't work anymore. And I shared this palace here with a man who also isn't with me anymore."

Mario nods; whatever he thinks he understands, it can't be the truth. "New job, new apartment, new man. Got it."

"Actually, just a new apartment, the thing with the new man isn't really working out." I cover the sadness in my voice with a deliberately cheerful wink.

"And what about the new job?" Curious, he tilts his head to the side and looks at me encouragingly. I know full well that for him there's no wrong answer.

"I'll probably have to look for one." Only once the words are out do I realize what they mean. My savings are as good as gone. If the realtor doesn't finally work a miracle, I'll have to work to be able to pay the next month's rent. "You work at a landscaping company, right?"

A friendly smile spreads across Mario's face. "I do, why do you ask?"

"Could you use some extra help?" An excited tingling spreads through me. This could be the solution.

"A damn big job just came in. You don't have a problem with hard work and dirty clothes, do you?" There's a hesitation in his words, but I don't let that stop me.

"Of course not." I can't help but smirk.

Mario nods, satisfied. "Very good. You'll be planting marguerite bushes, various ground covers, and tons of lavender."

While Mario claps his hands in anticipation, my heart

suddenly grows heavy at the thought of the fragrant, violet-flowering plants. I can't do anything about it. Even here in the cold kitchen of my old apartment, France and Philipp are constantly with me.

Mario's clearing his throat tears me from my thoughts. "All right, I'll get started in the study then." He speaks so carefully, as if he's afraid of disturbing me. Right after that he sets off, grabs the first box, and carries it toward the elevator.

I chase the memory from my head as best I can and grab one of the light boxes.

The most important moment is now. Get that through your head, Sarah.

Together we load the small van I rented at record speed. With everything I'm going to take to the new apartment, it won't even be half full. I'm only leaving ballast behind, which now also falls away from me in my mind; I feel as light as a soap bubble.

"That's it." I give the world a radiant smile and push a lock of hair out of my face. "Will you give me another moment?" I ask Mario, who is already heading for the driver's door of the small truck.

He studies me pensively. "Of course, take all the time you need. I'll wait here." His understanding moves me; I throw him a grateful look and disappear into the cool shade of the entranceway.

When I reach the top floor, I walk through the rooms one last time. In the kitchen corner the lion is still sitting there, and as always he stares at me with my mother's scrutinizing gaze. I run my hand over his head as if he were alive.

"Take care," I say, and I don't just mean the stone animal. "Who knows, maybe one day you'll still be able to forgive me."

A tear escapes the corner of my eye and runs hot down my cheek. Having lost my family is a shadow cast over my new life. Angular and dark, cold and deceitful. It will always be there, no matter how brightly the sun may shine for me otherwise.

I check whether we've packed everything and close the windows. Without the noise caused by the hectic hustle and bustle of the city, it is suddenly completely quiet. I pause for a moment at the patio door and let my gaze wander over the historic center of Vienna. A man in a suit is leaning against the light façade of the house at the end of the alley. From the way he runs his hand through his hair, I know immediately who it is.

Tom.

Now he lifts his head and looks straight up at me. Our eyes meet; for a few seconds we look at each other. Then he nods in farewell and turns to go. A gentle smile spreads across my face. Because I know it was the right thing to do. I was never happy with him, and I never would have been.

"Bye-bye, old life." My voice dies away in the room. Then I turn on my heel and leave the apartment without looking back one last time.

Mario is waiting, leaning casually against the driver's door of the truck, his feet crossed and his hands buried deep in his trouser pockets. He nods at me; I wipe the last salty drops from my cheeks. As if we could understand each other without any words at all, he pulls me into his arms and runs his hand over my back. From top to bottom, vertebra by vertebra, and then back again to the point where he started. He doesn't know my story, yet he doesn't ask about it. Everything he knows about me so far must seem strange to him, but he accepts me exactly as I am, and that feels wonderful.

"Thank you," I say, my voice choked.

A blaring honk abruptly yanks my attention away. "What the hell, move it!" someone yells at us angrily.

Mario realizes in a split second that our small truck is blocking the street. The furious man can't get through with his lorry. Gesticulating wildly, he signals for us to finally let him pass. A line of waiting cars has already formed behind him; encouraged by the man's honking, they're getting impatient too. At once I see the road to Les Baux-de-Provence before me, a slight tug makes itself felt in my chest. Mario lifts his shoulders apologetically, then jumps behind the wheel and starts the engine while I get in on the other side.

We drive off, the rush of air cooling my burning cheeks. As Vienna's city center passes by, I'm able to smile again. We leave the concrete buildings, separated only by asphalt, behind us and head out to the Sixteenth District. How my mother hated it, flashes through my mind. Too much riffraff, she always said, sticking her nose in the air.

If she knew that her daughter lives there now, her heart would stop.

Good thing she doesn't have a daughter anymore. I can almost taste the bitterness of the thought on my tongue, but I refuse to let it get me down. Especially not now, as we're already turning into the lane of my new home. Here I'll be moving into a two-room apartment on the first floor. At just under forty-five square meters, the rooms are tiny, but I have a terrace and even a bit of rooftop garden.

For me, that's more than enough.

We roll far too slowly down the lane. Impatiently, I squirm in my seat. Just a few more meters, then the light gray façade with the dark brown shutters appears before my eyes. But what's going on in front of the entrance today?

"What are all these people doing here?" I crane my neck to see better, and suddenly I spot Renate. "No!" I stare at Mario in dismay.

The grin on his face grows wider with every second. "I thought we could use a bit more help."

The way he drops that so casually sends a warm feeling curling through my stomach. All these people came just for me? That can't be. I shake my head vehemently. "But…"

Mario's laughter filled the cab. "Looks like someone's been struck speechless." He steered the small truck up onto the curb and pulled over.

In disbelief I looked at all the people waiting for me. Some I didn't know yet, some I knew very well. From the Snail's Shell. But it wasn't just Renate here; Helga and the parents of some of the kids had come too. With their little ones. They smiled at me expectantly, I saw the light in their eyes and the joy in their faces. Their energy washed over me and swept me along like a wave. I quickly jumped out of the van. I was so moved that I was completely lost for words.

"You're crazy," I stammered under my breath, over and over again, as I hugged them one after another. "Thank you, I don't even know what to say." Awkwardly I shrugged my shoulders; it was all too much for me. Tears of emotion blurred my vision, and Renate handed me a tissue. I dabbed them away and then I saw it clearly. The corners of her eyes were suspiciously moist too. She pulled me tight against her and rocked me back and forth, the way a mother would with her daughter.

"Hey, we're here to help, not to get cosy," eight-year-old Anna protested vehemently. With her hands planted on her hips, she looked at us demandingly.

I laughed and cried at the same time, crouched down in front of her and pulled her into my arms. "It's just so great to have you all here. That's all." I stroked her perfectly soft little cheek, took a strand of her pitch-black hair and tucked it behind her ear. Her uncomprehending look told me that none of this was anything special to her. Of course she couldn't begin to guess how extraordinary it was for me.

"Good, then we can finally get started." Motivated, the girl headed for the loading area, the others followed her and began unloading my boxes. For a moment I watched them, a wave of gratitude washed over me. I was surrounded by people who took care of me. Not because I did what they told me. But because they liked me just the way I was. I couldn't have been happier than I was in that moment.

"Sarah, keys." Anna stood in front of me, balancing one of the small boxes in her arms and looking at me expectantly.

I hurriedly fished the bunch of keys out of my pants pocket. "Of course," I said with a smile and unlocked the front door. "First floor, on the left."

Not even two hours later it was done. As busy as ants, my helpers had carried everything into the apartment, unpacked boxes and assembled furniture. Overwhelmed by what we had achieved together, I spun around exuberantly in the middle of my colorful living room. Renate had even thought to bring drinks and snacks for everyone. A little later we were already standing together on the terrace, raising our glasses.

"I can't thank you enough," I say solemnly as I look into the kind faces all around me. A lump forms in my throat, but it's nowhere near as big as the affection I feel for everyone here. I swallow it down and go on in a trembling voice. "You're the most wonderful people I've ever met. Without you…" I can't get the words out, my emotions are too strong, my feelings too overwhelming.

Renate speaks up. "It was just a little thing, not worth mentioning," she says with a dismissive wave of her hand. The others nod, but I can't and won't let it stand like that.

"No, it was more than that. Much more." I leave the reason unspoken; now is not the right time for gloomy stories. As if they can sense how much more it means to me than just carrying a few boxes, they smile at me encouragingly. "I'd like to invite all of you to dinner, tomorrow evening. As a thank-you for your help." Excited murmuring spreads, I hear enthusiastic agreement and lively discussions about what people could bring. "No one's bringing anything, is that clear?" I give the group a stern look and earn embarrassed nods all around.

"But we're allowed to help with the preparations, right?" Mario asks, with an expression on his face that makes it impossible for me to turn him down.

Still, I put on a show of reluctance, stringing him along by pressing my index finger to my lips and letting my gaze wander up to the sky. "All right, but only you. Everyone else, please be there at seven, good and hungry and thirsty."

"Yes, ma'am," I hear little Anna call out. Everyone starts laughing. My helpers raise their glasses to one another and sink back into their own conversations.

The mood is exuberant and cheerful as I lean, exhausted, against the house wall behind me. The evening light tickles my nose, and I take this moment for myself, right in the middle of the colorful bustle around me.

Everything will be all right, someday. With Nahla's voice in my ear, I watch the people who, in such a short time, have become more like family to me than my own ever was. That's when I suddenly know how right she was.

"Everything will be all right," I murmur to myself, so quietly that only I can hear it.

Chapter Forty-Four

Exhausted, I let myself drop onto the mound of earth Mario and I have piled up over the last few hours. The socks in my heavy work boots are damp, and the gardening gloves are so dirty that you can't even tell they used to be yellow.

"Looks great, now we can get started." Leaning on the handle of his shovel, Mario nods in satisfaction.

I shield my eyes with my hand against the glaring sunlight and squint up at him. "Haven't we been doing that this whole time?"

"What do you think we just dug all those holes for?" he asks, a grin on his face. Then he tilts his head. "Take a breather, I'll unload the plants for the hedge in the meantime."

Before I can even thank him, Mario is already on his way to the truck. Even though the work is nice, I secretly hope that planting this hedge will be the last task for today. My muscles ache and my stomach growls like a full-grown German shepherd. I take a sip of water and inspect our work. Where there was just an unremarkable lawn this morning, we've planted hydrangeas and rosebushes, laid a winding path of paving stones, and stacked bricks for a herb corner. Even though we're nowhere near finished, I can already start to imagine how great it will look in the end.

Far too quickly, Mario is back with two trees in terra-cotta-colored pots. "Smell this," he says, holding one of the pots out to me.

I don't even have to get close; the aroma of fresh forest air is already drifting into my nose.

Like an entire spruce forest. Just like Philipp back then on the plane.

I resist the urge to close my eyes and let the memory surface. I don't want to think about his dimples or the sound of his voice right now. Not about his hand on my cheek and even less about his lips on my forehead.

"You okay?" Mario studies me with furrowed brows.

I nod, maybe a little too vigorously. "Let's get started." Not very gracefully, I heave myself up and grab the first pot.

For a while we work side by side in silence. Mario makes one plant after another disappear into the ground, and I fill the remaining holes with soil.

Half the hedge is already planted when Mario stretches with a long yawn. "Is it okay with you if I don't take a look at your dripping faucet until tomorrow?"

"Already taken care of." I sound just as proud as I feel. I actually replaced the worn-out washer myself. "Wasn't all that hard," I say with a wink.

Mario gives me an approving nod. "You're full of surprises."

Even for myself, I add silently. Hardly anything I've managed in the past few weeks is something I would've believed myself capable of just a few months ago. My life has changed in so many ways, has become better and happier. Only one single thing has stayed the same: I'm still a lawyer.

Grinning at him in anticipation, I say, "I've got another surprise for you."

Mario immediately stops tapping the plant out of its pot and focuses all his attention on me. "Oh yeah?"

"The motions are ready." I've never been so happy about having produced paper and being able to take it to court soon. I throw my arms up and dance in a circle, no matter what I look like doing it. My excitement has to come out; everyone can see it.

Mario's eyes shine suspiciously, he comes over to me and hugs me so tightly as if he were a castaway and I were his lifeline. Then he lifts me up and spins me around. The freshly planted garden flashes past at the edge of my vision, speckled green, pink, and white.

"How can I ever thank you enough for this?" he asks breathlessly after setting me back down on the ground.

I wave it off. "Don't worry about it. Being able to help you is simply wonderful for me, and I'm really happy to do it."

An intense feeling of satisfaction spreads through my whole body, and with it a certainty as unshakable as an entire mountain range. This must be what life as a lawyer feels like. More and more of my new friends are asking me for help these days. Often it's little things, about applying for financial support or getting a work visa.

"I should make this my profession." The words just bubble out of my mouth, but in the very same moment I realize that this could be exactly what my next step should be.

"As a landscape gardener, you're not really much use

with those skinny little arms of yours, anyway." Mario lifts his shoulders apologetically, even though there's no need. I've known for weeks how unsuited I am to this physically demanding work.

I turn my idea over in my mind; I like it more and more. "Why on earth didn't I think of this sooner? I was probably too busy unsuccessfully trying to rent out my apartment."

A smile spreads across his face. "I think you should do it," he says in a tone as if he were just recommending I eat an apple instead of a pear today, even though it would be a damn big deal. Then he turns back to the hedge.

I follow his example, but even as he lets the next little spruce tree slide into the ground, my thoughts are back on my idea. Is it really conceivable? How could I make a living helping people who aren't able to pay for my services? What if I charged only a small amount, just enough for me to have enough to live on? Maybe there's even funding available?

The thoughts surge hotly inside me and ignite a fire of enthusiasm. The longer I think about it, the more clearly I can see it before me, down to the details.

The picture of my future is suddenly clearer than ever before.

Chapter Forty-Five

As I leave the courthouse, the hot, humid air forces sweat out of every pore. One look at the sky is enough to know how much I should hurry to get home. While I was busy filing the motions for Mario, thick clouds had piled up. On top they're white as cotton wool, but in their bellies, I can see it clearly, they're carrying raindrops down there, as heavy as his worries.

I march quickly toward the subway station, but after only a few yards the folders in my bag feel as if they were boulders. I try in vain to dry my sweat-soaked palms on the fabric of my skirt, which is already sticking to my legs like damp cotton candy. My body is screaming loudly for a break, and that's what it's going to get.

Leaning against a house wall, I catch my breath and use the moment to think about what happened just a few minutes ago. The appointment went brilliantly, the motions were accepted for review. I was a lawyer again and even had fun doing it. If only Philipp could see me now. In the one smart suit I still kept, with my hair casually pinned back. What would he say?

Inevitably, my thoughts wander back to where this new life began. Maybe I can help Suna and Nahla too. With more than just the money I send them. Suna has been trying for weeks to talk me into visiting her in Marseille again. I should fly over and see what I can do for them. Just thinking about it sends a surge of happiness flaring up inside me, while above me the clouds draw ever closer together with a rumbling thunder. The way the sky looks now reminds me of my former life. Dark and veiled. Without light.

Suddenly I realize how close I am to that life right now. On the other side of the street I can make out the display windows of my former favorite boutique. Just around the corner, in the narrow side alley, is the old apartment.

I have to see it one more time, I want to see with my own eyes how far I've come.

With the smell of warm summer rain in my nose, I hurry down the street and turn into the alley. Despite the oppressive heat, I have to smile when the prettily decorated façade appears in front of me like a memorial plaque. With my eyes I follow the winding ornaments up to the top floor. Then I step closer and let my fingers wander over the rough plaster of the wall. In this moment, right now, I can feel it very clearly. I was never happy here. Not with my life and not with Tom.

By now the air around me has gone completely still. One of my curls has come loose and is sticking to my forehead like a damp rag. Just as I try to blow it out of my face, a flash of lightning streaks across the horizon. The thunder isn't long in coming and immediately turns into a deep rumble. It takes a few seconds before I understand what's happening. Behind me a motorcycle is driving down the alley. My thoughts are with Philipp at once. I press my lips together and exhale in short bursts.

Will this never stop?

How much longer until I can smell lavender and eat cherries without feeling that wistful ache in my stomach? How many more motorcycle noises do I have to hear and how many trekking backpacks do I have to see before I can finally enjoy the memory of France?

The humming turned into a rattling, then it went quiet. At last.

One last time I looked up at the windows of my old apartment, then I turned away and sauntered off.

"Hey, Curly."

The soft, deep voice shot through my body like lightning through storm-laden air. I spun around, blinked and narrowed my eyes. No matter how often I repeated it, the image didn't change.

It really was true.

Just a few meters away from me stood Philipp. Leaning against the motorcycle in a black leather jacket. A wide grin spread across his face, his eyes sparkled.

He was here. Close enough to touch. With me.

Dream and reality blurred together. I was speechless, didn't know what to do. But all at once that didn't seem necessary anymore. Philipp only had to look at me to know everything. A glow spread over his face, so warm that I could feel it even across the distance between us. Then he came toward me with quick steps.

Without another word he took me in his arms and pulled me closer to him. My knees shook as soon as he kissed my cheeks. His stubble tickled my lips, and still they tingled no less than every other bit of skin his touched. Hastily I stepped back and took a deep breath.

With a careful movement of his hand, he brushes a lock of hair out of my face. His fingers stroke tenderly over my skin. Our gazes meet. Whether I want to or not, I feel as if I'm sinking into his eyes, like into an ocean. Far out, where the water is cool and refreshing.

With a sigh, I let myself fall into his arms. I barely even notice how the clouds above us give way with a groan. They release their burden, raindrops as big as walnuts burst on my head. Cold and wet, they soak the fabric of my clothes, stream down my legs like a waterfall, and form a lake right where we stand, tightly entwined.

I open my eyes and see beads of water running down his cheeks, glittering like diamonds. With a smile, he pulls away from me, but only far enough that the tips of our noses almost touch.

"Hey." His gaze is as relaxed as a Sunday morning.

Chapter Forty-Six

The downpour had long since passed over us, but I still couldn't find the words. A cool breeze left a shiver on my damp skin, my lips trembled. I was wet, everywhere, but I didn't care. Philipp was with me. As close as he hadn't been for far too long.

I searched his eyes for clues but couldn't find any. I didn't know what he was thinking and had no idea what he was feeling. "Why are you here?" I suddenly burst out, because I just couldn't wait any longer.

"What do you think?" His smile was warm. But his hands, which had just been resting on my arms, wandered back into his pockets. Standing in front of me like this, he reminded me of a schoolboy taking an exam. Was he actually unsure? Because of me?

Impossible, I was imagining it. I pulled my shoulders up. "Quick visit to your parents?" That would at least be logical.

For a moment, his gaze drifted past me to the horizon.

A watery film lay over his eyes, he bit his lip. “That too,” he said in a hoarse voice and took a deep breath.

Even though we’re trapped in the concrete hell of downtown Vienna, the sight of him catapults me back to France. To the beach at Le Saintes-Maries-de-la-Mer, surrounded by marshlands and flamingo families. With salty sea air in my nose and warming sunrays on my skin, we’re sitting in the middle of the wide beach in the sand. I let my hands sink into the warm ground while he stares at the water for minutes on end without saying anything, with exactly that expression on his face.

Back then I already couldn’t find any words, and even today it’s hard for me. How am I supposed to help him if I don’t know what’s weighing on him? I touch his forearm, wanting to stroke his skin to calm him down, just to do something at all.

Philipp jerks back and puts his hand over the spot I just touched. The very next moment he gives me a cheeky grin. As if he hadn’t just been miles away from me, lost in his thoughts. “We should get you dried off, Ice Princess.”

Did he just call me princess?

Smiling, I rub my fingers together. They’re icy cold. “All right. Take me to my palace.” I wave my hand like the Queen when she’s driven through the streets of London in an open-top car.

“Of course, Your Highness.” Philipp bows as if he were my servant and offers me his bent arm so I can lean on it.

Amused, I nod toward his motorbike. “I now reside in Ottakring,” I say and wink at him.

He immediately steers me toward his motorbike. “If I may, the carriage is ready.”

I give him the address and let him help me onto the bike. With a broad grin on his tanned face, he puts the helmet on me and drapes his leather jacket over my wet shoulders. A few seconds later the engine is already roaring. We weave our way through the city's alleys, passing historic buildings and carefully tended parks. But I don't pay attention to any of it. It's nothing more than background noise in my head, where a single sentence keeps repeating over and over. As if the needle of a record player had gotten stuck on the vinyl.

Philipp is here. Philipp is here.

Very slowly this realization seeped into my consciousness. By the time we arrived at my new home, countless questions were buzzing through my head. I held them back and handed Philipp a towel to dry his leather clothes. Then I made sure to get out of my wet costume.

A little later I stepped out of the bathroom in fresh clothes and with my hair dried. Instead of sitting comfortably on the sofa, Philipp was pacing between the kitchenette and the balcony door at the other end of the room. "Are you ready?" he asked before I could say anything.

This game of constant distraction didn't work anymore. It was my turn now to ask the questions. "Why did you come? And how long are you staying?" I fixed him with an unrelenting stare and didn't let him go.

Philipp looked surprised, but in the next moment his features softened. He gave me that smile that made the dimples in his cheeks flash. I had to stare right at them now, whether I wanted to or not.

"Why were you at my old apartment? And why don't you trust me?" The questions poured out of me, unfiltered and unsorted. Even though it was almost impossible, I didn't let his closed-off expression throw me off balance.

I wanted answers. Now.

To my astonishment, Philipp lowered his gaze as if he

couldn't withstand mine. Then he came toward me and put his hands on my shoulders. He raised his eyes again. I saw a plea in the deep blue, saw a silent request in his face. At once it became hard for me to breathe.

"You have to finally find out." His words were no more than a hoarse whisper. He bit his lower lip and furrowed his brow. "Everything."

I nodded; nothing more was necessary.

Still, Philipp shook his head. "Not here." In the next moment he pulled me outside to his motorbike and handed me the helmet. I had barely settled into the saddle when he hit the gas.

Wherever we go, once we arrive, there will be no more secrets. Not for me either.

Philipp is back. And this time he won't leave without knowing what he means to me, and how much.

Chapter Forty-Seven

Although we were only on the motorbike for a good hour, when we arrive I feel as if we're back in the rolling hills of France. Philipp parks at the foot of a rise where vines trace sweeping curves up the slope. All around us, the hazy dampness of the downpour rises from the tall meadows. But it still smells like summer.

As if it were the most natural thing in the world, Philipp takes my hand. "Come on, let's walk a bit."

I nod, a smile on my face that can definitely compete with the radiance of the sun. "Gladly."

Of course I could repeat my questions on the spot, put Philipp through the wringer as if he were a defendant in a trial. But where our arms are entwined, I can feel his heart beating.

Far too fast and with no discernible rhythm.

Several times his lips part and close again without a single word leaving his mouth. To make it easier for him, I set off and let my gaze wander over the vineyard on one side and the wide expanses of grass on the other side of the path. Memories of our visit to a winery push into my thoughts. The tasting had been extensive and had made Philipp as trusting as a little kitten.

In the shelter of the diffuse moonlight he nestles so close to me that I can feel him everywhere. His head rests in the hollow between my neck and my collarbone.

"I have to tell you something, Sarah," he mumbles, and I feel his lips brush against my skin as he speaks. "It's important. Really, really important."

"Then go ahead and shoot." I'm at least as drunk as he is. My head feels wonderfully light, my body feels as if it's made of cotton wool. And the wooden bench we're sitting on is our spaceship, with which we're drifting far out in the universe between the stars.

He jerks his head up and looks straight at me. "My heart doesn't beat anymore," he says, with a matter-of-factness in his voice that I can't understand.

"How is that supposed to work?" Shaking my head, I wrinkle my nose and feel my way with my fingertips to his carotid artery. There it is, the steady throbbing. "One, two, three. It's all there, you idiot."

Back then, high on that French wine, had he already tried to tell me what was weighing on him?

Like a loop on repeat, that evening plays over and over in my mind as we walk along in silence side by side. Only the crunch of the pebbles beneath our shoes and the murmur of the wind, gliding gently through the tall flower meadows, can be heard.

Then, finally, Philipp clears his throat. "This isn't easy for me," he says mechanically, without looking at me.

I squeeze his hand. "How can I help you?"

"Promise me you'll let me finish. Don't interrupt me and, above all, don't pity me."

Whatever he's about to tell me seems to weigh heavily on his soul. Even though I have no idea what's coming next, my heart grows just as heavy. He's suffering. My Philipp, the man who follows me into my most beautiful dreams, is suffering. "I promise," I answer with utter conviction.

Philipp took a deep breath, the air leaving his body in a shaky rush. His palm was damp, but I still didn't let go. On the contrary, I hooked my fingers even more tightly around his.

"In France you asked me what had happened in my life that made me leave. Do you remember?"

I nodded; of course I still remembered. Philipp had claimed there was no particular reason. But even back then I could feel that this wasn't the whole truth.

"The truth is, I just had to get away."

I didn't dare look at him and barely allowed myself to breathe. A why burned on my tongue, but I didn't let it out. For Philipp's sake.

We strolled along side by side in silence, and I lost all sense of time. Maybe minutes passed, maybe only seconds, before Philipp went on. "Vienna was my own personal hell, filled with feelings and memories that were destroying me. It was an escape. The goal was to turn my back on this city and never come back again. Somewhere else, or at least that's what I believed, I could be free. Free from what had happened."

A thousand questions whirled through my head; I held on to them as best I could and imagined my lips were sealed shut with superglue. Encouragingly, I squeezed his hand.

"Even thinking about it is hard for me, but no matter where I go, once a year there's no getting around it. Every third of August. Exactly when night starts to darken the sky. As if at the push of a button, the sharp stench of urine creeps into my nose. It mixes with stale, musty air and the reek of unwashed clothes. In the background a Nirvana song is playing, barely recognizable because the speaker crackles so much."

I saw Philipp in front of me with the neat short haircut he used to have. In a smart suit he was standing in the middle of a run-down building, holding a hand over his nose and mouth. His eyes were wide open, his forehead furrowed with lines.

"Then it hits me again, more real than any nightmare could ever show me. In my memory I'm holding him in my arms again, so tightly that my T-shirt is soaked with his sweat. His face is pale. Deathly pale. He's breathing, but only very shallowly. So many years later I can still feel his racing pulse in my fingertips. Just like the helplessness that seizes me. There's nothing I can do anymore to help him. My brother is dying. And I'm just crouching beside him, brushing the wet hair from his forehead and begging a God to help us, a God I've never believed in before."

Philipp presses his lips together so tightly that the skin around his mouth turns completely white. With his eyes closed, he exhales in short bursts and quickens his pace. As if he wanted to run away again. As if salvation were waiting for him at the end of this gravel path in the middle of nowhere. I stay with him, no matter where, how long, or how far he wants to go.

"It's pure horror. In my head he dies over and over again, every year on the third of August. Exactly 18 minutes past 8 PM."

His fingers dig into my hand. I can hardly bear not being allowed to say anything. Not being able to do anything, being no comfort to him. Gently, I run my thumb over his protruding knuckles, a sign that I'm here for him.

My other hand moves to his chest and stops his escape. We come to a halt. Then I dare to look at him. I'm sure that what I can see in his eyes now is all the anger and all the grief he has hidden from me until now.

"Even before we were born, we were already a team. It took years to understand that, but today I know it for sure. Not having my other half will torment me forever. I miss him, back then even so much that I tried to follow him wherever he had gone. I don't want to imagine what broke inside our mother when she almost lost her second son as well."

He shakes his head. Individual tears spill from his eyes and creep down his cheeks, thick as honey. They sparkle in the light of the evening sun and leave a bizarre picture of grief on his vacation-tanned skin. My fingers wander to his face all on their own and gently wipe the salty drops from his stubble.

"I push that behind my wall too. Along with the rest of the guilt. I can tell myself as often as I like that I tried everything to get my brother out of it. Away from the drugs. Away from those terrible people he called friends, who only dragged him deeper into the abyss. I took him in, got him help, stood by him through his attempts to get clean on his own. I wiped his vomit off the floor and endured his hatred. Still, it wasn't enough. Helping him with everything I had and still failing in the end, that broke me. Never again in my entire life did I want to feel that guilt. Or that unbridled hatred of myself. I didn't want to have to take care of anyone, and no one was supposed to worry about me. Since then I've lived like a lion, solitary and free. I don't let myself be tied down, not to any place and not to any person."

Now I finally understand, and even though I know the why now, his words stab me in the heart. So sharply that my thumb freezes on his skin and my legs feel as if they suddenly got stuck in the ground. My last spark of hope vanishes like a firefly in the darkness of a starless night. He didn't come because of me, he came to me.

Philipp looks at me as if it were the very first time. "Do you understand now, Sarah?" His voice is brittle. The man beside me, usually so tall and strong, suddenly seems small and weak.

I nod; how could I do anything else? Losing his twin brother is a pain that's beyond anything I can imagine. As if it were the most natural thing in the world, I place my hand on his cheek. "You know, a pretty smart man once told me we can't change our past." With my fingertips I stroke his temple, as if I could brush his worries away. "But we can decide about our future."

"And you think he was right about that?" Desperate hope and aching joy, all of it is reflected in his face.

"The proof is standing right in front of you." I smile at him with pride.

As if burned-out wood suddenly began to glow again, Philipp's face grows brighter.

I step closer to him and lock my gaze on his. "The time with you changed my life." My voice is steady; I'm not whispering or mumbling. It doesn't take any effort, and even less courage, to say what I feel. "For your brother, your help may have come too late. But me—" I tap my chest with my index finger "—you saved."

A smile flits across his face, warm and tender. He lays his hand on mine. "And yet something else entirely happened in France, didn't it?" he whispers.

He knows.

I see it in his eyes, recognize it in the way the muscles around his mouth relax. If there was ever a right moment for the truth, it's this very instant. For the blink of an eye we stand facing each other without moving, then the incredible happens. I don't hesitate any longer; I don't need courage or strength to finally say it.

"I fell in love with you."

Chapter Forty-Eight

Philipp's expression is like melted chocolate, sweet and seductive. Looking at him sends a shiver down my spine, tingling, as if champagne were trickling over my skin. His gaze flickers across my face. I wait, giving him all the time he needs. Enduring this silence costs me more effort than telling him what I think.

"Sarah ..." He looks at me helplessly, can't find words for what no one can say out loud. "I ..."

Not good. Whatever he's about to say will torment me. No, I don't want to hear it. I raise my hand defensively. "I get it." My words sound gentle, almost loving.

I turn away at once and keep walking down the path that won't lead anywhere anyway. On the horizon, the day is drawing to a close, the last rays of sun warm my skin. A pleasantly cool breeze carries the scent of freshly cut grass to my nose. It would be a perfect moment if Philipp's rejection weren't eating its way through my heart. Ruthless and lightning fast.

Behind me I hear Philipp's footsteps, they're getting

closer, but I march on undeterred. “Wait.” Suddenly his hand is on my shoulder. “Please!”

I stop, but I can’t manage to turn around to face him. My gaze fixed on the orange clouds, I fold my arms across my chest. “Don’t worry, I understand,” I say wearily, because nothing else makes any sense. No matter how much I want it. I can’t force him to love me.

In the very next moment, pebbles crunch suspiciously close behind me. Even though the sun is shining in my face, my back suddenly grows warm. All over. “No, you don’t understand anything.” He’s so close that I can almost feel the air vibrating between us.

I shrug. “Is that so?”

He pushes my hair back and puts his face so close beside my head that his lips touch my ear. Hot-and-cold shivers run from there down my neck into my chest, and there’s nothing I could do about it. I’m helplessly at the mercy of this longing, no matter how hard my mind drums into me to finally stop.

“Back then, in France, it wasn’t me who saved you,” he whispers and presses even closer against me. His voice trembles, and with it his whole body. “It was you who saved me.”

All the tension leaves my body, I let myself sink, nestling against his chest. “How?”

“By showing me who you really are. With every honest smile and every carefree gesture. Whenever I could see you without your mask, my wall started to crack. I knew it was only a matter of time before you would bring it down. With the same ease with which explosive charges bring massive high-rises to the ground in a matter of seconds.”

I swallow. My heart is pounding as if it wanted to escape the narrow prison of my body to be even closer to Philipp.

"I was panicking. What I never wanted to have again suddenly became everything I wished for."

Agitated, I turn to face him and search his features for signs I don't yet know myself.

Can this really be true?

I search my memory for clues, and I actually find them. All those moments when I thought I felt exactly that. Loving looks and tentative touches. His lips on my forehead, whispered words full of tenderness. Every single scene rushes past me like a film on fast-forward.

Then everything goes quiet, my thoughts stop spinning, my heartbeat falls silent.

As if someone had given us both a sign, we take a step toward each other at the same time and fall into each other's arms. On tiptoe I move so close to him that it feels as if we're no longer two people, but only one single human being.

I lift my head, and what I see now takes my breath away. Behind his face the sun sets, shining brightly on the horizon. The sky above us shows me all its colors. Red like love, orange like enthusiasm, and there, barely visible at the lower edge, it's as blue as my dreams.

Like in slow motion, Philipp bends down toward me. The air between us turns shimmering hot, the world around us blurs.

Any second now he's going to kiss me.

I look into his eyes one last time, then I close mine. His breathing is quick, hot air flows over my lips, salty and sweet at the same time. The heat shoots through my body, all the way to my toes and back again. His lips are so close to mine that I can almost feel them.

Then, finally, we kiss, as carefully as if it were our very first time.

Epilogue

Right after we reach cruising altitude, I fold up the armrest between our seats and snuggle up to Philipp. A pleasant feeling of safety spreads through every part of me. Not just because of the man at my side. Also because of myself. I've taken a thousand steps since we met on this very flight in early summer. Without him and with him, but always following the path of my heart. Today we're returning together to where it all began, to meet friends who were still strangers back then.

"Do you remember when we flew to Marseille together for the first time half a year ago?" There's a hint of wistfulness in my words.

"Mhm," is all Philipp says as he absentmindedly winds one of my curls around his finger.

For a moment I close my eyes and bury my face in his T-shirt. He still manages to smell different every single day. Today he smells like summer on the French coast, of lavender and red wine. I can't help but sigh with contentment, even though my thoughts wander back to a past in which my life was glassy and metallic.

"Back then everything was different."

I feel him gently shake his head. "Not everything was different."

Curious, I lift my head and look straight into the crystal-clear sea of his eyes. His loving smile grows so wide that I can see his dimples. I don't have to ask anything; he already knows what my frown means. His fingertips tenderly stroke my cheek and move on to my lips. There they pause, and suddenly it feels as if we're alone on this plane. I can hardly hear the drone of the engines, the cabin blurs at the edges of my vision. There are only Philipp and me, looking at each other.

"Then as now, there's this one thing I can't stop thinking about." He leans a little closer to me. Where the tips of our noses touch, my skin starts to tingle. "That I want to kiss you," he whispers hoarsely, "over and over again."

In a trance, I nod, the smile on my face turning into a radiant beam. There are no words in this world for what he does to me. And even fewer for what I want to say to him.

I can only show him how happy I am. How beautiful the picture of my life has become, how bright the colors are now and how free the brushstrokes.

Without taking my eyes off him, I close the last inch between us.

Our lips touch, ever so gently.

I sink.

In the blue of his eyes, in the warmth of his embrace, and in this one exact moment.

"Everything will be okay, someday," I hear Nahla whisper in my thoughts. And suddenly I know it for sure.

Someday is now.

Afterword

Dear readers,

I hope you enjoyed reading *Every Step I Take* and that you spent just as many wonderful hours reading it as I did writing it. Sarah's story accompanied me for so long and so intensely that I sometimes forgot she only existed in my head. But I'm not the only one who was part of this novel's creation story. Many fantastic people accompanied me on the road to publication, and to be honest, I don't know where to start. There's no "first and foremost" and no "last but not least." Every one of my companions is important to me; each of them deserves to be mentioned first here. Still, I can't put their names on top of one another, so I'll simply list them without any particular order.

A huge thank-you to my family, my test readers Anita, Eva, Janice, Mila, Sonja, and Sylvia, to the book professionals Anne, Constanze, Serena, and Steffi, as well as to my tireless helpers Antje, Celine, Chantal, Claudia, Debbie, Dana, Ina, Kara, Katja, Lea, Lily, Lina, Nicole, Petra, and Susi.

A very special thank-you also goes to you, dear readers, for buying and reading this book. I used to feel uncomfortable when authors asked for reviews in their books, because I didn't know why they did it. Now I know that ratings are vital for unknown debut authors. They enable us to keep doing what we love—writing books. So now I, too, would like to ask you for a recommendation on a book platform (for example: Amazon, Thalia, etc.) or in your private circle, even though I never wanted to do that myself.

Thank you very much!

If you still have questions or simply want to tell me something, I'd be delighted to hear from you.

Until then, all my best,

Belinda

More by Belinda Benna

vinci-books.com/thedreams

I was hired to care for his daughter... not his heart.

Single dad and world-famous pianist Josh Friedberg is focused, distant, and impossible to resist. Spending time with his daughter Sophia brings us closer, and the slow-burning spark between us is undeniable—but risking love could cost me my heart all over again.

Turn the page for a free preview…

The Dreams We Share: Chapter One

MAYA

A heart-wrenching whimper reaches my ears. Though barely audible amid the lively sounds of the kindergarten group, I am immediately alarmed.

It's Frida.

I look up from the cardboard butterflies I'm cutting out for the summer festival, blowing a strand of my long black hair away from my face. The bright June sunlight streams through the windows, casting a colorful glow over the whimsically decorated room. The glass beads of the mobile above the entrance sparkle with a rainbow of colors, and the vibrant red of the play kitchen glows even more intensely.

My gaze continues to wander until I find the crying girl, who shows up at the kindergarten day after day, only wearing tights and a T-shirt. Over in the corner with the building blocks, she buries her head between her tightly drawn-up knees.

"There she goes again." My boss, Nadine, shakes her head with an exasperated snort and reaches for the hot glue gun. "Can't this child go a single day without creating drama?"

I look into her icy-blue eyes. "Why did you become a preschool teacher, anyway?"

Of course, she's the boss, and if I've learned one thing during my internship here, direct criticism is unwelcome. Nevertheless, I can't help but ask her the question.

"That's none of your business." Nadine shrugs indifferently and crumples the red tissue paper in her hand into something that was supposed to be a lovingly shaped flower for the wall decoration.

If it were just about me, I wouldn't say a word. But her cold demeanor is directed at the little innocent beings we have the privilege of caring for.

"Not mine, but it is the children's business." I reply so quietly that she probably can't hear it, pushing the tiny wooden chair behind me as I stand.

I walk past the dollhouse, the construction workshop, and the painting corner. I almost stumble over a miniature train that one of the wild rascals left in the middle of the room.

A few seconds later, I sink onto the soft carpeted floor of the building corner and pull three-year-old Frida into my arms. Her red curls reek of cold cigarette smoke.

"What happened?" I ask the little one, stroking her back reassuringly.

She doesn't answer. I only notice how she plays with my oversized earrings, sparkling in all colors. Frida sure loves that.

"Together, we can solve any problem, you know," I whisper while gently rocking her back and forth. "You remember, don't you? We're both..."

"Superheroes." Frida's voice is so faint that I can hardly hear it.

I smile. Because suddenly, I feel strong too. "Exactly. And what do superheroes do?"

She pushes herself away from me slightly and looks up at me with her green eyes. "They can do anything." A conspiratorial grin appears on her freckle-covered face.

"So if a superhero can handle anything, nothing can happen to them that they can't fix, right?" I lovingly wipe the tears from her cheeks. In the corner of my eye, I see Nadine throwing her arms up in the air. Due to her sour expression, she looks completely out of place in the group room, which appears so cheerful with its yellow curtains and children's drawings on the wall.

"Do I have to do everything alone?" She rants in a volume she knows I can hear. Then she turns with a grim expression to the rainbow-colored stack of construction paper sheets on the craft table.

"Nadine is mad at you." Frida wrinkles her button nose.

Though I flinch inwardly, I mimic the little one's grimace. "So what?" I whisper back. Then I turn my face away so Nadine can't see it and contort my features until the little one giggles.

Experiencing her laughter is worth any sacrifice. No matter how difficult it can be having Nadine as my boss, time with the children makes up for it. With them, I am in a different world. A place where there's no pressure. They don't pretend; they don't lie. And they see the world just the way I love it. Like through a magical kaleidoscope that casts a rainbow hue over everything.

I nod encouragingly to Frida. "Do you want to tell me now why you were crying?"

She lowers her eyelids in shame. I can barely understand

what she murmurs, but as I also let my gaze fall, I don't need to understand anymore. She tries to hide the dark stain on her beige tights with her hands, but I can still see it clearly.

"Please, don't tell on me," she whispers with a voice choked with tears.

Instantly, I empathize with her. I feel her shame and guilt as if they were my own. Still, I smile at her reassuringly.

"You can rely on me. And you know what? Coincidentally, I brought a magic cloak with me today." I pretend to pull a cloth from my bright blue flowing skirt. "Anything this covers becomes invisible."

The girl's eyes widen. "Really?"

"Yeah, of course. What do you think?" I hold the nonexistent piece of fabric in front of her face. "My goodness, Frida, where's your head?"

She leans to the side as if peering out from behind a curtain. "I'm here!"

"Thank goodness. I thought..." I pretend to be relieved, wiping away imaginary sweat from my forehead. The numerous plastic bangles around my wrist make a dull clacking sound while I wrap Frida in the imaginary cloak. One last time, I hug her tightly. "Now you can follow me unnoticed to the restroom. On the count of three, okay?"

"Okay," she whispers almost inaudibly. She nods against my shoulder.

Hand in hand, we make our way through the group room. Fortunately, none of the other children take notice. Melinda and her best friend David are drawing ships, and the preschoolers are having a tea party with the dolls.

Only Nadine notices that we're sneaking outside. She scrutinizes me, the color of her eyes resembling an iceberg.

Without reacting to her, I turn toward the exit. Only Frida matters now.

After tending to the girl, I reluctantly take a seat next to Nadine at the craft table. I can feel her eyes on me as I reach for the scissors. Immediately, I'm filled with tension, which threatens to overwhelm me.

"Did she wet herself again?" Her thin eyebrows rise. The hot glue gun in her hand oozes, and the adhesive smell fills my nostrils.

I shouldn't lie to her; that has gone wrong several times already, leading to reprimands. "No, she just wanted to show me something," I say anyway. For Frida's sake. After all, I made her a promise. Hastily, I take the pine-green cardboard and place the leaf-shaped stencil on it. My brightly painted fingernails add a cheerful mood to the plain surface.

"Don't get too attached to the little ones, Maya. You supervise them, teach them something, and when they're old enough, you release them into their future lives." She lazily sticks a tissue paper flower onto the wire stem. "That's it. They're not your children."

Is it supposed to be that simple? Even though my intuition tells me otherwise? "I understand that, but..."

She raises her hand. "I don't want to hear it."

"Something may be wrong at Frida's home." I shouldn't speak that thought out loud, but I can't help it. "Her shoes are too small, and her clothes are frayed and rarely washed. Shouldn't we do something?"

Heat rises within me as I think about what could be happening in her life.

"Enough of that," Nadine warns me emphatically. "Maybe her parents don't have much money, but they're doing their best. And it's not uncommon for a three-year-old to forget to use the toilet while playing. I can recognize children with problems, and Frida isn't one of them."

Surprised, I let the paper and scissors drop. So she has been observing the little girl too. Has she been to her home or talked to her parents? Perhaps Frida's family isn't as bad as I imagined?

It's possible, yet I search Nadine's face for signs that she might be lying to me.

"You're just an intern." She suddenly sounds as if she pities me. She puts her hand on my forearm. "Why do you think that after a few weeks, you can assess a situation better than a seasoned educator?"

Ashamed, I lower my gaze. Because the facts can't be denied. She's the professional, and I'm the intern.

For now.

This internship is the foundation for my special education studies. Only if I accumulate the required practical hours, submit a written assignment, and pass the four partial exams for study eligibility will I be allowed to attend university. If I had completed school until graduation, it wouldn't be necessary. But that's just not how it turned out. At twenty-six years old, I haven't accomplished much in general.

That's about to change.

I want to help children with problems. Children like Frida. This dream has accompanied me my whole life, and a few months ago, I finally found the courage to pursue it.

I'd love to tell Nadine about it. But I don't dare. She wouldn't believe that I could follow through anyway.

Her strained cough doesn't bode well. "And one more thing: I would strongly advise you to dress like an adult. Just a tip." With a disdainful sniff, she scans my rainbow-colored T-shirt.

The children love my cheerful style. And so do I. "A little color brightens up anyone's life," I reply defiantly, but I can't even look her in the eye while saying it.

With a loud creak, Nadine pushes her chair back. "Did I ask you a question?"

No.

"Exactly." She stands up and tugs at her mouse-gray T-shirt as if trying to conceal her rounded hips beneath the fabric. Then she tilts her chin up and calls the children to the gymnasium at a deafening volume.

After all the children have been picked up in the late afternoon, I enter the group room. Completely alone, Nadine sits at the craft table, struggling to handle the decorations for the summer festival. She cuts the leaves so carelessly that I almost want to take the scissors out of her hand. I straighten my back and cross the room, which feels eerily quiet without the children.

"Where should I continue?" I ask as cheerfully as possible, taking a seat on one of the small wooden chairs next to my boss.

She doesn't respond.

Better to start working right away. But as I reach for the box with the pre-cut tissue paper flowers to assemble them on the wires, Nadine stops me.

"We need to talk," she says wearily.

I follow her into her office, which is more of a storage closet than an actual workspace. There, she gestures for me to sit on the chair in front of her desk, piled high with folders and books. I feel uneasy. She maneuvers past the table and rests her head on her hands.

Heaven, when she looks at me like that, I feel like I'm four years old again.

"Maya," she begins, letting out a heavy sigh. "This is an educational institution for children aged three to six."

Yes, I'm aware of that. I might be scrunching my face because I have no idea where she's going with this.

"For two months, you've been working here, and I've done my best to make this fact clear to you," she continues, leaning back in her chair. The squeaking of the backrest pains my ears. "I don't like to admit a mistake, but if you have made one, you have to own up to it."

What? Nadine wants to admit a mistake? Something stirs within me. A spark of hope that perhaps my future holds more for me than financial worries and temporary jobs that no one could endure for long.

Positive thoughts are the beginning of all good things, I hear my father's voice echoing within me. For years, I've carried his voice inside me, and whenever he whispers something in his warm bass, I feel a little stronger than before. Even today.

What if behind Nadine's rough exterior, there's a soft core? What if she's been testing me all this time? And what if I've passed the test?

With anticipation, I gaze at Nadine, barely able to contain myself and eager to finally hear what she has to say. She grabs a piece of paper on her desk with the blank side up.

This could be my evaluation.

My legs refuse to stay still any longer. With a fantastic internship certificate, the first step toward admission to university is taken. In just three days, I'll take the second step by completing the required biology exam. A warm tingling sensation runs through my arms, while my palms become damp and simultaneously colder.

Everything seems to be happening in slow motion. Nadine turns the paper over and places it directly in front of me. Curiously, I lean forward.

Termination.

Does it say termination?

No, that's impossible. I read the word again, but *termination* stubbornly refuses to turn into *evaluation letter*.

"Dammit, what's going on here?" Did I say that out loud?

"Your behavior has been unacceptable in this institution from the beginning. Today, you lied to me again. Frida did wet herself," Nadine says.

Dammit. How did she know...?

"The replacement tights had a different color." Nadine raises her eyebrows. "Did you really think I wouldn't notice?"

Dammit. She must have noticed during the changing for the gym class. I shouldn't have lied to her. But abusing the trust of the little ones would have been just as wrong. "I wanted to—"

"Enough," she interrupts me. Suddenly, she looks exhausted. "I've never witnessed such unprofessional behavior. Denying it only makes it worse."

But that wasn't my intention. "Let me explain," I stammer.

Nadine shakes her head. "That's not all. You can't handle criticism and consistently execute my instructions incorrectly." She looks at me, full of disappointment. "You know we've discussed this before. You're not suited to be an educator. In fact, you should be thankful that I'm telling you this early."

"But..." Nadine's words circle in my head, but I can hardly comprehend them.

None of our little charges has ever complained. I'm there for them, so it can't be wrong. Or can it?

What if my dream is bigger than I am? What if I'm not meant to help children?

Disappointed in myself, I lower my gaze. "I—"

Once again, she doesn't let me finish. "My decision is final. Today was your last day of work."

What? I can't even stay until the end of the kindergarten year?

What will happen to the summer festival? I had planned game stations and rehearsed songs with the children. And what about Frida? Who will remind her she's a superhero when I'm no longer around?

"How can I make it right?" The pleading in my voice is unmistakable. I slide forward on the chair, almost landing on my knees. "Give me another chance."

Nadine's body tenses up. "You've had too many already."

"I've learned my lesson, honestly. This internship means everything to me. Don't take it away from me." I look at her desperately. She has to understand that my entire future is at stake.

Nadine bites her lip. "Don't make it harder on yourself. Just sign it." She nods toward the termination paper.

Defiantly, I cross my arms in front of my body. "And if I don't?"

"You see, that's part of the problem. You're behaving like a child. Grow up already."

Grow up? Why should I? So that I can become as cold-hearted as she is? I shrink on the chair, feeling hardly taller than a Lego figure.

She stands in front of me and thrusts the pen into my hand. "Just sign it." Her index finger impatiently taps on the paper. "Working with children is not for you. You need a job that suits you."

I swallow hard. Even if my heart refuses to understand, at least my head has to. My goal is unattainable. It always has been; I was just foolish enough to hope it would be different.

"Go ahead." Nadine's tone leaves no room for argument. So I do it. Resignedly, I let the pen glide across the paper. My jagged signature seals in blue on white the end of my dreams.

It's over. I have failed. Once again.

The Dreams We Share: Chapter Two

JOSH

Warm air builds up under my jacket, and the headlights blind me. I turn my head so that I can still see the host of the television show. Maybe it would have been better not to because looking at her is anything but calming.

Her forced smile and the hair tightly tied up in a bun make her appear like a wax figure. Only one thing seems alive, and that's her eyes. They are alert like those of a tiger, and my gut feeling tells me that this predator in the little black dress will soon bare her teeth.

"We are live in three, two, one..." a voice calls out from the darkness behind the four cameras, all focused on the two of us. The lively murmur of the audience in the hall fades away.

This is the moment to check my posture once again. I run my hands through my short-cropped hair and straighten my shirt collar while the host greets the viewers at home and in the studio with her melodic voice.

"Tonight, I have the pleasure of introducing a special

guest to you." She pauses, presumably to build suspense. "As a composer and pianist, this thirty-year-old fills even the largest concert halls, and many female fans have already tried to win his heart." Another insincere smile, but this time, I see her teeth. "Good evening and welcome Joshua Friedberg."

The camera pans to me, and the audience applauds.

"Thank you for the invitation. I'm delighted to be here." I smile back. Not for her, but for the people who have come to see me.

She nods politely, then turns her attention to the cards in her hand. "Joshua, your rise in the past years could certainly be described as meteoric. What makes your success?"

Answering this question is routine, yet it always takes my breath away to utter these words. Because they are as important to me as nothing else in the world. "Playing the piano is my great passion. I owe being able to live it solely to my fans. Without the fantastic people who allow themselves to be touched by my music, I wouldn't be sitting here today."

The host's eyes suddenly glisten with tears. She quickly clears her throat. "Critics say your music cannot be categorized. It is neither classical nor modern. They call it nothing more than the naive background melody of an intermediate world that shouldn't exist. What do you say to these accusations?"

I hold her intense gaze. "My compositions are new and unlike anything that has come before. They don't require extravagant stage shows, nor do they belong in dusty opera houses. They belong solely to my listeners, whom I want to carry away from their everyday lives for a few minutes. If I can achieve that, I'm happy."

Unimpressed, she scrutinizes me. "As a child from an affluent background, it was easy for you to establish yourself with your new concept, wasn't it?"

Of course. Because talent and hard work can be easily bought. Actually, my wealthy dad just invested a few million, and that's how I became a successful pianist. Even if my father had ever believed in me, his money alone wouldn't have been able to do anything.

I suppress the rising memories of the dark sides of my childhood and smile at the host as composedly as possible. "My parents have always supported me, and I'm very grateful to them for that."

Although I have delivered an answer, the camera remains focused on me. I feel the pressure to keep speaking, but I stand my ground. These seconds of silence are a popular way to get the interview guest to reveal more than they want to. The woman sitting across from me also searches for a vulnerable spot. She needs an opening through which she can intrude and delve deep into my soul, in pursuit of scandal or sensational news. Anything that boosts ratings is welcome.

I endure the silence because I am just as professional as she is.

Now she wrinkles her nose. It's clear to her that she won't get as close to me as she would like. Internally, I relax. Interviews are always challenging. Words get twisted too quickly, opinions are formed, and wrong conclusions are drawn.

Her mouth curves into a triumphant grin. "Rumor has it that your first piano teacher was certain that you lacked talent," she says, raising her eyebrows and fixing her gaze on me, causing a murmur to ripple through the audience.

Dammit, where did she get this information?

I didn't see this blow coming. I have to respond. And appropriately. "I had my first piano teacher when I was four years old. You'll understand that I can't remember everything he said."

That was meager. We both know it. Now it's entirely up to her. Will she pounce on me once and for all? Or can she hold back? Beads of sweat form on my forehead. It's difficult for me to maintain a casual smile.

She straightens up in her cream-colored leather chair and leans slightly toward me. "Are you implying that false information has been fed to us?"

Actually, I mean to convey that there's nothing I desire more than to end this conversation immediately. She must not poke around in this wound, as it has yet to heal.

Feeling somewhat helpless, I raise my shoulders, my gaze flickering to the wristwatch. The interview will be over soon; I just have to preserve a bit more composure. "Do you have every detail of what you did or experienced as a child at the forefront of your mind?"

A crease forms between her eyebrows. "One never forgets impactful experiences," she says with a dangerous undertone.

I must refrain from nervously tapping my fingers on my thighs. In any case, I cannot show any reaction. I regulate my breathing, endure the silence once again, and focus.

Twenty-one, twenty-two, twenty-three.

Disappointed, she leans back in her chair, and the audience begins to buzz with excitement.

Twenty-four, twenty-five, twenty-six.

"Your divorce last year must have been an equally impactful experience for you," she continues mercilessly. "How did it come to this?"

Not that I enjoy discussing it, but at least my manager prepared me for this topic. "We grew apart, and I'm glad we were able to separate amicably, remaining the best of friends."

"For Sophia?"

"For everyone involved." I smile again, although I've had more than enough of it by now. When will this charade finally be over?

"Of course, our female viewers are particularly interested in your love life. An attractive, successful man like you..." Her gaze sweeps over my body as if I were every woman's dream even though I'm just an ordinary human.

The press has tried so many times in the past months to uncover something about my love life. But the truth is, it doesn't exist.

"My love belongs to music, and it will always stay that way," I respond.

A resigned sigh escapes her lips. "If that's the case, of course we want to hear you play now." She gestures toward the concert grand piano located on the side stage next to us. Its half-open lid glistens under the spotlight, the stool covered in blue velvet, and the keys magnetically drawing my fingers.

This is what I've been waiting for. Interviews are not my favorite pastime, but everything else becomes unimportant when I sit at the piano.

Relieved, I rise and approach the piano. I let my fingers rest on the pleasantly cool keys for a moment, close my eyes, and release all the tension from the interview through my breath.

Let's begin.

I cautiously play the first notes. My fingers dance across

the keys, finding their place and creating a melody that carries me away.

Every movement is perfect—no mistakes and not even the slightest hesitation. The sequence of tones becomes more and more intense, and everything within me begins to resonate.

I smile, no, I radiate, as I pour all my passion and emotions into this one piece. As I approach the grand finale, even my heart beats faster. The music permeates me, and I become one with it, forgetting the world around me. This is happiness in its purest form.

Another triplet.

The crescendo.

Then the final chord.

With my eyes still closed, I wait until the last notes have faded away in the room. This moment belongs to me and my listeners. We are all connected, experiencing the power of music and letting it affect us.

Only when absolute silence sets in does the audience begin to applaud. I hear enthusiastic cheers and open my eyelids. The lights in the hall turn on, allowing me to see the people in the audience. There's a little girl with thick glasses clapping devotedly. And an old lady, sticking her fingers in her mouth like a teenager and whistling so loudly that I can hear it from here.

I know I'm beaming. My eyes are moist, and my cheeks are glowing. Because at this moment, above all else, I am grateful.

After so many years of rigorous practice, of striving to be seen and never giving up despite countless setbacks, I am finally able to live my dream of playing the piano.

Shortly after, I leave the studio through the back exit, get into the car, and drive to the nearest shopping center. Once I arrive, I put on the dark baseball cap for safety and slip into the subtle gray sports jacket. That, along with my inconspicuous jeans, should be enough to stroll through the center unnoticed.

Walking along the wide corridor with glossy tiles, I focus on my mission today. My daughter, Sophia, will be spending the summer with me. I want to give her a warm welcome and provide her with everything she needs. That's why I make a stop at a toy store. My gaze searches the display. The horses and the horse stable might appeal to Sophia. Every little girl likes that sort of thing, right? Or does she prefer one of those wooden train sets?

Feeling more uncertain than I'd like, I enter the shop. The dusty smell of the carpet hits me, and a faint children's laughter can be heard amid soft background music.

"Please, Daddy, the pirate ship is so beautiful," says the little boy by the side shelf, unable to keep his legs still.

A man who is undoubtedly his father lovingly strokes his blond hair. Then he crouches down in front of his son. "We can build it together and go on an adventure. What do you think?"

"Oh, yes!" The little one's face lights up, and with a cry of joy, he throws himself into his father's arms. "You're the best dad in the whole world."

Hearing those words pierces my heart.

Because as much as I look forward to having Sophia with me soon, I mainly feel fear. Her mother always took care of everything, freeing me up to focus on my career. My daughter and I hardly know each other. Moreover, since the divorce, she has oscillated between two extreme emotional states: silent and quick-tempered.

Will she look at me the way the little boy looks at his father? Will she ever reach for my hand and hop alongside me like that little guy who now disappears with the man toward the cash register?

Longing and doubt simultaneously creep up within me. The fear of not being a good father threatens to overwhelm me.

To stop that, I hastily look around for a salesperson. The man at the cash register, who looks exactly like I imagined Santa Claus as a child, is busy. The lady with the knitted vest and oversized glasses is already assisting a customer.

In the back, I spot a young woman with long black hair, her top sparkling as conspicuously as the doll she holds in her hand. Indecisively, she looks back and forth between the doll and the shelf. The miniature Christmas tree ornaments on her extra-long earrings sway in rhythm. She appears nervous, almost desperate.

Helplessly, she looks around and places the doll on a shelf. It immediately falls out.

"No, no, no," I hear the woman murmuring in the distance, her voice growing increasingly panicked. She nervously brushes her hands against her expansive blue skirt.

She appears anything but competent. I doubt she can help me find the right welcome gift for Sophia. As I skeptically observe her, one of my pieces plays through the speakers. "Freedom."

The delicate notes begin to sound. Soon, the orchestra will join in. The music will swell, and the intensity will increase.

But it's not there yet. Only the piano can be heard, and although the melody is soft, the stressed woman's face suddenly relaxes. With the doll in her hand, she closes her eyes and sways to the rhythm.

A smile spreads across her lips. The clearer it becomes, the more the cute dimples flash on her cheeks.

Spellbound, I watch her. I see the peace that suddenly dominates her expression. And I realize how her chest rises before she exhales with a deep sigh.

Then she starts to dance. Right in the midst of the bustling shopping mall. Holding the doll tightly against her chest, she twirls around. She stumbles over her skirt, regains her balance, and laughs for a moment.

All of a sudden, I'm overwhelmed with emotion. Because I know it's my music giving this woman a carefree moment. It makes her radiate with such warmth that it reaches me despite our distance.

Her facial expression carries a special kind of bliss that I have never seen before. I feel connected to her.

Perhaps I shouldn't stare at her, but I can't look away. Not even as the last notes of the piece slowly fade away. And certainly not when she opens her eyelids and looks directly at me with a dreamy gaze.

Without any effort on my part, my mouth corners lift.

A fraction of a second later, her expression changes. It's as if she just woke up and realizes where she is. With a startled look on her face, she turns her back to me and tries once again to place the doll on the shelf. Her hands tremble, and her upper body shudders.

Strange.

Something like this has never happened to me before. Has she mistaken me for someone she fears?

Confused, I return my attention to the toy shelf where I still stand.

"How can I assist you?" a female voice asks from behind me.

It's the saleswoman with the cardigan, looking at me kindly.

"Um..." Why was I here again? Ah yes, Sophia. "I need a gift for a five-year-old girl."

"Well, let's see if we can find something." She claps her hands enthusiastically. "Mr. Friedberg, right?" she adds with a conspiratorial undertone. "I'm a big fan, you know."

The day has been long, and the interview drained my energy. But I'm happy to be there for the people who have contributed to my success. So I reveal my identity, give her an autograph card, and smile for a selfie in her phone camera.

Unfortunately, our interaction doesn't go unnoticed. Within a short time, more and more people surround me.

"When is your next album coming out?" an attractive woman with small dark curls asks, pressing her cheek close to mine for a photo.

Slightly dazed by her sweet perfume, I place a finger on my lips. "That's still a secret. But I can reveal that there will be news soon." My manager, Tamika, would expect me to convince the woman to subscribe to my newsletter or follow my social media accounts.

But that's not my style. Despite my success, it still feels like I'm imposing myself. So I discreetly pull out the pen again and turn to the other fans.

Only when everyone is satisfied do I bid farewell and quickly make my way to the car. Accompanied by the city lights, I traverse the evening streets of Vienna until I reach the driveway of the villa I've been living in since last autumn.

My house lies before me, deserted. The exterior lighting

enhances the intricate decorative elements and the bright whiteness of the facade, giving it an exquisite look. I've always liked Art Nouveau, and today, I have the privilege of living in such a magnificent estate.

I open the dark green wooden door and step into the entrance area, tiled in a checkered pattern. The key lands with a clink in the tray on the antique cabinet. The bright sound reverberates through the vast space, in stark contrast to my footsteps, barely audible despite the silence.

Like a ghost, I wander through the kitchen, the living room, and the dining room in semi-darkness.

In just a few days, the house will be filled with life. I look forward to it. Yet I can't help but wonder how I will manage to establish a connection with Sophia. My God, I should have figured it out by now. After all, she's my daughter!

The worries drive me farther into the music room. Once a library, this room still houses books, sheet music, and scores, reaching up to the high ceiling of the old building. I've removed the furniture, leaving only the piano and a leather seating group in the style of the thirties within the grand expanse of the room.

I lift the lid of the grand piano, sit down, and begin to play.

But before I can fully immerse myself in the most beautiful of my worlds, the doorbell rings.

It must be Tamika. No one else would pay me a visit at this hour.

As expected, my manager stands at the front door. She wears a mysterious grin on her bright red lips.

"Do we have an appointment?" I ask, confused as she bustles past me in her midnight-blue jumpsuit, making her way into the house.

She brushes back her perfectly smoothed platinum blond hair. "No."

"Please, come in," I say, even though she's already in the hallway. "Would you like something to drink?"

"Champagne, please." She'll be turning forty next year, but she looks like a mischievous little girl right now. "Come on, don't just stand there. Where are the glasses?"

"Kitchen," I say as I watch her practically float through the foyer. I follow her, and when I arrive, I see her standing in front of the open refrigerator. The light from inside makes her diamond-studded necklace shimmer.

"Perfect," she says, taking out a magnum bottle of champagne. "You could at least help me."

Even though I don't know why, I walk over to the glass cabinet and take two champagne flutes. "Will you tell me what's going on?"

Skillfully, Tamika pops the cork and fills the glasses. She hands one to me, and I can see that she's practically bursting with excitement.

I raise my glass. "What are we toasting to?" I scrutinize her.

"To you," she returns. "And..."

Raising my eyebrows in question, I urge her, "Enough now. Spit it out."

"And to your nomination for the International Music Award!" With an elegant gesture, she pulls a piece of paper out of the pocket of her jumpsuit and waves it in front of my face. Her cheeks are glowing. "You did it!"

I stare at her in disbelief. Did she really just say that, or am I dreaming? "You mean..."

She nods, her head bobbing wildly up and down and back again. Deep laugh lines form around her eyes. It's real.

The radiance, the joy, the triumphant clenched fist. Everything is real.

The nomination. It's real!

In a trance-like state, I lower my glass and take the letter. Indeed. In the upper right corner, the logo of the International Music Awards proudly shines. And in the subject line are the words I've been reading in my dreams every night.

"Congratulations! You are one of the ten nominees for this year's Best Newcomer category."

I don't need to read further, and it's not necessary. I know the process and rules of the most important music industry awards by heart. I know a shortlist of three contenders will be selected by mid-July. And that ultimately, in early September, during a magnificent show, the audience will decide who receives the award.

This prize means the world to me.

One day, I will be the greatest pianist of them all. Count on it. I made that promise to my father, but he just laughed at me.

He was convinced I would never be good enough.

But I am. If I win. Even he won't be able to ignore that proof. It's my chance to make him understand that choosing the piano was the right decision. And ultimately, to prove it to myself.

I barely notice Tamika jumping into my arms with a shout of joy. My thoughts are scattered, and emotions are overflowing. But gradually, a clear image forms in my mind.

"We should plan a tour," I say. Besides the musical concept, the jury values sales figures the most. But the fans, who will ultimately decide, can only be convinced by my music. I have to be better than I've ever been. I have to surpass myself; only then do I have a chance at this prize.

"Don't worry, preparations are already underway. Ralf and I are developing a new show. We need fresh compositions from you, preferably with a romantic touch, nothing too extravagant." Tamika's eyes light up. "We're planning an open-air tour, performing in all the capital cities and musical centers of Europe. Additionally, we'll ensure plenty of positive press coverage."

"Yes, yes, and yes." I can already vividly imagine myself sitting at the piano on the stage in the Arena di Verona, pouring my soul out. I hear the accompanying orchestra, see the fireworks rising behind the ancient arches of the amphitheater, and feel the energy of the moment. "That sounds amazing."

"The fans will love you. And they undoubtedly have to," Tamika grins mischievously.

I nod excitedly, but behind all my enthusiasm, a heavy thought suddenly emerges. "What about Sophia?"

Tamika shrugs. "She'll come with us, of course. She'll find this journey exciting, and in the fall, she can brag to her kindergarten friends about it."

Even though Tamika takes it lightly, my thoughts darken further. "But she's only five. Who will take care of her on tour?"

"We'll hire a nanny. I'll take care of that. Between rehearsals, performances, and press events, you can do something nice with Sophia," she says, casually uttering the words as if it's not a problem at all. As if there would be any time for anything during a tour.

I sink onto one of the kitchen stools, resting my head in my hands. How could I neglect Sophia like this when I finally have the chance to be a good father to her? This is wrong.

Suddenly, Tamika's forearm is heavy on my shoulders.

"Don't even start thinking that way," she says, as if she knows exactly what's going on inside me.

I look up at her. Her expression is serious.

"You've worked too hard to let up now. If there ever was a right time to give it your all, it's the coming months." She looks into my eyes intensely, her hand tightening around my shoulder.

"That's true..."

"Besides, you have many more summers ahead with your daughter. Next year, you can even take a whole month off and spend exclusive time with her. But you can only win the award this year, and maybe never again." It's fascinating how Tamika sees the world so pragmatically. But she's my manager for a reason. She knows what's best for my career.

However, no matter how right she may be in this matter, I can't give in to her urging without a fight. "Isn't there another possibility? A smaller tour, more concert breaks? Or we could skip the press events?" I look at her hopefully, but I can already read the answers to the questions on her face.

She hands me my glass again, somberly. "Your competitors will fight with all means necessary. If you don't go along, negative headlines will rain down on you. Your fans will turn away, and then you can forget about the music award."

Right. I have to deliver. This nomination is an honor, and if I don't do everything to win the prize, my father will be proven right once and for all. I would be forced to admit that I'm actually not good enough. And that I never truly was.

That must not happen!

I have to find a way to reconcile my most important career goal with the desire to be a good father. There's no other way.

"Well, it's settled then," I say, my voice firm as if I'm trying to convince myself that I can achieve both. I nod emphatically, then I place the champagne glass on the kitchen counter without taking a single sip.

Grab your copy…

vinci-books.com/thedreams

About the Author

Belinda Benna is an award-winning author whose moving romance novels are filled with emotion, allowing you to lose yourself between the lines and find yourself at the same time.

Experience stories that will make you cry, laugh, and fall in love—each with a message that will stay with you for a long time.

www.ingramcontent.com/pod-product-compliance
Ingram Content Group UK Ltd.
Pitfield, Milton Keynes, MK11 3LW, UK
UKHW010130110826
474298UK00003B/130

9 781036 734107